A Wyldhaven Christmas

THE WYLDHAVEN SERIES
by Lynnette Bonner

Not a Sparrow Falls – BOOK ONE
On Eagles' Wings – BOOK TWO
Beauty from Ashes – BOOK THREE
Consider the Lilies – BOOK FOUR
A Wyldhaven Christmas – BOOK FIVE
Songs in the Night – BOOK SIX
Honey from the Rock – BOOK SEVEN
Beside Still Waters – BOOK EIGHT

OTHER HISTORICAL BOOKS
by Lynnette Bonner

THE SHEPHERD'S HEART SERIES

Rocky Mountain Oasis – BOOK ONE
High Desert Haven – BOOK TWO
Fair Valley Refuge – BOOK THREE
Spring Meadow Sanctuary – BOOK FOUR

SONNETS OF THE SPICE ISLE SERIES

On the Wings of a Whisper – BOOK ONE

Find all other books by Lynnette Bonner at:
www.lynnettebonner.com

A Wyldhaven Christmas

Book Five
WYLDHAVEN

Lynnette BONNER
USA Today Bestselling Author

Pacific Lights

A Wyldhaven Christmas
WYLDHAVEN, Books 5

Published by Pacific Lights Publishing
Copyright © 2020 by Lynnette Bonner. All rights reserved.

Cover design by Lynnette Bonner of Indie Cover Design, images ©
    Depositphotos_21219423_DS – Texture
    AdobeStock_606424995 – Décor and Dividers
    Depositphotos_185393924 – Snow Overlay
    Depositphotos_4478911 – Flare
    Depositphotos_92519340 – Cabin

Other images generated by Lynnette Bonner using Midjourney and Adobe Photoshop.
Book interior design by Jon Stewart of Stewart Design
Editing by Lesley Ann McDaniel of Lesley Ann McDaniel Editing
Proofreading by Sheri Mast of Faithful Editing

Scripture taken from the New King James Version®. Copyright © 1982 by Thomas Nelson, Inc. Used by permission. All rights reserved.

A Wyldhaven Christmas is a work of fiction. References to real people, events, establishments, organizations, or locales are intended only to provide a sense of authenticity and are used fictitiously. All other characters, incidents, and dialogue are drawn from the author's imagination.

Sheriff Reagan's Christmas Boots

Novella One
Wyldhaven

Chapter 1

Charlotte tossed and turned fretfully for several hours before she heard the thump of Reagan's boots hitting the bedroom floor and felt the dip of the bed as he climbed in. He'd been dealing with a brawl at McGinty's Alehouse, and she'd partly been worried over his safety, but her mind was eased by the knowledge that he had his deputy, Joseph Rodante, and his mother's new husband, Zane Holloway, as backup.

But if she were honest, her main concern these past few days was because December was almost upon them and she didn't yet have a clue what to buy for Reagan's Christmas present.

Reagan reached over and squeezed her hand. "Hope I didn't wake you?"

She shook her head, then realized he couldn't see her in the dark, so said, "No. I've been awake. I'll sleep better now that you're home."

Reagan grunted and punched his pillow into a more comfortable position. "If you are going to have a difficult time sleeping every time I'm called out in the night, I'll have to look into making Joe or Zane handle all the late-night calls."

Charlotte socked his arm gently. "You wouldn't do that to Liora or your mother. Especially not your mother."

Reagan yawned loudly, and his voice was more muted when he replied, "Yes, but she's been doing a lot less worrying lately, have you noticed?"

"I have, indeed."

Reagan's response was a soft snore.

Charlotte sighed and flipped over on her back to stare into the darkness.

She, on the other hand, had been worrying a lot of late. What did one buy for their husband for Christmas? Last year had been fairly easy. It had been their very first Christmas, and so presents had been things they'd needed for their home. Reagan had bought her a new stove for the kitchen since old man Jonas, the previous owner of their house, had likely purchased his before the start of the Civil War. And she'd bought Reagan a new-fangled pen that stored ink right in the shaft and a new shaving bowl and razor.

But this year... She'd been racking her brain for months and hadn't been able to come up with an idea. Not because she didn't have ideas, but because, since she'd quit her teaching job to stay at home and be a wife, funds were much tighter this year than they had been last.

After a few hours of restless sleep, she woke, heart still weighed down by her predicament. She lay listening to Reagan's snoring until the sun pierced past the thin gap in the bedroom's calico curtains.

Reagan mumbled and turned over.

She threw an arm across her eyes and angled her head away. She needed more sleep, but thoughts of all she had to get done this day refused her the comfort of continued slumber. She eased from beneath the covers, doing her best not to disturb Reagan.

She hadn't taken two steps before she stubbed her toe on something hard and unyielding. Biting back a yelp and a grumble of irritation, she fumbled through the shadows to feel what it was. Reagan's boots. She gritted her teeth. In his weariness, he'd obviously discarded them without too much thought.

She grasped the boots by their tops to carry them to their proper place near the bureau. The shaft of light landed on them as she set them on the floor, and she felt her concern mount. The boots were worn and aged. The leather had definitely seen better days, but of greater concern was the large gap where the top of the shoe had separated from the sole.

Reagan had made no complaint, yet the days recently had been bitterly cold. It just wouldn't do for him to keep wearing such shabby shoes. Not only because his feet needed to be warm, but also because it simply wasn't a good image for the sheriff to be tromping around in shoes that were barely holding together. It didn't cast Wyldhaven in a good light.

She left the boots in their place by the bureau but smiled. And as she headed for the kitchen to start breakfast, she felt like a burden had been lifted.

Finally! She knew what her Christmas present this year ought to be. But her relief over knowing what to buy was mixed with worry over the how of it. They would be cheaper from the Sears and Roebuck catalog, but at this date, it was too late to have them shipped. She would just have to order a more expensive pair from Mr. Giddens at the livery.

Stepping to the cupboard, she pulled the teacup from the top shelf and dumped all the money onto the counter.

Two dollars and six bits. She was pleased. She hadn't realized that she'd saved up quite that much. It ought to be enough to buy a pair of boots, oughtn't it?

But in what size? Reagan only had the one pair of boots, and they were always on his feet unless he was sleeping, so she couldn't take them by the livery for a size comparison. She frowned as she stared at the scrambled eggs she was cooking. Maybe his mother would know? Yes. That was the solution. She gave a little nod. She would swing by her mother-in-law's later to ask her about the size.

Reagan woke an hour later and entered the kitchen with his boots in one hand. A large yawn stretched his jaw as he sank into one of the chairs at the table. He scrubbed a hand over his head, displacing his hair in all directions before he bent and tugged on the boots.

Charlotte poured a cup of coffee and set it before him. She grinned and scooped her fingers into his hair, combing it into some semblance of order. "Whatever did you do about your unruly locks before I became your wife, dear sheriff?"

"I combed it myself, but now I leave it messy to get you close enough to catch." He caught her wrist and tugged her onto his lap, looking up with a smile. He winked and raised his lips to hers.

Charlotte relished the feel of his strong hands at her back, the soft hair at the nape of his neck between her fingers, and the brush of his lips over hers.

Only a moment later, a knock sounded on the kitchen door. "Sheriff? Sheriff, you up?"

Reagan sighed and set her away from him. "Looks like my day is off to a rousing start." He opened the door.

Washington Nolan stood on the porch. "Sorry to bother you, sir! But you're needed in town."

Reagan grabbed two biscuits and pressed some eggs between them. Raising the makeshift sandwich, he said, "See you at dinner." Then he snagged his hat from the peg, stepped onto the porch, and pulled the door closed behind him.

Charlotte sighed and served herself a plate, sinking down at the table to eat alone.

Again.

Chapter 2

Charlotte hurried through her breakfast and the morning's house chores and then, with her coat tucked close about her neck and her breath fogging the morning, bustled through the cold to feed and water the chickens. She added wood to the banked fire in the old stove that Reagan had repurposed to keep the hen-house warm, and then hurried the mile into town to talk to Jacinda, Reagan's mother.

She felt a little nervous about the time frame. But if Jacinda knew the size and she got the order put in today, all should be fine.

Jacinda opened her kitchen door, wiping her hands on a towel. "Oh, it's you. Come in. It's colder than Belle's shoulder out here!"

With a chuckle over the reference to Belle Kastain's perpetual snootiness, Charlotte scooted into the warmth of the kitchen and hung her wraps on the hooks by the door.

Jacinda gave her a guilty look as she set a steaming cup of the herbal tea she kept just for Charlotte onto the table and nudged the sugar bowl her way. "Poor Belle. I really shouldn't have said that. She's gone through a lot in the past few years, and I'll be the first to admit that she's really stepped up to help her mother after William's passing."

Charlotte pressed her lips together, not wanting to agree that she shouldn't have spoken like that and condemn her mother-in-law, but also not wanting to reassure her, since it was true that they shouldn't speak at Belle's expense. Instead she offered, "I think I've figured out what I'm going to get for Reagan, finally!"

Jacinda pulled out a chair and sank down, gesturing for her to do the same. "Do tell."

"Boots!" Charlotte stirred a teaspoon of sugar into her teacup.

"Good luck getting him to give up his 'comfortable' pair." Jacinda grinned over the rim of her cup.

Charlotte tilted her head. "Am I going to have to make those old raggedy ones disappear?"

"Most likely."

"Well, the side of one busted out just the other day, so, hopefully, I won't have to fight him too passionately. But I came by for a reason. I don't know what size to have Mr. Giddens make."

Jacinda's eyes widened. "Oh, dear. I always just took a tracing of his feet to Bill. I never asked what size it corresponded to."

Willing away her disappointment, Charlotte set down her cup. "I see. Well, maybe Mr. Giddens will remember the right size. I'll pop over to the livery and ask him. What are you getting for Zane?" Since Jacinda and her US Marshal husband had only been married for a few months, this would be their first Christmas together.

With a swipe at some invisible specks on the table, Jacinda grinned and gave a pump of her brows. "Zane's old Morgan isn't as spry as he used to be. So I placed an order for an Appaloosa from the ranch we visited on our wedding tour. He admired both the dam and the sire, so I know he's going to be thrilled."

"That's so exciting! How are you getting it here?"

"It's scheduled to arrive on the train in a few weeks." She waved a hand. "I just hope everything goes smoothly. Deputy Joe has agreed to keep it in his and Liora's barn until Christmas morning."

Charlotte reached across the table and squeezed her hand. "Well, I can't wait to see it. For now, I'd better get going. I want to get my order in with plenty of time for Mr. Giddens to get them made." She stood and gestured to the cups. "Can I help you wash these?"

Jacinda brushed away the offer. "No, no. It won't take me but a moment. Thanks for stopping by!"

"Thank you for the tea." Charlotte wrapped her scarf around her throat and slipped into her coat before giving Jacinda a hug. "Have a good day. I'll let you know what I find out."

With that, she dashed out into the fat flakes that were now falling from the sky. Thankfully, Jacinda's house was on the same end of town as the livery.

Bill Giddens sat hunched near the potbellied stove in the livery tack room, cleaning a harness.

Charlotte got right down to business. "Hi Bill. I need you to keep a Christmas secret."

Bill set the harness aside and scratched at his long gray whiskers. "Beg pardon, ma'am?"

Charlotte smiled. "I want to buy the sheriff a pair of boots."

Bill's face lit up. "Oh! Yes'm. That there, I can do. I have all the fixin's just here."

He flipped a canvas cover off the table in the corner. On the table, several pairs of boots were lined up. Charlotte's gaze immediately settled on the pair on the end. Made of a rich brown leather, they had been hand-tooled and decorated with intricate stitching.

"Oh my. These are beautiful." She picked one up. The leather was as fine and soft as it looked, yet felt sturdy enough to last for a good long while. "Would you be able to have a pair of these made by Christmas?"

"Oh yes, ma'am. I can get right to it. That pair there, they would be seven dollars."

Charlotte dropped the boot as though it had just bitten her. Seven dollars! Her heart fell. She thought of the two dollars and six bits in her savings cup. Could she come up with four dollars and two bits before Christmas? She couldn't think how she would be able to do so.

"I didn't realize they would come so dear."

"Lot o' work goes into that pair, ma'am."

"Oh, I'm sure it does. I didn't mean to imply they weren't worth the cost."

Bill nodded. He pointed to a pair in the middle. "That pair there would only run you five dollars."

Charlotte twisted her lips as she studied the pair he'd indicated. They were fine; they just didn't have all the nice details the other pair had. She wanted Reagan to have the best. Her thoughts again flitted to the contents of the teacup on her top shelf, and she sighed. Her mother had always said she had champagne taste. The problem was, now that she was no longer teaching, she only had a beer budget.

So not only did she not know Reagan's boot size, but she didn't even have the funds for the ugliest pair of boots on the table. Her shoulders sagged.

At the reminder of the other fly in her ointment, she turned to Bill. "Do you happen to know the size of the sheriff's boots?"

Bill scratched his whiskered chin. "No, ma'am. Can't rightly say as I do. Been some time since Reagan ordered hisself a pair. But if you bring me a sketch of his foot, I can make that do just fine."

Charlotte picked up the boot once more and smoothed her thumb across some of the stitches. "How long will it take you to make a pair?"

"Depends on which pair you want. That fancy pair... I need at least four weeks to make those. These others can be done in three."

Charlotte's heart fell a few more degrees. She set the boot down once more. "I see. Well, I hope to order a pair. I have to—" her face flamed at the thought of admitting that she might not have enough money. Never in her life had she had that issue. Papa had always snapped his fingers and given her anything she wanted. But she and Reagan were determined to make a go of things on their own. They'd both determined that they would never ask a loan from anyone.

"Your pardon, ma'am?"

Charlotte came to and realized she'd left Bill hanging in the middle of her sentence. "I'll let you know by Monday if I plan to place the order. Will that give you enough time to get the fancy pair made by Christmas?"

He calculated on his fingers and then nodded. "Just enough time, Ma'am."

"Good. Then I'll let you know."

"Yes'm." Bill hunched onto his stool and took up his harness once more.

Charlotte bade him farewell and tucked her coat close around her throat as she stepped out into the bracing winter wind and snow.

She pressed her lips together in discouragement.

Today was Thursday. She had four more days to come up with the money and a plan. Even if she could figure out how to raise the money, how was she to get a tracing of Reagan's foot without raising his suspicions?

She sighed and headed toward Dixie's Boardinghouse. Maybe Dixie could help her figure this out. At any rate, she could use another cup of something hot to warm her up before she walked home.

Chapter 3

Dixie's dining room smelled like blueberry pancakes and bacon.

Despite the fact that she'd eaten a hearty breakfast, Charlotte's mouth started watering the moment she stepped through the doors.

Dixie glanced up from where she stood refilling a customer's mug. "Oh, hi! I'm so glad you stopped by! I could really stand to put my feet up for a few minutes." She rested one hand on her perfectly rounded belly, then swung her head toward the kitchen in a 'follow me' motion.

Charlotte smiled and trailed behind Dixie's ever-so-slightly-duck-like waddle. Dixie and the doctor's first baby was due any day now. Charlotte knew that Doc had been trying to get Dixie to take things a bit easier. He'd even hired both Susan and Belle Kastain to work full time in the kitchen after Susan's husband William had passed away last March, but Dixie still insisted on overseeing the breakfast cooking.

Dixie pushed through the batwing doors into the kitchen.

Steam rose in misty drifts from the double sink beneath the back window. Belle, whose hands were buried in the hot water up to her elbows, tossed a glance over her shoulder. She acknowledged Charlotte with a dip of her chin before returning to washing dishes.

Susan offered a smile from where she stood drying the plates Belle placed into the rack. "Morning, Charlotte."

"Good morning." Charlotte gave both women a quick squeeze. Then she sank down at the little kitchen table across from Dixie, who had dropped into a chair and promptly propped her feet on a nearby stool.

"Pardon my unladylike sprawl." She smiled.

Charlotte tugged off her gloves as she returned the smile. "I'm sure it must feel like a bit of heaven to put your feet up. How is the little one behaving today?"

Dixie rubbed her belly in a circular motion and loosed a sigh. "I'm not sure if it is elbows or knees, but someone has been gouging me in the ribs all morning!"

Charlotte chuckled and set her gloves on the table. "Only a few weeks and you'll be able to tickle little toes in retaliation."

Dixie laughed. "I do deserve at least a poke or two."

Motioning to the coffee pot Dixie had placed on the stove, Charlotte lifted her brows. "Can I pour you a cup?"

Dixie waved a hand. "Of course. And help yourself to the hot water. That blueberry tea you like is there on the shelf. In fact, I should avoid more coffee. I'll take some tea too." She glanced toward the sink. "Susan? Belle? Would you like to join us?"

Susan stepped over and set the sugar bowl and a pitcher of cream on the table. "Don't mind if I do. But I'm having coffee." She grinned.

"I'll just finish washing this last stack of plates." Belle's words weren't unfriendly, just all business.

Charlotte poured Susan a cup of coffee and fixed two cups of the herbal tea, then settled into her seat. She scooped a little sugar into her tea and relished a sip of the tart blueberry concoction. She appreciated the fact that Dixie kept the drink just for her. Both coffee and tea gave her debilitating headaches.

Chocolate too. "So, catch me up on all the news from town? Since I quit teaching, I feel like I miss out. By the time I hear about something, it's already days-old news."

Susan nodded. "You know Zoe's been helping to tutor the children after school each day."

"Yes. I'd heard that."

Dixie's lips thinned a little. "From what I've heard, she's been doing quite a bit of the teaching too."

Susan opened her mouth as if to reply, but then snapped it shut. She deliberately lifted her cup and blew on the black brew. But then she plunked the cup down. "Oh, I can't stand to keep it to myself any longer! Zoe has decided to take the teaching exam. I'm so proud of her!"

A thrill of joy bubbled up inside of Charlotte. "She has? Oh, that's such great news! I always felt she would be a wonderful teacher."

A plate crashed to the floor. Shards shot in all directions.

Belle gasped. "Oh, I'm so sorry, Mrs. Griffin. I can't think how that happened."

Susan leapt to her feet and hurried to fetch the broom in the corner.

Charlotte took in Belle's stricken face. "Are you injured, Belle?"

The girl seemed to give herself a little shake. "No, no. I'm fine. I'm just..." She raised her gaze to Dixie. "So sorry. I'll cover the cost from my next pay."

Dixie hadn't even moved. "Please, Belle." She waved a hand. "Accidents happen. I'm just glad you are unharmed. I'm not about to charge you for replacing a plate that was probably already chipped to start with."

Belle bent to pick up the larger pieces while her mother set to sweeping up the smaller bits. An uneasy silence settled.

Charlotte wanted to remove the scrutiny from Belle. "So, the teacher's exam! When does Zoe take it?"

Susan moved to the garbage bucket in the corner. "She goes to Seattle mid-December. I'll accompany her."

"You're making the trek to Seattle this time of year?"

Susan gave a nod. "The weather has been fairly mild this winter. We'll push hard so we aren't out in it for too many days. And Washington Nolan will escort us. Thankfully, he has time to make the trip before he leaves to join the cavalry."

"Wait! What? I hadn't heard that! He's joining the cavalry?"

Dixie sipped from her cup and gave a happy sigh. "He leaves just after the new year. He's to be stationed with the Seventh Cavalry Regiment in New Mexico."

"Oh my! Well, I'll certainly add him to my prayer list!"

With the clean-up of the broken plate complete, both Belle and Susan sank down at the table.

Belle smirked. "I guess the rest of those plates will have to wait. I obviously need a coffee break."

Everyone chuckled, and Charlotte quickly fetched the pot and poured another cup for Belle.

As she sank back into her seat, Dixie peered at Charlotte over the top of her mug. "So, what brings you by?"

Charlotte pulled a face. "I can't just swing by for a chat?"

"You know you can. Anytime. But I've never known you to do anything out of your routine unless you were on a mission of some sort."

"I'm that predictable?"

Dixie arched a brow. "Well?"

Charlotte chuckled. "Fine. I'm that predictable. I've decided to buy Reagan a pair of boots for Christmas, only I don't know his boot size. Nor do I have nearly enough money."

The other three women looked at each other.

Belle broke the silence. "How are you going to buy them if you don't have the money?"

Charlotte sighed. "That's why I'm here. I need help figuring that out."

Susan arched a brow. "And his boot size?"

Charlotte slumped back into her seat. "I need help with that too."

The ladies chuckled.

Chapter 4

Fixing Dixie with a look, Charlotte arched a brow. "Do you know what you are getting Flynn?"

A mysterious smile touched Dixie's lips. "I do." She leaned in. "Tell me."

Setting her cup back in her saucer, Dixie clasped her hands. "Let's just say that the 'shopping trip' I'm taking to Seattle in a couple of weeks isn't for new dresses as Flynn thinks." She grinned. "I've purchased him a sleigh from the premier sleigh maker in this region. He's going to love it. It will certainly make his trips out to the camps more comfortable."

"Oh, that sounds lovely! But Flynn is letting you travel to Seattle so soon before the baby is due to come?" Charlotte's brow furrowed.

Taking another sip of tea, Dixie brushed the concern aside. "Flynn says all is progressing normally, and I'll be taking the train. So only a day there, one day in town, and then another day back. Everything will be fine."

Charlotte blew out a breath. "Well, I'm glad you have everything figured out. Now, any ideas for how I should—"

A knock sounded at the back door.

Dixie made to stand, but Susan rose quickly and waved her back into her seat. "I'll get it."

Kin Davis stood outside the door, hat in one hand and a fishing creel in the other. Snow dusted his shoulders and hat, and he hunched his coat up around his ears.

Susan stepped back, inviting him in with a smile. Once he was inside and the door shut, she peered into his creel. "Well now, look here. Fresh fish for tonight's dinner. The loggers will be so pleased. Wait right here, and I'll get your payment." She bustled into the pantry where Dixie kept her money for such purchases.

Kin fidgeted a bit when he noticed the other three women seated at the table looking at him. "Ladies." He gave a little bow that was more nod than anything.

Dixie smiled at him. "Thank you so much, Kin. I always appreciate the addition of your fresh catches to my menu. I'm sure it was cold work, sitting still long enough to catch those."

He twisted his hat through his fingers, expression serious as usual. "You pay me well, Mrs. Griffin. I'm always happy to sell to you."

Dixie suddenly got a light in her eyes. She glanced back and forth between Charlotte and Kin. "Kin, you're an enterprising soul. Mrs. Callahan here was just sharing that she needs to make some Christmas money. What would you advise?"

Kin didn't even hesitate. His eyes softened just a touch as he said, "After the last community gathering, I heard several men raving about your apple pie, Mrs. Callahan." He dipped a nod. "Sampled a piece myself, and it was mighty tasty." His gaze pinged to Dixie. "Been awhile since Mrs. Griffin offered desserts because of—" His cheeks blazed, and he kicked at the floorboards with one toe. "Well, anyhow, I'm thinking that if Mrs. Griffin isn't opposed to the idea, that you could bake pies and sell them by the slice right here in the diner." He shrugged as if it was the simplest solution in the world. "Mrs. Griffin can likely even make a bit of profit for herself."

Charlotte blinked at Dixie, who blinked back.

Dixie was the first to break the silence. "That's a fabulous idea!"

Charlotte grinned. "Why didn't I think of that?! I've still got plenty of apples in the cellar! And I've enough money to buy the flour and sugar. It's the butter I'm not sure of. Mr. Hines does ask a dear price for it. We were buying our milk from Mr. King and making our own butter, but his cow has gone dry."

Belle cleared her throat. "Our cow is still giving a goodly amount of milk, and I'm sure Ma would be happy to sell you enough cream to make the butter you'll need."

"Of course, we will." Susan nodded as she handed Kin his payment for the fish. "And I can spare you a bucket of milk every other week after that too. What do you say to fifty cents for the month?"

"That sounds like a very good price." Charlotte eased back in her chair. "Oh, this is such a load off my mind! Now all I have to figure out is how to finagle his boot size out of him without raising his suspicions!"

Dixie chuckled. "And bake pies every day without him wondering why the house smells so delicious yet he hasn't had a bit of dessert for weeks!"

Charlotte laughed. "Oh, that's true! I'll have to bake them first thing in the mornings after he leaves so the smell won't still be lingering when he gets home!"

"If you don't mind my input on his shoe size, Mrs. Callahan, I might have an idea for you there too." Kin peered at her as he tucked his money away in his poke.

"I'm all ears!"

He shoved the drawstring bag into the inside pocket of his coat. "Heard Zoe talking to Wash about how she's having the kids down to the school do a project where they all line their feet up by size around the classroom."

"Line their feet up?" Charlotte couldn't figure out what he could mean.

"Yes'm. Tracings. They trace them, then cut them out and put them around the room by size."

"Oh!" She still felt confused. She glanced at Dixie who didn't seem to understand any better than she did. "How does that help me?"

Kin clasped his hands behind his back, and Charlotte had a feeling that if his face were more expressive, it would be showing a great deal of impatience with her density. But his tone was the epitome of patience when he spoke. "Zoe could ask the sheriff for a tracing of his feet to add to the wall."

"Oh! That's brilliant!"

"While she's at it, she maybe ought to ask a few other merchants so he doesn't get suspicious, and well...maybe," he gestured at Dixie, and his face turned red again, "Doc and Mrs. Griffin would like to have their baby's feet traced, soon as it arrives."

Dixie rested one hand on her rounded belly. "Oh Kin! That's an amazing idea. We can put it away in a keepsake box once Zoe takes them down."

He nodded. "Yes'm."

Charlotte couldn't help herself. She rushed across the room and threw her arms around Kin's neck. He stiffened, but she didn't let that stop her. She dropped a kiss on his cheek. "You're the best, Kin Davis." A thought hit her then. She pulled back and looked at him. "Where are you and Parson Clay going for Christmas? You are welcome to join Reagan and me."

He stepped back and waved his hat in a dismissive gesture. "Oh, no ma'am. The parson has plans to visit his family back east. Don't worry any about us."

Charlotte squeezed his arm. "Well, I'm sure that will be an adventure. I'm glad you have some place to go. And thank you, again."

"My pleasure." He offered a nod of farewell and then stepped out into the frosty morning.

Charlotte sank back down at the table. "My, that's a relief off my mind. Pure providence that Kin stopped by, I say."

Dixie nodded. "Agreed. I wonder how he and the parson will get along on a trip over Christmas? They've seemed a bit at odds with each other the past several weeks. I'm glad they have a place to go."

"Yes. I'm thankful too. That boy could certainly use some joy in his life."

Dixie adjusted the position of her feet on the stool. "Indeed."

"So, remind me how much you charge for a slice of pie?"

"Five cents."

"Eight slices per pie?"

Dixie nodded.

"And what would my cut of that be?"

Dixie tilted her head. "How about this. I haven't been selling any pies at all. And just having them back on the menu will make my customers so happy. So how about, for the first two weeks, you keep all of it. Then after that, we can see if you want to keep making them and discuss it further."

Charlotte did some quick calculations. And after deducting her costs for the cream, sugar, and flour, two weeks should just give her enough money to pay for the boots.

She squeezed Dixie's hand. "You're a gem!"

Dixie only smiled and sipped her tea. But after a moment she squirmed uncomfortably and adjusted her feet again.

Susan immediately stood. "You should go upstairs and rest. Belle and I will take care of the remainder of today's meals."

Dixie winced as she lumbered to her feet and rubbed her belly. "You know, I don't mind if I do. I'm suddenly feeling as though I could sleep for a week."

Charlotte took her cue and stood too. "And I'd best go talk to Zoe and put the plan into motion."

She gave first Dixie and then Belle and Susan quick hugs.

Susan stepped back. "We'll bring you plenty of cream and a bucket of milk tomorrow."

"Thank you. I'll swing by here to pick it up, first thing."

With that, she hurried out and crossed the street toward the schoolhouse.

Chapter 5

Kin settled his hat on his head and tugged his collar up around his ears as he stepped onto the street. If there was a God in heaven, he hoped the Almighty would forgive him for lying about having a place to spend Christmas.

It wasn't that he didn't appreciate Mrs. Callahan's offer. It was just that Christmastime was about family, and no one really wanted Wyldhaven's rogue orphan to spend Christmas with them, no matter how kindly stated their offers.

Parson Clay had, of course, invited him to return east with him to visit his family. But Kin could only surmise that the invitation had come out of duty. And besides, a week spent with the parson in the stuffy confines of a train car would mean a week of hearing stories about how God had given the man so much joy once he quit fighting for his own way. Kin was bone-weary of that, and it was especially not something he wanted to subject himself to on Christmas.

Not only that, but the parson was taking Tommy Crispin with him on the trip, and Kin could sure use a break from the simpleton's incessant questions and chatter.

When Wash had learned he wasn't taking the train with the parson, he had invited him too, but Kin had also put him off. Wash's family barely had enough money for presents of their own, much less for an extra. And they would feel obligated to get him something if he were to spend Christmas with them.

It was only one day. He would drink plenty to forget, spend the morning sleeping in, and let everyone else enjoy their families. Then the day would be done, and he wouldn't have to think about it again for a whole year. And no one would be the wiser. They'd all think he was at someone else's place.

Besides...he'd been thinking more and more about moving to Seattle to find more permanent work. Maybe he'd even see about becoming an apprentice in a law office. He'd read a few books about the law and wouldn't mind learning a little more about how the justice system worked.

McGinty stepped into the doorway of his saloon, drying a beer mug. He gave Kin a wave and lifted the mug with a little waggle.

Kin swallowed. A drink would be mighty satisfying right about now. But he'd promised Wash he'd try to cut back, and he'd been doing pretty good for the past few days. He rubbed his hand over the bulge of his money sack in his jacket. Even had a little bit saved up since he'd quit spending it all at McGinty's. But...he licked his lips.

McGinty smiled at him.

Kin took a step.

Movement down the street caught his attention. It was just the flicker of a white hat by the jailhouse alley. He watched.

A moment later, Sheriff Reagan poked his head out and scanned the street in both directions, then waved frantically for Kin to join him and withdrew again.

Kin's brow furrowed. He waved off McGinty as he headed toward the alley.

McGinty frowned and looked out in the direction of the alley but, when he didn't see anything, withdrew with a gesture of disgust.

Kin didn't let it get to him. He was too curious about what the sheriff could want. The sheriff was normally a very level-headed man, and he couldn't figure out what might have the man acting so crazy.

When he stepped into the alley, the sheriff was pacing back and forth. Near his feet were two bushel-baskets filled with...apples.

Kin's heart gave a thump of dread. He looked up and met the man's gaze.

Sheriff Reagan gestured in the direction of the dining room. "I saw Charlotte go into the boardinghouse earlier and then you go in after. Do you think she'll be busy with Dixie for a while? I've been trying to figure out how to get her out of the house so I could sell these apples to Mr. Hines. Money's been a bit tight this Christmas, and he's offered me a good price, but I don't want Charlotte to catch me hauling them across the street."

Kin swallowed. He stared down at the apples for a moment. He felt a bit like he'd just walked onto the stage in the middle of a theatrical drama and it was his job to instigate the resolution. He cleared his throat. Rubbed his jaw.

The sheriff frowned at him. "Was Charlotte in the boardinghouse kitchen just now?"

"Yes. Are these your apples?" More precisely, Mrs. Callahan's apples. The ones she planned to use to make pies so she could buy the sheriff a pair of boots.

The sheriff leaned a little closer and sniffed. "You been drinking again, kid?"

"No, sir."

The sheriff plunked his hands on his hips. "Of course, these are my apples. I wouldn't be trying to sell them if they weren't."

Kin worked his tongue over his lips. "What I mean to ask is...are these all the apples you have?"

The sheriff waved a hand. "Yes. But don't worry. This will be more than enough to buy her the bolt of lace she's been eyeing. So, do you think she'll be busy for a while?"

Heart falling, Kin glanced back toward the street. How did he fix this?

The sheriff stepped closer. "You are acting mighty strange. Is everything all right?"

"Yes. Fine. I was just—I'll buy the apples from you! What price did Mr. Hine's offer?"

The sheriff frowned. "He's offered me four dollars per basket."

Kin swallowed. Eight dollars! And he'd have to beat Mr. Hines' price to boot. But he didn't really have much he needed money for. And—he could hear the tinny piano in McGinty's plunking out "Clapham Town End"—it would likely save him from drinking the money away, anyhow. Besides his friendship with Wash, Mrs. Callahan had been one of the first bright spots in his entire life. She'd always encouraged him to do better, but never with the condescension that some had directed his way. And the sheriff was a kind man, even if he did enforce the law with exacting measure. Kin dipped his chin, decision made. "I'll pay you four dollars and fifty cents per bushel."

The sheriff blinked at him. "Why do you need this many apples?"

Kin shrugged. "It's Christmas." He grinned, hoping the sheriff would let the matter drop with that. He felt a sudden joy in what he was about to do.

The sheriff scratched his jaw. "Well, I guess I didn't promise Jerry I'd do it. We only discussed what his price would be, and I said I'd think on it." He stretched out a hand. "So you have yourself a deal."

Kin shook his hand and paid him, then watched as the sheriff, new-found cash in hand, carefully glanced both ways before dashing across the street to the mercantile.

Kin transferred his attention to the two bushels of apples stacked at his feet. He gave a little shake of his head, hefted them, and hurried toward the Callahan place. He needed to get these back into the Callahans' cellar before Mrs. Callahan got back to her place.

Chapter 6

"Yes, Miss Kastain!" the children chorused as Charlotte stepped through the back door of the church, which functioned as Wyldhaven's schoolhouse during the week. Surprised to hear the children addressing Zoe, Charlotte poked her head around the partition that separated the classroom from the back doors as she tugged off her gloves.

Zoe stood at the blackboard, instructing the children in long division.

Charlotte frowned. She searched the room but didn't see Mr. Haversham, the town's teacher. Where was he?

Noticing her, Zoe hesitated, which drew the attention of all the children to the back of the room.

"Mrs. Callahan!" Several of the older ones leapt to their feet and rushed to envelope her with boisterous hugs. Even though it had been months now since she'd last been their teacher, it felt good to know that some of them still remembered her with fondness.

Charlotte chuckled and coddled each of them for a moment, but then urged them all back to their seats.

She met Zoe's gaze. "Where's Mr. Haversham?"

Swiping at chalk dust on her fingers, Zoe couldn't seem to meet her gaze. "He, uh..."

"Mr. Haversham rarely makes an appearance before morning break." Grant, the youngest Nolan brother, piped up from the back of the classroom where his long legs were crammed beneath the too-small-for-him desk. He gave a definitive nod. "Zo—er Miss Kastain—does most of the teaching."

Charlotte felt her heart begin to thump against her breastbone. The town council wasn't paying the man to lay home abed while someone else did his work for him!

Zoe lifted a hand to ward off further questions. "It's not as bad as it might first seem. What brings you by today?" Zoe gave a pointed look toward all the children sitting enraptured at their desks.

Charlotte let her gaze drift over the students. She supposed Zoe was correct that this wasn't the time or place to have a discussion about Mr. Haversham's downfalls. "When you have a moment, may I speak to you outside?"

"Certainly." Zoe nodded. "Class, copy down your work and then focus quietly on your problems. I'll be back in just a moment." She tipped a nod toward the door.

Pulse pounding faster than ever in her ears, Charlotte went out and waited for her on the small landing. The moment Zoe made her appearance, Charlotte stepped toward her. "How long has he had you teaching for him?"

Zoe sighed. She folded her hands and seemed to contemplate her answer. "I don't want to get him into trouble."

Charlotte's lips pinched. "You won't be getting him into trouble. You'll only be telling me the truth."

With the toe of one boot, Zoe scuffed at the porch boards. "Since the beginning of the school year, I have been teaching all the morning classes."

Charlotte's teeth slammed together. "And?"

"He arrives at break time, checks to make sure all is going well, and then goes over to McGinty's till lunch."

"And Ewan hasn't said anything to anyone?!"

Still studying the boards at her feet, Zoe mumbled, "I asked him not to mention it. Just like I'll ask you not to mention it to anyone. I enjoy being able to help the kids and don't want to lose that."

"Oh, you won't lose it. I'll see to that. But I'll not stand by and let you do all the work and him collect all the money! And that's certain!"

Zoe's eyes widened a little. She held her silence.

Charlotte realized that she'd let her frustration boil over into her tone. She took a calming breath. "Sorry. It just makes me madder than a hungry bear fresh out of hibernation to learn he's been using you so."

"I wouldn't call it using." Zoe kicked at a knot in one of the boards.

"Well, it is. And as soon as you have your teaching certificate, I intend to let the board know I think you should have the job you've been doing all these months anyhow."

Zoe's eyes brightened. "You could do that? Oh, that would be such a relief to Ma and the family!"

"I can, and I will. I was so excited to hear that you were taking the teacher's exam!"

"I've been studying like crazy!" Zoe pulled a face. "But I'm still so nervous!"

With a wave of her hand, Charlotte dashed away the concern. "As smart as you are? I know you'll have no problem passing the test."

Zoe rubbed her hands together. "I hope so. Is that what brought you by today?"

Charlotte chuckled. "I heard that you are doing a project where you trace everyone's feet?"

Zoe's frown said she couldn't figure out why that would have brought Charlotte by. "Yes."

Charlotte explained her dilemma and Kin's idea for the solution.

Zoe chuckled. "That's brilliant! Yes. I can ask the sheriff to get his feet measured. In fact, I should ask all the Wyldhaven citizens! And maybe we can have everyone into the classroom to view the display and combine it with a Christmas party fundraiser for some larger desks for the bigger boys. Though it does give me a chuckle to see Lincoln and Grant sitting there with their knees up by their ears." She winked.

"That's a fabulous idea! I'm sure you could use some funds to buy more books too."

"That's certain." Zoe grimaced. "David Hines came to school the other day, and his arithmetic primer was completely torn in half and missing several pages. He said he'd accidentally dripped some butter on it and then had to rescue it from his dog."

Charlotte chuckled and squeezed Zoe's arm. "Reminds me of Jinx!"

Zoe nodded and rolled her eyes. "For a taste of butter, Jinx would eat Satan's socks. Anyhow, I'll go right down to the sheriff's office as soon as school's out for the day and get that measurement for you."

Charlotte thanked Zoe for her help and left with the promise to check back the next day to retrieve the drawing.

Chapter 7

Charlotte was still chuckling as she made her way toward home. But the longer she walked and the more she thought about what Mr. Haversham was doing, the angrier she became until her dander was all a ruffle.

By the time she reached the base of the hill, beyond which lay her house, outrage pumped through her. She hefted a double handful of skirts and stomped toward home. Of all the sneaking things to do! Well, as soon as Zoe had her teaching certificate, the school board would be hearing from Charlotte on the need for his replacement!

For now, Charlotte's immediate problem was taken care of. And maybe it was providence that had sent her to Zoe for part of her solution so that she could learn just exactly what Mr. Haversham was up to.

Charlotte crested the hill and paused to lean against a tree and catch her breath. She'd taken that steep road much too quickly! Hand propped against a trunk, she looked down on the little cabin she and Reagan had purchased from Mr. Jonas's son just after the old man had passed on.

Smoke rose in a thin wisp from the chimney due to the banked fire she had left in the stove. And with the mountains beyond, it created a picturesque scene. The barn could be in better shape, but they had worked on one end of it to make it warm and snug for Reagan's horse. Next year when they had enough money, they would finish the rest of it.

Movement caught her eye and she stiffened. Who was that coming up out of the cellar behind the cabin? She leaned in and squinted. It was a man. He dropped the heavy, sodded lid back into place, dusted his hands, and looked around.

Charlotte gasped and stepped to the side of the path behind a tree before he could see her. What had Kin Davis been doing in their cellar? She peered around the tree.

Kin jogged across the field behind their place. He disappeared into the trees beyond.

Heart heavy, Charlotte took the road down to the house. With a sigh, she realized that it was probably best she just go to the cellar and see what he might have taken.

Of all the shenanigans Kin had pulled in his day, she never would have pegged him to steal from her, or Reagan, for that matter. And she'd just watched Susan pay him a goodly sum for the fish he brought to Dixie's diner! He shouldn't be bad enough off that he needed to steal food.

Charlotte hauled up the door to the cellar and descended, lighting the lamp at the bottom of the steps. She shone the light into every corner, but nothing seemed to be amiss. She frowned. Not one jar was out of place. There were still six eggs in the basket of straw just as there had been this morning. The two bushels of apples were still in the back corner.

So, what had Kin been doing down here?

She returned to the house, but her heart was heavy all day, for she knew that she needed to tell Reagan what she had seen. No matter that he hadn't taken anything. He'd been trespassing, uninvited.

She had a simple meal of beef stew and biscuits ready when Reagan walked in the door that evening. He hung his hat and coat on the pegs by the door and then stepped to the sink to pump water for washing. He gave her a nod and a smile. "Evening. Sorry I'm a little late. Zoe came by right as I was leaving with a hair-brained idea for a last-minute Christmas fundraiser."

"Did she get the tracing of your feet?"

Reagan stilled and studied her. "How did you know about that?"

Charlotte's mouth went dry. Idiotic, Charlotte! She scrambled for an explanation with a wave of her hand. "I went to town earlier and stopped by the schoolhouse to chat with her for a bit. She mentioned it."

Reagan reached for the towel and set to drying his hands. "I see."

Charlotte spun away from him, blowing at a strand of hair in relief. She was such a terrible secret keeper.

Reagan was quiet as he hung the towel back on its hook, and Charlotte pulled the biscuits from the warming oven.

They said a quick prayer and then settled into silence as they ate.

After a moment, Reagan lifted his gaze to hers. "You aren't normally this quiet. Is everything okay?"

She sighed, heart pinching. She really hated to tattle on Kin when he seemed to have done nothing wrong. Yet, he also had no business being in their cellar.

"Charlie?" Reagan frowned at her.

Charlotte waved a hand. "It'll keep. Let's eat while the food is hot. What did Washington Nolan want so early this morning?"

Reagan spread butter on a biscuit. "Seems some bandits broke into his Pa's barn and stole buckets full of milk. The cow was nearly dry come morning, and the buckets were missing."

"Someone stole milk? How crazy! Do you have any leads?" Charlotte's mind flashed to the image of Kin coming out of the cellar. Could he have had something to do with it? But at the Nolan place? Surely not! He and Wash had been the best of friends since they were both in short-pants. And yet... she'd thought Kin respected her and Reagan enough that he would never do anything like that to them, yet there he had been, coming out of the cellar. She sipped her broth, reminding herself that she hadn't been able to find anything out of place. She tried to convince herself that there could be a perfectly innocent explanation for his trespass, yet logic seemed to defy that option. She came to and realized that Reagan had been speaking and she'd missed most of what he said.

After that, she tried to keep up her end of the conversation, but as soon as he had finished his last bite of stew, Reagan pushed his bowl away and tossed his serviette down on the table. "Come on, Charlie. Something is wrong. You've not been yourself all evening."

Charlotte curled her hands around her mug of hot apple cider and released a breath. She supposed the time had come. "I went into town this morning, as I already mentioned. And when I came back, I saw someone coming out of the cellar."

"What?" Reagan stood and reached for his hat, obviously intent on going out check on it immediately.

"You needn't bother going out. I've already been down to look, and nothing is amiss. But..." She hesitated. Did she tell him she knew it was Kin? What would happen to the boy? She clenched her teeth. In truth, Kin Davis was no longer a boy, but a full-grown man. One who should know better than to go skulking through others' cellars!

"But what?" Reagan urged.

Charlotte gave in. "I saw who it was."

Reagan searched her face, brows arching.

"It was Kin Davis."

Reagan's expression changed subtly. He returned his hat to the peg, and then sank back down at the table, fingers drumming. He frowned at Charlotte. "Nothing was missing?"

She shook her head. "Not a thing."

Reagan rubbed one hand across his jaw. "Maybe...he took...a few things that you didn't notice? Like...apples?" He lifted is coffee cup to his lips.

Charlotte shook her head. "No. I was just down there this morning before heading into town. Everything is exactly as I left it. The two bushels of apples are stacked right in the corner where they were this morning."

Reagan sputtered coffee and quickly swiped at it, snatching up his serviette to wipe his mouth.

Charlotte frowned at him. He must have inhaled wrong trying to talk and drink hot liquids at the same time. "You all right?"

He nodded. Batted away her concern.

She let it go. "Anyhow, like I said...nothing seemed disturbed. I have no idea what he was doing down there."

"Well, I'll swing by and talk to him about it first thing in the morning. For now, let me help you with these dishes." He rose and took his plate and utensils and the biscuit plate, leaving Charlotte to follow in his wake to the kitchen.

She frowned as she gathered the rest of the items. She tossed a glance toward where he was already pumping water into the sink. It was almost like he didn't want to talk about it anymore.

But why would that be?

Chapter 8

The banging on the parsonage door the next morning sent a nail straight through Kin's temple. He groaned and rolled over, tugging his pillow over his head. Blast, but his skull felt like a blacksmith had taken a hammer to it in the night. Maybe melted it down and tempered it a few times too.

He shouldn't have given Ewan that last dollar for that bottle of rot-gut.

Had the parson heard him come through his window in the night?

Whoever was at the door banged again.

"Coming. Coming." The parson's voice drifted through his door.

Kin pried one eyelid open.

And frowned.

Tommy sat on his bed across the room, palms pressed together and tucked between his knees as he rocked forward and back. He stared at Kin. "Y-You broke the chair."

The chair that he used to make late-night entry easier lay in several pieces beneath his window. Kin sighed. Tommy was right. He must have broken it somehow when he came in last night.

"P-parson is m-mad." Tommy's rocking increased.

Which meant the parson had definitely heard him come home.

The front door creaked, and low voices rumbled.

"Kin!" The parson's voice was none-too-gentle. "Law is here to see you."

Kin fought to think through the blackness that claimed all the memories of the night before. Had he done something stupid? Well...more stupid than drinking Ewan's home brew?

Tommy rubbed his head, a sure sign that his agitation was on the rise. "Tommy w-will stay here."

Coming.

He rolled to a sitting position and gripped the edge of the bed to steady himself. Spikes of pain made flashes of light cross his vision. He scrunched his eyes shut.

Bang!

Kin flinched, seeing Tommy do the same across the room.

Bang! Bang!

The parson's fist was like to bend the hinges!

"Wake up, son. Sheriff Callahan is here."

Tommy crawled farther onto his bed and curled his knees to his chest and his arms about his head.

"Coming!" Saying the word aloud made him realize that he might have only thought it the first time.

He fumbled his arms into his shirt sleeves and tugged on his pants and boots. Before he left the room, he paused to look at Tommy. "PC would never hurt you, Tommy. Not like those others before. Besides..." Kin crooked him a smile. "I'm the one he's mad at."

Tommy nodded vigorously. "Yep. He m-mad at you. Mad. Mad at you. Tommy stay here."

Kin reached for the doorknob. "That's 'cause you are smarter than me, Tom. A lot smarter."

Tommy cackled as he stepped from the room.

The parson and the sheriff were sipping coffee and speaking in low tones at the table when he approached, still working on his sleeve buttons.

Both men gave him a once-over.

"Morning." He squinted against the light coming through the window and turned for the coffee pot at the back of the stove. If he was going to jail, he might as well go with a mouthful of the parson's good coffee in his gullet, because he'd tasted the sheriff's, and his was downright awful. He sank down at the table and propped his head against one hand. "Whatever I did, Sheriff, just come out and say it because I got no memory of last night's doings."

Parson Clay's jaw bulged, and he folded his arms. But at least he held his silence.

The sheriff scrubbed one hand over his cheek. "I'm not here to arrest you. I'm here to ask you why you bought my apples and then put them back in my cellar."

"Oh. How did you find out?"

"My wife saw you coming out of the cellar. But she reported that everything in the cellar was just as she'd left it, including the two bushel baskets of apples."

"Oh." Kin's heart fell. So did Mrs. Callahan think him a thief, now? The thought was intolerable, yet he couldn't go to her with an explanation without revealing that the sheriff had been about to sell the apples to buy her present. Just like he couldn't tell the sheriff that his wife was making apple pies to sell so she could buy him boots.

"Well?" the sheriff urged.

Kin stalled by taking a large gulp of coffee. He fought through the muddy sludge of his memories from the day before searching for some plausible reason for his returning the apples. His thoughts stumbled onto the reminder of Mrs. Callahan throwing her arms around his neck, giving him a kiss, and then inviting him to Christmas. That could work. It was thin, but... it was all he had.

Both the sheriff and PC stared at him, waiting for a response.

He swallowed another gulp of scalding coffee. "It's just... well...you see...the parson is going back east to visit his family over the holiday. And your wife, sir, she...invited me to your house for Christmas. And she promised me apple pie. And she... well...she makes a mighty fine apple pie. I didn't want to miss out on that on account of you selling those apples to buy her some lace. Because...lace wouldn't be nearly as...tasty."

There was a moment of pause. Then both men burst out laughing.

"You spent over nine dollars so that you would be able to have a slice of pie come Christmas?"

Kin shrugged. "Well, and so's I wouldn't be tempted to spend it on drink." He tossed a guilty look at the parson in time to see the man's laughter fade into pinched lips.

"Guess you left a dollar too many in your pocket then, didn't you?" Hurt rimmed the edges of the words.

Kin ducked his head, guilt slicing through him. The parson was a good man who'd offered him nothing but kindness ever since Pa's death had thrown them together. But the man's patience with his drinking was wearing thin these days. And Kin couldn't really blame him. He was a might impatient with it himself.

The sheriff stood and lifted his hat from the chair spindle. He reached out and clapped Kin on one shoulder. "Well, I'll be certain you get the largest slice of pie, come Christmas, son. The very largest one."

The sheriff and the parson were grinning at each other again.

Hopefully they would just chalk all this up to the stupidity of youth and not see through to the lie beneath. He didn't want to ruin Christmas for the Callahans.

"Well, I'd best be going." Sheriff Callahan pushed his hat back onto his head. "I need to ride out to the Kastain place. Seems someone broke into their barn and stole a shovel and a bucket last night."

"Oh no!" Parson Clay stood. "Did they lose anything else?"

The sheriff shook his head. "No. Whoever it was left their cow in her stall, thankfully." He lifted a hand in farewell and stepped through the door.

And as Kin watched him go, he realized there was another spill of honey he'd just stepped in. He'd told Mrs. Callahan that he had other plans for Christmas, so she wasn't expecting him. But he supposed he could come up with an excuse to the sheriff later for why he couldn't make it for Christmas after all. He just had to hope that the sheriff didn't say anything to her about it in the meantime.

For now, he'd just have to avoid Mrs. Callahan so he wouldn't have to tell more lies.

And he'd make a point to let her know he wasn't stealing from her after Christmas, when the truth could come out without spoiling anything.

He glanced up to find the parson's piercing green gaze drilling into him.

He sighed.

Time for another lecture.

Chapter 9

Charlotte had placed her order for the seven-dollar boots with Mr. Giddens. And for two weeks she'd baked pies and delivered them to Dixie's by the back door so she wouldn't have to walk by the front windows of the jailhouse where Reagan might see her and question what she was doing.

She never had gotten a satisfactory answer from Reagan on what Kin Davis had said about why he was in their cellar. Reagan had merely said he'd spoken to him and that he wouldn't be prowling around their cellar again. Then he'd made a cryptic comment about Kin and Christmas just before he'd been called away to deal with another instance of things going missing from someone's property—in that case, the Hines had arrived at their store one morning to find that half a jar of penny candy was missing, along with a few candles and some soap.

And she'd hardly had a chance to pass more than a few words over dinner with Reagan since. Even then, he'd been so busy chasing about after this petty criminal that he was distracted and a poor conversationalist. She missed him. Hopefully, he would catch whoever was responsible soon, and their lives could return to normal.

Today she had awoken with excitement coursing through her. Yesterday, she'd delivered the last pies needed to complete her payment to Mr. Giddens. And Dixie had promised to have her money waiting for her just after the breakfast hour. They'd also made plans to discuss the future of their new pie-making venture. Charlotte had been combing through her recipe books for other types of pies she could bake because she was down to only a few apples at the bottom of the last basket. The lumberjacks would probably appreciate some variety in their desserts anyhow, so it wasn't such a bad thing.

Taking up her list and dawning her shawl, Charlotte slipped out into the drifting snowflakes and crunched across the squeaking snow toward town.

After the frigid walk, the warmth of Dixie's diner was a welcome comfort. Charlotte couldn't wait to wrap her hands around the warmth of a cup of tea.

Only patrons occupied the dining room, but that wasn't unusual. She would find Dixie, Susan, and Belle in the kitchen. And after her recent days of practical solitude, she was looking forward to some conversation.

"Dixie?" She pushed through the heavy batwing doors into the steamy kitchen.

And froze.

Across the room, two men with hats tugged low and bandanas pulled up nearly to their eyes stood holding the three women at gunpoint. Belle's raised hands dripped soap suds. Dixie's hands rested protectively over her baby. And Susan's hands were covered in flour. A batch of bread dough lay partially kneaded on the sideboard. Charlotte took in all this with a blink.

And then, one of the outlaws swung his gun in Charlotte's direction. She automatically lifted her hands.

His eyes were wide, and that was when Charlotte realized these weren't men at all, but youngsters. He motioned with his gun for her to join the other women in the corner.

Charlotte scuttled over to do as she was bid. What did they want? And were these the petty criminals that Reagan had been hunting down for the past couple weeks?

"You." The taller of the two pointed at Belle with the gun barrel. "Rinse your hands. You're going to fill a basket with food."

Charlotte and Dixie exchanged a look. That was a girl's voice. These were just a couple of children!

Belle glanced at Dixie.

Dixie nodded for her to follow instructions.

Belle pumped some water, rinsed her hands, and then led the way to the shelves that composed Dixie's larder and followed the girl's instructions to fill a basket with flour, lard, salt, and bacon.

"Sugar," the other one said, a boy by the sound of his voice. "Don't forget to get some sugar." He moseyed toward the table, all the while keeping half an eye on their little huddle, yet seeming to search the room for something too.

"Yes, sugar." The girl motioned with her gun. Belle added a packet of sugar to the basket.

The boy lifted one of Dixie's pots from its hook above the stove. "We should take one of these pots. Would certainly make cooking easier."

The girl gave a dip of her chin, and he set the pot on the table. His focus honed in on something on the sideboard, and beside her, Charlotte heard Dixie give a little intake of breath.

He reached for a small milk tin and gave it a shake. Metal jingled inside and he smiled satisfactorily.

Charlotte's eyes fell closed. Her boot money.

Dixie suddenly stumbled sideways and bent double, gripping the back of a chair with one hand and her belly with the other. She blew out a long breath that was part moan.

Charlotte's brows shot up. "The baby!" Anger surged, sure and certain. These ruffians had sent Dixie into labor! She snatched up the nearby broom and swung it at the boy before she even thought twice. It connected solidly with his shoulder.

"Ow!" He stumbled backward, tripped over his own feet, and sprawled to the floor. His gun tumbled away and slid beneath the wood stove. The red bandanna slipped, and, just as suspected, he was a peach-cheeked boy, probably no older than fourteen. His expression revealed shock over Charlotte's attack.

She left him lay there and turned her ire on the girl next. "Look what you've done!" Unfortunately, the girl was too far away to reach with the broom. "You've sent my friend into labor. You both ought to be ashamed of yourselves!" She chucked the broom aside. "Just take whatever you intend to take and be gone!"

The girl snapped her fingers at the boy. "Get up. Leave the money. We ain't here to steal. Only to take what we need to survive."

The boy rose with a grumble and readjusted his bandanna. "I weren't gonna take it all. Just a dollar or two so's we could buy some things proper, 'stead of stealing everything."

"Well, we ain't taking it! Get your gun."

He glanced toward the stove. "Can't. Stove's too hot."

Dixie blew out another groan.

Charlotte motioned toward the broom. "Use that." She couldn't believe she was helping the kid retrieve his gun, but at this point, she just wanted them gone so they could find Doc and get Dixie upstairs. She rubbed Dixie's back and bent to peer into her face. "You doing okay?"

Dixie only glowered at her, and Charlotte realized she probably deserved that.

Though the boy put the tin of money on the table, he kept glancing toward it, attention only half on the job of sweeping his gun from beneath the stove.

Charlotte didn't care at this point. She just wanted them to leave so she could help Dixie and find Doc.

The girl stepped away from the shelves with her knapsack so full that she could barely sling it over one shoulder. "We got what we came for. Come on!" Keeping the room covered by her pistol, she poked her head out the door and checked the street. "All clear. Let's go."

The boy gave one last glance at the tin of money, snatched it up and followed the girl out the door.

Charlotte's heart sank. All her hard-earned money.

But she couldn't bring herself to care about it right now. She was simply thankful that they were gone. "Come on, Dix. Let's get you upstairs. Belle, find Flynn."

Dixie released a long breath, hand on her belly as she bent double.

Charlotte rubbed her back, feeling a little bit terrified. She wished mother hadn't been so stingy with her information about childbirth. Every time Charlotte had asked her about it, she had brushed a hand through the air and exclaimed, "Oh, it will all be clear enough when the time comes, dear."

What if Dixie was too far gone to be able to move? If she had to deliver this child right here in the kitchen, she had no idea what to do!

But Dixie suddenly stood and smiled wanly. "All right. I think I can move now."

Charlotte realized Belle was still frozen in place. "Belle!"

Eyes wide, Belle nodded. "Yes. On my way." She lifted her skirts and spun toward the dining room door then back to the outside door, and then froze again. "Where should I start my search?"

Dixie waved a hand toward McGinty's. "I believe he's next door treating one of Ewan's tenants if he hasn't been called elsewhere. Start there."

Belle scurried out to the street, slamming the door behind her. Charlotte eyed Dixie. "Ready?"

"Yes. I think I can make it upstairs now."

Susan was washing her hands at the sink. "I'll be up in just a few minutes with warm water."

Charlotte gave her a nod. "Come on." She nudged Dixie toward the dining room door.

They were halfway up the stairs when Dixie paused, gripped the hand rail, bent forward, and loosed a long breath.

Charlotte hoped she couldn't feel her hand trembling as she rubbed her back again. "What do you need me to do?"

"Just. Give. Me a. Moment." Dixie panted.

Charlotte didn't want to give her a moment. She wanted to get her upstairs and into her bed and turn her over to Rose. If delivering a baby in the kitchen was bad, delivering one on the stairs was infinitely worse.

Slowly, Dixie unclenched her hand from the rail and straightened.

Charlotte literally bit her tongue so she wouldn't rush her on her way.

At that moment, the main doors of the boardinghouse burst open, and Doc rushed into the entry.

Oh, thank you, Lord. Charlotte released a sigh of relief.

"Dixie!" Doc was grinning from ear to ear. "You doing all right, darling?" Doctor bag in one hand, he rushed up the stairs.

Dixie ignored him. It seemed it was taking all her concentration to climb the stairs.

Doc thrust his bag into Charlotte's hands. He scooped his wife into his arms. "How long has she been in labor?"

She was supposed to know that? "I-I w-we were in the kitchen, and these kids broke in and—"

"What?"

Charlotte gave up on trying to explain that right now. He wouldn't be able to do anything about it, anyhow. "She went into labor in the kitchen about twenty minutes ago."

Dixie shook her head. "Five o'clock this morning."

"Five!" Doc peered into Dixie's face. "You knew you were in labor, and you let me go out on a call?!"

She gave a wave of her hand. "Just get me to my bed, Flynn, before another contraction comes."

"How far apart are your contractions? You been counting like I told you to?"

Dixie glowered at him. "I've had a few other things going on, Flynn."

He glanced back at Charlotte as he hefted Dixie past the last step to the landing. "Right. Kids broke in, you said?"

"They didn't harm us. Just wanted food, I think." And her money. Now that Flynn was here to take care of Dixie, Charlotte felt the full impact of what she'd lost. Reagan's Christmas present. Sure, she could bake and sell more pies, but the money wouldn't come in soon enough for her to have the boots under the tree on Christmas morning. Disappointment lodged in her throat. Now what was she going to give Reagan?

Charlotte realized she still stood halfway down the stairs with Doc's bag in her hand. She rushed to catch up to Flynn and Dixie. "Flynn, is there anything you need me to do? Susan's heating water in the kitchen."

He shook his head. "Thanks for bringing her this far. I'll take it from here." He bent and somehow managed to turn the door handle while still holding Dixie.

Unaccountably, disappointment surged through Charlotte. Only a moment ago, she'd been terrified that she might have to deliver this baby; now she was disappointed to be dismissed.

"All right. I'd better go let Reagan know about the ki—."
The door clicked shut in her face.

Shoulders slumping, she set his doctor bag by the door and turned for the lobby.

Chapter 10

Kin leaned against the corner of Dixie's boardinghouse, looking down toward McGinty's. He brushed a hand over the bills in his pocket and swallowed. He'd spent the past few weeks fishing long hours and then selling the meat in the logging camps come evenings. He'd been doing pretty good at not spending the money on liquor—keeping himself busy.

But then today, he'd decided to take a day to rest, and a couple hours ago that familiar powerful thirst had come on him. If he hadn't been in town when the wagon with Ewan's new supplies had arrived, he might have been okay, but from the moment he'd seen that crate of rum being hauled inside, he hadn't been able to think of anything else.

His gaze moved involuntarily to the church across the street and up on the hill. He owed a lot to Parson Clay. PC would be mighty disappointed if he had to come haul him out of Ewan's again. And Kin had no doubt that if he stepped through the alehouse doors, PC would come looking for him later.

But... He returned his focus to Ewan's. He could hear the music pumping from the old mostly out-of-tune piano, now. He loosed a breath, pushed away from the wall, and started toward the alehouse.

Just then, the front door of Dixie's Boardinghouse opened, and Charlotte Callahan stepped out into his path.

"Whoa!" Only then did Kin realize how quickly he'd been moving. He stepped back. "Sorry about that. I was—" He paused. "You okay?"

Mrs. Callahan quickly dashed at her cheeks. "Kin. Hi. I'm—no."

"What happened."

"Well, Dixie went into labor. That's a good thing."

Kin eyed her damp cheeks warily. "Is something wrong with her?"

She swiped at the moisture again with a little laugh. "Oh. No. I think she'll be fine. Doc is with her." She swirled a motion at her evidence of tears. "This is...because..."

Oh no. Was she going to start crying again? He looked around hoping to see someone he could hand the distraught woman off to, but it was only the two of them on the street.

Her face crumpled. "...a couple of kids broke into Dixie's and stole some things. Including the money I've been saving to buy Reagan's boots."

Kin's focus sharpened on her. "I'm sorry." His jaw clamped in irritation. The money he'd spent to save those apples had apparently been wasted. "So, you aren't going to be able to get the sheriff the boots?"

She shook her head. "Wasn't meant to be, I guess. I need to let Reagan know about the robbery, then I'll stop by and let Bill know I can't buy the boots just yet after all."

Kin remained where he was as he watched her walk past McGinty's and on into the jailhouse. He rubbed a hand over the bills in his shirt pocket once more. Glanced at the livery. Looked back at the church.

He sighed.

It only took him half a minute to find Bill Giddens. He was seated on the workbench in his tack room. The old man leaned over a saddle he was hand-tooling, face so close to his work, it was a wonder he could see anything.

Kin cleared his throat.

Bill sat up with a start, brows raising. Obviously, his ears worked just about as good as his eyes these days because he ought to have heard Kin's boots crunching over the sandy floor.

"Kin Davis. Lands, you've grown boy! What can I do ya fer?"

Kin tossed a glance over his shoulder. He needed to hurry if he was going to pull this off without getting caught.

He tugged the bills from his pocket. "Listen, Mrs. Callahan is going to be here in just a moment—"

"Eh? Speak up, kid."

Kin raised his voice. "Mrs. Callahan. She's going to come tell you she can't buy the boots, but," he held up the money, "you tell her someone covered it."

Mr. Giddens gave him an assessing look. "Where'd you get that kind of money?"

"I worked for it." Kin pressed the bills into the old man's hands. "And keep my name out of it, would you? Just tell her it was someone who appreciates all she's done for this town."

He hurried out the back slider of the barn so that if Mrs. Callahan was already headed this way, she wouldn't see him coming out.

And as he rushed toward the parsonage, he tried his best not to think about the sweet taste of the rum he was missing out on.

Charlotte dragged her feet toward the jailhouse, doing her best to get her sadness in check, but it was no use. By the time she arrived, tears streamed down her face.

The moment she stepped into the room, Reagan lurched from his chair and hurried toward her. "What's wrong?" He took her by the shoulders and bent to peer into her face. "You've been crying. What's the matter, Charlie?"

Charlotte couldn't bring herself to look him in the eye. Never had a Christmas gone by where she hadn't given those she loved a gift. And yet here she was, only in her second Christmas of their marriage, and she had failed to get her husband a gift.

Now not only would she not have nice hand-tooled boots to give him, but she didn't even have her original two dollars and change to buy him something mediocre from Jerry Hines' 'merkantile.' Perhaps she should suggest to Pricilla that she get her husband a correctly spelled store sign for Christmas, she thought grumpily.

Reagan's hands soothed up and down her arms. "You're scaring me, Charlie. Are you hurt?"

Oh! What was the use in hiding anything from him now? He wasn't going to get a present, and it would be better if he learned that now instead of after anticipating it for several weeks and then waking up on Christmas and finding no present, right?

She sank against the comfort of his chest, thankful that he had no prisoners in the cells at the moment so they were alone in the privacy of his office. "Oh Reagan, I'm so sorry."

Reagan's arms were strong and warm around her back. He pressed his cheek to the top of her head. One hand rubbed small circles into the muscles along her spine. "What are you sorry about?"

Charlotte sniffed, and a hiccup caught in her throat. "I've failed to get you a Christmas present. At least not one that will be under the tree on Christmas."

"Charlotte, I don't need—"

"Not that I haven't tried, mind you. I ordered a pair of boots for you from Bill Giddens. But I only had a couple dollars saved up, and they were more expensive than that." For a moment, her throat closed off, and she couldn't get any more words out.

"It's really—"

"But I went to Dixie's, and Kin Davis came by. He said I make really good apple pie."

"Yes. He told me the same." She heard a smile in Reagan's voice, even as his hand kept rubbing soothing circles.

Why was he finding humor in her confession of failure? The realization made her cry all the harder.

"Anyhow, I've been working for weeks, baking apple pies and selling them at Dixie's!" She felt him stiffen and hurried on before he could interrupt. Maybe if she could just explain all that had happened, he would understand. "And I was supposed to go and pay for them today—the boots, not the pies—but I was just at Dixie's to pick up the money, and these two children were there. And they s-st-stole all the money." She forced herself to lean back and look into his face. He at least deserved that when he heard the bad news. And she ought to see the expression on his face as penance for her failure.

He frowned. "Two children stole your money from Dixie's just now?"

She felt a fat tear drip off her chin and slide down her neck. "Yes. But they're long gone by now." She flapped a hand. "They sent Dixie into labor, and I thought I was going to have to deliver the baby, and Dixie was having a hard time making it up the stairs, so then I thought I might have to deliver the baby on the stairs."

Reagan looked appropriately appalled.

She nodded. "But Doc is with her now."

"I'll wait a bit to go ask my questions, then."

"Probably best. But there was a boy and a girl. They wore bandannas, but I could tell. The boy was maybe fourteen. I saw his face when I hit him with the broom and his gun fell under the stove."

Reagan's eyes widened. "They had guns? Wait, you hit him with a broom?"

"He sent Dixie into labor!" Charlotte brushed away his questions about the kids. "Anyhow, now I don't have money to pay for your p-present." A sob tightened her chest, and another hiccup shook her.

Reagan cupped her face and swiped away her tears with his thumbs. His eyes twinkled as he bent down and pressed a soft kiss against her lips.

She frowned. "Why are you smiling and kissing me when I've just confessed that I failed to get you a present?"

He stroked her cheeks again. "Because you are amazing."

Her face contorted. Had the man not heard a word she said? "But I'm not! I just told you—"

Reagan laid a finger over her lips. "Charlie, I didn't marry you for the awesome Christmas presents I would get. Giving gifts at Christmas is about the spirit of sacrifice. And I can tell by how upset this has made you that you've had that spirit in spades. You tried to get me a pair of boots, right?"

She nodded. "I tried really hard. I even asked Zoe to get a tracing of your feet so I would know what size to order." She couldn't help but smile at him through her tears.

He tossed back his head on a laugh and then rubbed his nose against hers. "You are a genius. And I love you more for wanting to give me a present than for any present you could or will ever give me."

She studied his face.

His blue eyes, filled with merriment, looked back at her frankly.

"So, you're really not upset?"

Reagan brushed another kiss against her lips. "I'm really not upset. It's all going to be fine."

She released a long sigh. She hadn't realized until just now how worried she was over how he would feel. "Well, I need to go tell Bill that I can't pay for the boots right away. But I want you to know, I'll keep baking and selling desserts until I get them paid for. They just won't be under the tree at Christmas."

Reagan stepped back and glanced down at his feet. He lifted first one split-out boot and then the other, and then he gave her a wink. "I can't see why you thought that was such a good present anyhow. This pair is so comfortable. Nice and airy too."

Suddenly feeling lighter than a feather, she laughed and gave him a playful smack. "Your mother warned me that I might have a hard time prying them off your feet, but be assured, Sheriff, those boots will disappear when the new ones arrive."

He gave a dramatic sigh and rolled his eyes. "Fine. If they must."

Charlotte started for the door but then paused and turned to face him. "Thank you for not letting Christmas be ruined because of this."

He tilted her a look. "How could Christmas be ruined when we have each other?"

Charlotte gave in to the temptation for one more kiss. She crossed the room and looped her arms around his neck, offering him a lingering one. "I really am spoiled to have found a man like you."

He grinned and rocked her from side to side. "Christmas will be amazing, boots or no boots. But Charlie?"

"Yes?"

"I think we should invite Kin Davis to the house. A slice of your pie is probably just the thing to make his Christmas."

"Oh, I asked him already, and he said he has other plans."

Reagan smiled mysteriously. "Go talk to Bill. And after that, I think you should ask Kin again. I have a feeling he'll say yes this time. Tell him I said he deserves some pie."

Charlotte shrugged and headed for the door. "Okay, I'll try. Oh, and Reagan?"

"Yeah?"

"Go easy on those kids when you find them, would you? I got the feeling they are just trying to survive."

Reagan frowned. "Trying to survive, or not, doesn't make it right for them to be stealing stuff around town."

Charlotte opened the door. "I know. But it is Christmas."

Reagan sighed. "I'll keep your wishes in mind."

She nodded. "That's all I can ask."

A few minutes later Charlotte stepped out of the livery feeling like a child on Christmas morning about to explode with excitement. She paused in the street. She propped her hands on her hips, despite the fact that her finishing school teacher, Miss Gidden, would chastise her for such an unladylike gesture. A glance both up and down revealed no one in sight. Who would have known about her money being stolen and had time to get to the livery?

She felt a bit as though she'd been tied to the end of a whip all day. One moment excited about picking up her money, the next having it stolen, worrying about Dixie, fearing she'd have to deliver the baby, and then being dismissed by Flynn. Confessing to Reagan that she wouldn't be able to give him the boots and now suddenly finding out that someone else had paid for them and she would be able to have them under the tree after all!

Who could have done it?

Her gaze snagged on the boardinghouse. Susan. It had to have been Susan Kastain. Or Belle? She shook her head. No. Belle gave all her money to her mother. But maybe it was something they had decided on together?

She strode purposefully and pushed through the boardinghouse kitchen door.

Susan must have already taken the pot of warm water upstairs, because she was once more at the table, swiftly shaping loaves out of the dough she'd kneaded earlier.

"How are things upstairs?"

"Doc seemed to think things were progressing as they should." Susan shrugged a shoulder.

Charlotte barged ahead with the purpose of her return. "Susan you are an angel, and I'll pay you back, honest I will."

Susan looked up, a blank look on her face.

Charlotte grinned at her. "You may look at me with that innocent face all you want, dear friend, but I know it had to be you."

Susan's mouth opened and closed a few times. Her forehead scrunched into a questioning slump. "Whatever you think it is I've done, I assure you that I haven't left the boardinghouse since you and I stood right here a few minutes ago. I heated the water and only came down from upstairs just a couple minutes ago." She gestured to the bread. "I've been working on these loaves since then."

Charlotte folded her arms and tilted her head, certain the woman had to be pulling her leg. "So, you didn't just go to the livery and pay Bill Giddens so I could give Reagan boots on Christmas morning?"

Susan's brows shot up. "Someone did that? That's wonderful!"

Charlotte plunked her hands on her hips. "It really wasn't you?"

A smile tugged at Susan's lips even as she shook her head. She brushed a lock of her autumn-red hair away from her face. "It really wasn't me."

Charlotte stepped to the door and scanned the street once more. "Well! If I believed in Santa Claus I'd say he just swept down from the sky in his sleigh!"

Susan chuckled. "Not knowing is killing you, isn't it?"

"It really is!" Charlotte nodded.

Across the street from Dixie's and up the hill, Kin Davis was just disappearing into the parsonage.

Charlotte gasped. No!

She thought back. Why...it had to be! There was no other explanation!

Tugging her coat tighter about her, she folded her arms and hurried up the hill. It only took a moment after her knock for him to answer the door.

He looked surprised to see her. "Mrs. Callahan. Hi." He stepped back. "The parson's not here right now, but...do you need something?"

She didn't enter. Instead, she searched his face. After her quick accusation of Susan that had turned out to be inaccurate, she was a little more hesitant this time. "Did you pay for Reagan's boots just now?"

He rubbed the back of his head. Confusion was written all over his face. "You just told me you weren't going to be able to afford them."

She nodded. "Someone paid for them without my knowledge. It wasn't you?"

His brow furrowed and he shrugged one shoulder. "Why would you think it was me?"

She searched his face. Was he pulling one over on her? "Not many people knew of my predicament." It had to be him, didn't it? "I simply wanted to say, thank you from the bottom of my heart."

Kin frowned. "Mrs. Callahan...surely Mr. Giddens didn't tell you it was me?"

"He didn't. Not a peep. He outright refused to tell me who it was."

Kin peered at her. "I think you need to keep after Mr. Giddens. He'll likely tell you who it was eventually. Maybe after Christmas. Whoever helped you, likely cares about you and the Sheriff a good deal and only wanted to spur on your Christmas cheer."

Charlotte searched his face. Surely, he would have confessed if he were the one who'd done it. Her shoulders drooped a little. She turned to scrutinize the houses of the town. Who else could it have been? Surely not Mr. Giddens himself? She stomped one booted foot. "Oh! It's going to plague me with curiosity until I figure out who it was!"

Kin smiled. "Perhaps you should simply accept the gift in the spirit I'm sure it was meant?"

Charlotte shook her head. "I will accept it for now, but, mark my words, I will figure it out and repay whoever it was, and that's certain!" She started back down the hill but then remembered and turned back. "Oh, and Reagan says that I should insist you come to our house for Christmas. He seems to think you'd like some apple pie."

Kin's eyes widened a little. "Yes, ma'am. I think I can arrange that."

"Excellent! We'll see you then!" Despite being foiled at finding out who her benefactor might have been, she felt lighter than air as she skipped down the hill.

Sheriff Reagan of Wyldhaven would get his Christmas boots after all.

Dear Reader,

I hope you smiled at least a few times as you read this story. And that this Christmas season, you'll remember that the heart of Christmas isn't about the hustle and bustle and stress of finding perfect gifts but about the Savior, King of all creation, who, being in very nature God, did not consider equality with God something to be used to his own advantage. (Philippians 2:6 NIV) Instead, He humbled Himself and was born in a lowly Bethlehem barn so that later, He could die for the sins of all mankind! What an amazing Love!

If you enjoyed this story, please leave the book a review. It doesn't have to be long, but every review helps spread the word, and the world needs more uplifting stories!

Wondering about the thieving kids in this story? Or about Dixie and Doc's baby? Or about how she is going to manage to get Flynn's sleigh now that the baby has arrived early? I invite you to read the next episode of this series titled Doc Griffin's Christmas Sleigh on the next page.

You can find all the books in the Wyldhaven series here on my website.

Merry Christmas!

Lynnette
BONNER

Doc Griffin's Christmas Sleigh

Novella Two
Wyldhaven

Chapter 1

Fat snowflakes drifted lazily against the gray pallor of the winter sky outside Dixie Griffin's bedroom window. She lounged against the pillows Flynn had propped against the headboard and studied the tiny round face of the newborn cradled in her arms. So much awe and wonder coursed through her. She'd never imagined she could feel a love like this—so protective, so fierce, so all-consuming.

She reached a tentative finger to caress the chubby cheek. Tiny rosebud lips just above a dimpled chin, and long dark lashes that lay on pink cheeks already had Flynn grumbling about how many times he was going to have to clean his shotgun to keep suitors at bay.

Dixie smiled. She had a daughter. *They* had a daughter.

Dixie looked up at Flynn, wondering if he shared in the feelings of overwhelming love washing over her.

The look on his face showed he did. He sat on the edge of the bed with one arm propped beyond her, his gaze fastened on their two-day-old daughter.

"I still can't believe how beautiful she is," he whispered. "Her face is shaped just like yours."

Dixie smirked. "Dr. Griffin! I know that I've put on some weight during the last few months, but there's no need for you to point out such."

His eyes widened a little as they darted to hers, but then he noticed her teasing expression and grinned at her. "I meant no such thing, and well you know it, woman." He leaned close to leave a lingering kiss against her lips.

Dixie sighed in satisfaction. She nestled her head against the pillows. "What are we going to call her? We really need to decide."

This time it was Flynn who reached out to caress one knuckle across the baby's cheek. "I've been pondering. And I like the name Ellery Rose."

Dixie smiled. "It's beautiful. And Rose will like that." Dixie's mother-in-law from her first marriage was more like a ma to her. It pleased her to honor the woman in this way.

He nodded. "It's a good name."

"It is, indeed."

Flynn stood then and gathered up the dishes from the soup Rose had brought a while ago. "I'll just run these down and set them to soaking."

Dixie felt her face heat. Cleaning up was women's work, even if Flynn was a doctor who'd likely done many more menial tasks for his patients. "I can do that later."

Flynn shook his head. "You just worry about taking care of that little one."

With that, he left the room.

Dixie returned her focus to the baby. This time, she stroked the dimple in the pudgy chin. She bent to whisper conspiratorially into the infant's ear. "So, Ellery Rose, you have no idea what your early arrival has done to my Christmas plans for your papa."

Dixie settled more comfortably into the pillows and turned her focus toward the ceiling.

The babe hadn't been expected for nigh on three weeks.

Earlier in the season, Dixie had convinced Flynn to allow her to take a quick trip to Seattle to do some Christmas shopping. She was supposed to leave the day after tomorrow. In reality, the trip was not to do Christmas shopping, for she had already done her shopping. The trip was to pick up the new sleigh that she had purchased for Flynn from the sleigh maker in Seattle. She'd planned to make sure it was loaded properly on the train and escort it on the return trip. Kin Davis had promised to meet her at the station with a horse and drive her to the Nolans' place since they had agreed to keep the sleigh until Christmas day. She had planned everything so perfectly, and the snows had even arrived right on time this year, much to her delight. Everything would have been perfect. Except she'd gone into early labor, and now here she was.

She blew out a breath. With the bitterly cold winds and potential for more snow any day now, she could not take the baby on such a trip, no matter that most of it would have been on the train.

Yes indeed, Miss Ellery's arrival had put a kink in her plans.

She tried to think what she ought to do. She would just have to send a wire. She would ask the sleigh maker if she could pick up the gift later in the spring.

But that presented her with another problem. She had hoped to give the sleigh to Flynn for this winter season. Well, for what remained of it. And not having the sleigh to give him meant that she would need to come up with some other gift. And she had no idea what that would be.

She spoke once more to the baby. "What are we going to do about papa's Christmas present, little one?"

Ellery Rose's only response was to slurp on her fist.

Dixie chuckled.

Dixie had hoped to get right over to the telegram office the next morning. Flynn normally left on his rounds first thing. But today, he had dawdled and fussed over the baby until Dixie was practically ready to shoo him out the door. Then, it had been time to help Susan and Belle with the boardinghouse breakfast, which she had somehow managed between bouts of feeding and changing Ellery. But the morning had slipped away, and now, it was almost noon! If she didn't go immediately, Flynn would be back from his rounds!

"You're sure you'll be all right with her for a few minutes?" she asked Rose.

Rose sank into the rocking chair by their living room's wood stove and stretched out her arms. "Of course, we'll be fine. We'll just sit here by the fire and have ourselves a little woman-to-woman chat."

Dixie smiled. She wasn't sure why she was so reluctant to leave the infant to simply walk across the street. She bent and laid the baby in Rose's arms. "All right. I'll be back just as soon as I can." She tapped the baby on her nose. "You be good for Grandma."

With that, she hurried down to the front door. She only felt a little guilty as she searched the street to make sure Flynn hadn't returned earlier than expected. After all, what was the Christmas season without a few secrets? And that man was a hard one to keep secrets from since he knew everyone and talked to so many people every day. It was why she'd purposely ordered his gift all the way from Seattle, so that no one would accidentally let something slip.

Seeing he wasn't in sight, she dashed across the street. The bell above the post office door jangled as she opened it.

Ben King looked up from where he stood sorting mail into the delivery pouches. "Mrs. Griffin. Good morning, ma'am. I hear congratulations are in order and that she's a real peach of a gal."

Dixie clutched her shawl closer at her throat and turned to give the street one more searching look before she closed the door and stepped fully into the room. "She is that. All that and more." She smiled at him, knowing how much wistfulness his congratulations must contain since he and his wife, Ethel, had tried for the last several years to have children without success. "Flynn says it will be fine for us to bring Ellery to church on Sunday, so you should be able to see her then."

He nodded. "Ethel will look forward to it. As will I." Complete sincerity shone in his gaze.

"Yes, well..." Dixie took another step into the room. She fiddled with the hem of her shawl, trying to figure out exactly how she should word her message to quickly sort out this mess with the sleigh.

Ben King leaned his elbows on the board and tilted his head. "What is it I can do for you this morning, Mrs. Griffin?"

Through the window, Dixie gave the street one last glance before she stepped all the way to the counter and forced herself to focus on the task at hand. She clenched her fingers together. "I need to send a wire to Seattle."

Ben nodded, licked his forefinger, and lifted a telegram form from the stack. He took up a fountain pen and held it at the ready for her message.

"It's to Mr. Fordham of Stewart Street Sleighs."

Mr. King nodded and jotted the pertinent details in the form's correlating boxes. "And the message is?"

Dixie hesitated. "Well you see... It's just that... I'm not quite sure how to proceed."

Ben King's blond brows slumped over his eyes. "Perhaps you should tell me what the problem is, and then maybe I can help you figure out how to word your request."

Dixie nodded. "I ordered a sleigh for Flynn. And I was scheduled to pick it up later this week. But with the arrival of Ellery there's no possible way for me to make the trip. So, I suppose I need to ask them if I can pick up the sleigh at a later date. But I'm not sure when that will be. After the snows clear in the spring, maybe? Once the weather is a bit warmer."

Mr. King nodded. "Yes. Yes. I see. So how about something like this..." He jotted words on the paper as he spoke them. "Early arrival of infant daughter prevents travel. Still want sleigh. Possible to pick up in March or April?"

Dixie felt relieved. "Yes. That conveys everything. Thank you." She reached for her reticule. "What do I owe you?"

Mr. King deposited his pen in the jar next to his cash register and counted the words on the telegram. "Eighteen cents."

Dixie clamped her teeth against the tip of her tongue to keep from grumbling about the dear price of telegrams these days. She extracted the coins and handed them over.

He gathered them into his palm and gave her a nod. "I'll send this straight away. And will get you the reply as soon as it arrives. Likely, early this evening."

"Thank you I appreciate that very much. Oh, and Mr. King?"

Mr. King lifted his brows and met her gaze.

"The sleigh was supposed to be a Christmas gift for Flynn. And I would like to keep it a surprise if at all possible. So, if we could keep this just between you and me?"

Behind them the bell over the door rang as someone stepped into the room.

Mr. King shot her a wink. "I'll keep it our little secret. We wouldn't want word getting back to Flynn."

"Thank you." Dixie clutched her shawl tightly and turned to make her exit. She stopped.

Mrs. Pricilla Hines stood in the doorway, brows almost buried beneath her feathered, purple hat. She glanced back and forth between Ben and Dixie.

Dixie wanted to moan. How much of their conversation had the town's biggest gossip overheard? After all her trouble to keep this a secret, if word got back to Flynn... She gritted her teeth and forced a smile. "Good day, Mrs. Hines."

"And to you, Mrs. Griffin." Mrs. Hines gave her a minimal curtsy, and Dixie could feel the woman's chilly curiosity like a palpable presence in the room.

She stepped toward her. "Listen, if you could please keep what you may have overheard to yourself, I'd really appreciate it. We don't want to ruin anyone's Christmas."

Pricilla's lips rounded into a small, tight O.

Reassured that the woman seemed to have caught on, Dixie gave her an encouraging nod.

Pricilla snapped open her fan and flapped it so rapidly that it wasn't much more than a blur before her face. "Of course. You don't want Flynn to know." She made a little motion as though locking her mouth. "My lips are sealed."

Dixie puffed out a breath. "Thank you. And now, if you'll excuse me, I'd better get back home to Ellery before Flynn catches me over here."

Pricilla stepped to the side and swept her skirts out of the way. "Yes. Don't forget about the little dear. I'm quite surprised to see you out and" —her gaze swept to Ben— "about, so soon."

Dixie smiled and scooted past her. Even though she knew she should pay Pricilla's words no mind, she felt the need to defend herself. "I haven't left her for long, and she's with Rose. I just needed to have this little chat with Ben."

Pricilla gave a conciliatory bob of her head. "Well, don't let me keep you."

Ben lifted a hand. "See you tonight."

Dixie gave a parting wave, checked the street, and then rushed across to the boardinghouse.

She gave a sigh of relief once she was safely back inside without catching a glimpse of Flynn. At least she wouldn't have to come up with a plausible explanation about why she'd been "out and about" so soon.

Chapter 2

Thankful to have finished his rounds a little early, Flynn left his horse in the livery and walked up the street. He was anxious to get home to cuddle that new little bundle, but he needed to stop by the mercantile first to see if the new cooking pots he'd ordered for Dixie for Christmas had arrived yet.

However, when he stepped inside, Jerry was not behind the counter, and no one seemed to be in the store. Just as he was about to decide to check back later, he heard a shuffling sound from the storeroom behind the mercantile counter.

A long green curtain cloaked the doorway, so he couldn't see who it might be, but sometimes Jerry stepped in to fetch one thing or another. He would probably be right back.

Not wanting to call out and disturb him, Flynn opened the Seattle newspaper Jerry kept by his register for customers to peruse.

"Do stop pacing and spit it out, Pricilla. I came over at your insistence. What is it you need to tell me?"

Flynn lowered the newspaper and frowned. That was Ethel King's voice. What was Ben's wife doing in the Hines' mercantile storeroom? And why would Pricilla have taken her in there?

He heard footsteps and could see a shadow passing beneath the hem of the curtain. "Oh, Ethel, I'm just not certain how to break the news to you."

Flynn's lips pressed together. With the two women involved he might have known it would be a gossip session. He folded the newspaper and returned it to its place. Looked like he probably needed to come back later after all. If Jerry had left Pricilla in charge of the store, she wouldn't be any help with checking on the order. He knew that from experience. He started for the door.

"Just spit it out, Pricilla."

"Fine. I think your husband might be having an illicit affair with Dixie Griffin."

Flynn froze. Blinked. Frowned. Anger surged hot and sure. He spun back to stare at the curtain. What under all of heaven?

Ethel King gasped. "Pricilla Hines! Of all the tales you've told, this might just take the cake!" Ethel's hand came into view. She was leaving the storeroom and going to catch him here listening!

"No, wait!" Pricilla snapped.

Ethel stilled, her hand gripping the curtain.

"I'm telling you as a friend, Ethel. I don't know what is going on, but Dixie Griffin and Ben King have some sort of secret. I overheard them talking about it!"

Flynn took a breath. Scrubbed a hand over his face. This was simply another of Pricilla's tall tales. He should walk away right now. Yet somehow, his feet seemed glued to the floor.

Ethel's hand disappeared. "My husband is not having an affair with Mrs. Griffin! Whatever would make you say such a thing?"

Priscilla Hines *tsk*ed. "Darling, I'm not saying anything other than what I overheard and saw just a few minutes ago."

Flynn felt every hackle on the back of his neck rise. Of all the dirty lies that Priscilla Hines had ever spread, this had to be the worst. He was of a mind to march behind the counter and demand that Pricilla be truthful for once in her life! And yet...though Pricilla was quite a teller of tales, every story he'd ever heard her tell had a small nugget of truth at the center. So...how had Dixie come to be at the center of this one?

"And just what did you overhear and see?" Ethel snapped.

Pricilla must have leaned closer to her friend, because her words were much quieter when she said, "I went to the post office because I needed to mail a letter to my mother. But when I stepped inside, your husband and Dixie appeared to be in a *very intimate* conversation. And I distinctly overheard him say 'I'll keep it our little secret. We wouldn't want word getting back to Flynn.'"

Flynn studied the floor at his feet, working his jaw from side to side. Why would Dixie and Ben be conspiring to keep information from him?

Ethel gasped her exasperation. "Pricilla, this is ridiculous. Word of what getting back to Flynn?"

"That's just it. I don't know. But then when Dixie saw me standing there, she asked me to keep what I'd overheard to myself until after Christmas."

Ethel released a chuckle. "Well that explains it. Christmas! She must have ordered a package for Flynn!"

Flynn's eyes fell closed, and he smiled. He was an idiot. Of course! That explained everything. He turned once more toward the door. He'd better get out of here before Pricilla spilled the news of what Dixie had gotten him.

From the storeroom Pricilla trilled a note of negation.

Despite himself, Flynn hesitated with his hand on the doorknob.

"That's what I thought at first too," Pricilla said. "But then, as Dixie was leaving, Ben *winked* at her and called out that he would see her tonight."

Flynn frowned, but he was determined not to listen to any more of this gossip. With a quick jerk he yanked open the door and lurched onto the steps.

He pulled in a calming breath and studied the street, willing himself to put the troubling story behind him.

And yet... Dixie had deceived him for months when he'd first known her. She'd been married—granted to a man that she'd been forced to run from for her life, but married nonetheless—and she hadn't told anyone in town. Not even him. Not until her husband ended up, gun-shot, as Flynn's patient.

Flynn sighed. He thought he'd gotten past all that. Forgiven her. But...could she be deceiving him yet again?

He shook his head. No. She was a different woman now. Had given her life to God. And they'd put all that behind them after her husband's death.

And yet...

His heart felt like a rock in his chest as he started, once more, toward home.

He wished he'd never walked into that mercantile today.

Chapter 3

Maude and Seth Carver hovered near the fire at the front of the little lean-to shelter they'd built. Their older brother, Kane, lay at the back of the shelter on a pallet made of pine boughs and all three of their bedrolls.

Though Seth held his hands toward the flames, his gaze remained fixed on Kane. "He's shivering again."

Maude swallowed, eyeing Kane worriedly. "Maybe we should take him into town to the doctor?"

"They saw my face when we robbed that boardinghouse a couple weeks ago. If I show up there, they'll arrest me. But... You think he's gonna die? Because—"

"Not if I can help it." She gave a firm shake of her head. "And you're not going to jail, either. You done shucking those ears of corn? This water's boiling."

Seth banged together the two ears of corn they'd stolen from the storehouse of a farm earlier today. "This corn is harder than rocks."

Maude snatched the ears from his hands. "Will have to do. Kane needs food. We'll just let it boil until it's tender."

Seth huddled into his thin coat, eyeing the blankets piled around his brother with a touch of jealousy. "He needs some meat."

Maude sighed. "We ate all the bacon we got from that boardinghouse kitchen. You think you could catch us some fish?"

Seth thought back to the wave of warmth that had enveloped him when they'd stepped into that kitchen. Even though that woman had attacked him with the broom, he wouldn't have minded staying there. She could whack him all she wanted, so long as he was warm. But they couldn't have left Kane on his own. Though Maude had never admitted it, it was a good thing he'd taken that tin of money despite her telling him to leave it, because that was what had allowed them to buy the three bedrolls from the mercantile in Cle Elum. She knew it, and he knew it, but he would never dare say it.

"Hello?" Maude waved a hand before his face. "You hearing me?"

He considered her question. "What would I use for fishing line? Or a hook?"

Maude pondered for a moment and then shrugged out of her sweater.

Seth's eyes widened. "What are you doing? It's freezing out here."

Maude tied the sleeves of the sweater into knots on the wrist ends. "Saw a man once who had a basket that was a fish trap. The fish swim in one end and can't get out the other or turn around. You go to the creek and see if you can use my sweater to catch us some fish."

Seth hesitated. It was mighty cold out there away from the fire. Not to mention that her plan sounded like he'd have to wade into the water to get it to work. She may have just given up her last piece of warm clothing to make it happen, but he'd have to get wet.

He thrust the sweater at her. "You need warmth more than we need fish."

She pushed it back at him. "But not more than Kane needs it." She gave him a pointed look.

Seth sighed. Looked like it was December creek waters in his future instead of the warmth of a fire. "Fine. I'll see what I can do."

Before he left, he stepped to the back of their shelter and squatted next to Kane. He reached out and laid a hand over Kane's forehead. Still burning up.

Kane shifted and mumbled something unintelligible.

Seth gritted his teeth. "Don't you die on us, Kane. We need you to live, you hear?"

Kane made no reply.

Feeling the heavy burden of despair, he hefted the axe that they had placed by the pallet, both for protection at night and also so the blade wouldn't get wet and rusty. On his way out, he handed it to his sister. "While the corn boils, you'll need something to do to keep you warm. Chop some more pine boughs and see if you can't weave a few more into the sides and front of the lean-to and pile as many on top as you can. It's fixing to snow again tonight. We're going to need all the insulation we can get."

Maude grunted. "Yes, boss."

Seth rolled his eyes at her. Maybe she would have thought of it on her own, but the truth was, she'd never liked being told what to do.

As he trudged toward the creek, Seth tossed a glance at the heavens. "I know with all the stealin' we been doing lately, You might not be feeling exactly kindly toward us. But if Kane were able, he'd whup both Maude and me for the thievin'. So, if You could see fit to bless us with some warmth and some food so he can recover, it would really be for his account. And Maude and I would appreciate it."

A clap of thunder rolled through the cloudy sky. Seth flinched.

He wasn't sure if he should take that as a good sign or as a bad sign. But maybe it was, at the very least, a sign that God had heard his prayer.

When Flynn stepped into the living room, Dixie was in the rocking chair near the wood stove. With Ellery tucked into the crook of one arm, her head tipped back, and her eyes closed, she gently rocked the chair using one foot.

Across the room, Rose sat on the settee, reading a book. She glanced up and gave him a smile. By some unspoken agreement, they didn't converse, allowing both mother and babe to continue their rest.

But Dixie must have sensed his presence because it was only a moment before she lifted her head. "Hi." She spoke quietly. "You're home early. How were your rounds?"

Flynn bent to drop a kiss on her brow. "Good. Thankfully, the incidents of winter illnesses have been fairly low this year." He carefully eased the blanket away from his daughter's face, feeling his heart melt all over again at the sight of her.

Ellery thrust one tiny fist from the blankets and arched her little back into a stretch.

They both smiled.

Flynn set his doctor bag in its place by the door and eyed her. "And how was your day?"

Dixie gave a nonchalant shrug, but didn't meet his gaze. "Oh, you know... A bit of a challenge what with getting used to working around Ellery's schedule."

That was a bit evasive. Hang it. He was just going to ask her outright. "Did you go anywhere?"

Dixie lurched from the rocking chair. "You know, I think Ellery needs changed." She rushed from the room with the baby.

So...not a lie, but not an answer either. He looked to his mother-in-law.

She suddenly seemed fastidiously interested in her novel. She wouldn't cover for Dixie if something untoward was going on, would she? No. Surely not. All this was likely a Christmas surprise, just as Ethel had pointed out.

Flynn paced to the wood stove and opened it. As he tossed in a couple pieces of wood, he considered.

Why was he even giving Pricilla's story any credence? He knew what kind of woman she was. He also knew that Ben King loved his wife. And Dixie had never given him any cause to distrust her since she'd given her life to Christ. More importantly, he knew that Dixie loved him.

He closed the stove and sank onto the settee next to Rose. Sweeping a hand over his face, he leaned against the cushions and stared blankly at the wall.

Dixie bustled out of the bedroom. "There. All dry and ready for some time with her pa." She held the baby out to him. "I'll run down and fetch us a tray of supper. I can't say how thankful I am that Susan and Belle have agreed to take on a few more hours of work. It will be a great relief. In the next few weeks, especially."

Setting aside her book, Rose stood. "I'll run get the food. You sit and enjoy the evening with your husband. Your family." She smiled.

Dixie hesitated. "I really don't mind. We can both go."

Flynn cradled Ellery against one arm and eyed the two women. Were they both trying to make an escape?

He looked down at the baby and pressed his lips together, weary already of his swaying emotions. He either trusted his wife, or he didn't. There was no in between, so what was it going to be?

"All right," Dixie suddenly said. "Thank you. I do confess to being rather exhausted. But I don't want you to think that we expect you to serve us now."

Rose flapped a hand to bat away Dixie's concerns. "Nonsense. I don't feel that way at all. I'll return shortly."

And as Dixie sank onto the settee next to him and curled against his side, Flynn suddenly knew the answer to his question.

He trusted his wife. Without a doubt. He smiled down at her and wrapped one arm about her shoulders.

This was the good life. Inside where it was warm. His daughter in his arms. His wife by his side. The good life, indeed.

Besides, Pricilla had said Ben told Dixie he would see her this evening, and that obviously wasn't happening.

He felt his concerns release their hold.

Everything was fine. He was just tired. That was all. He needed to renew his efforts to entice another doctor to this area. Most days, he was practically run off his feet, and he didn't remember the last time he'd gotten a full night's sleep—all of which was only bound to get worse now that they had a baby in the house.

Yes, everything was going to be fine. He dropped a kiss against Dixie's temple.

And then, a knock sounded at the door.

Chapter 4

Dixie had just settled onto the cushions next to Flynn when the knock came.

"I'll get it." She leapt up, not wanting to disturb Flynn. He rested so seldomly.

Kin Davis stood on the other side of the door with a piece of paper in his hand. "Evening." He gave her a nod. "Ben King sent me over with this here message for you."

Dixie's heart surged and seized all in the same moment. She tossed a glance toward Flynn. She didn't want him getting curious and asking questions about why Ben was sending her a message at this time of night. She should have thought to tell Ben she would come by for the message in the morning, but she certainly hadn't expected a reply this late.

Flynn's brows arched and his expression turned stony.

Dixie took the note and held it up. "Must be my reply from Seattle. I had to wire that I wasn't able to make the trip due to Ellery's early arrival." She held her breath. Would he buy it? If she didn't calm down, she was going to give away the surprise herself.

Yet her story was true enough. Only she'd wired a sleigh maker and not a dressmaker as he would suppose.

For some unaccountable reason, Flynn was suddenly grinning from ear to ear. "Of course! That explains everything."

She frowned. "What explains what?"

He shook his head. "Never mind. I'm just exhausted is all." He returned his focus to their daughter, but he suddenly seemed at ease.

On the stoop, Kin's feet shuffled. "Well... I guess that was all." His gaze met Dixie's as though he were trying to tell her something.

Dixie glance at the message from Mr. Fordham and her heart sank. He said he couldn't hold the sleigh for her till spring because he had buyers lined up and waiting. She would have to place another order come spring and make her payment in full before he began the work. She pressed her lips together. She'd obviously upset the man.

Flynn cooed softly at the baby, then lifted his gaze. With his little finger grasped firmly in his daughter's grip, he glanced between the two of them. "Thanks, Kin, for bringing the message."

Kin nodded, shuffled his feet again, and then tipped his hat. But when he had retreated into the hallway enough that Flynn couldn't see him, he motioned with his head that she should follow him.

There was obviously something he wanted to tell her. Something he couldn't say in front of Flynn.

Rose returned just then, and angled her tray of food past Kin on the landing. He stepped out of her way. "Evening, Miss Rose."

She smiled. "Evening, Kin. Would you like to stay for dinner? There's plenty."

His gaze darted to Dixie's, again conveying some sort of message. "Ah, no ma'am. Thank you, just the same."

Rose stepped past Dixie and into their apartment. She set the tray of food on the table, and when Dixie looked back, Kin had started down the stairs, but he again gave her a 'follow me' gesture.

Thinking quickly, Dixie reached for her shawl. "Kin? Do you mind waiting a moment?"

Kin paused, a relieved look flashing over his expression. "Yes, ma'am. I'd be right happy to."

Dixie turned to Flynn as she tucked a few loose curls into her chignon. "I have a delivery of pies that Liora ordered for a Christmas party she's having at their place in a few days. Since Kin is here, I'll just run down and give it to him to take out to them."

Flynn frowned. "This time of night?"

"Well, he can keep the order at the parsonage for the night if he likes and run it out in the morning, but to work around Ellery's schedule, I think it will be easier to hand it off to him now, since he's here."

Flynn rubbed his hand over his jaw and then tossed it in the air. "All right."

She frowned. Had she upset him somehow? "I shouldn't be long." She hoisted her skirts and stepped onto the landing, following Kin down the stairs. But the whole way to the kitchen, she couldn't quite shake the feeling that she'd somehow irritated Flynn.

Once they were alone in the kitchen, Kin grinned at her. "Good thinking about the pies."

Dixie brushed away his comment. "I could tell you wanted to say something." She lifted the telegram and couldn't help the slump that weighed down her shoulders. "Mr. Fordham says he won't hold the sleigh for me till spring."

"But that's not going to be a problem."

Dixie's brows rose. "Why not?"

Kin folded his arms and leaned into his heels. "I don't mind making the trip to Seattle to pick up the sleigh for you."

"Oh, Kin!" Before she thought better of it, Dixie threw her arms around him and pulled him into a tight hug. It was like the weight of the world had just been lifted from her. "That would be such a relief! I've been pondering what else to give him and just didn't know what to do. Let me give you those pies and my final payment for the sleigh and a train ticket. Tomorrow, I'll wire ahead to let them know that you are picking up the sleigh for me. You should be able to drop the pies by Liora's on your way to the station. But the train leaves at ten sharp, so don't be late."

"Yes'm."

She hustled into the larder and tugged her tin of money from the top shelf. Extracting the amount she'd been saving, she carefully folded it together, then returned and handed it to Kin. "There's a little extra to buy yourself some food once you reach Seattle."

Kin tucked the money into his back pocket. "And the pies?"

"Oh!" Dixie tossed her hands in the air and returned to the pantry. She carefully settled two pies into the bottom of a crate, then inserted a board across the slats and settled two more pies on that layer. Tucking a towel over the whole thing, she hefted the crate and returned to hand it to Kin along with the delivery fee.

"Thanks."

She nodded. "Thank you."

He settled his hat and tugged on the brim. "I'll be on the train at ten."

"You've lifted a great burden."

Dixie couldn't believe how relieved she felt as she watched him cross the street and head up the hill toward the parsonage with the crate of pies held carefully in his hands.

Everything was going to be fine, and Flynn would get his sleigh after all.

What a relief!

***

As Dixie and Kin disappeared down the stairs, Rose Pottinger shut the door. She bit back a smile as she watched Flynn bounce baby Ellery, all the while frowning at the living room door.

Dixie never had been very good at being secretive.

Flynn glanced over at her. Seeing her humor, his own lip quirked up at one corner. "She didn't have any beaus back east other than her husband that I should know about, did she?"

Rose gave him a look. "Flynn Griffin, you know better."

Flynn stood and settled baby Ellery into the cradle near the stove. "Yeah, I suppose I do. I just don't like it when I can tell she's keeping a secret from me."

"You do remember that the Christmas season is only a few weeks from now?" Rose handed him his plate of sandwiches and set a cup of milk at a place on the table.

He nodded gloomily.

With a chuckle, Rose settled down with her own plate.

Flynn sank into the seat beside her, and after a quick grace, they ate in silence. When he'd polished off his sandwiches, he pushed the plate back and looked over at her.

"So, I don't have anything to worry about? Because earlier I overheard Pricilla Hines say that she thought Ben King and Dixie were... Well..." His face turned red.

Rose huffed. "Pricilla Hines? And you found that credible?" She made sure he could read the censure in her expression.

Flynn lifted his palms in a don't-shoot-me pose.

Rose made sure she had his full attention before she spoke. "It's Christmas, Flynn. Dixie loves you more than anything. She would never betray you like that. And neither would Ben do that to Ethel. Frankly, I'm shocked that you would even briefly consider Pricilla's drivel. And that's all I have to say on the matter." It was probably more than she should have said already.

Flynn nodded. "Yes. That's what I've been trying to tell myself, but..." he waved the rest of the thought away. After a few minutes, he yawned expansively and scrubbed both hands over his face. "If you don't mind watching Ellery until Dixie gets back upstairs, I think I'm going to catch some shut eye. I was called out at four last night to tend someone wounded in the alehouse, and my short night is catching up to me."

"Of course." Rose sighed as she watched him disappear into his and Dixie's room. It wasn't the first time that the long hours he kept had raised her concerns. If he weren't half exhausted, he wouldn't likely have given any credence to Pricilla's tales.

Rose gathered up their empty plates.

One of these days, Pricilla Hines was going to end up starting a rumor that would be her undoing.

Chapter 5

Seth woke to soft gray morning light filtering in through the small hole they'd left in the roof to let out the smoke. His nose was so cold, it felt numb, and the top of his head felt as if it had been pressed against a snowdrift all night. But it was warm beneath the bedrolls.

He and Maude had crawled in next to Kane the night before. And even with the pine boughs and one bedroll beneath them and two on top, and the heat of Kane's fevered body beside him, it had taken him some time to get warm after his fishing misadventure in which he'd caught no fish, but gotten wet feet. Thankfully Maude had an extra pair of dry socks for him when he'd returned to the lean-to last night, and his other pair should have dried by the fire now.

Maude suddenly sat bolt upright on the other side of Kane, taking the covers with her.

Seth gasped at the slap of frigid air. "Maude! Blast! It's freezing! What are you doing?"

She ignored him and clapped a hand against Kane's forehead. "He's burning alive, Seth!"

He laid his hand next to hers and grunted. "Jail or no, we have to take him to the doctor in that little town."

Maude worried her lip. "We got no money for that."

"I know, but we have to try. Maybe the doctor will let you work to pay for his care."

She squinted at him. "Me work? What about you?"

Seth sighed. "I'll likely be in jail."

"They're going to know I was your accomplice the moment we arrive in town together."

He pondered that. She was likely right. "Well, then maybe we'll both be in jail, but hopefully they'll help Kane."

Tears filled her eyes. "True. We have to try."

Seth reluctantly left the warmth of the pallet. Before he could even tug his boots on, Kane was shivering violently. Seth's concern mounted. "He's not going to be able to walk."

Maude pressed her lips together. "We'll make a travois, then."

Seth nodded. "Give me the hatchet."

It took him half an hour to chop branches and fashion a travois, and by that time, Maude had their meager possessions all packed.

Kane barely had the strength to scoot from the pallet over to the travois, but with the two of them helping him, he made it.

With Maude pulling on a branch on one side and him the other, they started down the road.

Seth sucked in a big gulp of the cool mountain air and took a moment to appreciate the delicate lace the snow had made of the bare branches of a small oak. If he was breathing in his last morning of freedom, it was a good one to go out on, he supposed.

And Kane would have made the same sacrifice for him if their roles were reversed. Except...Kane wouldn't have stolen anything in the first place.

Kin felt like a little kid on Christmas morning as he trotted his horse through the snow toward the Rodante place with the crate of pies balanced carefully before him. He hadn't been able to believe his luck when Mr. King had explained Dixie's situation and asked if he'd be willing to take this trip to Seattle. Since he'd been thinking about moving to the city, this would be the perfect opportunity to look the place over and see if he felt he really wanted to move there.

Parson Clay wouldn't be happy with him leaving, but things around here had started to feel confining. He appreciated all the parson had done for him over the past few years, he really did. But he was a grown man now, and it was time he freed the parson from the burden of caring for him, especially now that he'd taken on Tommy's care.

His horse's breath fogged the air, and the sun, just cresting the horizon, lit the bare white branches of a large maple with golden stardust. A few inches of snow had fallen during the night, and the landscape all around was covered in a soft sparkling-white blanket.

On a cold morning like this, he didn't expect to see anyone, so he was surprised when he came around a corner and saw two people tugging a travois toward him down the middle of the road.

"Whoa." He pulled his mount to a stop and eyed the ragged group. None of them appeared to be in very good health. The girl and boy who were pulling the travois looked like they were about one missed meal away from starvation. And he couldn't really see the person on the pallet for all the blankets piled around him, but if he was being hauled toward town in such a manner, he couldn't very well be in too good of a shape.

The girl huddled into a sweater thin enough that it was likely meant for a warm spring day, not a bitter cold winter morning. Her dress hung on a scarecrow-thin frame, and a hank of mahogany red hair dangled over one of her dark eyes.

They stopped, both of them looking up at him with wary expressions.

Kin swung down and settled the crate of pies onto the road bank. "Howdy. Looks like you could use some help?"

The girl shook her head. "Our brother is sick, and we're taking him into town. We'll be fine."

Kin resettled his hat as he scanned the road in both directions. Of course, there was no one else in sight. But if he helped them get to town, he was going to miss the train. "You sure you can make it?" He scanned their scrawny frames once more.

The girl lifted her chin. "We'll be fine."

Her brother, however, eyed Kin's horse. "We'd get to the doc faster if we could manage to hitch this travois to your horse—"

"Seth, hush up," the girl snapped.

Seth paused. His gaze narrowed at his sister for a moment, before he kicked at a clump of snow.

Kin realized that he must be concerned about the amount of time it had taken them to get this far. He sighed. Mrs. Griffin wasn't going to be happy, but neither would she want him to leave people freezing and—he glanced at what he could see of the sick man's pallid face—maybe dying, on the road. He had to help them.

He stepped forward and held out his hand. "Name's Kin Davis."

The girl hesitantly accepted it, dipping her knees in a little curtsy of greeting. "I'm Maude Carver. Our brother, Kane, is the one who's sick. This is my brother, Seth."

The boy nodded.

"Seth." Kin shook his hand next.

He led his mount around 'til it faced the opposite direction. And realized with a bit of dread that not only was he going to miss the train, but he was going to have to abandon the crate of pies as well. Mrs. Griffin might never hire him to do a job again.

He retrieved a length of rope from one of his saddlebags. "So that's your brother on the pallet? How long has he been sick?"

Seth shuffled his feet. "He's been sickly for nigh on three weeks, but only in the last couple days has he been taken by it so badly. We're going to the doc, but we don't have any money."

"Shh." His sister hushed him with an embarrassed smack to his arm. She huddled into a tight, tense hunch, and wouldn't meet Kin's gaze.

He took the travois from the siblings and searched the sick man up and down as he set to lashing his rope around the front branches. "Is he contagious?"

Maude's eyes widened. "Will the doctor not treat him if he is?"

Kin swallowed. What had he gotten himself into here? Had he just exposed himself to some disease? He shook his head at her question and dragged the travois a little closer to his horse. "The doctor will treat him no matter what; it's just, he has a brand new baby, so if your brother is contagious, I hate to take you right to the doctor's house."

"I see." She eyed him as he worked. "What about payment?"

Kin motioned for Seth to help him. "Take that branch and put it into the stirrup on that side while I do the same over here. Then hold it till I can come around and lash it in place." He worked for a minute before giving Maude a quick look. "I've never heard of the doc turning anyone away, no matter their circumstances. He'll work something out with you, I'm sure."

She expelled a little breath, and he saw her shoulders ease. "I don't know if he's contagious. But neither Seth nor I have come down with whatever he has, and we've been around him all this time."

That was good to know, still, with the new baby, it was better to be safe. As he worked at tying the rope on Seth's side of the horse, he considered.

The Kastain place wasn't too far from here. And all three of these people looked like they could use some warmth sooner rather than later. He knew the Kastains had a finished room at the back of their barn where Mr. Kastain used to house a stable hand several years go. It had an old wood stove and a bed. That might be the best place to take them for now. He could ride into town from there to fetch Doc.

Once the travois was securely lashed to the stirrups, he pointed through the trees. "Friends of mine live just over that ridge. I'll take you there. They have a room, and that will get your brother out of the cold. And I know they'll be happy to let you stay for a few days without pay."

The siblings looked at one another. Seth shrugged one shoulder.

Maude sighed. He could tell that she didn't like the idea of charity. "All right. Thank you." She strode to the crate on the embankment. "I'll carry this for you."

That was a relief. Maybe he could salvage part of this morning's tasks at least. "That would be a help, thank you."

As Kin led them along the path toward the Kastain place, he thought about the money for the train. If he couldn't go to Seattle today, he could just catch tomorrow's train. He'd still be back with the sleigh in plenty of time for Mrs. Griffin to give it to her husband as a present.

His hopes lifted.

Maybe all was not lost after all.

Chapter 6

Dixie hurried across the street to the post office, joy coursing through her. Everything was going to come together, and Flynn was going to be so pleased with the sleigh that would allow him to travel a little faster and transport more of his medicines on his trips to the camps.

From their living room window earlier this morning, she'd seen Kin ride out of town with the crate of pies. And he'd left with plenty of time to drop them off and make it to the train station in time. She was so pleased that she didn't need to change her Christmas plans!

Now she just needed to send a wire informing Mr. Fordham that Kin would be arriving later today to get the sleigh after all.

Mr. King looked up when she entered and offered her a smile. "Morning! From the look on your face, it seems that Kin took my suggestion to go pick up the sleigh in Seattle for you?"

"That was your idea? Oh, it was such a relief to me!" Dixie reached across the counter to shake his hand. "Thank you so much."

Ben gave her hand a friendly pump. "My pleasure."

From behind her, a loud throat-clearing startled her.

Dixie snatched her hand back and spun around.

Mrs. King stood at the base of the steps that led up to the King's apartments above the post office.

"Oh, hello, Ethel! Are you coming over for your morning cup of coffee at the diner? Just give me a minute, and I'll walk with you."

For some strange reason, Ethel's eyes narrowed on her husband beyond Dixie's shoulder. Dixie turned slowly to look at him. She pressed her lips together wondering what the poor man could have done to upset his wife. From the look on Ethel's face, she'd best hurry along with her mission and get Ethel out of here before she said something to her husband that she might later regret.

"Ben, if you could just wire Mr. Fordham again and let him know that Kin will arrive on this afternoon's train? As you know his wire last night informed me that he couldn't hold the sleigh till the spring, so I want him to know that Kin is able to pick it up today." She dug for some change in her reticule. "Will eighteen cents cover it again?"

Ben and Ethel were still having a stare down. But Ethel's expression suddenly seemed a little less stony. In fact, almost contrite. Dixie glanced between them as she held the change toward Ben. She was obviously missing something here.

"Ben?"

With a start, he drew his attention back to her. "Yes, eighteen cents will cover it. Thank you. I'm sure everything will be fine."

"I hope so!" She looped her arm through Ethel's, giving it a squeeze as she offered her friend a smile. "Ready?"

Ethel lifted a hand to her husband and spoke softly. "I'll see you at lunch?"

Ben snatched up his fountain pen and set to scrawling on one of the telegram forms. "Yes, you will." His lips pinched into a firm line.

Ethel's eyes shimmered with tears as she stepped through the door with Dixie. They paused at the top of the stairs.

Dixie looked over at her. Could this be about Ellery's birth? It really wasn't her place to pry, but she'd known Ethel ever since she and Rose had arrived in town. She wanted to offer a gesture of friendship for whatever might be going on in the woman's life. "Is everything all right?"

Ethel seemed to ignore her question. "Did you visit the post office yesterday?"

Dixie frowned. "Yes. I did. I had ordered Flynn a present from Seattle, and when Ellery arrived early, I was unable to travel and pick it up as planned. I had Ben send a telegram."

Ethel sniffed. Her countenance paled, and her eyes fell closed. "I'm such a fool."

Dixie blinked. "Pardon me?"

Ethel sighed and, unaccountably, threw her arms around Dixie and pulled her into a firm embrace. "And I owe you an apology."

Now Dixie was truly confused. "You do?"

"Yes. You see, Pricilla came in yesterday just as you were finishing up. She witnessed the exchange between you and Ben, and, well, I'm afraid she jumped to...conclusions."

Dixie's confusion mounted. "Conclusions about what?"

Two splotches of pink bloomed on Ethel's cheeks. "About you and Ben."

Dixie's mouth fell open, and, for a moment, she couldn't quite grasp what Ethel might mean, but then, it hit her. "About me and Ben!"

"Yes." Ethel withdrew and wrapped her arms around herself. "And I'm afraid that Ben and I got into a bit of a row over it last night."

Dixie took a step back. "Ethel, I assure you that Ben has never even so much as—Wait!" A thought struck her. She remembered Flynn gasping out last night that her getting a telegram explained everything and then getting grumpy again later. "Was Flynn part of that conversation?"

Ethel frowned and shook her head. "No. He wasn't there. But I suppose Pricilla could have shared her concerns with him like she did with me."

Concerns!? Dixie had a mind to march down to the mercantile and give Pricilla a very large portion of her mind, but, in her present state, that was probably a very bad idea.

"Can you forgive me for even wondering if it was true?" Ethel asked.

Realizing how her expression must look to the woman, Dixie turned and pulled her friend into an embrace. "Of course, I can. What an awful thing for you to have been told. I'm sure it was quite a shock."

Ethel's hand trembled where it fiddled with the brooch pinned at her throat. "It was, indeed."

"But I assure you, there is nothing between Mr. King and me."

"Yes. I believe you." Ethel's hands trembled as she straightened her sleeves.

Dixie gave her a sympathetic look. "I'm sure you could use a cup of coffee, but I think right now, what's more important than your usual one at the diner is perhaps sharing a cup with your husband?"

Ethel blew out a breath and released a tremulous smile. "I think you are probably right."

Dixie squeezed her shoulder and started down the steps. "I'll see you in the diner tomorrow."

Ethel raised a hand, smiling now in true joy. "Yes. Tomorrow."

Dixie pressed her lips together. She wasn't certain if Flynn had heard the same tale from Pricilla, but she needed to find him to make sure everything was all right between them.

Where would he be this time of morning?

Chapter 7

Kin tromped up the Kastains' kitchen steps and knocked on the door. Belle and Susan were, of course, in town at the boardinghouse, where they both worked in the kitchen. But Zoe ought to be home with her younger siblings.

She answered the kitchen door with a towel in her hands, and Kin swept off his hat, wishing he'd remembered to do it before she answered. He motioned with it toward the little family huddled in the yard. "Hi, Zoe. These are the Carvers."

Zoe's quick gaze swept over them before she smiled. "Hello."

He swallowed. Zoe was quite stunning when her face lit up like that. Her red hair was piled high on her head, but several strands had escaped to tease her face. And her eyes… Had he ever noticed how blue they were before?

"Kin?" She was frowning at him.

"Uh, yeah." He cleared his throat and stepped back. "The older brother is down with something serious. They were going into town for Doc when I came across them. I wondered if they could stay in that room at the back of your barn?"

To Kin's relief, she immediately took charge. "Of course." She turned to the Carvers with a smile, tossing the towel she'd been holding onto the kitchen sideboard before she stepped out onto the porch. "We'd be happy to have you stay in our barn. I'm so sorry your brother is sick." Zoe bounded down the steps and reached for the crate Maude was still holding. "Here, let me take that from you. Is this your stuff?"

"Be careful not to tilt that," Kin rushed to say. With Zoe's propensity to act first and think later, he didn't want to end up losing the only part of this morning that might still be salvaged.

Zoe stilled and met his gaze, then glanced down at the crate with curiosity.

"Those are some pies I was supposed to be delivering out to the Rodante place on my way to the train station this morning."

"Oh. Well, we will get the delivery taken care of for you." Zoe propped the crate haphazardly against one hip.

Kin winced, imagining the contents of Mrs. Griffin's pies sliding right on out of the pie tins.

But Zoe didn't seem to notice. She snapped her fingers at her little brother, Aidan, who had appeared in the doorway with the twins behind him. "Aidan, you get some kindling chopped and get a fire going in that old wood stove in the room at the back of the barn. Shiloh, go into the house and get a set of sheets and every extra blanket we've got. We'll need to make up the bed in that room. Sharon, here." She thrust the crate at her younger sister, and Kin was much relieved to see that Sharon handled the cargo with much more care. "You take this down the road to the Rodante place for Kin. Make sure that Mrs. Rodante knows what it is. And make sure you don't bobble it. We don't want the pies to get ruined."

Kin almost grinned at that instruction.

Thankful that Zoe was taking over the organization, he realized he'd better hurry to town and fetch Doc. He strode to the travois and leaned down to look at the man lying there. Kane, his sister had said, wasn't it?

The man's eyes opened partway, but then he squinted them shut again and lifted a hand against the light as though it hurt his eyes.

"Hey there," Kin said. "Name's Kin Davis. I'm going to help you get inside where we will be able to get you warm. Get you some food. And have a doctor look at you."

The man frowned, shaking his head weakly. He moistened his lips. "Seth? Maude?" His voice was a barely audible whisper.

"They are right here. Just relax," Kin reassured him. "Do you think you can stand?"

"Don't want to be a burden."

"Nonsense." Hands propped on her hips, Zoe leaned over him. "No one is being a burden. Don't you worry about a thing." Her gaze lifted to the porch. "Oh, good, you're here with the sheets. Hurry and help me make up the bed while Kin and," her gaze flitted to the siblings, "Seth, was it?"

The boy nodded.

Zoe gave a satisfied dip of her chin already shooing Shiloh into the barn. "While Kin and Seth help the patient."

Kin slung one of Kane's arms around his shoulders, and Seth did the same on the other side. Kane barely had any strength. They mostly carried him between them, and, by the time they got Kane into the back room, Zoe and Shiloh had the bed made.

Zoe plumped a pillow and laid it at the top of the bed. "There you go. Just rest yourself right here. My brother is getting the fire going. The room will warm up in two shakes of a lamb's tail; then I'll bring you some soup."

Kin left her there, still chattering, and hurried back to the yard. The sooner Doc saw that man, the better. He rushed toward his horse, mindful that he needed to untie the travois, but he paused when he saw Maude still standing in the yard, huddled into her thin sweater.

He stepped toward her and motioned to the barn with his hat. "Zoe's got a room all ready for you. Fire going and everything. She said she'll bring you some food in just a bit."

Maude glanced around the place. "We stole from these people."

Kin frowned. "That's..." He was at a loss for words. "A rusty bucket and a spade. But we left their nicer pail and newer shovel. We wanted to take a bucket of milk, but they had so little. Just the cow and," she swept a gesture to the little cabin, "what with the chinking needing so much repair, we figured they might be nearly as bad off as we were."

Kin followed her gaze to the cabin. Part of the foundation must have given way at some point because the back corner of the house was canted at an angle. And Maude was right. Much of the chinking was missing from between the logs. A window that must have gotten broken somehow was boarded up. And several shingles were missing from the roof.

Maude shrugged, drawing his attention back to her. "They have so little, and yet they're willing to share? With complete strangers?"

"That's just the kind of people they are."

"Why?"

Kin's feet shuffled. He looked down and worked the toe of his boot into a patch of snow. He knew the answer. Had been forced to sit through enough of PC's sermons to know what the Good Book said about hospitality and such. "They're church-going folk."

Maude's brow puckered in curiosity. "Church-going folk?"

Kin was saved from needing to explain when Zoe rushed up and drew Maude to her side. "That's right. We are. And the Good Book tells us that when we entertain strangers, we might be entertaining angels." She giggled as she skillfully turned Maude toward the barn. "You aren't an angel, are you?"

Maude cast him a wide-eyed glance over her shoulder, and he gave her a smile along with a you're-on-your-own wag of his head before he turned to freeing his mount from the travois.

By the time he trotted out of the yard, smoke poured from the back-room chimney, and Zoe was headed back across the yard to the house. Based on her no-nonsense stride, the Carvers would soon be filling their bellies with hot soup.

Dixie was just crossing the street and trying to decide where to search for Flynn first, when a rider turned the corner by her boardinghouse and trotted toward her.

It was Kin!

With two fistfuls of skirts clutched firmly in her hands, she froze and gaped at him. He was supposed to be on the train on his way to Seattle right now! "Kin?"

He reined to a stop in front of the alehouse and tossed his reins around the hitching rail, then swiped off his hat and lifted his hands. "I'm really sorry. I was on my way to the Rodantes' with the pies and right on schedule to make that train, when I came across these homeless siblings. One of them is real sick, and the other two looked so haggard that a stiff breeze might have done them in. I couldn't just leave them there. I took them to the Kastains'. I'll be on the very next train, but right now, I need Doc. Do you know where he is?"

Dixie felt torn between frustration that Kin hadn't gone to Seattle and pride because he'd made the right decision.

Kin gripped the back of his neck. "I know you're probably upset with me, but—"

"No, actually." Dixie shook her head, pride suddenly winning out. "I was just standing here thinking what a wonderful man you've turned out to be."

Kin smirked. "PC might take issue with your assessment. You're not upset about the delay in picking up the sleigh?"

She waved a hand. "A little yes. But it will still be there in a couple days. As for Parson Clay, if he gets upset with you for breaking his rules, it's only because he wants a happy life for you and he knows that the choices you sometimes make are not taking you down that path." She gave him a pointed look.

"Yes'm." Kin paused for only a moment before he averted the subject with, "So, do you know where Doc is?"

Dixie decided to let the change of topic go. The reminder that she still needed to speak to Flynn about what she'd just learned made her shoulders slump. "Unfortunately, no." She turned her focus to the buildings along the street. "My guess is we start in the alehouse. He treated someone there last night."

"Okay. I'll check. I'm sure you need to get back to your place."

Dixie sighed. She did need to get back to Ellery and Rose, but what she really wanted to do was have that talk with Flynn. It looked like that would have to wait.

Kin started toward the alehouse.

"Kin?"

He stopped and looked at her over his shoulder.

"When you find Flynn, will you give him a message from me?"

"Of course."

Dixie pondered what to say. "Tell him I love him."

Kin's face turned a red to match the apples Jerry Hines had recently started selling in the mercantile. "Beg pardon, ma'am, but...how about I tell him you're looking forward to speaking with him when he gets back home?" He gave her a hopeful wince.

Dixie smiled. "I suppose that will have to do."

Kin blew out a breath of relief. "Good."

He rushed off, and she had a feeling he was worried she might change her mind.

Chapter 8

Kin found Doctor Griffin in the alehouse, just as Mrs. Griffin had suspected. He was concluding his examination of the patient he'd tended the evening prior.

Doc glanced up. "Howdy, Kin. What can I do for you?"

Kin explained about the Carver family.

"At the Kastains', you say?"

"Yes."

"I'll head right out there." Doc set to washing his hands in a basin, but, just as Kin turned to leave, he stopped him. "You don't think these kids could be responsible for all the stolen things over the past few weeks, do you?"

Kin paused by the door and swallowed. He had a good idea that they *were* the ones responsible, but he didn't want to get them in trouble when they were only kids and had been trying to keep their older brother alive, so all he said was, "I can't say for certain."

Doc gave him a look. "Well, best you mosey on down to the sheriff's office and tell him what you just told me. He can ride out and ask them a few questions for himself."

Kin considered on that. "Truth is, I'm supposed to be running an errand for—" He bit off the words just in time as he realized that it might ruin Doc's Christmas if he mentioned that he was taking a trip to Seattle for his wife.

"For who?"

Kin waved a hand. "Just for one of the townsfolk. But I'll let the sheriff know if I see him." He hurried out before Doc could question him further.

And he checked the street carefully before stepping out onto the alehouse porch. If he didn't see the sheriff, he couldn't very well report to him, now could he?

He leapt onto his horse and trotted it out of town. He would just ride to the train station and stay the night there. PC already expected him to be gone for a few days. And the truth was, Lord forgive him, he could use a break from Tommy's incessant prattling tonight.

And he wouldn't let himself do any drinking, because it was imperative that he be on that train in the morning.

Mrs. Griffin had been kind to him over the years. He didn't want to let her down.

Kin rented a stall and bought feed for his horse and then tossed his saddle blanket onto the hay and sank onto it. Thankfully, he'd escaped Wyldhaven without running into the sheriff. Hopefully, the Carvers wouldn't have to face the wrath of the law anytime soon, though Parson Clay would say that people reaped the seed they sowed.

Maude and her brother were young, and hopefully now that they'd seen how willing the people of Wyldhaven were to help them if they only asked, they'd do a little more asking and a lot less taking in the future.

He passed a restless night and was grateful to see the hint of new day touching the sky the next morning.

The closer he got to Seattle, the more excited he grew. Maybe he'd have time to line up a job and a place to live. Then when he went back home, he'd tell Parson Clay that he was moving on.

As the train chuffed into the Seattle station, he peered through the grimy window, and his anticipation grew.

Everywhere, the streets teemed with people. Pushing carts, pulling carts, hawking wares, selling newspapers. The sound of all the hubbub crashed over him as he stepped from the train car.

An old woman stood on the platform with a basket of apples around her neck, and Kin paid her the requested five cents and munched on the juicy tart fruit as he stepped to one side and checked the address Mrs. Griffin had given him.

He looked at the old woman. "Which way to Stewart Street?"

She gave him a once-over, as though trying to determine if she could extract any more money from him, then must have decided she couldn't, for she tilted her head to the north. "Thet way."

Kin tipped his hat. "Obliged, ma'am."

It only took him a few minutes to walk the blocks to Stewart, and the store was easy to find. He tossed his apple core into the gutter, where several birds immediately converged on it. The bell above the door dinged a welcome as he stepped into the warmth of the interior.

There were sleighs in every stage of completion throughout the workshop. But one at the front stood complete with a new coat of glossy red paint making it shimmer in the light streaming through the big picture window.

Kin smiled. That must be Mrs. Griffin's order.

At the counter, he offered the proprietor his hand. "Name's Kin Davis. I'm here from Wyldhaven to pick up the sleigh that Mrs. Dixie Griffin ordered."

The man didn't take his hand. In fact, he didn't move. Only blinked.

Apprehension seeped into Kin's excitement. "She wired you that I was coming."

Finally, the man stepped forward and took his hand. "I'm Walt Fordham. But you were supposed to be here yesterday."

Relieved that the man had at least been expecting him, Kin loosed a breath. "Yes, sir. Something came up, and I couldn't make the train yesterday. But I'm here now."

"I sold the sleigh to someone else."

Kin stared at the man. "What do you mean, you sold her sleigh to someone else? We told you we were coming for it."

Mr. Fordham shrugged. "She telegrammed to say her plans had changed and she wasn't going to be able to pick it up right away."

"But then she sent another, telling you she was sending me."

He gave another indifferent lift of his shoulder. "You were supposed to be here yesterday. I sold it this morning."

Kin gripped the back of his neck. "Well, do you have another? One substantially similar?" His gaze turned to the one shining in the light of the front window. "How about that one?"

The sleigh maker shook his head. "Afraid not. That one's spoken for. And it's a busy time of year. I've sold everything I've made this year."

Kin's stomach clenched. He hated to go back to Wyldhaven with such disappointing news for Mrs. Griffin. He glanced around the man's shop. How did he fix this? "Well, I need to get Mrs. Griffin's money then."

The sleigh maker folded his arms, leaned into his heels, and glowered down the length of his nose. "And how do I know that she actually sent you, kid?"

Kin sighed. Was this what compassion got him? If he hadn't taken the time to help the Carvers... But could he really have done anything else? "You said yourself that she sent you a telegram saying that I would be picking up the sleigh for her."

"Yes. But I have no way of knowing if you're him. The man she said was coming."

Kin tossed his hands in the air. "Who else would I be? If I'm not him, how would I know about you having her sleigh?"

The sleigh maker gave his habitual shrug that was beginning to wear thin on Kin's nerves. "Suppose you could've knocked this Kin Davis fella out and come for the money yourself."

Kin clenched his teeth. "And I suppose you could be attempting to swindle a woman who is simply trying to give her husband a present at Christmas."

Mr. Fordham shook a finger at him. "Aw, no you don't. Don't go trying to lay the blame for this at my door! Prove you are the fellow she sent, and I'll give you her money, certain sure."

"Look, I don't appreciate being called a liar."

The sleigh maker shook his head. "Can't be helped. I've got a business to protect here."

Kin would have liked to reach across the counter and take the man by the front of his shirt, but instead he forced himself to take a breath. Parson Clay would be mighty proud of him if he could see what he wanted to do and how he actually responded. "What's something only Mrs. Griffin and her messenger are likely to know about? Ask me anything."

Mr. Fordham narrowed his eyes. "Why did she send a messenger to pick up the sleigh in the first place?"

Kin lifted his chin and rose to the challenge. "She gave birth to a baby girl. Ellery Rose, her name is, if you must know."

Mr. Fordham grumbled his acquiescence to the fact that was true. "Fine. I'll give you her money. But not before I take down your name and description. If she doesn't get it back, I'll be sending the law to hunt for you."

Kin folded his arms, more to clamp his fists in place than anything. "She'll get her money."

Now he just had to figure out how he was going to salvage her Christmas present for Doc.

His gaze settled on a shiny pair of red runners on a shelf behind the counter, and, suddenly, he had an idea.

Chapter 9

Dixie stood in the kitchen of the boardinghouse looking at Kin in disbelief. With Ellery resting comfortably in the crook of her arm, she stirred the pot of stew she was making for the diner with one hand. "He sold my sleigh to someone else?"

Kin nodded. "I'm afraid so. But...I've been thinking and...I have a solution."

"You do?"

"Yes, ma'am." Kin folded his arms and settled more comfortably into his heels. "That is, if you are interested in hearing it."

Dixie waved a hand. "I can't see as I have any choice other than to listen at this late date." Too late, she recognized the hurt on Kin's face. "I didn't mean that I expect your solution to be bad. It's just, I had all this planned out for months, and now everything has fallen through. Please, tell me your thoughts."

"Well..." Kin laid an envelope on the kitchen table. "I did get him to return the money you put down."

Dixie nodded. "That's a big help. Thank you."

"And..." Kin got a little smile on his face. "I got him to throw in a pair of sleigh runners for free."

Dixie frowned. How were sleigh runners supposed to make her happy when she had ordered an entire sleigh? "You'll have to explain."

"Well I've taken a look at several sleighs both in Seattle and here in town, and I don't see how they would be too difficult to re-create. In fact, most likely, I could improve on them. So, if you'll allow me, I'd like to build your sleigh. And I'll do it for less than you planned to pay that sleigh maker in Seattle."

Ellery began to fuss, and Dixie despaired of ever getting the diner's evening meal ready. "Here." She passed the baby to Kin without giving him a chance to decline. "Hold her for a moment, would you? Just watch her head. She doesn't have any strength in her neck yet."

Kin's eyes widened, and he gingerly held Ellery from him like she might be a newborn piglet he was assessing for market.

She squirmed and cried a little harder.

Dixie grinned at Kin from where she bent over the oven, pulling out the fresh loaves of bread. "She's not livestock. Tuck her close. Bounce her."

Kin awkwardly curled the baby against his chest. He carefully adjusted Ellery to a more comfortable position, curling his big hand behind her head and jigging across the floor. "Let's just say I am much better at making sleighs—which I've never done before—than I am at watching babies." He gave her a self-deprecating grin.

Dixie smiled as she set the bread onto the trivets on the table and brushed a strand of hair off her forehead. She had thought she could handle having a newborn and cooking at the same time. But this wasn't going as smoothly as she would have liked. Thankfully, Rose would be done with her nap in just a few moments and would come down to get the baby, but, if things continued the way they were, she was going to need to hire yet another worker for the kitchen. Saving money by hiring Kin to make the sleigh might be just what she needed right now.

She pierced him with a look. "You're certain that you can make it in a quality fashion?"

He nodded and bounced Ellery gently, looking awed that the baby had stopped fussing and set to slurping on a thumb and two fingers. "Yes, ma'am."

"All right then. I'm happy to hire you. I've never known you to do a slipshod job, so I'm sure you'll make a beautiful sleigh."

"I'll do my best, ma'am. I'll ride to Cle Elum this afternoon and purchase the wood."

"Here, I'll take her." Dixie swiped a gesture at the envelope on the table. "You better take what you need as an advance so that you can buy the supplies."

Kin nodded, looking a little disappointed to return the baby. "She's a peach," he said.

Dixie saw a distinct line of red creep up his face.

He stepped back quickly and opened the envelope to extract a few dollars, which he held up so she could see what he'd taken. "This ought to cover it, but there's one thing we're going to need."

"What's that?"

"A seat. Joe and Liora have an old wagon that they never use by their barn. The bench is in good condition. I could use it for the sleigh. Would you have time to ride out there and make the deal?"

Dixie gave him a nod. "I'll find the time later today."

"Thanks. I'll let you know when I'm back with the wood."

A thought struck her. "Will you be able to get it done in time?"

He nodded. "I'll make certain of it."

Dixie worried her lip as he left the kitchen. She wasn't going to be able to relax until she saw this completed sleigh with her own eyes.

Even if they never got it done, she supposed she would have a good story to tell Flynn come Christmas morning.

Speaking of which, she still needed to find time to speak to him about what had happened at the post office. He'd arrived home very late the evening before and left again first thing this morning.

Tonight. As soon as she got home from the Rodantes'. She would make sure of it.

With Ellery tied snuggly beneath her coat, Dixie pulled into the yard at Liora and Joe's and swung down from the wagon.

Liora stepped from the cabin. She was wiping her hands on a kitchen towel. "Dixie! What a pleasant surprise."

She stepped up onto the porch and pulled her friend into an embrace. "Sorry to drop by unannounced. Is now a bad time?"

Liora shook her head. "No, no. Please, come in. The girls and I were just finishing up this week's bread."

She led the way into the cabin and motioned for Dixie to have a seat at the kitchen table. "Can I get you some coffee?"

Dixie chuckled. "Always." She pulled a face as she extracted Ellery from beneath her coat. "Especially now that we are getting so little sleep each night."

Liora chuckled. "Oh, I'm so glad you brought her! I've been so excited to get that little one in my arms!" Liora poured the coffee and joined Dixie at the table. But she didn't sit. Instead, she reached for the baby. "Oh my! She's beautiful! Look at all that dark hair!"

Dixie smiled and relinquished Ellery to her. "Yes, isn't it adorable? I think she's going to have Flynn's curls."

Liora bent and chattered to the child. "You are just so beautiful. Yes, you are. Look at your big eyes and those rosy cheeks. Your daddy is going to be kept busy fighting off the callers. Yes, he is."

Dixie chuckled. "Flynn has been perusing shotgun ads in the Sears and Roebuck catalogue."

Liora laughed. "I'm sure Joe will do the same when our time comes."

Excitement trilling through her, Dixie swept her with a glance. "Are you—"

"Oh! No!" Liora blushed. "Not yet." She pressed her lips together. "So, what brings you by today?"

Dixie let the subject change go, and stirred half a teaspoon of sugar into her cup. "Christmas." She pulled a face. "Can you hear the bitterness in my tone?"

Liora chuckled. "Do you need help figuring out what to give to Flynn?"

Dixie shook her head. "I know what I'm giving him. But with Ellery's early arrival, I've had a few setbacks."

Liora glanced down at the baby in her arms tucking the blanket away from her face. "Have you put kinks in your Ma's Christmas plans?"

Dixie chuckled and rolled her eyes. "Oh, you have no idea."

Liora looked up at her. "Really?"

Dixie nodded. "I was supposed to pick up a sleigh in Seattle, but I can't take her on that long of a trip. And when Kin arrived to get it for me, the sleigh maker had already sold it to someone else." She waved a hand. "It's been quite the ordeal. But, thanks to Kin's ingenuity, I hope that we are on our way to a solution."

"How can I help you?" Liora cocked her head.

"Kin tells me that you and Joe have an old wagon, and the seat is in fairly good condition?"

Liora squinted her eyes. "Well, 'fairly good condition' might be a bit of an exaggeration. But I'm more than happy to let you look at it and decide. In fact, it's just been sitting out by the barn. If you want it, we would be happy to give you the seat. Joe's mentioned several times that he needs to just chop it up and burn it."

Dixie brushed away the offer. "No, no, no. I would definitely want to pay. But yes, I would like to look at it if you have time to show me?"

"Of course. We can go out right now." Liora led the way through the kitchen to the side of their barn. The old wagon canted at an odd angle because it only had three wheels. But just as Kin had said, Dixie could see that the seat was in fairly good shape. With a little bit of padding and upholstery it would work just fine for what they needed. She gave a satisfactory nod and patted the seat like it might be an old friend. "Yes. This is just the thing."

Ellery fussed a little, and Liora bounced her. "Oh, good. I'll have Joe unbolt it just as soon as he gets home this evening."

"Perfect. And I'll have Kin drop by to pick it up." Dixie reached her arms to take Ellery. "If you'll forgive me for rushing off, I have to go visit with Jacinda to see if she has any material that would be appropriate for upholstering the seat. I'm trying to squeeze all these errands in while Flynn is out at the camps on his rounds." She gave Liora a wink. "Which reminds me, I never asked what you are giving Joe? Do you know yet?"

Liora nodded and gave a surreptitious glance around the yard. "Would you like to see it? I'm really very excited about it." She laughed. "Probably a lot more excited than I have a right to be."

Dixie smiled. "We get a lot of joy from giving gifts to those we love, don't we? I would love to see it."

Liora led the way to the small building where the women she and Joe had helped to escape the camp brothels stayed. In a small side-room, Liora approached a sheet-shrouded crate, and, when she pulled back the lid, Dixie couldn't help but give a small gasp.

The saddle was indeed the most beautiful piece of workmanship she had ever seen. Crafted from a beautiful mahogany leather with red overtones, the seat-housing and flaps were hand tooled and embellished with brass. Dixie reached out and stroked a hand over the seat. The leather was smooth and soft and stretched over a firm padding. "Oh, Liora. He's going to love it."

Liora smiled in satisfaction and pressed the lid of the crate back into place. "I know. I can hardly wait for Christmas Day to arrive." She chuckled.

Dixie tucked Ellery into the warmth of her coat. "Well, I'd really best be on my way. Thank you, again. So much." She held out a few bills for payment.

But Liora refused to take them. She smiled. "Like I said, no payment necessary. Truly. Our pleasure."

Dixie gave her a quick hug. "Very kind of you. Hopefully I can make it up to you one of these days."

Dixie's relief carried her all the way into town where it doubled again upon seeing the perfect red upholstery material presented to her by Jacinda. She reached out to touch it. "Oh Jacinda, It's lovely."

Jacinda smiled. "It's left over from the benches at the bank. Good and sturdy and should last for years to come."

After settling on a price, Dixie promised that Kin would stop by to pick up the material and then hurried toward home. It was almost time for Ellery's feeding. But more than that, Flynn should be home by now. She could hardly wait to see him and throw her arms around his neck.

Thank the Lord for her wonderful neighbors in Wyldhaven. Flynn would get his Christmas present after all.

He was there, waiting for her, when she stepped back into their apartment above the diner. He hurried forward with a bit of a frown, and she was reminded that she still hadn't spoken to him.

He took Ellery and glanced toward the frosty window. "You've been out in this cold?"

"Yes." Dixie tugged off her gloves, her gaze never leaving his beloved face. "I kept her tucked inside my coat the whole time to ensure she stayed warm."

A slight furrow still puckered the skin between his brows, and Dixie was thankful that Rose was down helping out in the kitchen, because she'd never wanted to kiss her husband more than she did right now.

She stepped right into his space and looked up at him, reaching one hand to soothe his frown. "Flynn, there's something I need to tell you."

He swallowed. "Okay." Concern darkened the hazel-blue of his eyes.

She realized that instead of calming him, she'd only raised his concerns, so she hurried on to say, "I spoke to the Kings today. Ethel apparently had a conversation with Pricilla Hines yesterday that concerned Ben and me."

A muscle in Flynn's jaw ticked. "Yes. She did."

Dixie tilted Flynn a look. Had he truly been afraid that she would cheat on him with Ben King? She clasped her hands behind his neck. "Ben King has been helping me with a Christmas project and nothing more."

The light returned to his eyes. "Oh." One corner of his mouth lifted. Ellery fussed a little but settled right down when he bounced her.

"Were you really worried?" Dixie couldn't help but feel a little hurt by his doubt.

He swallowed. "I'm tired, Dixie. So tired. I think my exhaustion clouded my judgement."

Which was partly why she had wanted to get him this sleigh so badly. It would save him several hours each week.

She quirked him a smile. "And there was that little incident where my husband showed up in town a few years ago as your patient."

Flynn smiled but shook his head. "And where I was tempted not to treat him but to hurry him to his death. But, just like I'm no longer that man, I know you aren't that woman. Can you forgive me for doubting?"

"If you'll forgive me for acting in such a manner that caused your doubts."

His eyes crinkled at the corners. "It is the Christmas season."

She nodded. "It is."

He grinned. "So, what did you get me?"

She laughed. "Wouldn't you like to know?!"

He lifted one shoulder. "It was worth a shot." He leaned past their daughter to dally his lips over Dixie's.

And, as Dixie released a sigh of contentment, she couldn't help but be thankful for the season of Christmas that had brought her to this place in her husband's arms.

Dear Reader,

I hope you smiled at least a few times as you read this story. And that this Christmas season you'll remember that the heart of Christmas isn't about the hustle and bustle and perfectly kept surprises, but about the Savior, King of all creation, *who, being in very nature God, did not consider equality with God something to be used to his own advantage.* (Philippians 2:6 NIV) Instead, He humbled Himself and was born in a lowly Bethlehem barn so that later He could die for the sins of all mankind! What an amazing Love!

If you enjoyed this story, please leave the book a review. It doesn't have to be long, but every review helps spread the word, and the world needs more uplifting stories!

Wondering if Kane Carver is going to recover and if Sheriff Reagan is going to figure out they've been the ones causing trouble? Or about what's going to happen to Joe's saddle? (Because you *know* it wouldn't be a story without something going wrong, right?) I invite you to read the next episode of this series titled *Deputy Joe's Christmas Saddle* on the next page.

You can find all the books in the Wyldhaven series here on my website.

Merry Christmas!

Lynnette
BONNER

Deputy Joe's Christmas Saddle

Novella Three
Wyldhaven

Chapter 1

When Liora woke on this early December morning, Joe was just leaving for his rounds.

She yawned and worked up the courage to push back the covers and face the cold. "I'll get you some breakfast."

Joe bent over her and placed a kiss on her forehead. "Stay in bed. I'll take some of those hard-boiled eggs you made last night and a couple slices of bread."

She squinted one eye. "You sure that will be enough?"

"Plenty." He reached for his boots. "I'll build up the fire, and the house will be nice and warm by the time you need to get up."

Liora wasn't going to argue. She couldn't linger in bed too much longer, but she would take a few more minutes of leisure any day of the week. "Be safe," she cautioned him.

"Always." It was his usual reply. And she knew that he did approach his job with thought and wisdom. None of that prevented her from praying for his safety throughout the day.

As a deputy for the town of Wyldhaven, Joe was kept pretty busy out at the logging camps. Especially with them growing as rapidly as they were. Cities all along the west coast were booming, and that had increased the demand for wood, which had, in turn, increased the amount of workers living in the camps.

Yes, she often fretted about him, and the town really needed a few more lawmen, but today she would be kept so busy she really didn't have time to worry.

After giving herself another few minutes of rest, she tossed back the covers and hurried into her dress, thankful that Joe had so thoughtfully stoked the fire, because, just as he'd said, the house had warmed considerably.

Thinking of Joe's thoughtfulness brought to mind the Christmas present she'd purchased for him—a brand new saddle that boasted hand-tooled leather and brass accents. His current saddle had seen better days, but he'd been putting off getting a new one, claiming his current one sufficed. But, with the many long hours he spent riding for work, Liora knew this new one with the thickly padded seat was going to be much more comfortable. She could hardly wait to give it to him. He was likely going to chastise her for the amount she'd spent, but she'd been saving her egg and cream money all year, and he was worth the price and more.

She tamped down her excitement and focused on today's preparations.

They were hosting a Christmas gathering at their place on the morrow, and she still had so much to finish for it.

At least she had Aurora. Liora blessed the day that God had given Aurora the gumption to run from brothel owner John Hunt before he could press her into service.

And she had Ruby too, she reminded herself. Ruby may have come to them a little later in life, with a bit more reluctance, and after a good many mistakes, but the Lord had brought her out of the brothels and into their lives, and Liora kept praying for ideas of how to reach her with a deeper Truth.

She bustled into the kitchen, snatched up her apron, and looped it over her head. As she tied the strings behind her back, she studied the list she'd created to make sure she didn't forget anything for the party.

The sweet-roll dough she'd left to rise in the cool of the windowsill all night was just about to spill over the lip of the bowl, just the way she liked it. She tossed some flour on the table, scooped the dough from the bowl and set to kneading. Joe had insisted that her sticky buns were a must for the party. She smiled at the thought.

The kitchen door squeaked open, and Aurora stepped inside, closed it, and leaned against it. "Ah, Liora?"

Liora looked up from the dough. "Yes?"

Aurora, bundled up in her thick winter coat and scarf, had a basket of eggs clutched in her hands. "There is something you need to see."

Liora blew at a strand of hair. She could almost feel the Christmas party breathing down her neck. And, with so much on her list still to do, she really didn't have time for interruptions. "Can it wait? I'm just about to put these cinnamon rolls in the oven."

"No. I'm afraid it can't. Ruby has run off in the night."

"What?!" Liora stepped to the sink and set to pumping water so that she could rinse the dough from her hands. "I thought we were really starting to make progress with her."

Aurora set the basket of eggs on the counter and shrugged out of her wraps. "That's not the worst of it. And you're not going to like it."

"What could be worse than her running off?"

Aurora grimaced. "She stole a bunch of stuff, including the saddle you planned to give to Joe for Christmas."

Liora gasped. "She didn't!"

Aurora tilted her an apologetic wince. "Afraid she did."

Liora dried her hands and then massaged at the rapidly blooming headache burgeoning behind her temples. "How long has she been gone?"

Aurora shrugged. "When I woke up, she wasn't in our room. I thought maybe she had gone out early to do her chores. But she's not in the barn, and she's not chopping kindling either."

Liora racked her thoughts, trying to decide how to proceed. Normally, she would call on Joe and have him track down the missing girl. Though they never forced any woman to stay with them, they did always try to have open communication with each one they came in contact with through their ministry of helping prostitutes escape their lifestyle. So usually, if a girl ran off, they did at least try to find her to see if they could talk her into staying. But, in this instance, if she asked Joe to hunt down Ruby, he would see the saddle. And she had worked so hard to keep the gift a secret. She didn't want to ruin the surprise if at all possible.

Though, of course, if Ruby got to a place where she could sell the saddle, there would be no surprise at all.

Aurora stepped close and gave her a hug. "I'm so sorry."

Liora was ever so grateful for the friendship the Lord had given her in the person of Aurora. She set the woman back from her and tilted her head. "What else did she take?"

Aurora winced and wrinkled her nose. "I'm not exactly certain. Though she did take all the coins I've been saving in that bowl in our room."

Liora's shoulders slumped. "Oh, I'm so sorry she did that to you."

Aurora shrugged. "I suppose if we are trying to reach the lost, we ought to expect a little bit of maltreatment now and then. Hurting people tend to hurt others."

Liora sighed. "That's the truth." She herself had been in that position not many years ago.

Much as Liora was concerned about the missing saddle, she was even more concerned about Ruby. The woman was old for her profession, almost fifty from what she had told Liora. And, though she had unhesitantly left her work when Liora had spoken to her about the love of Christ, breaking a long-held pattern was always a difficult prospect. Liora feared that Ruby was likely returning to work in a brothel at one of the camps.

If she could report her for stealing, Joe could go and arrest her, and maybe Liora would be able to talk some sense into her before she returned to a way of life she had so desperately wanted to escape. But, since she didn't want to involve Joe this time, she'd just have to find a different way.

Liora pressed a hand to her forehead. "Okay, we can deal with this. But first, I have to get these rolls in the oven. Rinse the eggs while I finish these, then we'll scout around and see what else she might have absconded with. Maybe that will give us a hint as to where she's going."

Aurora's lips pinched together. "I think we both know."

Liora sighed. "Yes, I fear you are right. But we can't know for sure until we find her."

Taking the basket of eggs to the sink, Aurora put the pump handle to work. She tossed a glance at Liora over her shoulder. "She may have already sold the saddle. And it's not like you ever force anyone to stay here. You really still want to try to go after her?"

Liora felt tears prick the back of her eyes as she sprinkled a generous amount of sugar and cinnamon over the dough. "Yes. If the saddle is gone, it's gone. But I at least want a chance to speak to Ruby. Do you know of anything that might have happened to make her unhappy here?"

Aurora shook her head. "She seemed fine last night."

Liora rolled the dough and set to slicing it. "I'd rather not get Joe involved, just in case I can get the saddle back. I want to speak to her. But I have so many responsibilities here today that I really don't have time to go traipsing after her. And I don't want you going after her on your own, either."

"I could ask Kin Davis if he has time to help me find her. He is always looking for odd jobs to do. Isn't he coming by later today to get that wagon seat for the sleigh he's making Dr. Griffin?"

Liora felt relief at just the mention of Kin possibly helping. "Yes, yes. He should be here in a bit. He and Joe unbolted it last night, and Kin said he would come with a wagon today to pick it up."

"So, should I ask for his help?"

As she laid the rolls on the baking sheet, Liora tried to think. Why today of all days? Of course, Ruby would have known about her busy day. It was likely the reason she had chosen today to disappear. It really was her responsibility to find Ruby. Yet... She tossed a glance at her list on the table and sighed.

Aurora waited quietly.

After a few seconds, Liora waved a hand. "Fine, yes. Ask Kin. Hopefully, he will be able to help us."

Aurora nodded. "I'll talk to him."

The pain of what Ruby had done hit her then. Liora blinked back tears. "Why is it so hard for some people to have faith in God?"

Aurora shook her head. "I'm not sure. What I am sure of is that you loved Ruby to the best of your ability. We all did. And we each spoke truth into her life as best we could. This is not our fault."

Liora supposed that was true enough. All she could do was hold out the truth to people; if they chose not to accept it, then what more could she do? Keep loving them, of course. But she also had to draw the line. Have boundaries that protected the rest of the people here. She blew out a breath. What she really wanted to do was talk to Joe about this. He always had such a godly perspective.

She pinched her lips together and made a decision. If they hadn't found Ruby by this evening, she would speak to Joe, even if it ruined Christmas.

Liora opened the oven and slid the rolls inside. "For now, what chores do I need to help you with that Ruby normally does?"

Aurora brushed her offer away. "I know you still have some baking you want to finish. And that you hoped to go to the Mercantile today to pick up your order. I'll cover the chores and get those evergreen wreaths hung up."

Liora pulled the girl into an embrace. "I don't know what I would do if the good Lord hadn't sent you, dear Aurora. You are always such a blessing."

Aurora blushed and batted away her praise.

A wagon trundled into the yard.

"Oh, I think that's Kin now." Aurora hurried into her coat. "I'll go talk to him and let you know what he says."

Chapter 2

Kin Davis folded his arms and looked at Aurora in disbelief. What was it with people having trouble with their Christmas presents this year?

He shook his head. "I'm sorry, Aurora. But as you know, I am helping Dixie build a sleigh for Flynn right now. I simply don't have time to track Ruby." He felt bad, but there were only so many hours in the day.

Aurora's shoulders slumped, and she rubbed at her temple with a little frown. "All right. I understand. I just wish there was a way for me to help Liora. I feel somewhat responsible for not realizing that Ruby planned to run off. She and I shared a room, you know."

Kin leaned into his heels. "Seems like she has kinda been trouble for you all since she moved in."

Aurora nodded. "A little bit. And there were some things that maybe I should have mentioned. That's why I feel partially at fault for her running off."

Kin's awareness prickled down his spine. "Things like what?"

Aurora swept a hand through the air. "She never seemed content. She was always grumbling about Liora and Joe behind their backs. She often mentioned how rough it was to be poor and what a privilege it must be to live like Joe and Liora. Things like that."

Kin frowned and rubbed one hand over his cheek. "She obviously didn't look around." He swept a gesture to encompass the property.

Aurora took in the place. Suddenly, she saw the property with new eyes.

Where before she had only seen the cabin as a loving home, she could now see that the porch steps were canted at an odd angle and the front rail was loose and hanging down. The yard needed a trim, and the garden weeding had fallen behind. The barn had started out more as a lean-to. It had been built onto over the years, and the original portion had lost all of its chinking. True, they mostly only used that part for tool storage now, but she knew that both Joe and Liora would want to have the place looking better if either of them had the time or money to make it happen.

Aurora returned her gaze to Kin's. "Yes, I see what you mean."

Kin nodded. "They sink all their extra money into helping women."

He realized too late how insulting his words must have sounded to her when she folded her arms and dug her toe into a clump of snow.

"I didn't mean you. You are more like family to them than a ministry. And I know you've been busy yourself, helping PC at the church with the music. Anyhow, my point was that if Joe and Liora were so well-off, they could afford to hire the upkeep done."

Aurora nodded. "Yes. I understand what you meant. Which is why it's such a tragedy that Liora's present for Joe—that she saved all year to buy—has been stolen."

Kin thought for a moment. Then he stretched out a hand. "Tell you what. I don't have time to go tracking her down, but you're a smart girl—even passed yourself off as a man for a while." He tossed her a wink.

Aurora felt her face heat. "Kin Davis, don't you go bringing that up. What's your point?"

He chuckled. "I can show you how to track. I think you'll be a quick study. No time to give you all the finer points, but maybe just having the highlights will help you find her. She's probably not trying to cover her trail too well. Moving as fast as she likely is with stolen goods."

"I suppose that's true."

Kin strode to a muddy patch of moist ground in front of the barn doors. "Here, come take a look."

Aurora sank down next to Kin and admired the way the light played off of the rippling muscles in his forearm as he stretched a hand to point out a footprint to her. It amazed her that she had never felt the awkwardness of attraction around Kin. But truly, ever since she had posed as a lad and spent several weeks living with Parson Clay and Kin, she had only ever thought of him as a big brother.

If only she felt the same about Parson Clay. She felt the heat of the thought in her cheeks.

Kin looked over at her. His brows lifted. "Are you paying attention?"

"Yes, yes." She grinned at him. "But tell me again."

He chuckled and elbowed her. "Pay attention, little brother."

He showed her the set of footprints he had found and how he could tell that they were Ruby's. "You see here how the heels of her boots are shaped? And this notch right here? That's because she has a crack in the sole of her right boot. That's how you'll know it's her footprints you're following. She also has that bit of a limp, and you can tell that because this right footprint is a little bit deeper than the left."

Aurora looked between the two tracks. She couldn't see any difference, but figured she would take Kin's word for it.

Kin stood and motioned down the path into the forest. "She went that way. And judging by how fresh these are, not more than a couple of hours ago."

Aurora frowned at the tracks. "How do you tell how fresh they are?"

Kin pointed to the outer edges of one print. "The perimeter is crisp. On older tracks, the wind or rain knocks bits of shale and dust around and decays the precision. It's something you'll take note of the more you read sign. Sort of like the difference between a freshly penciled letter and one that's been floating around for a while where the wording is a bit fuzzy. Course, now with the ground as damp as it is, and the weather freezing nights, the tracks will take longer to decay." He stood and reached down to help her up. "All that to say, you should have a good, clear trail."

"All right." Aurora accepted his help and stood to her feet. "Thank you. I'll see if I can find her."

Kin reached out and gave her a gentle sock in the arm. "Don't forget about your pistol and everything PC and I taught you about how to use it."

Aurora rolled her eyes at him. "I'm not going to have to use a pistol on Ruby. She may complain a lot, but she's never been violent."

"Better safe than sorry. Speaking of which..." Kin gave her an assessing look. "You sure you should be going after her on your own?"

Aurora shrugged. "We don't have much choice. Liora has that Christmas gathering tomorrow, and—"

"No." Liora spoke from just behind her. "He's right. You can't go off tracking her on your own. I've set aside the baking. It will just have to wait. Finding Ruby is more important right now."

Aurora could not deny that she was relieved to have someone joining her on the hunt. If she were honest, Ruby had always given her a bit of an uneasy feeling.

Aurora reached out and gave Liora a one-armed squeeze. "I'll help you with the baking as soon as we get home. I'm sure everything is going to work out just fine."

Liora heaved a sigh. "I hope so."

Chapter 3

Kane Carver sat on the edge of the bed in the back room of the Kastains' barn. He couldn't believe how much better he felt after only a couple days of staying indoors near a warm fire and being fed three square meals a day. The doctor from the local town, Wyldhaven, had encouraged him to simply rest and had given him some medicine to help with his high temperatures. The man had assured him that rest was the fastest way to full recovery, and it looked like he'd been correct. Kane had slept like a baby for hours on end the past couple days, and his fevers were mostly abated now, coming only sporadically and usually after he'd been up and about for too long.

But after so many days of being cooped up, he was going to go mad if he didn't stretch his legs.

Seth lay sacked out on one of the bedrolls near the wood stove, jaw gaping like a fly trap. And Maude sat in a patch of light streaming through the room's only window, reading a book.

Kane smiled. Maude and her books. How many times had she read that one, he wondered?

He roughed a hand over Maude's hair. He knew both she and Seth had been burning the candle at both ends with worry over his recovery. He spoke quietly so as not to wake Seth. "Take a nap on the bed. I'm going for a walk."

She looked up, worry immediately creeping into her expression. "But—"

He lifted his hands to stop her protest. "A short one, I promise. I'll be back in thirty minutes."

Maude eyed the bed pillow with undeniable desire. "All right. Just don't go too far? And bundle up in that wool coat they gave you."

Kane nodded and lifted the long gray double-breasted overcoat from the peg by the door. The Kastain family, who they were staying with, had apparently lost their father not long ago, and Mrs. Kastain had insisted that Kane have this coat, stating that none of them needed it right now. He was thankful for their generosity. Just as soon as he was back to full health, he needed to find a local job so he could repay them.

The snow of the barnyard crunched beneath his feet as he strode toward the narrow trail he could see leading into the trees to the south. Though the sun was out today, the crisp chill of the winter air made his breath cloud the way before him. Here and there a lonely Autumn leaf still clung to a maple branch, but mostly it was bare limbs that stretched to the heavens. That and evergreens. There were plenty of evergreens, just like back home in Montana.

He took the path slowly, enjoying the play of sunlight and shadow against the snow drifts. And the way the snow had piled up against the leeward side of the trees. This trail must be well-used because the snow along it lay hard packed by several footprints.

A family of deer caught his attention. They grazed in the shelter of a tree-shrouded meadow.

He paused to lean a shoulder against the trunk of a birch and watch them.

Delicate hooves pawed at the snow, and agile black lips nibbled the brown grasses beneath. One deer lifted its head to reveal a little pile of snow on the end of its nose. Kane smiled and eased away so as not to disturb them.

The path angled into an incline, and ahead, he could hear the burbling waters of a creek. He quickened his pace. He'd always loved the sight of a river cutting through freshly laid snow. As he climbed, he kept his gaze on the placement of his feet. The last thing he needed was to misplace a step and take a tumble down this slope. The Kastains didn't need to have to form a search party to come after him.

He had nearly reached the top of the incline when he heard the rapid crunch of footsteps.

A woman barreled over the crest, running full out but looking over her shoulder at the trail behind her.

"Whoa!" He tried to leap out of her way, but wasn't in time to avoid her. She crashed headlong into him. He took a bracing step to catch his balance, but, in his weakened condition and with how fast she was running, he wasn't able to absorb her weight. Plus, she was running with a saddle, of all things, clasped in her arms.

He tumbled backwards, clutching her to him as they careened down the hill. The saddle flew off halfway down, but he and the woman kept tumbling until they crashed into the base of a large cedar.

The woman's shoulder rammed into his bread basket, and Kane's breath left him in a whoosh.

She slumped beside him, unresponsive and limp.

Kane tried to inhale without success. Snow had pushed beneath the collar of his coat. and he shivered as he rolled to his hands and knees, coughing hard. Finally, sweet air filled his lungs. He gasped a couple more breaths as he crawled toward her.

He pushed her hair off her face. "You all right?" His words were not much more than a wheeze.

The woman stared wide-eyed at the branches overhead. For a moment, Kane followed her gaze, wondering what she was looking at, but then he realized she wasn't breathing.

And that was when he saw the blood.

On the snow and all over him.

Chapter 4

Liora followed Aurora through the crisp chill of the winter morning with her coat tugged snuggly about her.

Ruby must not have thought about the fact that they could follow her footprints, because she hadn't bothered to hide the fact that she'd taken the main trail toward Wyldhaven. And Aurora had easily been able to pick out her footprints among the others.

But about two miles into the trek, Aurora stopped and studied the ground with a frown.

"What is it?" Liora bent and tried to see what was bothering her.

Aurora shrugged. "It might not be anything, but there's suddenly two other sets of footprints, and then it looks like Ruby cuts off this way." She pointed to the north.

"Toward the Kastains?"

Aurora nodded. "Looks that way."

Liora frowned and studied the trail behind them. "If she'd wanted to go to the Kastains, it would have been quicker for her to choose the other trail leading away from our place."

"Yes. But her footprints are farther apart now and heavier. Like she might be...running?" Aurora stooped to point out something on the trail. "And look. These other much larger sets of footprints seem to be following her."

Liora bent to get a closer look. "Could they have been laid down before she got to this spot?"

Aurora wobbled her head from side to side indecisively. "I don't think so. I'm no tracker, but these new ones look to be over top of hers; see how her prints are almost smudged out here?"

Liora blew out a breath as she glanced in the direction Ruby was now apparently headed. She didn't want to lead Aurora into danger. "Maybe it's best if we just go into town and fetch one of the lawmen. Those appear to be men's footprints, don't you think?"

"Yes. But we'd need to go this way anyhow in order to get to town from here."

Liora pressed thumb and fingers to her temples. That was true enough, she supposed. "All right, but we proceed with caution."

Excitement sparked in Aurora's green eyes as she trotted down the trail leading the way. "I've never assisted in the capture of a criminal before."

Liora hurried after her. "Slow down! That's not with caution."

"But we don't want to let her get away! Not when it took you a whole year to save up for that saddle! I can't believe she did this after all you did for her."

Liora winced a little at the reminder, but couldn't help a small smile. She was thankful to have Aurora so incensed by what Ruby had done.

"I do have to confess that I maybe should have seen this coming." Aurora's voice drifted back over her shoulder as she continued following the footprints. "She was never content at your place, and, even though I know you won't want to, I hope you will press charges against her. Maybe sitting in jail will help her see how good she's had it all these months."

Liora worked her teeth over her lip as she hurried along behind. It was true, she supposed. She would have to decide whether to press charges against Ruby once they finally caught up to her. It was also true that she hoped it wouldn't come to that.

Maybe Ruby would be repentant, and this would be a breakthrough moment in her relationship with the Lord.

They crossed the little bridge that spanned Wyldhaven Creek and hurried up the incline on the other side. The Kastain place was not too far ahead.

Up ahead of her, Aurora still chattered about how she felt that maybe she should have foreseen Ruby's plan to run off, but Liora wasn't paying her too much mind because none of them truly could have expected this.

Aurora's chattering stopped so suddenly that prickles lifted on the back of Liora's neck. She glanced up to see Aurora at the crest of the hill with a hand covering her mouth. She hurried forward. "What is it?"

Aurora made no reply, only stared wide-eyed into the valley below.

Liora surged the last little way to the top of the hill and felt her breath leave her as though someone had punched her.

※

Kin finished manhandling the bench seat into the back of his wagon and stepped back to wipe his hands on a rag.

Seemingly of its own volition, his gaze wandered to the path that led toward the Kastain place. It was true that he really didn't have time to help track down Ruby, but he'd had an uneasy feeling in his gut ever since the two women had walked off on their own. And it really hadn't been very gentlemanly of him to leave them to find her themselves.

Sure, he'd promised Mrs. Griffin that he'd get this sleigh finished post haste, but if he had to put in a few late hours because of helping Mrs. Rodante and Aurora, that wouldn't hurt him too much.

With a sigh of resignation, he set to unhitching the team. He would leave the draft horses in the warmth of the barn and borrow the extra mount Deputy Joe kept here. He'd catch up to the women faster that way.

At first, the trail clearly showed only Ruby's prints with Liora and Aurora following her. But when Kin caught sight of the boot tracks, his heart thumped hard in his chest. He swung down from the horse and bent to study the path.

Ruby had been running, but then she'd stopped, and, judging by the melee of footprints, she and the men in the boots had circled around each other for a few minutes, likely having a conversation.

Here, one set of boot prints and Ruby's stood very close together, and then, for some reason, Ruby had turned and run. He could tell because her prints were much deeper and farther apart.

Aurora and Liora's prints overlaid the others, so it was clear they were still on Ruby's trail.

But as Kin jogged along, bending every so often to make sure he was still on the right track, he saw something that jolted him upright and dropped his hand to his gun.

He searched the forest all around him.

Everything lay in silence.

He frowned. Had he read the sign right?

He bent to look again.

Yes. No mistaking it. Along this section of the trail, the boot prints overlaid Aurora and Liora's!

Whoever had caused Ruby to run was now trailing after all three women!

Chapter 5

Kane knew he was in trouble the moment he looked up and saw the two women standing at the top of the hill. Even so, he raised his hands to indicate he meant them no harm.

He still couldn't quite fathom what might have happened.

The woman had come running at him over the top of that hill. And yet, she was very clearly dead at his feet with a knife in her chest. Had she been holding the knife? Not likely, since she'd been hugging that large saddle that now lay half way up the hill.

The two women descended toward him. One of them, a slight little thing with dark hair and snapping eyes that were a light color he couldn't quite make out from here, now had a gun leveled at his chest. She motioned with the pistol. "Back away from her."

"I know this looks bad," he offered as he complied. "But I didn't kill her."

The blonde hurried forward and touched the dead woman's neck. She shook her head at the one with the gun and stood. "Who are you?" She asked, tucking her arms around herself as she took in the scene with wide eyes.

The other maintained her distance, but her aim with that pistol was disturbingly steady.

"Name's Kane Carver. My siblings and I have been staying at the Kastain place for a few days. I've been sick. Dr. Griffin from Wyldhaven has been treating me. He can corroborate my story."

"Can he corroborate that you didn't kill her?" The brunette snapped.

Kane sighed. "No. I'm not even sure I know what happened. I was out for a walk. Almost to the top of the hill. She careened into me, very much alive, and we fell together down the hill. She was dead when we landed at the bottom. She was carrying that saddle there when she crashed into me." He frowned as he searched the brush around them. "You didn't see anyone else nearby, did you?"

"No." The women answered in unison.

"But we did see a couple sets of footprints that seemed to be chasing her." The brunette dropped her gaze to his boots. "They were wearing boots."

Kane's hopes for making a good life for Seth and Maude plummeted. Why was it that, no matter how hard he tried, he couldn't seem to get ahead in providing for his brother and sister?

Yet, his only option was to cooperate. Hadn't Pa always said that a man never needed to fear if he had the truth on his side? *Yeah, and look where that got him.* The bitter thought careened through his mind like a hawk with talons outstretched.

Still, he would like to know what had happened here as much as the next person.

He kept his hands where the women could see them. "I'll be happy to go with you to talk to the law. Tell my side of things."

The women exchanged a glance.

The blonde spoke quietly. "We should take him to the Kastain place and send Aidan for Reagan and Joe.

The other woman nodded, then motioned with the gun. "Walk."

Kane carefully took the trail so they wouldn't think he was going to try any funny business. "Might I have the pleasure of your names?"

"You may not." One of them snapped. Likely the saucy brunette.

He walked quietly after that, and it was only a few minutes later that they stepped into the yard at the Kastain place.

The woman with the gun motioned for him to sit himself down on a log round near the corral.

Mrs. Kastain and Zoe bustled out of the house.

"Heaven's!" Mrs. Kastain exclaimed. "Aurora, why are you holding Mr. Carver at gunpoint?"

"Is that blood?" Zoe gasped.

Kane suddenly realized that the blonde woman had tears tracking down her cheeks.

She swiped at them as she said, "Susan, do you think you could have Aidan ride into town to fetch the law? Tell them Ruby has been killed."

Mrs. Kastain's hands flew to cover her mouth. "Oh my! You don't think Kane—" Her gaze settled on him, filled with horror and a whole lot of uncertainty. "He's been staying here for several days and has been a model guest. Both he and his siblings."

Kane pressed his lips together. Looked like she was trying to figure out how a perfect gentleman had turned murderer.

"Aidan!" Zoe called over her shoulder, and, as soon as the boy hustled out of the house, she spoke a few quiet words to him. A few moments later the boy galloped from the yard bareback.

Kane's shoulders slumped. His only hope was that the law in these parts was fairer than it had been back in their hometown in Montana.

After completing his rounds of the town, Joe Rodante was just getting ready to step into the sheriff's office to warm himself when he saw Parson Clay ride onto Main Street.

He lifted a wave to the man. "Want to join me for a cup of coffee?"

The parson reined up at the hitching rail. "Don't mind if I do." He swung down and tied off his mount. "Just getting back from Camp Sixty-Three. Man out there sliced his leg pretty good with an axe. You seen Doc?"

Joe opened the door and held it for him. "Not this morning, and I just got done with rounds." His gaze landed on David Hines, who sat on the porch of his pa's mercantile, just across the street. "David!" Joe called to the boy. "Take word to the boardinghouse that, as soon as they see Doc, he should ride out to Sixty-Three and tend to—" Joe arched a brow at the parson.

"Thornton Bowling," the parson called to the boy.

"Yes, sir!" David scrambled to his feet and trotted toward the boardinghouse, which was run by Doc's wife.

They stepped inside.

"Thank you." The parson huddled over the jailhouse stove, stretching his hands to its warmth. "Mighty cold out there today."

Joe frowned and gave the man an assessing glance. It was cold, but the sun was out, and they'd had many a colder day in these parts since the parson had come to town. Joe's concern rose a notch when he noted the man trembling a little.

He stepped to the stove and poured a cup of coffee into one of the tin mugs and handed it over. "You all right? Look a little worse for wear."

Parson Clay accepted the mug, wrapping his hands around it with a grateful exhale. "Just can't seem to get warm today."

Joe took in his face. "You look a little flushed. You sick?"

The parson waved a hand. "Can't afford to be sick. Too much to do. I've just been cold since I rode out at dawn." He blew on the coffee and took a hearty sip. "You know how it is when you can't seem to warm up. I'll be fine now that you've blessed me with this." He lifted the cup in salute.

Joe smiled and reached to pour himself a cup.

The door burst open.

Aidan Kastain stumbled over the threshold. "You gotta come quick," he gasped.

Pulse spiking, Joe plunked his cup onto his desk and reached for his coat. "Slow down, Aidan. What's going on?"

"You gotta bring the sheriff! Ruby's been killed! Aurora's got Mr. Carver at gunpoint!"

The parson straightened. "Aurora? Where?"

"Our place." Aidan gulped for air. His gaze flicked to Joe. "Your wife is crying! Everything's a real mess"

Joe's heart seized. "Liora's at your place? Why's she crying?"

"I think because Ruby's dead." Aidan shrugged. "Where's the sheriff?"

Joe was already heading out the door. "He went home for lunch. I'll get him, and we'll be right out."

"I'm coming too." Parson Clay gulped another swallow of coffee and then followed in Joe's steps.

Joe willed himself to be calm. Breathe. Liora crying? Ruby apparently shot, and Aurora holding someone at gunpoint? And what were they doing clean over at the Kastain place? Everything had seemed fine when he'd left the house this morning. And as far as he knew, Liora's only plan for the day had been to finish preparing for the Christmas shindig they were putting on.

Sheriff Reagan's place was only a little out of the way, and since he was only home for his lunch hour, his horse remained saddled by his back door. Within a few minutes, they were all galloping toward the Kastain place.

And Joe was never more thankful to be a praying man.

Chapter 6

Kin moved as quickly as he could while still maintaining caution. As he crossed Wyldhaven Creek, voices up ahead set him on alert. He crouched low and eased to the crest of the ridge to peer into the gully below.

His focus immediately went to Ruby, laying in the snow, eyes staring sightlessly, and then traced the blood that started halfway down the hill and ended where the woman lay. Aurora and Liora stood facing a man who stood near the body with his hands raised.

Kin's first instinct was to charge down the hill to the women's defense, but something held him in check.

Besides, Aurora seemed to have the man well in hand. She stood, with her legs braced wide, and her pistol pointed at— Kin blinked as he focused on the face of the man. Was that Kane Carver? He'd helped Kane and his brother and sister get to the Kastains' and get Doc's help just the other day. What was he doing here?

Liora said they should take him to the Kastains', and then Aurora snapped at the man to walk.

He should go make sure the man knew that he was here so he wouldn't try anything crazy, but there was something tugging at the recesses of his consciousness. What was it? He let the party of three walk away and continued to lay motionless, studying the scene all around, searching for whatever it was that had put his senses on alert.

It was then that he recognized the hush all around him. No birds chirped. No squirrels chattered. The forest lay in an uneasy silence.

Five minutes went by. Then ten. Fifteen. Still nothing happened.

He frowned. Maybe whatever he'd sensed was only in his imagination. He probably ought to give up and head to the Kastain place.

And then movement caught his eye.

He took shallow breaths and made sure to make no moves that might draw attention.

The man slunk from beneath a bush in plain sight. He had a Winchester rifle in one hand and a pair of Colts tied low at his hips.

And Kin had a feeling that if he had moved first, he would now be lying dead.

The man moved to look down on Ruby. He gave a shake of his head and squatted to feel Ruby's throat.

Kin found that odd. Did the man really think that Liora and Aurora would have left her there if she was still alive? But... his eyes narrowed...he wasn't feeling for a pulse. He'd pulled something from her neck and now stuffed it into the pocket of his worn wool coat.

Kin frowned. Was this one of the men who'd been trailing the women? Or had that been Kane? Either way, this man was up to no good. Even now, he strode toward the saddle.

It was time to act.

Liora had said they were taking Kane back to the Kastain place, so that was where the law would come first. If he could get this man there to meet them, maybe they could all have a sit-down, as Sheriff Reagan would call it, and figure out what had happened here.

Where was the man's partner? An uneasy realization slipped down Kin's spine. Maybe he'd gone after the women! He needed to hurry, but this man had to be dealt with first.

Kin tugged from his pocket the deputy star that Marshal Zane Holloway had given him when he'd been sworn in for a short time last year. Technically, the Marshal hadn't revoked his status as a deputy. And they'd never asked for the star back. He figured they wouldn't mind him pinning it back on now.

Kin quickly stuck it to his shirt pocket and then rose to full height and cocked his rifle. "Freeze right there, mister."

The man paused his reach for the saddle, which was just how Kin wanted him—with his arms stretched full out away from his weapons.

The man slowly lifted his hands by his sides. "I'm just minding my own business here."

Kin moved a few steps down the hill. "Sure, you are. Stealing from dead bodies always indicates a man minding his own business."

The man's shoulders sagged a little. "I wasn't stealing. She was my wife."

Kin felt the shock of those words. Ruby? The whore Liora had rescued from the brothel out at Camp Sixty-Five? A wife? She'd lived with the Rodantes for over a year, and Kin had never heard her mention a husband. Of course, she likely wouldn't.

"You can explain it all to the sheriff."

The man turned to face him then, his gaze dropping to the tin star briefly, before rebounding to Kin's face. The man's eyes narrowed. "Little young to be a lawman, ain't you?"

Kin kept his gun steady, despite the quavering in his midsection. "Deputized last year. And young or not, this gun speaks just as clearly as any other. Now drop your weapons, slow-like."

Following orders, the man inched his hand toward his Colt, but just before his hand wrapped around the handle, his gaze flickered to something beyond Kin's shoulder.

The barest hint of sound behind him made Kin realize his mistake.

Without further thought, he tucked his head and hit the slope in a summersault. The reports of two weapons chased him, bullets kicking up snow so close that he could feel the sting of it on the back of one hand, his cheek, his neck.

He crashed past the place where Ruby lay by the big cedar and snaked his arm out to grab a small sapling that had grown up between the roots of the larger tree. But he'd slid too far! He searched the hill. Above the cedar, he could see the man he'd been speaking to on one side and the new assailant on the other. Both of them were sighting down on him.

Kin lunged for the cedar.

And then his back was pressed against the coolness of the bark, and he gulped great lungfuls of the cool air.

He was safe for the moment, but he wouldn't be for long. One of them would flank him, and then he'd be done for.

He had to think!

No, scrap that.

He had to act!

He closed his eyes. Visualized how far that saddle had been up the side of the hill and where the first assailant had been standing in comparison to it.

Then he spun to his left, leveled the rifle, and squeezed off a shot.

The man cursed and dove behind a tree.

Without waiting to see if he'd actually hit the man, he withdrew to his cover.

Then before he could talk himself out of it, he spun in the other direction and assessed the hill on that side.

Something red moved behind a scraggly juniper bush three quarters of the way up.

Kin squeezed off a shot.

Severed juniper branches exploded in every direction.

The man bellowed, and the scrap of red disappeared.

A waft of air whipped past Kin's cheek. And only then did he hear the report of the gunshot. Ruby's husband had nearly shot him in the head!

He jerked into the sheltered safety behind the cedar. But he couldn't just stand here. He had to keep them pinned down or he was going to lose his cover!

Spinning to the other side of the tree, Kin bobbed his head out trying to catch a glimpse of Ruby's husband.

A flash of movement drew his gaze to where the man dashed from his position toward a flanking spot. But he'd made a mistake. He'd left his cover, likely because he'd expected Kin to cower behind the tree for longer than he had.

"Freeze!" Throwing his rifle to his shoulder, Kin squeezed off two rapid shots, placing one on each side.

Ruby's husband was smart enough to do as he was told. With his back to Kin, he thrust his hands—one still holding his Winchester—into the air.

"Toss down that rifle and clasp your fingers behind your head." Kin was mindful of the fact that, though he had wounded the other attacker, he still didn't have him in sight.

Grudgingly, Ruby's husband tossed down his Winchester and did as Kin had said.

"Now, you tell your partner there to come out where I can see him."

"Shade's his own man. He don't take orders from me."

Shade. Kin felt the name like a punch. Was he Bobby Shade? Kin had wrestled with the man and his partner Victor Sloan when he'd posed as a drifter in order to lay a trap for their outlaw gang with false information. After they'd caught the gang, Shade had been sentenced to a year in jail for his part in all those doings. Had he gotten out early?

"Shade?" Kin raised his voice. "You value the life of your partner here, you'll step out in the open, nice and easy like." He hoped they couldn't hear the tremor in his voice. Neither of them needed to know that he'd never done anything like this before. Nor that he had no plan to follow through on his threat and shoot Ruby's husband in the back.

"Can't move," the man called Shade hollered. "You busted my leg up good."

"Just because I hope that's true doesn't mean I'm going to believe you." Kin squinted, trying to think what his best course of action would be.

"I ain't lyin'."

Kin loosed a breath. "That's just what I would say if I was hoping to shoot a man the moment he stepped out from cover. If you're actually shot and want help to stop the bleeding, then you toss your weapons from behind that bush now."

A six-shooter sailed over the small juniper, followed by a Bowie.

Kin's brows lifted. Maybe the man was telling the truth. But when was the last time he'd met a man who only carried one pistol and a knife?

"All your weapons!"

"Don't got no more, honest, deputy. Lost my rifle down the hill a ways when I fell. I'm bleedin' awful bad. Please come help me."

Kin squinted. Did he believe the man? He could be telling the truth, but there was no way Kin was going to trust his word.

Kin remained where he was behind the cedar, keeping his rifle leveled. "Ruby's husband, what's your name?"

"Saunders. Ab Saunders."

"All right, Ab. You use two fingers, and you take those pistols of yours out nice and slow and toss them. Any sudden moves, and they'll be the last ones you make, understand?"

The man did as he was instructed.

"Good. Now, back towards the sound of my voice nice and slow." Kin talked Ab down the side of the hill and instructed him to kneel before him. That allowed him to keep to his cover while tying the man's hands tightly behind him with some strips of rawhide he always carried. Then he grabbed him by the back of his shirt, and, using him for cover, moved to the place where Shade was.

He halfway expected Shade to shoot Saunders to take away his cover, but when he reached the juniper, he saw that the man had indeed been telling the truth. He also noted that this was a different man than the one he'd dealt with last year. But there was a resemblance. A brother maybe?

Kin's shot had taken him through the calf, and he was trembling so badly that Kin figured he might be in shock. He thrust Ab into a seat against the base of a pine and yanked his belt off. Wrapping it above Shade's wound, he cinched it down tight.

Shade's face was dotted with moisture, and his lips had turned a little blue.

Kin shucked out of his jacket and laid it over the man's legs, then helped him take a drink from his canteen.

He sat back against his ankles and considered his next steps. He didn't want the man to die. He still had dreams about Lenny

Smith, who he'd been forced to shoot in that gang takedown last year.

He looked at Ab. "You two got horses nearby?"

Ab nodded and jerked his head to indicate the direction. "Just that way about fifty yards."

Kin leveled the man with his gun. "On your feet."

They found the horses just where Saunders said they would be, and Kin led the animals back to Shade, forcing Ab to walk in front. There was no way to get Shade into the saddle other than to trust Saunders to help him with the task.

"I'm going to untie you so you can help me get him on the horse. Don't try any funny business."

Saunders nodded.

And, thankfully, he followed through on his word. They draped Shade over the saddle and covered him with Kin's coat.

After allowing Saunders to mount his own horse and lashing his hands to the saddle horn, Kin led the way down the trail toward the Kastain place.

He hated leaving Ruby lying in the forest alone, but he knew the sheriff would want to see the scene undisturbed.

Chapter 7

Fiora felt like her world had just fallen apart. She sat at the Kastains' pine-board dining table, twirling the cup of coffee Susan had given her but not drinking it. If she put anything in her stomach right now, it was bound to come right back up.

She had failed Ruby. Somehow, she hadn't been able to reach the woman's heart, and now it was too late. What ought she to have done different? What did she need to change so that next time she wouldn't fail? She didn't know. And that paralyzed her. How could she run a ministry if she didn't know how to reach the lost who were most like she had been? Joe had known nothing about her lifestyle, and yet, he'd somehow managed to reach her. So why was it, that she, a woman who should intimately understand what each soiled dove in her charge was feeling, hadn't been able to reach Ruby?

She had no answers. Could barely think past the thick fog of grief that had left her dry, tearful, despondent.

She glanced around the room.

Zoe and Susan bustled around the kitchen, hands moving in a flurry over some canning they were finishing. Early strawberries, it looked like. Bright red fruit in the blue canning jars made them a pretty shade of purple.

The three younger Kastains huddled near the kitchen sideboard that separated the table from the stove and sink. The twins whispered to each other behind cupped hands, staring at Kane Carver.

Kane and his siblings sat on a bench against the far wall.

Aurora shifted in her seat next to Liora. Her pistol lay on the table in front of her. And from the glower she kept giving the Carver family, Liora doubted any of them would try anything.

Kane had his head tipped against the wall, and his face seemed pale. A shiver shook him. The poor man was racked with fever.

Liora rose and fetched the afghan from the couch in the sitting room and handed it to him.

He gave her a nod of thanks, and his sister did the same. She helped Kane work the blanket around his shoulders.

"Do you need any medicine?" Liora was surprised she found the nerve to speak to him. Had he really risen from his sickbed and killed Ruby this morning? Or had it been an accident, as he claimed?

The sister's lips thinned. Maude, Liora thought her name was. "The doctor gave him some medicine, but it is out in our room in the barn." She angled a glower at Aurora and her gun.

"I'll get it." Liora gave her a nod. It would give her something to do besides sit here keeping company with her glum thoughts.

As she crossed to the barn, she thought through Kane's story. He'd said he didn't kill Ruby, yet she'd clearly had a knife in her chest, and he'd been the only man in the area. So, what had happened?

She wasn't quite to the barn when Joe, Sheriff Reagan, and Parson Clay galloped into the yard with Aidan.

The tears that she'd somehow managed to keep at bay for the past few minutes burgeoned, and, the moment Joe dismounted, she rushed toward him and threw herself into his arms.

"Hey, I'm here now," he soothed, pressing a kiss against her hair. "Everything is going to be all right. Tell me what happened."

Liora shook her head. "I'm not sure." The softness of his suede leather coat welcomed her cheek, and she inhaled his familiar scent of leather and spice as she tried to gather her thoughts.

His hands stroked her back. "Start at the beginning. From when I left the house this morning."

Liora tucked her thumbnail between her teeth and pulled in a calming breath. Her Christmas surprise was going to be ruined, but there was nothing for it. A Christmas present paled in comparison to Ruby's death. She filled him in, leaving nothing out to the point when they'd made the Carver siblings sit on that bench in the Kastains' dining room to await the law. And when she got done with the telling, she stepped back and swiped at her cheeks.

Sheriff Reagan and the parson had stood by listening to the story too. Both men looked at Joe.

Reagan's feet shuffled. "'Twas a boy and a girl that broke into Dixie's a couple weeks back. Could be the same family, maybe."

Joe nodded and set Liora back from him. "I guess we should go in and talk to them." He looked down at her. "Where were you going when we rode in?"

She motioned to the barn. "The oldest brother is sick. Doc apparently gave him some medicine. It's in the room where they've been staying in the barn."

"Go ahead and get it, and we'll meet you back inside."

Liora nodded.

It only took her a moment to find the brown bottle of medicine right where Maude had said it would be, but by the time she got back to the house, the lawmen were already grilling the siblings. Parson Clay had moved to stand next to Aurora's chair, but he was focused on the interrogation.

Reagan stood over the Carvers, arms folded. "You've been staying here for several days?"

Kane nodded. Maude and Seth only studied their knees.

Reagan continued in a hard tone. "We've had a string of misdemeanors round these parts for several weeks. Interesting thing is, they stopped a few days ago. You all wouldn't know anything about that, would you?"

Kane sat a little straighter, giving his siblings a sideways glance. "Misdemeanors?" He returned his focus to the sheriff. "What kinds of things?"

Realizing she still hadn't given Kane his medicine, Liora pumped a glass of water, accepted the teaspoon that Zoe handed to her, and then approached to offer him the bottle.

Joe snaked out an arm. "Liora, stay back."

Startled, Liora looked at Joe. She knew his harsh words had been issued out of fear for her safety. But it was in that moment she realized she believed Kane Carver's story, because she didn't have an ounce of fear of the man.

Joe took the medicine from her and handed it over.

Reagan didn't miss a beat of his interrogation. He waved a hand through the air. "Missing bucket and shovel from right here at the Kastain place."

Maude and Seth both shifted.

"A bucket of milk stolen from another local farm—their cow was mysteriously dry when they went to milk her in the morning. And," Reagan's firm gaze seemed to pin Maude and Seth right to the wall, "a boy and a girl broke into the boardinghouse in town and stole food and money."

Kane was still holding the medicine, spoon, and cup. His gaze had never left his siblings. "Tell me that wasn't you two."

Maude picked at something beneath one fingernail. "You were so sick, Kane. We didn't know what to do. We were just trying to keep you alive."

Kane's shoulders slumped. "By stealing?" He coughed, and another shiver worked through him.

Maude's lips pressed into a thin line. "We tried to only take things that could easily be replaced—like the milk. Except for the food and money at the boardinghouse. But Seth took that money so's we could buy those bedrolls to keep you warm."

Kane's head tipped against the wall. "That don't make it right. You could have asked any of these folks for help and I'm sure they would have been happy to help! And now, because you two did all that, do you think they're going to believe me when I say I didn't kill that woman?"

Both Maude and Seth got tears in their eyes. Their gazes bounced from their brother to flit over the faces of the lawmen and the parson.

Maude's lower lip trembled. "Kane would never do anything like what we done. And he certainly wouldn't kill anyone."

"I believe you," Liora blurted. She brushed past Joe and took the bottle of medicine from Kane, tipping some into the spoon and handing it back to him. "Take the medicine. It will help you feel better. We'll get to the bottom of all this."

He gave a sigh of resignation. "Thank you, ma'am." He swallowed down the medicine with a grimace and handed the spoon back to her, then chugged down the water. "Now what?"

Reagan and Joe looked at one another.

"We should go look at the scene," Joe said.

Reagan nodded.

Kane pushed to his feet. "I'll come with you so I can show you just exactly what happened from my perspective."

"That might not be necessary."

Every eye in the room turned to find Kin Davis standing in the outer doorway of the kitchen.

Chapter 8

Liora felt her curiosity rise. What was Kin doing here?

He swiped his boots on the mat but didn't enter. He tilted his head toward the yard. "Got some other men who might be able to shed some light on the situation."

Reagan and Joe exchanged a look and then were the first to follow Kin as he stepped off the porch.

Everyone else crowded to follow.

Kin stepped over to a man draped over a horse. "I need some help to get him down. And it would probably be good if Aidan rode for Doc."

Susan Kastain hoisted her skirts and turned for the house. "I'll fix a bed. Aidan—"

"I know. I know," the boy groused before she could get another word out. "I'll fetch the doc." He stepped off the porch and dragged himself toward the barn. "I always miss out on all the fun!"

Liora and Aurora stepped to one side of the porch as Reagan, Joe, and the parson moved to help Kin, and the Carver siblings gathered on the other side of the porch.

A second man sat with his hands lashed to the saddle of a nearby horse, but Liora noted that Kin had tied his mount off to the hitching rail.

"Who are these men?" Joe asked as they helped the wounded and moaning man down. Reagan and Kin had the man drape his arms around their necks, and then they lifted him, each carrying one leg.

"This one is named Shade," Kin puffed as they shuffled toward the porch.

Reagan gave the man a second look. "Any relation to Bobby Shade?"

After they'd seated him on the porch steps with his busted leg stretched out before him, Shade folded his arms. "Bobby is my cousin. My given name is Dorian. But just because he's an outlaw that doesn't make me one."

Kin rolled his eyes and launched into his tale of how he'd waited and how the men had tried to ambush him.

"We weren't going to shoot at you until you made a run for it," Shade groused, rubbing a hand over his face.

Kin pointed at the man on the horse. "That man is Ab Saunders. He claims he's Ruby's husband. He took something from her, and it's in his coat pocket."

Reagan gave Joe a nod, then shucked his pistol and held it on the man as Joe strode over and cut Ab's bonds.

Moving slowly, the man dismounted.

Joe motioned for him to lift his hands. "No funny business. I'm going to check your pockets."

Ab sighed. "It's a locket. I gave it to her on our wedding day."

Joe extracted and held up a chain with an oval locket on it, just as the man had said.

Joe opened it, then lifted his gaze to Reagan's. "Picture of him on one side and her on the other."

Ab turned his palms to the sky. "I wanted it as a memento, is all."

Kin folded his arms and narrowed his eyes on the man. "You loved her enough to want a memento, but were just going to leave her in the woods, unburied? More to the point, how did she get that knife in her chest?"

Ab shook his head, and Liora was surprised to see tears mound up in the man's eyes. "Honest to God, I don't know."

Every eye turned on Kane Carver.

He shook his head. "I didn't stab that woman. I didn't even know her. I already told the women, she ran into me full tilt, and we fell down the hill. Next thing I know, she has a knife in her chest and those two are coming at me with a pistol leveled." He swiped a gesture toward Aurora and Liora.

"What were we supposed to do?" Aurora glowered at him.

And suddenly several people were talking at once.

Liora expelled a breath. None of this was going to solve anything. They needed to get to the details from the beginning. "Everyone, hush!" She surprised even herself with the forceful command.

Everyone quieted and focused on her.

Liora propped one hand on her hip and squeezed at the headache behind her temples with the other. "We're going to start at the beginning of the day and go from there, and each of us is going to give information in an orderly fashion. Aurora, you go first."

Aurora looked a bit startled to be called upon, but rose to the challenge. "When I woke this morning, I noticed that Ruby wasn't in our room where she normally is. Then I noticed that..." Here, she hesitated and gave Liora a look.

Liora waved a hand. "I already told Joe about the saddle."

Aurora nodded and gave a little apologetic twist of her lips. "Fine, then. I noticed that the saddle was missing. Liora had stashed it in our quarters since Joe never comes in there. That was what made me realize she'd run off. And then I noticed that she'd taken the coins I kept in a bowl on our dresser. We talked to Kin, who showed us how to track, and we went after her."

Joe and Reagan frowned at Kin.

He lifted his palms. "I was busy, and I didn't know there were murderers on the loose!"

Liora raised a hand to prevent them from getting sidetracked. "So, Ruby took the trail toward town. But from what we could tell, she met these two men next. What happened at that time?" She bounced a glance between the two men.

Ab and Shade exchanged a look.

Ab tossed one hand in the air. "I've been searching for Ruby for nearly three years now. She left me and our boy and disappeared. I work a few miles from here at Camp Sixty-Five. I had no idea she was this close the whole time."

Liora frowned. "She's only lived with us for a year."

Ab nodded. "Yeah, and before that she spent two years as a whore, apparently." His jaw bulged.

"Yes, that's what I was trying to save her from by bringing her to live with us. But I had no idea she had a family."

"Well. She does. Did. Our boy was nine when she just up and left us one day. Anyhow, Shade, here, heard that someone by Ruby's description lived with you all. I was coming to your place this morning to try to talk sense into her. But then, there she was, walking toward us on the trail with that fancy saddle. I got her to stop for a few minutes, but she wouldn't listen to sense. She said she was going to sell the saddle and use the money to move back east where she'd finally be happy. And then, she ran from me like I might try to kill her..." His voice trailed away as he obviously realized that was probably not the best analogy to use in this moment. "I didn't want to kill her, mind you," he rushed to say. "Anyhow, after three years of not seeing me and then she didn't want anything to do with me,

I was upset." He lifted his hands. "Again, not upset enough to kill her. But I let her run."

"It's true, he did." Shade concurred.

Ab continued. "Shade and I were headed back to Sixty-Five, but I figured I shouldn't give up so easy, so we doubled back to try to talk to her some more. When we arrived, those three were exchanging words." He pointed from Kane to Aurora and Liora. "And Ruby was dead at the bottom of that gully with her knife in her chest. I hung back to see what I might overhear. But after they rode off, he showed up." He stabbed a finger at Kin.

Everyone turned to look at Kin, but Liora raised a hand. "Wait. You said *her* knife."

Ab nodded. "That's right. I gave her that knife myself, our first Christmas together. She kept it on a length of leather cord around her neck. It hung beneath her blouse."

"She did wear a knife around her neck." Aurora concurred. "I've seen it many times. I should have thought to mention it."

Sheriff Reagan pinned Kin with a look. "How do you fit into all this?"

Kin's lips thinned. "I finished loading the wagon bench Joe and Liora donated for Mrs. Griffin's sleigh. And then I got to thinking that I shouldn't have sent the women off on their own. So, I followed. I arrived just as Liora and Rory were making Kane walk this way, but I sensed someone else, so I waited. Ab came out of the brush awhile later, and I was going to bring him here for questioning, but then Shade came up behind me. I tucked and rolled, and they both tried to shoot me."

"Only because we thought you were going to try to shoot us first," Shade reiterated.

Kin tossed up his hands. "We're right back to where we started with none of us knowing how Ruby got that knife in her chest."

But with the added information about Ruby wearing a knife around her neck, Liora had a thought. "Not necessarily. I think I know what happened."

Everyone looked at her.

"Kane said he was nearly to the top of the hill when Ruby barreled into him and they fell, tumbling into the gulch. I think in the jarring and jolting of that, her knife somehow jostled loose of its sheath and then she probably fell on it." She turned her gaze on Joe. "Would there be a way to tell if that was the case?"

Joe tilted his head and angled Reagan a look. "If the sheath was still beneath her blouse and the knife was still on the cord around her neck... We'd have to see the scene."

Reagan looked first at Kane then at Liora and Aurora. "Did any of you notice a cord?"

Kane shook his head. "I was in such shock to see her lying there dead. I couldn't say."

Liora also was uncertain. "I was trying not to look at her."

"All right. For now, here's what we're going to do. Kane, Shade, and Saunders, you three are going into handcuffs. You can go into the warm room in the Kastains' barn where the Carvers have been staying, and Parson Clay and Kin will stand watch while Joe and I ride out to assess the scene. After that, we'll know a little more." Reagan and Joe handcuffed the men as he spoke, and Kin and the parson walked with them toward the barn.

Tugging her shawl tighter about her shoulders, Liora met Joe's gaze across the yard.

He lifted a hand and gave her a nod, and then he and Reagan rode away.

Chapter 9

Joe followed Reagan up the trail until they found Ruby's body. They dismounted and approached carefully so as not to disturb any of the evidence.

Squatting, Joe rested his forearms against his thighs and simply took in the scene for a few minutes. It had been cold and snowy this year, but, thankfully, it had warmed up the last few days, and the ground here beneath the shelter of the forest showed clear footprints in the icy mud of the trail.

After a moment of taking in the scene, he scouted wide and came out on the trail at the top of the hill. He found the place where Saunders and Shade had headed back to the camps just as they'd claimed, and then where they'd come back a little farther on, which again, corroborated their story.

Reagan pointed out that Kane's footprints never made it beyond the crest of the hill which also substantiated his story.

Joe released a breath, only then realizing how tense this had made him. It was good to know they likely didn't have a killer in their midst.

He glanced at Reagan. "I guess an examination of her body will hopefully tell us the rest of the story. You think Liora's theory could be right?"

Reagan led the way. "We can hope."

They both sank down next to her and didn't allow themselves to touch her until they'd given her and the area around her a good searching.

After getting a nod from Reagan, Joe carefully tugged aside the collar of Ruby's blouse.

Just as Saunders had claimed, the knife was indeed on a leather cord around her neck.

Reagan gently patted her down and hesitated over one area near her waist. He untucked her blouse and withdrew the object that had made him pause.

Just as Liora had theorized, the sheath from the knife had fallen to her waist. It was a flat sheath with no strap to hold it fast to the handle. In her regular day to day work, it probably never had been an issue, but running as she had been and lugging that saddle...

"And look." Reagan pointed.

The handle of the knife protruded from a rip in the silk of her blouse.

Joe rubbed at his jaw. "They were probably all in such shock earlier that they didn't see the rip. But that would add further credence to the fact that this was likely all an accident. She was running. The sheath somehow came off her knife—maybe bumped by the saddle—and then, when they fell down the slope, she accidentally got stabbed."

Reagan blew out a breath. "I concur. There's nothing here that tells me we need to hold any of those men over for trial. All the evidence I see matches what we heard from them earlier. You?"

Joe nodded. "Agreed."

Reagan pushed to his feet. "All right. Let's get her wrapped up. I'll take her into town, and we can bury her tomorrow."

"We already had that Christmas gathering planned. I think Liora would like it if we turned it into a wake for Ruby. Maybe everyone can bring something for her husband and son?"

"I'll spread the word."

After they loaded Ruby's body onto one of the horses and Reagan led her away, Joe walked up the hill to where the saddle lay in the snow. He ran his hand over the plush softness of the seat, took in the intricate embossing of the leather, and gave a little shake of his head. Liora had spent a pretty penny on this gift. It was more a work of art than a working man's saddle. He loved it. But now it would be a bad memory. He didn't want to keep it if it was going to cause her sadness each time he used it.

With a sigh, he hefted it and slung it up behind his old worn saddle. His mount balked at the unexpected load on its hind quarters, but he was a good horse and settled down after only a moment.

Joe mounted up and headed toward home. He would drop the saddle in the barn and then go back to the Kastains to pick up Liora and Aurora.

Liora bustled through the sitting room with the blue enameled coffee pot, making sure each guest at the gathering—now a wake—had enough refreshments. She tried not to glance at the coffin, but it was hard to avoid since Ab had requested it be placed beneath the front window.

The time of sharing about Ruby earlier had been awkward, since few of them knew her well. She'd mostly been standoffish and hadn't accepted anyone's offer of friendship, though many of them had tried—especially those from the church.

All of that only added to Liora's burden. She should have tried harder. Spent more time attempting to connect with Ruby. Offered more love.

The tears she'd been withholding all day threatened, and she hurried to the kitchen to make more coffee.

A moment later, Jacinda Callahan hurried in, checking over her shoulder. She lowered her voice and leaned toward Liora. "I wanted to let you know that the train with Zane's horse arrives tomorrow. Kin is going to help me get it from the train to here and—" She tilted her head. "You doing all right?"

Liora dashed at her cheeks and sniffed. "Yes. Fine." She scooped grounds into the top of the percolator. "I'll let Joe know to expect Kin. I'm sure Zane's going to love the horse!"

Jacinda strode to her side and wrapped one arm around her shoulders, stilling her furious activity with her other hand. "The world's not going to come to an end if you allow yourself to grieve."

"I know." Liora dropped the measure back into the coffee tin and smoothed her palms over the coolness of the sideboard. "It has been a crazy few days is all. And I haven't been feeling well on top of everything. I'll give myself time to rest tomorrow."

Jacinda pegged her with a look. "Haven't been feeling well?"

Liora waved a hand. "It's nothing. Just a queasy stomach. I'm sure I'll be feeling fine in a few days."

A sparkle lit Jacinda's eyes for just a moment, and Liora felt her brow furrow. Was Jacinda finding humor in her illness? Surely, she'd misread. "What?"

"Have you spoken to Doc?"

"No. I'm certain it's nothing too serious." Liora pressed the lid back onto the coffee tin.

Jacinda took the pot and moved to the pump. "I think you should. In fact, why don't you go lie down, and I'll have Doc come see you?"

The truth was, Liora had thought of making an appointment with Doc a few times in the last couple weeks, but the symptoms were slight—only nausea that was generally gone by noon—and each time, she'd told herself she'd be feeling better in a day or two. Joe kept so busy that she hadn't wanted to burden him with extra concern over her health.

She added a piece of wood to the stove. "I'll see him if I'm still feeling under the weather in a couple days."

Jacinda plunked the coffee pot onto the stove. She smiled at Liora and then tossed her a wink. "After you talk to Doc, you come see me about the dresses we'll need to be letting out."

Liora glanced down at herself. "Why would I—" Eyes widening, she lifted her gaze to Jacinda's.

Jacinda nodded. Smiled. Hugged her. "You should rest. And you should talk to Doc."

A wave of exhilaration swept in, mixing with her grief in a swirling eddy of confusion. She rested one hand over her stomach. "Yes. It could be, I suppose. I've just been so busy that I never even considered..." Liora clapped a hand to her forehead.

Heavens, she really needed time to absorb this.

Jacinda nudged her toward the door. "Go rest. Everyone has had plenty of refreshments, and the food is still laid out on the table. If anyone needs anything beyond that, I'll see to them. Besides, I heard Ab talking about needing to get his son back home. I think people will be leaving soon."

"Okay. Thank you. Maybe for just a few minutes." Liora made her way through the living room where Ab and the men were just carrying Ruby out to a wagon Liora could see through the window. Ab had requested that he and his son be allowed to have a private burying with just the parson out at the camp where they would be closer and able to visit her grave from time to time.

That made Liora all the more thankful that she'd had this time to say goodbye.

Not wanting to watch them place her in the wagon, Liora stepped into her and Joe's bedroom. She sank down on the edge of the bed and folded her arms around herself. Juxtaposed to the excitement of a baby on the way was the hollow feeling that had come over her the moment she had seen Ruby's broken body in the bottom of that gully.

What was she really doing, trying to be a minister of God's? Who was she to think that He would want to use a woman like her? It was obvious from all the tragedy that had happened since she had started this ministry that maybe the Lord was trying to send her the message that she should give up. Tess, the very first woman she had ever tried to help had died in the church fire. And now Ruby.

She laid one hand over her stomach. Would she fail a child in the same way? The thought drove uncertainty to her very core.

Moisture dripped onto the back of her hand. She swiped at her cheeks. Rolled her eyes at herself. She had cried so much in the past twenty-four hours that one would think the well of her tears ought to be dried up by now.

The door to their room eased open, and Joe poked his head inside. Upon seeing her, his brows lifted, and he quickly stepped in and shut the door behind him. He came and sank down beside her.

Wrapping one arm about her shoulders, he gently tugged her toward him.

She gladly sank into the comfort of his embrace.

He rested his chin on top of her head. "I know your heart has to be breaking. I'm so sorry."

Somehow, the shelter of Joe's arms always gave her the strength to face the next moment, take the next breath.

She needed to tell him about the baby, but she wanted that news to be shared on a joyous occasion. Right now was not the time. She would talk to Doc first. And then, if she truly was expecting, she would find the right time to share the—if she were honest— terrifying news with Joe.

Joe shifted, one hand sweeping over her back. "Talk to me. What's the matter?"

She dragged her thoughts back to her feelings about Ruby. Today was the day to deal with those. "I just feel...worthless. Why couldn't I help her?"

Joe tucked her in a little closer. "Some people just...don't know how to be helped, I guess."

Liora gave a little huff. "Or maybe I'm just not very good at helping them."

She felt Joe shake his head. "That's not true. You have an amazing, caring heart, and, in the end, that's all we can offer people. The Bible says Light came into the world, but people prefer the darkness because their deeds are evil. Our responsibility is to shine the light, and you've done that so well. Even Jesus had Judas among his disciples."

She took a moment to ponder. "That's true." What kind of a man had rejected the perfect love of Christ? A love that had walked with him daily? And yet, wasn't that the very same thing Ruby had done? "I just feel like God might be trying to tell me this isn't the ministry for me."

"Why's that?"

"Well, first there was Tess dying in that fire."

Joe's hand smoothed over her hair. "Tess died in that fire because she went in to save David Hines. I don't think you can count that as a failure. She sacrificed herself to save another. The very definition of love and what you try to model every day."

Liora considered. "Again correct, I suppose. But this incident with Ruby...I just keep feeling like I maybe should have done something different to reach her."

Joe set her back from him and cupped her face. "Listen. I'm not saying you did everything perfectly. But you tried your best. And that's all any of us can do. Jesus said for us to remember when the world hates us that it hated him first."

Liora pressed her lips together. How had she been so blessed to find a man who constantly reminded her of the foundation she wanted to build her life on? "So, you're saying I shouldn't give up trying to reach women?" She allowed a hint of a smile.

Joe's thumbs stroked over her cheeks. "That's exactly what I'm saying. Love keeps reaching, even when it is rejected."

Her smile bloomed more fully. "Like you did for me."

He tilted his head. "Well, like God did through me."

Leaning forward, she placed a gentle kiss against his lips. "I'm sorry your Christmas present got ruined." But her smile remained as she suddenly realized just exactly what Joe's real Christmas present would be.

He dipped his head for another kiss. "You are the only Christmas present I need."

"Am I?" He would soon feel differently, she felt sure.

"You are." He nodded. "I've decided to get rid of the saddle. I don't want you feeling sad every time you see it."

Liora shook her head. "No. You know what? Every time I see it, I might think of Ruby, but more than that, I'll take it as a reminder of what we talked about today. Not to give up. Keep holding out my hands in God's love, even when they are pushed away."

Joe tugged her close once more and pressed his lips to her temple. "You're sure?"

She nodded. "I'm sure."

"I'm so proud of you. And I'm sorry about Ruby."

She laid a hand against his chest. "Yes. Me too. Speaking of which, I'm sure Jacinda is cleaning. I should go help."

Joe stood and held his hand out to her. "We'll go together."

And despite her heavy heart, as Liora laced her fingers with his and followed him into the main room, she couldn't help but feel lighter. Freer.

Ready to search out the next woman God had for her to love.

And, she smiled softly, ready to love this new little one God was about to send into their lives.

Dear Reader,

Christmas is supposed to be about hope, love, joy. But the truth is, sometimes all we can see is rejection, loss, and sorrow. Maybe someone is missing from your gathering this year. Or you can't seem to get past a harsh word that's been spoken. Maybe your godly advice has been rejected and you can see the pain and destruction it is causing in someone's life. When you are rejected, hurt, left behind, or mistreated, don't give up. When you are tempted to despair, tempted to give up, or tempted to withdraw into your shell and never reach out in love again, remember the One whose very birth the season is about. The One who *chose* to be born into a world that He *knew* would reject Him. Yet Love compelled Him. And like Jesus, we are to take up our cross and walk in the way of His example. (Matthew 16:24-26) Love on, dear ones. Love on!

If you enjoyed this story, **please leave the book a review**. It doesn't have to be long, but every review helps spread the word, and the world needs more uplifting stories!

Wondering what's going to happen to the Carver siblings now that Sheriff Reagan knows their identity? Or about what's going to happen to Zane's horse? I'll just drop a big hint and tell you; it's going to take a miracle for that horse to make it to Wyldhaven this year! ;) I invite you to read the next episode of this series titled *Marshal Zane's Christmas Horse* on the next page.

You can find all the books in the Wyldhaven series here on my website.

You can also join my newsletter to be kept up to date on all future releases.

Merry Christmas!

Lynnette
BONNER

Marshal Zane's Christmas Horse

Novella Four
Wyldhaven

Chapter 1

Jacinda Holloway woke with a thrill of joy zipping through her. Today was the day she and Kin Davis were set to meet the train and take delivery of the Appaloosa yearling she had ordered for Zane's Christmas gift.

It was Zane's day for rounds out to the camps, so she should have plenty of time to make it to the station with Kin and back again. Kin was then going to take the colt to the Rodantes'. And early on Christmas morning, Joe would bring it to the house.

She could hardly wait to see the look on Zane's face! He'd admired both the dam and the sire when they'd seen them at a ranch while on their wedding tour last spring. And Jacinda just knew he was going to be thrilled with the gift—especially since his own mount was getting up in years.

She thrust off the covers and bounced to her feet, hustling into her dressing-gown. Mindful that Zane still slumbered on his side of the bed, she strode to the window and parted the curtains just enough to see what the weather was like but not enough to disturb him.

"Oh my!" She gasped and raised both hands to shove the gap wider. Her shock made her forget Zane's peace for just a moment. "Must have snowed a foot last night!"

And it was still coming down! She pressed a hand to her throat, heart squeezing. Would so much snow affect the train's schedule?

From his side of the bed, Zane grunted and squinted one eye open.

"Sorry!" Jacinda tugged at the curtains, but too late. Zane was already climbing from beneath the covers. He came to stand behind her, wrapped his arms around her waist, and rested his chin on her shoulder, then reached to push the draperies all the way open.

He breathed out a hum of satisfaction. "I love the way a layer of fresh snow cleans up the world, don't you?"

Despite her concerns about the train, Jacinda relished the feel of his arms about her. And even if the train was late, it wouldn't be the worst tragedy the town had seen recently. It was good to remind herself of the positive side of things. Something she was trying to do more of.

She pondered the misfortune that had rocked their little town this week. A prostitute who Liora Rodante had been ministering to had run off from the Rodante place, and a tragic accident had befallen her and taken her life. "I guess the town needed the fresh outlook after this week's happenings."

He rocked her a little, taking a moment before responding. "Do you think Liora will be okay? I'm sure Ruby's death hit her hard."

Jacinda folded her arms around Zane's and tipped her head against his shoulder, reminding herself once more to see the beauty in the snow even though what she really wanted to do was lift a fist and rail at the heavens. Why this storm, today of all days?

Yet, there was even something positive out at the Rodante place.

Realizing Zane still waited for her response, she said, "Yes. I know she's devastated by Ruby's passing. But I also know that she and Joe have something very exciting to look forward to, and I think that will help her through the grief." She smiled up at him with a little pump of her brows.

Zane's expression filled with excitement. "Really? When?! I can't wait to congratulate Joe!"

"No!" Jacinda spun to face him, gripping the front of his night shirt. "You can't say a word until they announce it. I don't know if she's told him yet. She hadn't recognized the signs herself until I pointed them out to her yesterday at the wake."

He eased comfortably into his heels, drawing her closer. With a languid smile, he searched her face. "All right, I'll keep my trap shut, but it won't be easy with such good news. And it hardly seems fair that I know about it before he does."

Jacinda poked him. "It's only unfair if he *finds out* that you knew before he did." She winked.

He chuckled. "Upon my honor, my lips are sealed."

"I know they are. Besides..." Jacinda smoothed her hands over the wrinkles she'd made by grabbing his shirt. "I could be wrong."

"Hang on, let me write this down." Zane stepped to the little leather-bound notebook he kept on the table on his side of the bed. He lifted it and the fountain pen and opened to a blank page.

Jacinda frowned. What did he need to write down?

He removed the cap of the pen, and then started scrawling. "December seventh, in the year of our Lord 1894..." He gave each number a bit of a flourish. "Jacinda Holloway admitted that she might be wrong."

Jacinda gasped and advanced on him, snatching the pen.

He laughed and ducked away.

She joined his laughter, but plucked his notebook from his fingers and tossed it onto the bed. "You are impossible."

His hands settled against the small of her back, and he grinned down at her. "Am I?"

"Indeed, you are." Beneath the material of his shirt, the muscles of his chest were firm against her palms.

Lowering his head, he whispered, "I do believe you could coax the incorrigibility out of me. But it will take a good amount of time and many a long, persuasive lesson."

She felt her face heat in anticipation, even as her gaze dipped to his mouth. "Is that so?"

"Mmmm." He closed the final distance between them, and his lips swept over hers like gliding silk. "This is a good start to the first lesson, don't you think?" He trailed a few kisses the length of her jaw and back again. "Rule number one: to prevent incorrigibility, keep busy."

She chuckled and closed her eyes against the pleasant temptation of him. And heavens, he was a temptation! But they were both grown adults who had business to attend to. Kin would be here inside half an hour. "Don't you have to go out on rounds?"

"Good news..." He rumbled distractedly between kisses. "Can't ride to the camps with a foot of fresh snow on the roads."

Jacinda jolted. "What? Wait." She pushed back from him, forking her fingers into her hair and trying to think through the fog his attentions had instigated.

He reached for her. "No work. Didn't you hear?"

She dodged his grasp and snatched up her day dress, taking it behind the privacy screen with her. She peered at Zane above the divider, hoping he wouldn't be too put out with her. "*You* may not have to work today, but that doesn't mean that *I* can take the day off."

Zane frowned and curved one hand around the back of his neck. He seemed to be rehashing all that had just happened, then he lifted his gaze to hers. "Have I upset you somehow?"

"No. Of course not."

"I see," Zane said. But his tone proclaimed that he very much did not see.

Jacinda pushed away her guilt and quickly finished buttoning her cuffs. She was going to have to come up with an excuse to be gone from the house for so long this morning, but she didn't want to lie, even for such a worthy cause as a Christmas surprise. And she couldn't just send Kin to the station on his own, because she still owed the rancher the final installment of money for the Appaloosa. She needed to pay him at the train station upon acceptance of delivery.

Zane grumbled a few words under his breath, then spoke for her benefit. "Well, I suppose I'll just mosey on down to the Sheriff's Office and see if there is any paperwork that needs done." She heard his gun-belt buckle clank and, a moment later, his boots strike the floor as he stomped them into place.

The hurt in his tone was almost her undoing. But there was nothing for it if she was going to get this horse picked up and paid for. She could give him an explanation on Christmas morning after he saw the magnificent creature.

But for right now, she couldn't let him leave without an explanation of her absence, in case he came home early from the office. "You should go to the boardinghouse for lunch. I have some errands that I need to run this morning." Behind the screen, she winced, holding her breath. Would he buy her excuse without questions?

"Errands? What kind of errands?"

No, don't offer to come with me.

"I could come with you. I don't like the idea of you roaming around in this weather on your own."

Jacinda's eyes fell closed. Perfect. Now she had to hurt him even more. "No, no." She bustled into her apron, thankful that the screen hid her from his scrutiny. Her expression would likely give her away. "I had already asked Kin Davis. So, he should be here at any moment to ride out with me."

Zane frowned. "How come you didn't mention these errands of yours until now?"

Jacinda tamped down her irritation. Couldn't the man recognize that it was almost Christmas? She needed to put a stop to all his questions! "Well"—she stepped from behind the screen and rushed toward the bedroom door—"I thought you would be riding your rounds. So, I planned to get these done while you were away for the day. I'll run down and get breakfast underway."

She made her escape, leaving him sliding his arms into his jacket. Hopefully, by the time he came down to eat, he'd have resigned himself to the way of things.

Chapter 2

Zane did his best to temper his irritation. Jacinda had run from the room like she was escaping a brushfire. But, hang it, a man couldn't be blamed for wanting to spend a little time with his wife on an unexpected day off.

What had he done to upset her? One moment things had been going along just fine, and the next she was jumpier than a green-broke filly.

He roughed a hand over his face and stepped over to the mirror. He took up his shaving brush and bowl. Maybe it was for the best at any rate. He lathered on the soap and took up his razor.

Reagan would be bringing the Carver siblings in to the office this morning, and it might be good if he was there as backup in case anything went sideways. Just because the oldest brother had turned out not to be a murderer didn't mean there wouldn't be some other shady dealings in their history. After all, the younger siblings' first reaction to hardship had been to steal from strangers.

It only took him a few minutes to shave, yet, by the time he reached the dining room, Jacinda had placed scrambled eggs, toast, and thick slices of ham on the table. She hurried in with the coffee pot in her hands.

With a frown, he took in the three place settings before he pulled out his chair and sat. Must be for Kin?

She poured him a cup of coffee, but before he could ask his question, a knock sounded from out front.

"That'll be Kin. I'll get it." She rushed toward the door.

Zane grunted. He'd assumed that her errands were to deliver dress parcels to clientele. But there were no packages on the table where she normally stacked them.

He remained in his seat. Considering that third place setting, Jacinda didn't plan to leave without offering Kin a cup of coffee and some breakfast.

"Kin, good morning," Jacinda greeted.

Zane couldn't see the entry from his seat, but he could feel the sweep of a chilly wind rush in around his legs.

There came the sound of stomping feet and the rustle of Kin shucking out of his long leather coat. "Quite the storm we had last night, isn't it, ma'am? I only hope that the train—"

"Won't you join *us* for breakfast, Kin?"

Zane frowned. Why had she put such emphasis on the "us" in that sentence?

Only a moment later, they both stepped into the room.

Kin's eyes sparkled just a little too much. The lad was up to something. But then when was he *not*?

"Kin." Zane nodded toward the seat across the table.

"Marshal. Morning, sir."

Zane rose and held Jacinda's chair for her. And he supposed that if she'd been expecting Kin this early, he had to grudgingly understand why she'd fled their bedroom so hastily a bit ago. His mood suddenly improved by a drastic measure. He dropped a hand to her shoulder before resuming his seat.

They said grace, and then Zane passed Kin the plate of ham. "Did you mention something about the train?"

Kin bobbled the platter, almost losing the fork off the side before he snatched it from mid-air. "My, this ham looks downright sinful, Mrs. Holloway. Where'd you get this one?"

Jacinda didn't miss a beat. "Why thank you, Kin. This came from one of Mr. Hines' sows. He smoked it to perfection, I'd say. Eggs?"

"Yes, ma'am. You make the best eggs in town, if you'll promise not to tell Mrs. Griffin I said so." He grinned, trying to act at ease, but the quick dart of his eyes in Zane's direction spoke of the fact that he was covering something.

Zane looked at Jacinda. "I know a snowstorm when I see one." He allowed his humor to show in the quirk of his lips. What were they so all fired determined to keep from him?

Jacinda's gaze widened innocently. "Yes! I know I said a foot earlier, but I think there might actually be closer to eighteen inches out there."

Kin nodded. "About that, yes, ma'am."

The reality of the weather distracted Zane momentarily from his quest to figure out what her errands might be. In truth, he was concerned about them riding off for even a short distance in this storm. "I'm not sure I want you going anywhere in this. Can't your undertaking wait?"

Jacinda's mouth gaped, and she flashed Kin a look that was near panic.

Zane sat back, perplexed. What was he missing here?

Kin swallowed a bite of ham and lifted his coffee cup. "Actually, there is blue sky to the west, and that's where our weather generally comes from. I think the storm is just about to pass." He sipped his coffee and methodically lifted a bite of eggs. "It's a Christmas surprise, see? The parson, he's very hard to buy for. So, Mrs. Holloway is going to help me with a little shopping." He stuffed the eggs into his mouth and reached for his toast, never meeting Zane's gaze. "Mmmm. This breakfast is mighty fine, ma'am. Mighty fine. The parson, he always burns the toast. This is just right."

"Thank you, Kin. Please help yourself to more, if you like."

"Don't mind if I do." He reached for another slice and slathered it with Jacinda's strawberry preserves. His gaze flicked to Zane's. "Saw the Carvers riding in as I was on my way here. Sheriff Callahan met them at the office."

Zane sighed and pushed his plate back. He didn't have the stomach to eat more, anyhow. There was no shopping out near the station. And he'd clearly heard Kin mention the train. These two were keeping something from him.

He glanced at Jacinda. She wouldn't be helping the boy cover up something, would she? Helping him keep it hidden from the law?

With a wince, he took himself in hand. This was Jac, he was thinking about. She wouldn't do something like that. He would just have to trust her, he supposed. For now, he needed to get to the office to help Reagan. "Guess that mean's I'd better get on my way." He bent to place a kiss on Jacinda's cheek. "Till this evening."

With that, Zane headed for the entry. He took down his duster and shoved his arms in the sleeves, then yanked his scarf around his neck and stuffed the ends inside. Snatching his Stetson from the peg by the door, he plunked it on his head and stepped out into the blustering wind.

He paused on the top step. Why was it that his mood was suddenly right back to where it had been when Jacinda had left him standing in their bedroom?

He rolled his eyes at himself.

Married life was reverting him to a moody adolescent.

Jacinda blew out a breath and sank against the slats of her chair as Zane banged out the front door.

She gave Kin a look. "I don't like to be deceptive. I'm not helping you shop for the parson."

"You are now." Kin grinned at her, then stuffed his last bite of toast into his mouth.

Jacinda laughed. "Very well, I can do that. But I hope you weren't being deceptive about the weather?"

He shook his head, wiping his fingers on his napkin. "No, ma'am. The roads will be a bear to traverse, but the weather should hold until we make it back home."

"That's such a relief. All right." She stood. "Give me five minutes to clear the table, and then we can be on our way."

Kin stood with her. "I'll get your horse from the livery."

"Perfect. I'll be ready when you get back."

Fifteen minutes later, they were on their way out of town, and Kin was proven right. The sun had come out, and all around them the snow sparkled with dazzling diamond dust. The wind that had driven the storm slid cold fingers around her neck, and she tucked her coat a little tighter. Though the snow was mounded higher along the embankments, it was still knee-high to the horses in most places, and the going was hard.

They came to a spot where the wind had blown most of the snow clear and paused to let their horses catch their breath.

Jacinda tipped back her head and inhaled long and slow of the snow-scrubbed morning air. The sky domed above them, as blue as denim, but when she turned to look back at the receding storm, the clouds were stacked up like black sheep at a trough. "Oh my, Kin, look at that!" Jacinda pointed. "Isn't it beautiful? Imagine the awesomeness of a God who could turn something like that"—she waved at the bank of clouds—"into this." She swept a gesture to the blue sky and sunshine before them.

Kin cleared his throat. "Yes, ma'am."

Jacinda angled him a look. She knew he was still uncertain whether he believed in Jesus. Floundering through the process of letting go of his own will and surrendering to God's. She tried to broach the subject with him gently as often as she could, but she decided that today, she would let the matter drop.

He was a good boy. She only hoped he didn't keep putting off the surrender until he could no longer hear the still small voice of the Lord calling to him.

Even though it took them longer than normal to reach the train station, the tracks lay empty when they arrived. They'd beat the train.

With a frown, Jacinda glanced at her pendant watch. "The train should have been here five minutes ago."

"You know how these things go," Kin said. He stretched a hand for her to precede him up the platform steps. "They're not late for at least another thirty minutes." He smiled and motioned to a bench. "Shall we?"

"Thank you." His reassurance eased some of Jacinda's tension, but by the time another forty-five minutes had gone by and still no train in sight, her anxiety had climbed even higher than before. Several others had been waiting with them, and now, down the platform, a group raised their voices in agitation.

Jacinda studied them. One man had just come from inside the station, and he was gesticulating a tale. The others seemed to be upset, but they were too far off for her to make out their exact words.

Kin slapped his hands to his knees and stood. "I'll check with the station master to see what's going on."

Jacinda couldn't sit another moment, or she just might scream. She rose. "I'll come with you. I could use the walk."

She followed him through the large double wooden doors into the station. The domed ceiling caused every conversation to echo, and she was glad they'd been sitting outside enjoying the sunlight instead of in this loud chamber, despite the warmth that emanated from the large wood stove along the back wall. They stepped to the end of a long line before the only manned window, and, as Jacinda looked around, she noted with growing unease the number of other passengers who paced the area, many of them repeatedly checking the time.

Something had happened to the train. She pressed a hand over the crimp in her middle. She'd already wired the rancher a princely sum for this horse. She prayed the train hadn't derailed. What if the animal had been killed?! Not to mention all the people who would have been on board!

Ahead of them, a man pounded the counter with the side of his fist. "An avalanche! How we s'posed ta travel east fer Christmas if'n the trains can't pass through?"

The station attendant responded in a voice too low for Jacinda to hear.

Wide-eyed, she met Kin's gaze. "This can't be!"

His lips pressed into a grim line. "Let's just wait until we have the full story before we panic."

Too late for that.

Chapter 3

Maude Carver pressed her hands together and followed her brothers to the bench the sheriff motioned them toward. Sinking down, she tried not to tremble as the sheriff sat in a chair behind the imposing desk.

The outer door banged open, and another man with a star on his chest that read "Marshal" tromped in. Maude didn't remember seeing him before, but he was large and imposing, and his eyes were striking—the color of the forget-me-nots on the china Ma used to have.

She remembered how Ma would carefully unwrap each piece from the old flour sacks she kept them in. She only brought the good dishes out on Christmas or Easter, or if the squinty-eyed parson was calling. Otherwise, the plates were kept in the bottom of the cabinet.

Beside her, Kane cleared his throat quietly, and Maude came back to the present with a start. She realized she'd been staring at the marshal and forced her gaze to her clenched hands.

The man strode to the stove. "Any of you want some coffee? Mighty cold out there today."

Kane nodded with his typical deferential politeness. "Yes, sir. Thank you."

Coffee sounded heavenly. When was the last time she'd had a cup? The Kastains always brought Kane a cup but brought her and Seth tea, and she'd manners enough to know better than to ask for something different. "Yes, thank you."

The marshal pinned his silvery-blue gaze on Seth, one eyebrow quirked.

Seth nodded too. "Thank you."

With a dip of his chin, the marshal lifted the coffee pot. "I'll get water from McGinty's and be right back."

As he headed out the door, the sheriff rose, opened a drawer in his desk, and withdrew several tin cups. They clanked together as he gathered them by the handles and then strode over to place them on the little table beside the stove. "I don't have cream, but there's a little sugar here, if you like."

Maude licked her lips. Sugar. She hadn't had a taste of sugar for nearly two years.

The sheriff plunked himself back into his chair and clasped his hands behind his head as he propped his boots on one corner of his desk. "While Marshal Holloway finishes up with the coffee, why don't we get down to business?"

Dread dropped into the pit of Maude's stomach, making her forget all about coffee and sugar. She knew this scrape they were in was all because of her.

The sheriff pinned Kane with a look. "How long have you been in this area?"

Kane met the sheriff's gaze in that straightforward way of his. "Longer than we intended to be. We were headed through to Seattle when I came down sick."

Worked himself into a sickness was more what he ought to have said.

The marshal returned. The pot's spout already wisped steam. The water he'd fetched must have been heated. He scooped a generous portion of grounds into the pot and set it over the burner of the wood stove.

"Where are you from?" Despite the sheriff's casual tone, his eyes seemed able to cut right to the bone.

Kane shifted.

Maude clenched her hands in her lap. She held her silence, content to let Kane do their talking and also knowing that she'd have plenty of her own questions to answer soon enough.

"We grew up out Montana way. Little ranch near Fort Benton."

The first waft of percolating coffee filled Maude's senses. Her mouth watered.

"And what brings you our way?" There was a hard edge to the sheriff's words.

Kane leaned forward and planted his elbows against his knees. Only because she knew him so well could she see the tension in his posture.

"Short version is that our Ma and Pa were both killed, and I needed to get my siblings out of town for their protection." Kane's jaw bulged.

The sheriff dropped his feet to the floor and sat up. "I've got time for the longer version." His flinty expression made it clear they wouldn't be going anywhere until he'd heard it.

Kane sighed. "My pa ran cattle up in the hills near Fort Benton. Had about three thousand acres of prime land. Problem was, it was just a little too prime." He sat up and pushed his palms against his thighs as though he were drying them. "Few years back, the area had a drought. People were barely scraping by. But there were a couple of deep springs on our property that kept us going when everyone else went bust. Big outfit came in and started buying up all the smaller places around us. Most everyone was happy to sell at rock bottom prices just to be shut of the place. But Pa didn't want to sell."

The marshal quietly set about to pouring several mugs of coffee.

Maude wished she could block out the rest of Kane's story, or maybe make him stop telling it, but there was no escape from the bleak past.

Kane accepted a cup from the marshal and took a sip before continuing. "Problem was, Vince Stoke didn't want to take no for an answer."

"What happened?"

Kane glanced at Maude. She knew he was concerned about her hearing the tale again on account of how she'd panicked the last time he'd told it to someone.

She sipped her coffee, not even caring that the marshal hadn't added any sugar. She gave Kane a nod, then took a breath, closed her eyes, and prepared herself to revisit the horror.

As Kane told the story it was as though she had traveled back in time.

"There was an evening sing-along at the schoolhouse," Kane said. "But our ma was suffering from a headache, so our pa stayed home with her, and the three of us went."

Maude remembered her excitement as she had dashed from the house. Heard the squeak of the screened porch door and Ma's voice calling for them to have a good time. Had she replied? She'd never been able to recall.

"The schoolhouse was a thirty-minute ride from home."

She could smell the decaying leaves of that autumn day. Hear the horse's hooves crunching through them and the wagon wheels grinding over the gravel of the road. She remembered how Lucy Paxton had run to meet her and tugged her into the coat room, chattering gossip about Brody Frederick.

In the auditorium, the piano was especially out of tune that night. Maude wondered if the Frederick brothers had somehow sabotaged it.

"After the singalong was done, we arrived home to find our house on fire."

Both the marshal and the sheriff seemed taken aback by that. As they should be.

Before they had turned the corner to their ranch, she'd been studying the starlit sky, enjoying the jangle of the horses' harnesses. The first waft of smoke had drifted to her on the night air, bringing her focus to the road ahead. Had Pa set the pig they'd slaughtered earlier that day to smoking? She tested the smoke again. No. Something didn't seem quite right. Then she'd seen the black belch of soot and cinders blocking out a column of starlight.

Kane yelled at the horse, his voice sharp, panic-filled. Maude clung to the seat, and a few moments later the wagon skidded into the yard. Bright flames clawed at the night sky, feral, blistering, and unapproachable.

From his seat in the wagon bed, Seth's cries pierced high above the devouring crackle.

Kane's breaths puffed in a rhythmic percussion as he raced from the inadequate water trough to the house with the too-small bucket.

Despair sapped the strength from Maude's legs. The damp ground pressed cold against her knees, and the smoke-scented wind cooled the tracks of her tears. The salty taste of despair still stung the tip of her tongue.

Kane's hand settled at the back of her neck. "Breathe, Maude. Just breathe."

She blinked and realized that the taste of tears was such a reality because she was crying. "Sorry." She dashed at her cheeks, fixing her gaze on the pot-bellied stove and doing her best to push the anguish away.

The sheriff folded his hands and sat quietly for a long moment before he finally spoke. "You think the fire was set purposely by this Vince Stoke?"

"I know it was." Kane's jaw worked from side to side. "But I don't have any proof. We had nothing but the clothes on our backs. All the papers had been destroyed in the fire. And the local magistrate was bought off because, even though he knew our family had owned that land for years, he wouldn't help. I had these two to think of. So, I sold the horse and wagon, and we started west. We worked doing odd jobs for anyone who would hire us, most times just for food. Then I took powerful sick. I don't remember much of the next few days." Kane glanced at her.

And the sheriff's narrowed gaze followed.

Maude swallowed. "After Kane took sick, we couldn't find anyone who would hire us. They all said we was too young to do an honest day's work. And the one place I explained that our brother had taken sick, the lady clapped her apron over her mouth and shooed us away with a broom. By the time we got here, Kane was so fever-racked that he couldn't travel anymore, and the weather had started to turn cold. We needed more than just food." She hesitated, plucking at her skirt as she worked up the courage to keep speaking. "I knew it was wrong—"

"We knew it was wrong," Seth inserted.

Maude nodded. "But we were afraid Kane was dying. In fact, I think he *was* dying. If it weren't for Mr. Davis helping us find that warm room at the Kastains, I don't know what we would have done."

The marshal and the sheriff smirked at one another.

The marshal said, "Mr. Davis. There's something we haven't heard before."

Maude frowned. She didn't like the way their tones disparaged the kind—and okay, handsome—man who had helped them. She lifted her chin. "He was downright gentlemanly."

The lawmen both composed their features.

"Yes. I'm glad he was able to help you find lodging. However, that doesn't negate the fact that I have several people in town who were wronged by your theft."

Maude's shoulders slumped. "Yes, sir. I know. We'll be happy to work to make it up to them."

"The Kastains have said we're welcome to keep renting the room in their barn for a dollar a month," Kane said.

Maude lifted her gaze. She hadn't even known her brother had spoken to them about that.

He continued. "I like it here. Good community. If I can find work, we'd like to stay. And we are happy to pay back more than what was taken from anyone my brother and sister wronged."

The sheriff scrubbed a hand over his jaw and met the marshal's gaze. They both nodded at each other.

"Well, all right then. I'm satisfied that it was a culmination of bad circumstances that resulted in poor judgement." The sheriff bounced a look between her and Seth. "I hope from now on you'll realize that just because a few people treat you badly, doesn't mean everyone will." He stood and stretched his hand first to Kane, then to Seth, and finally to her. "We're happy to have you join our community. Now, how about we make a list of everyone you took something from and go from there?"

Maude released a breath of relief. The magistrate back home likely would have had them pilloried and flogged.

This hadn't been nearly as painful as she'd feared it would be.

Chapter 4

After they spoke to the attendant and learned that there had indeed been an avalanche on the tracks to the east, Mrs. Holloway slumped morosely onto a bench near the stove.

Kin was trying to decide how best to encourage her when he noticed a man wearing a conductor's uniform organizing a group near the station's entrance. "I'll be right back."

He jogged through the crowd, hoping he wasn't going to miss what the man was saying.

"—heading out in fifteen minutes. If you've got a shovel, bring it. Those who don't have one can spell the ones who do from time to time."

A man at the back of those gathered raised his hand. "How big was the slide?"

The conductor shook his head. "Small enough that the train seemed undamaged, from what the rider who brought the news said. But that's about all we know at this point. If we can, we hope to shovel out the tracks enough that the train can get here. It's not too far down from here."

This was good news. He made his way back toward Mrs. Holloway. He could go with the group to help shovel. Hopefully that would ease her mind some. Kin propped his hands on his hips as he waited for a man pushing a large cart piled high with luggage to pass.

A thought occurred to him, and he smirked. From the way the rest of the Christmas presents he'd been asked to help with had gone this year, he probably should have known that he ought to decline to help with this one. Seemed it was his year to have to repair the gone-awry Christmas plans of every woman in Wyldhaven.

When the cart of baggage passed, he looked up to see Parson Clay and Tommy standing next to Mrs. Holloway. He'd forgotten that today was the day they were supposed to leave to go be with PC's family back east for Christmas.

Agitation twisting his features, Tommy rushed toward him. His hands wrung. "Th-the train got a bunch of s-snow on it. W-we d-don't get to go to PC's m-ma's house no more."

Kin settled a hand on Tommy's shoulder. "I'm sorry. I know you were looking forward to that."

Tommy nodded. "L-looking forward to it. To C-Christmas."

"We can still have Christmas Tom, you'll see."

"Still have Christmas?" A new hope lit Tommy's expression.

Kin nodded. "Of course. I'll make sure it's a good one, all right?"

Tommy jumped up and down, hands flapping. He grinned at PC. "K-Kin will m-make sure it's a good C-Christmas!"

Kin transferred his focus to the parson and felt his concern rise. The man didn't look good. He'd been fighting a cold for a few days now, but today his eyes were all red and puffy.

"Sorry about your trip," Kin offered.

PC blew noisily into a hanky. "Might be for the better. I feel like I was on the receiving end of that avalanche. Achy and cold." A shiver worked through him as if to emphasize his statement.

"Sorry. You should go home and sleep."

"Maybe I can now. I've been too busy getting ready for this trip." He offered a droll tip of his lips.

"Good news is they are saying the train seems undamaged."

Mrs. Holloway dropped her head back. "Oh, praise the Lord."

Kin motioned back to the group getting ready to leave the station. "Thought I might go help shovel out the train. See what I can learn."

She stood. "Thank you, Kin. You've no idea how grateful I am for your help."

"Happy to be of service." He transferred his gaze to the parson. "Could you escort Mrs. Holloway back to town?"

PC nodded. "Of course. If that's all right with her?"

The marshal's wife had a bit of a blank look on her face. "I... Yes. I hope everyone on the train is okay."

PC shoved his hands into his coat pockets and hunched into his shoulders. "I'm certain we would have heard if there were any serious injuries."

She touched the lace at her throat. "I suppose that's true. At least that's something. A comfort."

Kin stepped back and started them all toward the entrance. "Yes, ma'am. I'm sure PC—Parson Clay—is right. And I'll make sure the horse is taken care of. Don't worry any more about it."

PC frowned and mouthed to Kin above Mrs. Holloway's head. "A horse?"

Kin gave him a little nod and placed a finger over his lips. He could tell PC all about it later.

The group near the door started to exit.

Kin moved toward them. "I'll be home later this evening." With his next glance at PC, however, he hesitated. He looked at Tommy. He was dressed warmly, with a pair of sheepskin gloves on his hands and a wool hat on his head. "Tommy? You want to come with me to the train? Help shovel?"

Tommy's eyes brightened. He nodded excitedly. "Tommy sh-shovel!"

Kin looked to the parson for permission. He figured taking Tommy with him would give the man a better chance for some rest.

PC waved him onward. "Thank you. Yes, Tom, you can go. But remember, no running off. You have to stay right with Kin the whole time."

"I s-stay with Kin." Tommy nodded. "Y-you see h-her home. We go sh-shovel."

Kin couldn't suppress a little smile. Tommy had made that sound as if their work was by far the more important.

PC gave Kin a little roll of his eyes when Tommy wasn't looking. And Kin suddenly realized what a sacrifice the man had made when he'd taken Tommy under his wing. It wasn't easy living with someone who needed constant monitoring and attention. Even he'd escaped the house on occasion just to avoid having to listen to Tommy's prattle.

Kin lifted a hand of farewell and then motioned for Tommy to follow him. Hopefully the parson would take advantage of his afternoon of solitude and be feeling better by the time they returned home.

Zoe Kastain eyed her older sister across the dining room table. She was supposed to be finishing the corrections on the last few math assignments the students had turned in, and Belle was putting the finishing touches on a watercolor painting she planned to give one of the twins for Christmas.

They sat in companionable quiet, but Zoe had sensed a wall between them for the last few days. Just after Pa had passed, they'd gone through a rough patch, but she'd thought they'd made it past it. Yet, for several days, Belle had been short in every reply and distant in her demeanor. Zoe didn't like it, but she hadn't been able to think of a subtle way to approach the subject.

She looked at Belle's painting. It was a picture of Hijinks, the family dog, stealing a drink of milk from a pail that Aidan carried. Aidan had his hand to his eyes and was studying a V of geese in the sky, bucket of frothy milk hanging forgotten by his side. The red barn in the background and the pink curl of Jinx's tongue gave the painting just the right balance of bright shades to balance out the greens and the blues.

Zoe smiled at the image and shook her head. Every time she saw a new painting of Belle's, she was in awe again of her sister's talent. "Did you really see Jinx do that?"

Belle wrinkled her nose. "I really did."

Zoe felt her stomach turn. She quirked her lip. "Did we drink it?"

Her sister's laughter tinkled through the room. "No. I made sure that the pig got that bucket along with her slops."

"Thank heavens!" Zoe fiddled with her pencil. "Are you mad at me?" The question popped out without her permission. She rolled her lips in and pressed them together.

Belle frowned and lowered her paint brush, meeting her gaze. "No! What makes you think so?"

Zoe shrugged. "You've just seemed...off, recently."

With a sigh, Belle set the small paint brush onto a plate and used her rag to wipe her fingers. She worked at the task for so long that Zoe thought she wasn't going to continue the conversation, but finally she looked up. "Do you remember right after Pa died, how I told you I wanted to go to Seattle to study art?"

"Yes. To the university. Their first graduate was a woman, you said."

Belle nodded. "And I still want to go."

"So why don't you?"

Belle waved a hand. "Ma needs me here. Wants me here. I just keep waiting for the right time, I guess."

"So, you are unhappy?" Zoe slid the math papers into a neat stack and leaned on her arms against the table.

"No. I'm content. I'll go to Seattle one of these days when the time is right. In the meantime, I can buy a book or two about art from the Sears and Roebuck catalogue when I get a little extra money from work."

Zoe tilted her head. "What has made you upset the last few days, then?"

Belle pushed aside her paint paraphernalia and leaned forward, all her focus on Zoe. "Do you want to take the teaching exam? Or are you just doing it because Ma wants you to?"

A wave of relief crashed over Zoe. "Is that what this is about? You think Ma is forcing me to stand for the test?"

"Is she?"

"No. Not at all." Excitement surged through her. "I am so thrilled and terrified all at once. But Ma didn't make me do this. I can't imagine anything I'd love more than to be a teacher."

Belle still looked uncertain. "Okay, good. But you know you can be anything you want to be, right, Zo? Like, anything."

Zoe grinned. "I know." Her thoughts trailed to a wistful memory. "When I was little, Pa asked me what I wanted to be when I grew up. We were sitting just there in front of the fire. I told him I wanted to be a Grizzly Bear. He threw back his head and laughed." She paused, recollecting the joyful sound of it. "Do you remember his laugh, Belle?"

Her sister's expression softened. "I do."

"He told me that if I were a Grizzly Bear, I would have to eat raw fish."

Belle chuckled.

"I told him that was okay because if I were a Grizzly Bear, I would like it."

Belle reached across the table and squeezed her hand. "I have to amend my earlier statement." She smirked.

Zoe frowned. "You do?"

"You can't actually be anything you want to be."

Zoe grinned and covered Belle's hand with her own. "I really do want to be a teacher, Belle. Truly."

"All right, then. I'm happy for you. And I'll quit being upset with Ma for making you take the test." She winked.

"That's good. Just promise that you won't put off your dream of art school for too much longer?"

Belle gave her hand a pat, then withdrew and picked up her brush once more. "I promise, Zo."

Satisfied, Zoe returned to the final pages she needed to grade and tried not to worry about the thought that had plagued her for the past several weeks since she'd made the decision to take the test.

What was she going to do if she didn't pass?

Chapter 5

Crisp snow crunched beneath Jacinda's boots as she and the parson strode toward her horse, with him carrying his and Tommy's bags.

She felt uneasy and knew she wouldn't be able to relax until this whole issue with the horse was resolved. Her mind was still spinning with a hundred different scenarios—all of them dire situations that could end up with her losing her investment. Then what would she do for Zane's Christmas present?

They descended the platform steps, and Jacinda stopped next to her mount and untied it from the rail.

Parson Clay set the bags down, shoulders slumping.

"What is it?" she asked, eyeing him.

He gripped the back of his neck, staring down the road toward Wyldhaven. "Jerry Hines dropped us off. But he had to get right back to his store. I'm obviously not functioning at my peak. I don't have a ride."

"Oh dear." And in his current state of health, it wouldn't be safe for him to walk the whole way back to town. Especially not with the deep snow on the roads. Her horse was too small to carry both of them and would already be exhausted with the work of simply getting her back to town.

Yet...she glanced to where the party of men were just starting out in the direction of the train, then back to him. The parson was in far worse shape than she was. He needed to get home and get into his bed.

Making a quick decision, she shoved the reins toward him. "You take my horse. I won't be comfortable until I see that the Appaloosa I bought for Zane is fine at any rate. I'll go with the other party and return to town later."

The parson frowned. "No. I couldn't take your mount. I'll just walk."

"Nonsense. They have a sleigh. See?" She pointed. "I'll ride on it, and once we get the tracks cleared and meet up with the train, we'll have the extra horse that I can ride home. It's the perfect solution." She thrust the reins at him once more, hoping he wouldn't realize that she wouldn't have a saddle or bridle. She would figure out that hurdle later. Right now, the parson's health was more important.

Thankfully, his condition seemed to be muddling his thoughts because he didn't protest further. "All right. Thank you." He sneezed. Then sneezed again.

She was suddenly torn. "You sure you'll make it back to town fine?"

He gave her a half-hearted smile. "The day I can't sit a horse, I'll be dead."

Her brows rose as she gave him a once-over. She only hoped that today wouldn't be that day. She didn't want to live with the man's death on her conscience. "Okay. I'll check on you tomorrow and bring you some soup."

He touched the brim of his hat. "Obliged."

She left him then and hoisted her skirts to dash toward the departing group. She didn't want to be left behind!

※

Kin had kind of forgotten that Tommy wouldn't have a mount, but when they caught up to the group of men, several of them were piling onto the back of a large sleigh.

Relieved, Kin helped Tommy find a seat, and then swung into his saddle.

The party took leave, but at the pace they were traveling, Kin couldn't help but think that they might not reach the train till next spring. However, they'd only gone a few feet when from behind them, he heard Mrs. Holloway's voice.

"Kin!"

Wondering what she could have forgotten, he turned to face her.

Skirts hoisted to skim the snow, she worked her way through the deep drifts toward them. "Help me onto the sleigh."

"What?"

She flapped a hand. "I'm coming with you."

Kin didn't move. "Ma'am, it's going to be hard work to clear those tracks."

"I know, but I won't rest until I see for myself how that Appaloosa is. And I'll find things to keep myself busy. I can heat water. Make coffee for the men if there's some on the train."

Coffee did sound like a grand idea, but before he could move to dismount, Tommy had already leapt from the sleigh. "Y-you c-can have my s-seat!"

Mrs. Holloway smiled and took Tommy's helping hand. "Thank you, Tommy. There's room enough for both of us there, I believe." Once she was on board, she leaned down to help Tommy back up.

Tommy settled onto the seat beside her and grinned at Kin over his shoulder. "PC'd be h-happy I remembered my m-manners."

Kin gave him a nod. "Yeah. Good job, Tom." He tried not to let it grate that Tommy had acted the gentleman before he had.

As they started off once more, Kin had another thought. He hoped the marshal never found out about this little trip because he would have Kin's hide for letting his wife jaunt off on such a venture.

※

Back at the Kastain place, Maude paced in the little room in the barn. Her relief at the lawmen's gentle treatment had soon turned to despair as she realized they didn't even have a penny to their name.

How were they to pay back everyone they'd taken from?

Sure, she'd only let them take food, except for the time Seth had taken that tin of money. But food didn't come cheap, especially in the dead of winter. And that tin of money had contained over seven dollars!

She stopped and spun to face Kane. "How are we going to get money to pay everyone back?"

He shook his head. "I don't know."

"It's the middle of winter in logging country, and you're a rancher."

"I realize that, Maude."

From his stool by the fire, Seth dropped his head into his hands. "We never shoulda stolen anything. We should have tried again to ask for help."

Maude gritted her teeth. Just because she knew he was right didn't mean she had to like having her failure shoved down her throat.

Kane was irritatingly calm. "God will provide something for us. You'll see."

Maude clenched her teeth and set to pacing again. Kane and his infernal belief in God. "Where was God when Ma and Pa were being murdered in their beds and our house burned to the ground?"

Kane rubbed his hands over his face. "I don't know."

She tossed her hand in the air. "That's what I thought. You don't know, because He wasn't there. Because He doesn't care!"

"That's not true." Kane shook his head. "It may seem that way sometimes, but if there's one thing I know for a fact, it's that God loves us more than we could ever know. Just look how He sent Kin to you and Seth just when we needed Him and this place"—he swept a gesture around the room—"the most."

"Coincidence."

"And was it coincidence that when you broke down and decided to start stealing it was in the territory of lawmen who are fair and just and understanding?"

She turned her back on him without reply. They could play this game all day, going rounds with each other about whether God really existed and loved humankind. Neither of them would win, and neither of them would change the other's mind.

"We're coming up on Christmas." Kane apparently wasn't ready to let this round of the fight go. "That's what the celebration is all about. The fact that God loved us so much that He sent His Son to be born. Out of His love for us, He chose to come! Knowing He would eventually be required to give His perfect life on our behalf."

Maude didn't reply. Maybe she was too focused on the fact that they would have to come up with so much money to enjoy their philosophical debate. The list they'd made at the sheriff's office had been quite substantial when all was said and done.

"Tell you what." Kane was still talking. "We are going to pray right now." He stretched one hand toward Seth and the other toward her. "Come on." He waggled his fingers. "If you don't believe in God, it can't hurt any to talk to Him, right? We'll pray, and we'll ask for help in paying this all back. And you'll see, He's going to answer. It's going to be great."

Maude rolled her eyes, but she knew he would just pester her until she agreed, so she stepped over and took his hand. Seth completed the circle, and she swallowed down the lump that bulged in her throat. This was so reminiscent of the way Ma and Pa had them end each day back home on the ranch. And look what good that had done them!

Kane's voice was a low rumble when he spoke. "Father in heaven, I know that You see this predicament we find ourselves in. We'd like to make amends for the wrongs we've committed to the good folks in this community. You know this time of year, it won't be easy to find work. Please, we ask that You provide a way. Amen."

"Amen," Seth agreed.

Maude only clamped her teeth together and stepped over to look out the window at the late afternoon sun.

If Seth and Kane were relying on God to do something about their situation, she feared they were going to be stuck in Wyldhaven for a very long time.

───※───

It took them nearly an hour to reach the train, and Jacinda was ever so thankful that the sun still shone brightly in the sky.

This whole situation would be so much worse if the weather was gloomy.

The train tracks, though covered with enough snow for the sleigh to ride on them, were clear enough that the train could make it through without issue since the cow-catcher would simply plow the snow off to the sides. But a little less than a quarter of a mile from the train, they came upon the scene of the snow slide.

A great section had sloughed down the mountainside, but, thankfully, most of it had not reached the rails. Only a length of track about a hundred yards long was covered in deep snow that would need to be shoveled. Still, it was a lot of snow to move. She was thankful so many men were with them!

The men set to, and Tommy grabbed the first spade and dove in with gusto, sending huge shovelfuls of snow flying over his shoulder—right back onto the tracks behind him.

"Tommy! Tommy!" Laughing, Kin waded into the fray, dodging scoops of flying snow as he tried to get Tommy's attention.

Tommy tossed a shovelful right into Kin's face.

Kin blustered and blinked and swiped to clear his eyes.

"S-sorry." Tommy hung his head.

Jacinda hid a smile behind her hand. How would Kin respond?

With bits of snow still clinging to the stubble on his face, Kin clapped one hand to Tommy's shoulder. He gestured to the pile Tommy had made behind himself. "You have to toss the snow to the side, okay Tom? Not right back onto the tracks."

"N-not onto the t-tracks."

"That's right. Throw it that way."

Tommy nodded. "That way."

"Good. Now show me how it's done."

Tommy scooped and tossed with enthusiasm, and Kin nodded, satisfied that he wasn't recreating their work this time.

When Kin glanced her way, Jacinda gave him a nod of approval. He'd handled that situation just right. *My what a good man he was growing into. If only he'd see his need of a Savior.*

Kin raised a finger with a swipe as if to say his kindness was no big doings. Then he tugged on his gloves and went to work with a spade of his own.

Jacinda, still standing on the back of the sleigh and high enough up that she could see over the mound of the avalanche, eyed the train for a moment. It was so close, and yet, with all this snow between them, it might as well be miles away. She was so curious and excited to see the horse she'd purchased. The rancher she'd communicated with had assured her that she was getting a top-notch horse that might even make her some money in stud fees. She knew Zane would appreciate that. He'd often talked of starting a small spread, come the day that he no longer wanted to ride for the marshals.

But her curiosity would have to wait. This mountain of snow was standing in the way.

With a sigh, she jumped down from the sleigh and went in search of some wood. Despite the hard labor that would keep them warm, the men who didn't have shovels would appreciate a fire to stand next to between shifts of digging.

She had just cleared a spot large enough for a fire and found an armful of sage that should burn fine once they got it started, when she heard a piercing whinny and then a man's yell.

She jolted, eyes widening.

"Shut that slider! Are you crazy? That devil will bolt!"

Every muscle tense, she straightened and looked toward the sound.

A flash of gray and white bounded from one of the cars and floundered through the snowy field next to the tracks.

"No!" she gasped.

Zane's horse was on the loose!

Chapter 6

Kin heard Mrs. Holloway's sharp inhale and looked up just in time to see her toss down an armful of wood and wade onto the mound of snow. But there must have been five feet piled up in places here along the tracks. It was only a moment before she floundered to a stop as one of her legs sank through the top layer of icy crust.

Kin rushed to her side and took her arm. "Come back, Mrs. Holloway."

"If it puts its hoof into a hole in that field, it could break a leg and need to be put down before I have even taken possession of it!" There was an edge of panic in her tone.

Kin tugged for her to come down. "Look, they've caught him." He pointed to where several men had surrounded the Appaloosa, which hadn't gotten very far due to the deep snow along the side of the tracks. The horse whinnied and pawed the air, but settled a little when a lasso cinched around its neck.

Mrs. Holloway gripped the bridge of her nose and took a deep breath. "Kin, if I ever tell you again that I'm thinking of buying a horse for a Christmas gift, will you please remind me what a terrible idea that is?"

He smiled at her. "We'll be through this in under an hour, and then you'll see for yourself that this is going to be worth it. That horse looks to be a fine creature, ma'am, from what I saw of him just now. A fine creature."

"Well I hope so." Her eyes widened a little. "He looked somewhat wild, don't you think?"

Indeed. Probably only green broke. But he didn't want to add to her discomfiture, so all he said was, "A horse with some life to him, yes ma'am. But those are the best kind."

With all the men pitching in, Kin's estimate of under an hour was just about right.

Tommy wanted to throw the last shovelful, and everyone cheered him on as he did so.

He grinned and thrust his fists into the air as if he'd just won an exhausting race.

Jacinda couldn't help but chuckle. The boy's personality had flourished since Parson Clay had taken him under his wing and brought him to live in Wyldhaven.

She hadn't been able to find a pot to heat water. Neither had she been able to reach the train to see if they had one or some coffee. Nevertheless, the men had appreciated the warmth of the fire. However, they had been out of fuel for the past several minutes, and all that remained were a few coals. Since their job had come to an end, one of the men swept a clump of snow onto the coals with the side of his boot, and the heat disappeared with a sizzle.

The engineer had come around to shake everyone's hands and thank them for helping clear the way. He'd also offered that they could all ride back to the station in one of the cars. The man whose sleigh they'd ridden on had left a few minutes earlier, and now the rest of them piled into the Pullman.

Jacinda hadn't realized how chilled she'd become. She rubbed her hands together in appreciation of the heated car as she admired the gorgeously appointed interior. Large overhead bins, where luggage could be stored, were covered by glossy red-wood doors with intricate gold detailing. These were offset to perfection by the muted green ceiling. A carpet the color of forested hills lay plush beneath her feet, and padded benches, clustered in groupings of two facing each other, stretched the length of the car on either side of the aisle.

"Oh my! This is beautiful!" She ran her hand over the floral and fleur-de-lis pattern in the fabric of one of the bench seats.

Beside her, Kin studied the car, a bit wide-eyed. He nodded. "Yes, ma'am. I almost hate to sit on one of those."

"Well you'd better sit because none of the rest of us can get by you," a man behind them groused good naturedly.

Jacinda and Kin hurried to clear the aisle.

Even with the snow on the tracks, it only took the train half an hour to reach the station. And it was only in that moment that she realized she still hadn't seen the horse, other than at a distance.

Kin looked at her with a grin. "You ready to go meet this wild beast?"

She swallowed. "I'm afraid you might be right. What if it is still wild? I can't give Zane a horse that can't be ridden as a Christmas present!"

Kin nudged her. "We'll never know until we go see it for ourselves."

Jacinda took a breath. He was right. It was time to go see this horse that she'd purchased sight unseen.

Whyever had she thought that was a good idea?

———

Kin stepped from the Pullman car and reached a hand to help Mrs. Holloway out.

That compartment was sure something fancy. He couldn't recall ever seeing anything like it before. Was that what everything would be like in Seattle? He still hadn't worked up the courage to tell the parson that he planned to leave. Was *itching* to leave, if the truth were known.

He loved the people of Wyldhaven, but he wanted something more exciting in his life than the small, mundane town offered. Wanted to be something more than a handyman, or a logger, or a parson—he shuddered at that thought.

Mrs. Holloway pressed her hands together. "His letter told me he would meet me with the colt out front where the wagon lot is."

Kin suppressed a sigh. This day certainly had been a lot of fuss about a Christmas present. But thankfully it was almost over, and he'd be able to go back to Wyldhaven and maybe swing by McGinty's for a drink.

No.

He pushed the thought away. PC was sick and needed him to take care of Tommy.

Tommy!

The thought had him turning back toward the car, only to bump into his charge.

"W-whoa, Kin. Right here. I's r-right here."

Kin socked Tommy in the arm. "Good job, Tom. Way to remember to stick with me." He and the parson had lost Tommy a time or two at the very beginning when PC had first taken over as his guardian, and Kin hadn't liked that feeling in the least.

But it looked like Tommy might finally be learning his lesson about staying close.

"Want to go see the horse?" Kin asked, leading the way.

Tommy's boots clomped down the platform behind him. "Tommy n-not sure 'bout that h-horse. L-looks w-wild!"

"Oh dear." Mrs. Holloway settled one hand over her stomach like she might be feeling sick.

Kin hurried down the platform steps, swept off his hat, and reached a hand to help her descend. "Don't worry, ma'am. I'm sure the horse was simply tired of being cooped up. He's probably as gentle as a kitten." He smirked as an idea came to him. "In fact, I think you should name the horse Kitten." He'd love to see the marshal riding around town on a horse so named.

Mrs. Holloway gave him a look. "I'm not certain the marshal would go for that."

Disappointment seeped in. "No, ma'am. Likely not."

They heard the horse before they could see it. A large covered wagon stood in the lot, and, from behind it, they heard a couple of shouts.

"Get him!"

"Hold that rope."

"Hang it! You devil of a beast!"

Mrs. Holloways eyes widened. "I hope that's not them revealing the true name of this creature!"

He took her elbow and urged her forward. "Let's get the lay of it. But if your deal was for a mount ready to ride, then don't be afraid to do a little negotiating."

As if by mutual agreement, they both froze at the end of the wagon.

Tommy bumped into him from behind. "S-sorry."

Kin waved away his apology as he leaned to peer around the wagon at the scene taking place on the other side. Mrs. Holloway followed his lead.

Two men, obviously working ranch hands from their dress, stood on either side of a wild-eyed horse, each with a rope wrapped around their forearms. Despite their best efforts to hold the Appaloosa steady, it pranced and danced, bobbing its head, pawing the air, and whinnying in protest. It swung a nip at first one man, and then spun to try to kick the other, then screamed in protest when both efforts failed.

Mrs. Holloway withdrew and fanned her face. She moaned a little. "Oh Kin, what am I going to do? I've purchased an unbroken colt!"

Kin didn't reply. He was still studying the scene.

Another man stood near, with a bored look on his face. He was impeccably dressed in a black suit with a smart round bowler atop his head. He adjusted his sleeves, lips pressed into a thin line. "She's likely to be here at any moment! Can't you calm him?"

Kin turned his focus to the horse and pulled in a breath of awe.

It was magnificent! White faced, it had a black muzzle and black intelligent eyes that emphasized the sleek curve of its nose. The white of its head faded into speckled silver-gray that was darker over its haunches. The horse had dark fetlocks, and its mane and tale were long silver threads dipped in whitewash.

"He's beautiful." Mrs. Holloway breathed, and Kin realized that she had peered from behind the wagon again.

"Indeed," he agreed. "Don't pay another penny for that hellion of a horse."

Chapter 7

All Jacinda's irritation over the day's craziness surged to the fore. The truth was, she never would have bought this horse if she hadn't been assured from the beginning that it would be well-trained and ready for use.

Tugging at her gloves, she marched from behind the wagon and stormed toward the dandy in the bowler. Her breath fogged the air in a cloud before her, and her steps crunched across a layer of hardened snow.

The man looked up, pasting on a smile.

"Mr. Chesterton, I presume?"

He nodded and stretched out his hand, but Jacinda's ire was so high that she ignored it.

"What is the meaning of this?" She swept a gesture to the still prancing horse.

Too late, she realized that hadn't been the smartest move.

The horse threw back its head, eyes wild. With a screech, it dropped into a crow-hop and then shot into the air with a great twist, legs, mane, and tail flying.

"Look out!" The men holding the ropes dove for safety.

And the next thing Jacinda knew, the horse landed with a great *whump* and charged directly toward her!

She flinched, only having time to duck so that her shoulder would take the impending impact.

"Whoa!"

Jacinda kept herself tucked, braced for the collision.

It never came.

Slowly, she uncurled.

Her focus went first to Kin, who stood next to her, jaw slack. She followed his gaze.

Tommy stood between her and the horse, arms outstretched.

The Appaloosa shifted quietly, nostrils flaring, but no longer panicked and wild.

"There you go. See? No need to be afraid," Tommy cooed.

Jacinda looked back at Kin. Her brows lifted. Tommy hadn't stuttered once in that sentence. She'd never heard the young man speak so clearly before.

"You're okay," Tommy continued. "No one wants to hurt you." He inched his hand to take the hackamore, and once it was securely in his grip, he angled to face her. "H-he's r-ready to go n-now."

Everyone released a collective sigh of relief. The two men who'd been responsible for holding the horse scrambled to their feet and dusted themselves off. Mr. Chesterton straightened his bolo tie and adjusted his sleeves.

Jacinda placed a hand on Tommy's arm. "Thank you, Tommy."

He grinned. "H-he's not so b-bad."

She wasn't so sure about that. She angled Mr. Chesterton a look. "You assured me in all our communications that the horse I was buying would be ready to ride."

He stretched his neck, again touching his tie. "Yes, well... we had a problem. The horse I planned to deliver came down with a bad case of colic last week. It was too late to let you know, and I didn't want to disappoint you by not showing up at all." He turned to look at the Appaloosa. "In all honesty, this creature is twice the animal of that other. Once you break him, he'll be the best horse you've ever owned. He's from the same lineage as the other."

Jacinda folded her arms. "Yes, but I now have to go to the expense of hiring a trainer. Not to mention finding someone in our area. This is a logging community, Mr. Chesterton, not a ranching one."

His feet shuffled. "I'm prepared to forgive the rest of what you owe, if you still want him."

His focus returned to her.

Was that hopefulness in his eyes?

She sighed and studied the horse once more.

It thrust its black muzzle into Tommy's hand and whickered softly. What was it about the simple-minded young man that had calmed the creature? Whatever it was, she never would have guessed this to be the same horse as she'd seen only moments earlier. Maybe there was hope for it after all?

She looked at Kin. "What do you think?"

He twisted his hat through his fingers and walked around the animal, studying it from all sides. Then he motioned to Tommy. "Open its mouth, Tom. I want to see its teeth."

Tommy pried the horse's lips back, and it gave no protest.

Kin came to stand by her. He shrugged. "It's a beautiful horse. And I heard Kane Carver mention that his pa was a rancher. Could be he could help with the breaking of it. Joe and Liora's place isn't too far from the Kastain place, where he's staying. He's got three weeks between now and Christmas. And I know they could use the money. Might be worth asking at any rate?"

Jacinda checked her timepiece. "Too late to get out there today. I suppose I could come up with a reason to visit the Kastain place tomorrow. But..." Her gaze lifted to the sky. "It looks like another storm might be blowing in this evening."

Kin rubbed a hand along his jaw. "I have to deliver the horse to the Rodantes, anyhow. Wouldn't be anything for me to swing by the Kastain place and ask him. I could come by tomorrow and let you know what he says."

Relief swept in. Maybe she would be able to salvage this Christmas present for Zane after all. "That's a great idea, Kin. I can pay him with the money I'm saving on the purchase price."

He nodded. "Yes, ma'am."

Jacinda held her hand toward Mr. Chesterton. "I'll take him."

"Heaven be praised," one of the ranch hands mumbled under his breath.

Jacinda's doubts resurged, but Mr. Chesterton grabbed her hand before she could withdraw it. The deal was sealed.

"You won't be sorry, Mrs. Holloway. You won't be sorry."

Jacinda only hoped he wasn't lying.

After the Carver siblings left the sheriff's office, Zane caught up on all his paperwork and made several rounds of the town. But it was clear that the weather had kept any troublemakers at home today, and since his horse wouldn't make it out to the camps and back, he returned home.

The house was cold and dark. The breakfast dishes, though washed, remained on the drainboard, something very unlike Jacinda, who was meticulous about the way her kitchen looked.

He stood quietly for a moment, hands on his hips, staring at the dark floor. Surely her errands hadn't taken this long? Shopping for the parson's Christmas present, Kin had said. But they'd also mentioned the train. Where would she be?

He strode to the back door and yanked it open, checking the sky to the west. A small bank of dark clouds hung on the horizon. Another storm was on its way.

He closed the door and banged through the process of making a fire and putting on a pot of coffee. Then he dug through the icebox and took out the pan with yesterday's stew and plunked it onto the stove. It hadn't been so long from his bachelor days that he'd forgotten how to make biscuits, so he whacked together a batch and thrust them in the oven.

Jacinda still wasn't home by the time the meal was ready.

His irritation melted into concern. Why hadn't he asked more questions this morning? What if something had happened to her? He didn't even know where she and Kin had gone! And with his horse's age, even if he did know where they were, he might not be able to ride after them.

No matter. He would rent a horse from Bill at the livery. Maybe he would know where she and Kin had gone off to.

Leaving the food on the table, he strode toward the front door.

Chapter 8

Kin was amazed at how the horse calmly followed Tommy down the path to the Rodante place. Clouds had been sweeping in from the west all afternoon, and the evening had settled into a gray gloom. But, thankfully, the winds were mild.

After dropping Mrs. Holloway off on the outskirts of town, he and Tommy had traded off riding his mount and leading the Appaloosa back to the Rodante place. At first, he'd been concerned that the horse wouldn't respond to him with Tommy riding, but the horse seemed content to simply have Tommy near.

Tommy had taken over leading it about five minutes back. Every once in a while, he would coo something nonsensical to the Appaloosa, and it would whicker at him as though they might be carrying on a conversation.

Kin shook his head. He'd never seen the like. But if there was one thing he'd learned in the months that Tommy had lived with him and PC, it was that the boy was very special. He was talented in ways most would discount at first glance. It shamed Kin to think that a few years ago he might have treated someone like Tommy dismissively.

They crested the hill just before the Rodante place, and Deputy Joe was just coming out of his barn.

Seeing them, he paused. His expression brightened. "Is that the new horse for Zane?" He released a whistle. "It's a beauty."

Kin eyed the horse, half expecting it to bolt at the whistle, but it continued to step softly in Tommy's wake, ears pricked in curiosity of its surroundings.

"It spooks fairly easy. But Tommy seems to have a calming effect on him." As he spoke, Kin swung down, let his mount drink from the trough, and then looped his reins over the top corral pole. "Turns out this isn't the horse they'd planned to sell her. That one came down sick. And this one is green broke."

Joe gave the Appaloosa a once-over. "Looks calm enough."

Kin nodded. "You should have seen it kicking up a fuss before Tommy got hold of it. I think until we see how it responds that we'd better keep it on a lead rope, even when it's in the corral. I saw it jump from a standing position up into a train car, so I don't think that fence is going to stop it."

Joe nodded. "All right. When I have it outdoors, I'll be sure to put a lead on it."

Kin nodded. "I'm going to the Kastain's right now to speak to that new man, Carver, about breaking it. Be all right if he agrees, if he comes here to do the work?"

Joe shrugged. "Don't see why not. Plenty of room here in the corral."

Kin dipped his chin in agreement. "I'll tell him." He motioned for Tommy to hand the hackamore to Joe. "We'd better be going, Tommy. We still have one stop to make, and then we need to go check on PC."

Tommy hung his head, reluctant to give up the rope.

"You can come see him again. I'll bring you myself."

Tommy looked up with a hopeful expression. "Tonight?"

Kin and Joe chuckled.

Kin shook his head. "Not tonight. We have to go home and get you warm. But I'll bring you back before the week is out."

Tommy's shoulders slumped, but he did hand the rope off to Joe this time. "O-okay."

Joe dropped a hand onto Tommy's shoulder. "See you later in the week, partner."

Tommy nodded, but his wistful gaze was still fastened on the horse.

Kin grinned and patted the saddle. "Come on. It's your turn to ride." They'd get to the Kastain place faster with Tommy in the saddle.

He lifted a hand of farewell to Joe and started them down the trail.

Since the path to the Kastains' was under the overhang of trees for most of the way, which had kept it clear of snow, the trip didn't take them much longer than normal, and the sun was still hanging above the horizon when they arrived.

Zoe stepped out onto the porch, wiping her hands on a towel. "Hi, Kin. Hi, Tommy!"

Kin looked up. He wished she'd put as much enthusiasm into greeting him as she had into greeting Tommy. He'd bet if Wash were here, she'd hail *him* with a little more excitement in her voice. Realizing how bitter the thought was, he brushed it aside. He could hardly complain when he'd never really tried to woo her, now could he?

He pressed his hat over his heart and gave her his most fetching grin. "You are looking pretty as a picture today, Zoe."

She blushed and looked down. "Thank you."

From behind her, Zoe's ma cleared her throat loudly. She stood in the shadow of the doorway, and he hadn't even noticed her there. "What can we do for you, Kin?" There was a little bit of vinegar in her tone.

Right. Best he quit thinking about wooing the fair Zoe and concentrate on business. "I'm here to speak to Kane Carver if he's around."

Mrs. Kastain nodded. "He's in their room in the barn there." She pointed. "Go on and talk to him."

With a little bow, Kin backed toward the barn. "Yes, ma'am. Thank you." As he continued to mosey backward, he let his gaze linger on Zoe. She certainly was mighty easy on the eyes.

His heel banged into something, and he suddenly found himself flailing his arms like a windmill to avoid sitting in the Kastains' watering trough.

Zoe giggled, and then her Ma's arm snaked out the door and yanked her inside.

When Kin finally regained his balance, Tommy looked at him, head shaking. "Y-you should watch wh-where you're g-going."

Kin chuckled. "That I should, Tom. That I should."

When he knocked on the door at the far end of the barn, Seth Carver opened it and then stepped back to invite him in. All three of the Carvers were there. And speaking of gals who were easy on the eyes, Maude was something to behold. Her hair had tints of red, but was nearly as dark as coal. The color fascinated him. It brought to mind the darkest hues of sand plum tree leaves in autumn. As petite as she was, when he'd first seen her out on the road, he'd taken her for a girl just in her teens. But now that she was wearing clean clothes and had enjoyed a few days of rest and food, her color was healthier and her eyes a little brighter. He now realized she was older than he'd first thought.

Kane glanced from Kin to Maude and back again with a little frown on his face. "How can we help you?"

Kin motioned for Tommy to step all the way inside so they could shut the door against the cold.

He reminded himself once more that he was here on business. "I'm actually hoping you can help me."

For some reason Kane gave his sister a smile that had the essence of an I-told-you-so. "Oh yeah?"

"You know anything about breaking horses?"

Maude gasped. Face paling, she sank onto the edge of the room's only bed.

Kin frowned. "You all right? Did I say something wrong?"

She shook her head. "No." Her voice was thin.

Kane was grinning from ear to ear when Kin looked back at him.

"I must be missing something."

Kane looked ready to dance a jig. "You believe in the power of prayer, Kin?"

Taken aback, Kin bounced a glance between the brother and sister. "Can't say for certain."

Kane still looked as excited as a kid on Christmas morning. "Well I do. And not an hour ago we stood right here and prayed that the Lord would provide work for us. Can you guess what I did on my father's ranch for all my growing up years?"

Kin felt a prickle along the back of his neck. "Bronco busting?"

"That's right!" Kane swooped down on his sister, wrapped her in a big bear hug, and swung her in a circle. "What do you think about the Lord answering prayer now, little sister? Huh?"

"Kane, put me down!" Face red, Maude beat against her brother's shoulders.

"Nope! Not until you admit it! This is a blatant answer to prayer. He didn't even know that's what I did!"

Maude threw back her head in exasperation. "Fine! I'm willing to concede this might be more than coincidence!"

"Ha ha! Indeed!" Kane set her down and stretched a hand toward Kin. "I'll take the job."

Somewhat befuddled, Kin shook. "But I haven't even told you what it pays yet."

Kane shook his head. "Don't matter. If the Lord sent the job, I'm willing to do it."

Kin gave him the details of the job, and, as he and Tommy left, he was still pondering the man's crazy reaction to such a simple thing.

"I l-like him!" Tommy proclaimed, and then broke out into his characteristic tuneless whistling.

And as Kin trailed in his wake toward the parsonage, he couldn't help but feel the same.

Zane was in the entry reaching for his coat when the door opened and Jacinda bustled in.

"Oh!" she gave a little jolt. "You startled me." With a chuckle, she laid a hand over her chest.

And then she breezed into the house as if it were the most natural thing in the world for her to be hours late returning home. All of this was so uncharacteristic of her.

"Mmmm! That stew smells divine! Thank you for heating it up. I'm sorry I wasn't back sooner."

She bustled to the cupboard and took down crockery, scooped some silverware from the drawer, and had the table set almost before his heart had settled into a calmer beat.

"Oh, and biscuits! Goodness!" She sidled toward him and looped her arms behind his neck. "I didn't know what a talented man I'd married."

He thinned his lips and narrowed his eyes. "I was getting worried about you."

"I'm sorry. There was an avalanche that blocked the train." She bit her lip as though she hadn't meant to let that slip.

"Surely you weren't dealing with the parson's present this whole time? And what was Kin buying that had to do with the train? You mentioned it this morning too."

"Listen, I don't like to see this interrogating expression, Marshal. You get that certain expression. I'm not one of your outlaws!" She offered a pretty pout that was deliberately exaggerated.

He couldn't help but smile. "And what does my interrogating expression look like?"

She touched his forehead. "You get a little pucker between your eyes right here, and here"—she touched the outer corner of his eye—"the skin wrinkles up just a smidge. Then your lips purse ever so slightly. It's really quite intimidating."

He supposed he was going to have to let this go. It wasn't like he didn't trust her. It just grated on him to have her keeping secrets.

She huffed and tilted her head. "You do realize that Christmas is almost upon us, don't you, Marshal?"

"Ah!" Just like that, everything fell into place. "So, whatever came on the train had nothing to do with Kin and the parson but with you and me. Why didn't you just tell me you were off on a Christmas errand this morning?"

She opened her mouth as if to reply and then hesitated. "In truth, I don't know. Except that you get all interrogatey."

He laughed. "Do I?"

"I rest my case," she said dryly, then smiled. "I should have told you. I apologize."

He grinned, but he still had questions. "So where was this avalanche? And did you leave Kin buried beneath it?" He winked.

"No. Kin is with Tommy. Which reminds me, the parson and Tommy couldn't catch their train to the east today because of the avalanche. They are now supposed to catch one next week, but the parson did not look well. Not at all. I need to go check on him in the morning."

"I can go over there after dinner with some stew."

She gave his chest a little bump. "That's a very good idea. So, am I forgiven for keeping secrets?"

He grinned. "Did you get me something good?"

To his surprise she blew out an uncertain breath. "I hope it will turn out that way, yes."

He threw back his head on a laugh, enjoying the feel of her small waist in his hands. "Now you have me curious for sure."

She tapped his nose. "Well, I'm not saying another word. Let's eat."

Deciding to quit teasing her, he pulled out her chair and held it for her, then took his own seat across from her.

And after they'd said grace, he was dismayed to learn that he'd obviously forgotten quite a bit about how to make a decent biscuit. But he had a wife who loved him enough to ride out into a bitterly cold winter day to procure him a present. He would happily eat dry biscuits every day to keep things just the way they were.

Dear Reader,

Have you ever tried to do something nice for someone, only to have one thing after another go wrong like Jacinda had in this story? Or maybe it's a series of things that just aren't going your way like Maude and the Carvers are experiencing. Especially at Christmas, with all the stress and bustle, it can sometimes seem like we'll never get that to-do list finished. Or maybe your stresses are more significant than that.

This holiday season, try to take a moment to simply rejoice in the true meaning of the season. Plant your feet firmly on that solid foundation and claim the victory over whatever is going on in your life. Resting in Jesus brings us peace.

Philippians 4:4-7 puts it this way. *Rejoice in the Lord always. I will say it again: Rejoice! Let your gentleness be evident to all. The Lord is near. Do not be anxious about anything, but in every situation, by prayer and petition, with thanksgiving, present your requests to God. And the peace of God, which transcends all understanding, will guard your hearts and your minds in Christ Jesus.*

May that peace fill your hearts this season!

If you enjoyed this story, **please leave the book a review**. It doesn't have to be long, but every review helps spread the word, and the world needs more uplifting stories!

Wondering what's going to happen to Zoe and Washington on the trip to Seattle for Zoe's test? And what about poor Parson Clay, sick and stuck in Wyldhaven for Christmas, or Kin's plans to move to Seattle?

I invite you to read the next episode of this series titled *Washington Nolan's Christmas Watch* on the next page.

If you would like to read Zane and Jacinda's romance where they first fall in love, you can find it in the book, *Consider the Lilies*. All the books in the Wyldhaven series are here on my website.

Merry Christmas!

Lynnette
BONNER

Washington Nolan's Christmas Watch

Novella Five
WYLDHAVEN

Chapter 1

When Zoe awoke on the morning she was to leave for her teaching exam, she couldn't decide if her queasiness was from butterflies or great lurking bats.

What she did know was that she wanted to get on the road so they wouldn't be late. She planned to arrive early for the train and to the testing venue tomorrow. She hoped punctuality would allow her to relax—well, relax as much as possible with such a life-changing test looming.

She dressed hurriedly in the chill of her room and rushed out to help Ma finish breakfast. But it seemed Ma might be just as nervous as she was, because it was obvious Ma had been up for several hours.

Pancakes and eggs already sat steaming in the middle of the table, and Ma was hurrying Aidan into his frock coat. "Hustle up now, or you'll be late for school." Ma quickly thrust an apple and a paper-wrapped sandwich into each of the three lunch pails on the kitchen sideboard.

The twins bustled in. Before they could sit at the table, Ma lined them up against the wall next to Aidan. She made sure she had captured the focus of each of the youngsters before she spoke again. "Each of you, listen up. Belle is going to be working at the boardinghouse when you get done with school. I don't want any of you walking that path home alone that time of day.

You are to go straight from the school to the boardinghouse and wait for Belle's shift to conclude. I've already spoken to Mrs. Griffin, and she said you can sit at a table in the dining room to work on your homework while you wait."

Sharon nodded. "Yes, Ma. I'll make sure we all get there."

Ma gave her shoulder a squeeze. "That's my girl."

When Ma turned her back to finish packing the lunches, Shiloh rolled her eyes and stuck her tongue out at Sharon.

Zoe suppressed a chuckle and arched one brow at Shiloh. She hoped she would get the message without her having to say a word. But Shiloh only wrinkled her nose and rolled her eyes again.

Zoe narrowed a glower at her sibling but then turned from the confrontation. She didn't have time or energy to spend on dealing with Shiloh's attitude today. Thankfully, everyone seemed ready to go because she knew Ma wouldn't leave the house until she got the kids off to school and Belle off to work.

She ticked through her mental checklist of everything she needed to remember to take with her on the train today. Her glance at the clock on the wall showed that Washington Nolan would be here inside thirty minutes. Thankfully, the storm from earlier this week seemed to have abated. Sunshine currently streamed through the dining room windows to cast golden rectangles across the table and floor.

She only hoped there would be no more avalanches. Heavens! She pressed one hand over her middle. "Ma, what if there's an avalanche?!"

Belle stepped into the room then with her work apron over one arm. She turned and placed both her hands on Zoe's shoulders, giving her a sisterly shake. "There's not going to be an avalanche. Stop it, or you'll make yourself sick."

"She's right, Zoe. Come on now, sit down." Ma rushed the twins and Aidan into seats at the table too. "Everyone, eat your breakfast quickly."

Belle took her jacket from the hook by the front door. "Actually, Ma, if they are walking to town with me, we need to go."

Ma plunked her hands on her hips. "Aren't you going to eat some breakfast?"

Belle shook her head. "No time today. I need to be at the boardinghouse first thing since you aren't going to be there to help."

Zoe gave Belle a second look. Had there been animosity in that statement? But after only a moment, she gave herself a little head-shake. No. Belle had been a bit snippy about her taking the teaching exam at first. But they'd had a good talk, and, ever since then, Belle had changed her attitude. Her sister had merely stated a fact. And she appreciated Belle doing extra work so Ma could go on this trip with her.

"Well, all right." Ma scooped eggs into the middle of one pancake and rolled it up, tucking one end in. She thrust it at Aidan, then repeated the process for the twins. Shiloh frowned. "But there's no syrup."

"It will have to do for today," Ma said. "Get your lunches." She hurried to Belle with one as well, then tugged her into a quick embrace that might have squished the pancake to Belle's blouse if she hadn't thought quickly and thrust it off to one side. "I don't like to see you going without breakfast."

Belle lifted the pancake roll, and Zoe could see her tucking away her humor. "Thanks, Ma."

"Of course. And thank you for seeing to the young ones for the next couple of days. It's a blessing that I can count on you."

Belle nodded. "Of course. I'm happy to help." She strode to Zoe then and pulled her in for a quick one-armed hug. They shared a humorous glance over Ma's insistence that none of her children leave the house without breakfast, and then Belle said, "You will do amazing. Don't be nervous."

Zoe laughed apprehensively. "I'm afraid there's not much I can do about that."

Belle gave her shoulder a squeeze, then flapped her hands at the kids to get moving. "Just remember how smart you are and that Mrs. Callahan always said you were one of the brightest pupils in the room."

Zoe tilted her a look. "She said that about you too."

Holding the door open with one foot so the kids could file out, Belle gave an exaggerated sweep of her hair. "Of course, she did."

Joining in with Belle's chuckle, Zoe flapped a hand. "Get on with you."

"Right. Everyone ready?" Belle said to the kids. "Let's go." She pulled the door shut.

Zoe blew out a breath, undeniably thankful to have them off for town. She and Ma could share a bite to eat and still have a couple minutes before Wash arrived.

"Aidan?" Belle's words drifted in from the yard.

Footsteps slapped against the porch boards, and then the door burst open. Aidan flung himself across the room and into Ma's arms. "Don't go, Ma! What if I never see you again?"

Ma's lips pressed together, even as tears filled her eyes. She wrapped her arms around Aidan and held him close. "There, there. Nothing's going to happen to me, love. I'm healthy and whole, without any ailment whatsoever. And no one is going to shoot me."

They were Aidan's recurring fears, ever since their pa had been shot by an outlaw and died last year after a long bout of illness.

"I don't want you to go!" Aidan wailed, hugging Ma tighter.

Zoe felt a wave of hopelessness crash over her. Because when Aidan got into one of these fits, there was no changing his mind. He was as stubborn as a mule and twice as dogged.

Zoe clenched her fists. Oh! Why today of all days!?

She forced herself to pull in a long, slow breath and then push it out on a measured exhale. But it didn't do anything to quell the storm that had arisen in her middle.

Aidan! The little jackanapes! He was probably only trying to get out of school! She didn't even feel guilty for being irritated with him.

This was definitely going to make her late!

Chapter 2

Washington Nolan dipped a double handful of water from the icy bucket on the back porch and doused it over his hair. He gasped at the frigidity of it. This was good. He could come back to the memory of this moment every time he thought of Zoe Kastain as more than simply his childhood friend during this trip.

He'd made a really big mistake last spring and kissed her. And it had been nice. *Really nice.* But nothing could come of it. He wasn't ready to settle down and start a family. Had no idea how he would provide for one. No. He definitely needed to get back to thinking of her as only a friend.

As if to solidify the thought, he dashed another handful of water into his face. He couldn't suppress a shiver. That water hadn't gotten any warmer in the past few seconds.

His father chuckled from where he stood next to the door peering into the small mirror while shaving. "Guess it might be time to start bringin' the bucket inside nights." He jutted his jaw to one side and stretched his skin tight as the razor scraped over his cheek.

Wash fumbled for the piece of toweling. "Seems so, yes." He dried his face and scrubbed at his hair.

Pa set down his razor and held out a hand for the towel.

Wash handed it over.

Using it to wipe the remaining bits of froth from his face, Pa asked, "So they got the trains runnin' again?"

"From what I understand. It took them nearly two weeks to clear the tracks though. There were slides in several places." Wash glanced at the pocket watch Pa had given him last Christmas and decided to forgo his own shave today. He tucked the watch into his pants pocket and reached for his shirt. He still could hardly believe that Pa had given his great-grandfather's watch to him. It was a beautiful piece with an intricately engraved gold housing.

Pa made a *tsk*ing noise. "Every modern convenience comes with its own set of problems."

"Yes, sir."

"So, you'll be back in two days?"

"Yes, sir." Wash worked at his shirt buttons.

Pa took up his hat. He stopped on the top step and stared out across the yard for a few minutes, and Wash could tell he was pondering on something he wanted to say. Pa was thoughtful like that. Never uttered a word he didn't think through first. Finally, he settled his hat on his head and offered, "Just remember that a gentleman never leaves hisself behind." He gave a little dip of his chin, as though giving approval to what he'd just said.

He strode toward the barn then, leaving Wash to stare after him.

He chuckled. Never leaves himself behind? It was such a Pa thing to say. Something that sounded so meaningful and packed a punch, yet didn't really mean anything at all.

Wash tucked in his shirt, pushed his hair back, and then settled his Stetson on his head. He grabbed his jacket from the hook inside the door. It was time they got going. He knew how Zoe fretted about being on time for things like this.

"Jax! We need to go!" he called into the house.

"We don't need to leave for half an hour yet!" his brother hollered back.

"Yeah. But Zoe likes to be early."

"Zoe likes to be early." Jackson mimicked as he tromped past. "Fine. Let's go."

Wash rolled his eyes, hefted his small valise, and trailed his brother to the barn. Jackson had been in a real snit ever since Pa had demanded that he drive Wash, Zoe, and her ma to the train station so he could bring the wagon back home. But thankfully, Jackson knew better than to disobey Pa's orders.

The quiet of the frosty morning was broken only by the jangle of the harness bells, the crunch of the wagon wheels over the snow-packed road, and the occasional twitter of a bird. Wash had always loved cold mornings like this with the sun shining and steam rising from every place the rays touched. Crisp, blue sky above and the snow-dusted winter branches stretching upward as though glorying to be alive.

The trip didn't take them long, but the moment Jackson pulled to a stop in the Kastains' yard, it became obvious that something wasn't right.

Belle and the twins, bundled in coats and scarves, stood off to one side. Belle kept checking her timepiece, and it was obvious she was feeling impatient. The twins stood with books in one arm and lunch buckets dangling by their sides. They all watched Mrs. Kastain and Zoe, who were on the porch with Aidan.

Mrs. Kastain took Aidan by the shoulders and bent to look right into his face. "You have to go to school. Everything is going to be fine. I promise we will be home in just a couple days."

Aidan fought through the restraint of her grip and flung himself against her. "No! You can't go! You just can't!"

Mrs. Kastain rested one hand on Aidan's head and gave Zoe an apologetic look. Zoe gave a little bounce on her toes, the only thing that revealed her impatience with the situation.

Washington jumped down from the wagon and strode onto the porch. "Hey now, what's with this fuss?" He squatted down so that he was on Aidan's eye level when Aidan turned from his ma to see who'd spoken.

Aidan tilted his head a bit sheepishly. "I don't want Ma to go. Or Zoe either. I won't be there to protect them. I'm the man of the house now. I'm supposed to protect them."

Wash scratched his jaw. "I see. And what if I told you that I was going to be along to protect them? Would that suffice?"

Aidan shook his head. "No. You can't stop a bullet." Large tears brimmed on his lower lids.

From the corner of his eye, Washington saw Zoe lift one hand to cover her mouth. A quick glance showed her own tears brimming. And Mrs. Kastain had lifted her gaze to the ceiling of the porch and was blinking rapidly. Washington couldn't imagine what a burden little Aidan had been carrying since the death of his pa.

He worked his teeth over one side of his lip. He didn't figure it would do much good to point out to young Aidan that he wouldn't be able to stop a bullet either. This was one situation that he'd best let Mrs. Kastain handle herself. He glanced at her as he stood back up.

She dropped one hand against the top of Aidan's blond mop and gave his head a bit of a ruffle. "Right then, you can come with us and be our protector."

From across the yard, Shiloh gasped. "What!? If I throw a big conniption and demand to come with you, do I get to skip school too?"

"Absolutely not." Mrs. Kastain leveled her with a look that, to Shiloh's credit, she was smart enough not to buck. "You and

Sharon get on to school and please let Mr. Haversham know that Aidan won't be there for a couple days."

Belle nudged the twins. "Let's go, girls." She lifted her hand and waved to her mother and sister.

Aidan had already scrambled into the house, and Mrs. Kastain followed him. "I'll need five minutes to pack him a few things."

Zoe paced the porch rubbing her temples. "This has made us late. Are we late? What time is it? Are we going to miss the train?"

"Zo!" Wash stepped into her path and bumped her with his hat to stop her pacing. "I made sure to get here half an hour early. We aren't going to be late."

Zoe rolled her eyes and paced away from him. "What you mean to say is, we aren't going to be late so long as nothing else delays us."

Washington bit back a grin and decided it was probably the better part of valor not to reply to her comments. "How about we load your bags into the wagon while she gets Aidan ready to go?"

"Right." Zoe motioned to the pile just inside the kitchen door. "These are what we are taking."

Washington eyed the mound of luggage. Did they think this trip was going to last for a month? How much stuff did one woman need? Again, deciding to exercise discretion, he simply hefted two bags and went to the wagon.

Quietly, he said to Jackson, "Best you come help me, or we won't get on the road until next week with all the luggage they've got."

Jackson pressed his lips together, but he did swing down from the seat and come help him.

They were just loading the last piece of baggage into the back of the wagon when Mrs. Kastain stepped from the cabin with Aidan and a small cloth knapsack.

She motioned the boy toward the wagon. "Go on. You get in the back there."

Grinning like a monkey with a pile of bananas, Aidan scrambled to do as he was told. He sank down next to the luggage, swiping the remnants of tears from his cheeks.

Wash couldn't help a little smile as he helped first Zoe's ma and then Zoe up onto the seat next to Jackson. He had a feeling that Aidan had just pulled a good amount of wool over his ma's eyes. But it wasn't his place to say anything. He hauled himself up to the seat, and by the time he sank down next to Zoe, Jackson already had the wagon rolling. Wash tossed him an irritated glance, but with both Zoe and her ma between them, he decided to let a reprimand go. Jackson wouldn't listen to him at any rate.

Realizing how crowded they were, Wash tried to scoot as close to the arm of the bench as possible, but it was no use. They were crammed onto the bench like so many peas in a pod.

Beside him, Zoe shifted a little. And hang it, if just the feel of her arm brushing his didn't bring to mind that springtime kiss. It had happened just down the road a little way from here.

Mrs. Kastain adjusted her skirts, tucking them tighter about her legs. Then she reached over and did the same for Zoe.

"Ma!" Zoe brushed her mother's hands back. "I've got it. I'm fine."

"Well, we don't want you catching your death of a cold the night before your big exam."

"I'm not going to get sick. I'll be fine."

"Yes, well... Better safe than sorry."

Washington decided that he had better save Zoe from her ma's ministrations. He swept a gesture to the sunlight all around them. "Lovely day for a trip, isn't it, Mrs. Kastain?"

The woman blinked and glanced around. "Why yes. I guess it is a beautiful day. I've been running like a hen in cracked corn all morning. And I suppose I haven't noticed until just this moment."

"I like cracked corn," Aidan piped up from the back.

Something about the muffled quality of the boy's words drew Washington's gaze.

Aidan was hanging from the side of the wagon by one arm, leaning out as far as he possibly could and trying to grab handfuls of snow from the drifts piled up along the embankment.

Eyes widening, Wash leaned over the back of the seat to grab him just as the wagon hit a good-sized bump. It was a good thing Aidan wore a belt, because it was the only thing Wash could catch. He hauled Aidan up like a book he'd grabbed by the spine.

"Whoa!" Aidan gasped, arms and legs dangling.

"Aidan! Do behave!" Despite Mrs. Kastain's curt words, Wash did see her give the lad a once over to make sure he was unharmed before she returned her focus to the fore.

Wash lowered Aidan to the safety of the buckboard once more.

The boy looked up from beneath his brows. "Thanks."

Wash gave him a nod. "I think it might be a good idea if you set your backside down right there and didn't move."

Aidan gave a sigh of resignation. "All right." He sank against the pile of luggage and rested his wrists against his knees. And with his mussed hair and tear-tracked face, he looked for all the world like a discarded waif in a New York slum.

Wash quickly faced forward before the boy could catch his grin.

Zoe gave him an elbow in the ribs. She leaned close and spoke in a low voice. "Don't encourage him. He's already incorrigible enough without prodding."

Washington made no reply, but he well remembered the days just after his ma had passed when he had often felt like he might come apart at the seams for no reason at all.

The horses bobbed their heads in the cool winter morning, causing their harness bells to jangle melodically. A tree branch snapped from just behind them.

Wash twisted to see that Aidan had broken a branch from a bush they had just passed. But the kid was seated, and what harm was there in letting him have a bit of wood to play with?

Next to him on the seat, Zoe seemed to have relaxed a little, and well she might for they still had plenty of time to make it to the station. After they crossed the Wyldhaven Creek bridge just ahead, the station would only be five minutes farther on.

Wash was doing his best to ignore the pleasant feel of Zoe sitting so close to him. He studied the clear cerulean sky. He looked across the field to the lacework of the bare winter branches. He picked at a rough spot on the arm of the wagon's bench seat. None of it served to distract him.

Behind them, Aidan methodically snapped little pieces off of the branch he'd grabbed. Wash couldn't help but envy the kid a little. Oh, for the carefree days when he hadn't been thinking about growing up, creating a family, or how to provide for them. Certainly for the days before his nearly every waking thought was of Zoe Kastain and the softness of her lips against his under the trees of the Wyldhaven forest.

"Come on, now." Jackson spoke softly to the horses.

Only then did Wash realize the wagon had come to a stop.

Pa's team never had liked crossing this bridge. Maybe it was the loud thumps their hooves made on the old plank boards, or the hollow rumble of the wagon's wheels behind them, or the fact that there were no rails along the sides. Whatever it was, it always took some coaxing to get them across. They bobbed their heads and pawed at the ground snorting and huffing in protest as Jackson clucked to them and tried to get them moving again.

Zoe squeaked out a little sound of misery. She pressed one hand over her stomach.

And Wash knew she was worrying again about being late.

He leaned close, and was just about to give her a bit of a hard time over her anxiety, when from the back of the wagon Aidan lurched to his feet. "I can get them moving, Zoe!" The eight-year-old loosed a great feral bellow. "Hiyah!" He scrambled up to lean over the back of the bench and Wash's shoulder on the right, and proceeded to throw a handful of the broken bits of branch. They pelted the rump of the off horse. "Let's go!"

Despite the fact that Pa's team was a bit skittish, Aidan's yell might not have caused any problems. But his yell not only startled the horses, it also startled a white rabbit that must have been sunning itself on the riverbank. It darted out into the middle of the road right beneath the horse's feet and then shot off the other side to bound away across the field.

Aidan leaned up on his tiptoes and angled a little farther so he could keep an eye on the critter. "Golly! Did you see that, Ma?"

"Aidan! I will not tolerate such language!" Mrs. Kastain lunged to snatch a handful of Aidan's hair, just as, with a sound that was more screech than whinny, the bays leaped forward. The nigh horse whinnied and rose up on its back legs, causing the off one to shy away from it. The wagon skated on the snow.

"Whoa!" Jackson yelled.

But it was too late.

The horses had surged too close to the edge of the bridge! One wheel slipped off the side!

The wagon was going over!

Chapter 3

"Aidan!" Zoe screamed, clutching at the bench seat as the wagon tipped precariously.

The rear right wheel slipped off the bridge, and Zoe could hear the axel scraping along the lip as the wagon slowly swung farther over the edge.

Aidan, who had been flung to the side when the wagon tipped, hung precariously from the arm of their bench with the icy waters of Wyldhaven Creek waiting below!

The wagon slid another few inches.

Zoe lurched across Wash to grab Aidan, but Wash beat her to it.

"I've got you!" He leaned as far down as he could to grab Aidan's belt again.

Zoe leaned farther, trying to see over his shoulder. "Do you have him?!"

A loud *crack* shot through the morning as the arm of the seat broke away!

Extended and off balance as he was, and with Aidan's weight hanging from his arms, Wash lost the battle with gravity.

"No!" Zoe grasped his jacket, and tried to haul them back. But their combined weight was too much for her.

All three of them tumbled over the side!

The ice-cold, black waters of Wyldhaven Creek enveloped her.

The creek was so cold that for a moment she wouldn't have been able to breathe even if she hadn't been underwater.

So dark! She turned, twisted, twirled, trying to see which way was up. The current tugged at her, and panic pulsed through her. She needed air!

A hand grabbed her. Propelled her toward the surface. It was Wash. With him beside her, she gulped a great breath of sweet oxygen. Thankfully, though the water was moving at a good clip, it wasn't much more than waist deep here. She found her footing, and none too soon, for Wash was pushing her upstream.

"Move! That way!"

The wagon! Was it about to fall on them?

"Go Zo!" He shoved her harder, and she blindly surged against the current.

What about Ma and Jackson? What had happened to them? And Aidan?!

"Aidan!" Zoe stopped and spun, searching the water.

"He's right here." Wash's voice emerged gritty and grim.

And sure enough, with Wash gripping a firm handful of the boy's jacket collar, Aidan thrashed right next to her. "Oh!" She grabbed him and tugged him close, helping him get his feet.

From above them, there came a loud scraping sound.

"Ha! Ha!" Jackson stood, slapping the reins against the horse's rumps and yelling at the top of his voice!

Ma sat wide-eyed, clutching the seat.

Zoe immediately saw Jackson's plan. If he could just get the wagon across the bridge, the wheel that was hanging over the edge would hit the embankment and right itself. But with each passing moment, the wagon slipped a little farther over the edge.

Jesus, please!

Zoe didn't have time for more of a prayer than that before the horses gave one last valiant effort, and then the wagon's wheel connected with solid ground on the north side of the creek. The wagon trundled a few more feet to the middle of the road.

"Whoa!" Jackson pulled to a stop and collapsed onto the seat. Snatching his hat from his head, he swiped his forehead with his arm and looked back at them.

"Good job," Wash said.

Jackson nodded.

Relief coursing through her, Zoe huddled into the curl of her arms.

"Are you okay?" Wash placed one hand at her back and peered into her face.

How warm his hand felt. It struck Zoe as odd, drenched to the skin as they both were. She nodded. "I'm fine."

But they all needed to get out of this water. They were closer to the southern embankment, so they would have to climb out there and then cross the bridge to get back to the wagon.

"Can you take him?" She nudged Aidan toward Wash.

"Happy to." With an aggravated press of his lips, Wash took her brother by his collar and his belt. He flung the boy onto the snowy embankment without much ceremony.

Aidan gasped and floundered in the snow to gain his feet. He wrapped his arms about himself and shivered uncontrollably. "Whadya do that for?!"

Zoe bit back a grin. Washington had obviously lost much of the sympathy she'd seen in his eyes for Aidan back on the porch a bit ago.

Ignoring Aidan, Wash took her by the arm, and together, they slogged their way toward the embankment.

The cold hit her like a slap as they reached the shallows. Her dress clung to her like a sausage casing, and the water had swept away most of her hairpins because her hair cascaded across her shoulders. She clenched her teeth against the impulse to whimper. That wouldn't be proper.

On the embankment, Aidan had no such compunctions. "I'm freezing! I want to go to school!"

Zoe was suddenly too angry to care about propriety. "Aidan William Kastain! If you had gone to school this morning like you were supposed to, none of this would have happened! When will you learn to think before you act!" She slogged another couple of steps closer to the bank.

Ma rushed toward them across the bridge. "Zoe. Don't speak to your brother in such a manner."

Aidan thrust his chin into the air. His reply emerged as a wail. "Weren't my fault! How was I to know those horses were spookier than ghosts!"

Ma reached Aidan and wrapped her arms about his shoulders. "Come on darling, we have to get you out of these wet things!"

Zoe gritted her teeth.

Washington clambered up onto the embankment and reached down to haul Zoe out as well.

With her feet planted firmly on solid ground again, Zoe felt panic welling up inside her. "What time is it?" Everything shook. Including her chin when she said, "We're going to be late for the train." Tears blurred her vision.

"Nonsense." Wash settled his hand to her back once more and nudged her toward the bridge. "The train station is only five minutes from here, and it will be faster to go there than to try to go back to your place, anyhow." He swept a hand for her to precede him to the wagon.

Ma was already hustling Aidan into the wagon bed and climbing in after him.

"Thankfully, none of the bags seem to have fallen out. I was even able to save my hat." He lifted it as though she might need to see it in proof. His lips lifted wryly. "Once we check into our seats, we'll find a berth where we can all get changed."

"I'm cold!" Aidan's whine caused Zoe's jaw to jut to one side. She didn't dare speak to him again, or she would surely be ashamed of what she said later on.

Ma's eyes sparked at her with frustration, but she didn't reprimand, only tugged Aidan close to her side. "Here, huddle next to me for warmth."

Washington mumbled something under his breath. But then he seemed to gather himself in hand. He held one hand to help Zoe into the back of the wagon at the same time as he motioned for Ma to look in the corner of the buckboard with the other. "There are a couple horse blankets there. We should all try to stay as warm as possible between here and the station."

Jackson looked back from his place on the driver's seat. "Are we still going to the station?"

Wash smiled at her. "Of course, we are. We aren't going to let a little thing like a winter dip in Wyldhaven Creek stop Zoe from becoming a teacher. Just think of the stories she's going to have to tell in the future!"

Zoe rolled her eyes at him and reached for one of the blankets.

Jackson set the team into a fast trot, and Zoe almost gasped at the shock of the cold wind against her wet clothes. She scrambled to sit next to Ma and Aidan, feeling Wash do the same.

They all four huddled against the front wall of the wagon bed, trying to avoid as much of the wind as possible. Ma and Aidan shared one of the blankets, and she and Wash shared the other. And despite the fact that she had daydreamed many a time about being this close to Wash again, she couldn't seem to do anything but try to concentrate on warm thoughts. That and push away her worry over whether they would make it to the station on time.

Chapter 4

Zoe followed Ma into the train station with Aidan's hand clasped firmly in her own. Her wet boots squeaked across the tiles, and she heard Wash shuffling along behind her.

She glanced over her shoulder. The poor man was not only still soaking wet, but burdened down with their plethora of bags. He even had one tucked beneath his arm. She had offered to help, but he'd insisted he'd be fine, and really, with her skirts as wet as they were, she needed one hand to hold them so she could walk.

The beauty of the station's architecture had always fascinated her. With the decorative plaster dome overhead and the hammered bronze accents, she could stand and study the art for hours.

But today, the moment they stepped inside, conversations all around them ceased. A woman to her right gasped and covered her mouth with one hand as she swept them with a horrified look.

After that, Zoe only had the gumption to study the small space directly in front of her feet, never mind the grand ceiling. She heaved at her skirt to take a few more steps. What a sight they must be! Leaving a trail of drips in their wake and hair all a straggle. Even Ma, who was the most presentable of them all, had a large wet splotch on her dress from where Aidan had sat on her lap between the creek and here.

As they followed Ma across the room, Aidan tugged for the release of his hand, but Zoe tightened her grip.

"Lemme go!"

Zoe bent and whispered fiercely, "Aidan Kastain, you've made enough trouble today! Stop! You will hold my hand until we get on the train, and that's final!"

His shoulders slumped, but at least he quit fighting her.

Zoe stood behind Ma, who handed their tickets to the man behind the counter. He was speaking to his colleague in the next booth when they stepped to his window. He took the papers methodically and looked them over. Then he glanced up. His eyes widened, and he actually leaned to see around Ma. His curiosity focused first on Wash, and then on her and Aidan.

Ma cleared her throat sharply. "I need to add one ticket for my son." She motioned to Aidan.

After taking Ma's payment, the attendant handed back their paperwork. "Give this to the official in car seven. But..." He paused as though hesitant to offend her with his next words. "Would you like to pay an extra dollar to have a private berth?"

Zoe's eyes shut. Of course, a private berth would cost extra. Where were they going to find a dry place to change? Because she knew Ma didn't have a spare dollar. They'd counted their money last night and had only enough for the train fair, the boardinghouse rooms in Seattle—one for their family and one for Wash—and a bit of food along the way. Zoe wasn't even certain where Ma had come up with the money for Aidan's fare.

Ma tossed her a fretful glance.

Behind Zoe, cases clunked to the floor, and Wash stepped to the counter. "Yes. We would." He thrust his hand into his inner coat pocket. His jacket was so wet that his hand got stuck as he tried to extract it. With a grunt he gave it a yank and withdrew a wallet. He wrenched it open and slapped a dollar bill onto the counter in front of the attendant.

Without a word, the man slid the bill from the counter and handed Wash a key on a placard. "Give this to the steward in car seven, and he'll show you the way." A sympathetic smile and another sweeping glance accompanied the instructions.

Wash gave the man a curt nod and then set to loading himself down with all their bags again.

Zoe and Ma waited without a word until he had all the luggage in hand, then Ma led the way to car seven.

This official was just as curious about their appearance and less polite about it. He smirked as Ma handed over their papers and the key to the berth, but didn't move. After a prolonged scrutiny, he broke into a chuckle. "Had a little trouble on the way here, did we?"

"Astute observation," Wash groused dryly.

Apparently realizing his error in judgment, the attendant turned and hurried down the aisle. "Right this way. I'm sure you'll be pleased that you spent the extra three dollars for our largest birth."

Zoe exchanged a look with Ma. Wash had only paid a dollar. But the moment the attendant pushed the door of their compartment open and she saw how small the interior was, she thanked Jesus for the Christmas generosity of that first man in the station. Even this more expensive berth would be a bit cramped with all of them in it. But blessed heavenly mercies! Against the outer wall of the berth stood a small coal burning stove! The remainder of the compartment consisted of two padded benches that faced each other and a tiny coat closet with two hangers.

"Thank you," Wash said as the attendant left to return to his post. His tone was contrite, as though he realized he'd been a bit short with the man.

Ma led the way into the room, and Wash stacked all their bags in a pile in the little closet, then stepped back. "I'll wait out here till you all are situated." He closed the door as he left.

"Aidan, quickly now." Ma hurried to dress Aidan in dry clothes, while Zoe huddled near the stove. As soon as she was done, Ma tossed Aidan's wet clothes over the stovepipe and then stepped into the hall with him, leaving the room to Zoe.

She tried to hurry so Wash wouldn't be stuck in his wet clothes any longer than necessary, but soaked as she was, everything was heavy and clingy. She felt like a caterpillar shedding its skin as she peeled off the traveling dress and petticoats. When she slipped into her dry everyday dress, nothing had ever felt quite so good. She took one of the hangers from the closet and hung her clothes from the berth's curtain rod. The weight of the wet dress bowed the rod in the middle, but it seemed to be holding okay. Satisfied to let her hair dry a little before she did it up, Zoe hurried out to give Wash the space.

Wash didn't take long to change, and soon they were all seated on the room's two facing padded benches—Ma and Aidan on one bench and Zoe and Wash on the other. Wash had followed her example and used the other hanger to hang his jacket, shirt, and pants from the rod. The wooden bar bowed low in the middle, but that would place their clothes closer to the heat and hopefully help them dry quicker.

Zoe touched her temple and tried to think. She'd planned to use this time on the train to look over some geographical terms, but that would mean pulling her satchel from the bottom of the closet, and she had to work up the gumption to move away from the warmth of the stove.

"What time is it?" she asked.

Wash stretched out one leg and reached into his pocket. He withdrew a gold pocket-watch and flipped it open. But he didn't offer the time, only stared at the timepiece with his jaw working back and forth.

"What's the matter? Is something wrong?"

With a sigh, Wash clicked the cover shut and thrust the watch back into his pocket.

Zoe was puzzled. "Aren't you going to tell me the time?"

"Can't," he said. "Watch must have got wet during our little swim. It's not working."

"Oh no!" Zoe would have liked to give Aidan a good thrashing right about then. If Pa were here, he would do it. "Was it very expensive?" They would have to replace the piece or give Wash payment for its ruin at the very least.

Wash shrugged. "Not exactly sure. It was my great-grandfather's watch."

"Oh, Wash." Zoe laid a hand on his arm. "I'm so sorry."

Wash glanced down at her hand, and Zoe quickly snatched it back into her lap. What had she been thinking to touch him like that? And in front of Ma, no less. She could tell by the narrowed scrutiny Ma was even at this very moment giving her that she would have some explaining to do later for the lapse in propriety. But Aidan had ruined Wash's family heirloom!

They would definitely have to do something about fixing it. She considered their meager funds. Maybe she could give up some meals in order to have money to pay for the repairs.

After that, none of them said a word. They simply sat. Like refugees who'd recently escaped a war zone. Not even Aidan made a sound, and he normally chattered worse than a squirrel.

Across the room the curtain rod *snap*ped! Zoe's clothes splatted into a heap next to Wash's as the two ends of the rod pinged from the ceiling to rattle on the floor of the compartment.

None of them even flinched. They all simply stared.

Then Zoe glanced sideways. "Why would a three-dollar train berth have such weak curtain rods? Couldn't the designers foresee that people might need to use it to hang things on?"

Wash quirked one eyebrow, gaze fixed on the pile of steaming clothes. "There is a closet."

Zoe conceded. "Right. I suppose they would expect things to be hung in there. They likely couldn't foresee that three travelers would arrive soaking wet and need to hang their things by the stove. Especially not a dress that weighs a gazillion pounds when wet. I don't suppose they could have anticipated that." She sighed. "Now what?"

Wash burst out laughing.

Ma followed suit.

And then they were all laughing—long and deep until they each had tears streaming down their faces.

Chapter 5

Thankfully, after their terrible morning, the rest of the trip to Seattle was uneventful. Wash was never happier to see the first leg of a trip coming to a close.

After the incident with the curtain rod, Zoe had fretted that they might have to pay for it, but the conductor had apologized profusely, saying it must have been faulty to begin with. And when Mrs. Kastain had offered him money, he'd waved her away, much to her relief. Neither Zoe nor her ma had said anything, but Wash had a feeling their funds were running tight on this trip. He was glad they'd asked him to come along. Hopefully, he could pay for a few things that would ease their purse strings a mite.

After the conductor's reassurance, they had all managed to rest a little, and Zoe had even settled down enough to do a little studying. And if he'd done a little studying of his own—watching her while she concentrated on her books—well then, no one seemed to have noticed.

But now, as he followed her down the train aisle toward the exit with her ma and Aidan trailing, a knot cinched tight in his stomach. Just the few glimpses that he'd seen out the windows so far showed so much commotion and chaos! His every protective instinct screamed at him not to let them off the train.

He clenched his teeth and reminded himself to breathe. The Lord would watch over them. After all, He had called Zoe to teach, and in order to do that, she had to take this test.

In front of him, Zoe adjusted her grip on the valise that she'd insisted he let her carry. She navigated past a table and chairs in the main part of the lavish Pullman car and didn't even comment on the beautiful furnishings, which was so unlike her. If she weren't so nervous about her test, she would be thrilled beyond containment by this moment.

Realizing the exit lay just ahead, Wash touched her shoulder. "Let me go first." She moved to one side, and he squeezed past her, stepped down to the platform, and turned to help her descend. As she placed her small hand within his and settled onto the platform beside him, she took in the area with a sweep of her blue eyes, and her expression brightened in excitement.

Of course, she would be excited by all the activity. He, on the other hand, felt like he might turn sick. If anything happened to this family, he'd never be able to forgive himself. He'd best keep a close eye on Aidan so he didn't get lost in the bustle.

He reached to help Mrs. Kastain from the car, but his focus was more on their surroundings. Everywhere he looked, chaos reigned. How would he ever find their boarding house in a city this big, much less the testing venue Zoe needed to get to in the morning?

"Isn't this amazing?!" Zoe clasped her hands beneath her chin, eyes sparkling.

That might be one way of putting it, but it wouldn't be his first choice. Loud. Bawdy. Not a place for a lady—especially not one as naive and gentle of heart as Zoe Kastain. All those were more apt descriptions of this place.

Here, an old woman hawked apples, but beside her, a woman of another type sauntered through the crowd with everything she offered on full display.

"Oh heavens!" Mrs. Kastain gasped.

Wash jerked his focus to where a young boy ran through the crowd yelling at the top of his voice about newspapers for sale. Then onto a group of Chinese businessmen who trotted by, discussing something seemingly very important at the top of their lungs.

Wash gathered their bags, and thankfully, with Aidan carrying his knapsack and one other small bag, and Mrs. Kastain and Zoe each carrying one also, the task was easily accomplished. He only had to carry two bags in each hand.

"Let's go this way." He nudged Zoe in a direction that seemed to have the least activity. They could pause in a moment and gather themselves to figure out where they needed to go.

"Get out of here, you scurvy mutt!" Just ahead, a butcher in a bloody apron surged from a storefront swinging a broom. A yelp drew Wash's gaze to the dog receiving the brunt of the man's anger. It skulked away from the butcher shop, so skinny its ribs could be counted. With one last muttered threat, the butcher returned inside.

"That poor dog!" Zoe bent to get a better look.

No. The last thing they needed was for Zoe's compassion to have them feeding every stray animal in the city.

"Zoe don't touch it!" Mrs. Kastain cautioned.

"Ma it's starving. And with all these people around! How could everyone be so cruel? We have to help it!"

Wash pulled in a lungful of the rank air. "Zoe we can't—"

Her pleading eyes cut him off mid-reprimand. He swallowed. How had her pa ever said no to her?

Thankfully her ma seemed to be on his side. She nudged Zoe in the back. "We can't help it right now, Zoe. We need to get you to the boardinghouse so you can get a good night's rest."

"But ma, we can't just leave it here. Look at the poor thing!"

The dog seemed to realize she was speaking about it. It scooted a little closer and settled to its boney haunches, ears pricked hopefully.

Wash pressed his lips together.

The dog did have soulful eyes that were hard to ignore. It was white with black splotches and dark eyes. One of its ears flopped to the side, while the other remained at attention.

Tugging Aidan behind her, Mrs. Kastain prodded Zoe again. "It's a full-grown dog, Zoe. It has survived this long. It will be fine."

Zoe's shoulders slumped a little. "Are there any biscuits left in the lunch pail?"

"I ate the last one." Aidan scuffed his toe at the boardwalk, looking sorry about his revelation.

Hang it all, this was no good. "Over there." Wash herded the little family into a clear space next to the wall of the brick building. He set the bags at their feet and gave Aidan a firm look. "Watch the bags and the ladies. I'll be right back."

Aidan straightened a little, and Wash was glad to see he seemed to be taking his order seriously.

He stepped through the door, and a bell dinged above his head. The man looked up, and a large smile spread across his face. "What can I do for you?"

He still wore the blood-smeared apron, and the store smelled so rank that Wash wondered if he'd be doing the dog any favors by buying it a bone in here. He glanced the length of the table, which had cut after cut of meat laid on it out in the open. Some of them with flies crawling across them. Wash swallowed. "I need a beef stew bone. A fresh one."

The man tilted his head. "I have a good meaty one, but fresh costs extra."

"Just give it to me." Wash dug out his wallet and plunked the requested amount onto the counter while the butcher wrapped the large bone in brown paper. He couldn't believe he'd just paid good money for a bone for a dog—meaty or not.

But only a moment later, when he gave the dog the bone and it trotted off, tail wagging, Zoe stepped to his side and clasped his arm in gratitude.

She looked up at him, eyes soft with appreciation. "Thank you."

And as Washington looked down at her, he knew he hadn't purchased that bone for the dog.

Not at all for the dog.

***

Susan Kastain studied the way Zoe clutched Wash's arm and the way Wash looked at Zoe, and her stomach gave a slow turn. She remembered the way Zoe's hand had fallen on Washington's arm so naturally back in the train car. A sigh slipped free. She was not ready to lose her baby to a man, even if he was a man as good as Washington Nolan. And it was clear from the way they looked at one another that their attraction was mutual.

Why had she thought it a good idea to bring Wash along on this trip?

She hefted her valise and motioned for Aidan to do the same. "We'd best get a move on if we are to find this boardinghouse. The owner telegraphed instructions for us to arrive before six if we expect to eat the meal provided with the room. She doesn't serve after that." In truth, they had plenty of time before that deadline, but maybe if they were moving, Zoe and Wash would put a little space between themselves.

As she'd hoped, they separated and took up their part of the luggage.

Susan tugged the paper she'd written notes on from the hem of her sleeve. "It says we need to find Yesler Way."

A man approaching must have overheard her comment, for he paused before her and pointed. "You'll find Yesler just that'a way."

Susan dipped her knees. "Much obliged to you."

He tipped his hat but didn't step out of her path. "Yes'm." His gaze swept over her, and Susan wasn't so old that she'd forgotten what it was like to have a man appreciate her in such a way. She felt her face heat. "My *children* and I thank you."

He glanced past her then, and a smile nudged at his lips. He moved to the side and tipped his hat once more. "All the best to you and your *family*, ma'am."

Indeed. In this instance the mention of her progeny had given her the desired consequences. But what about the day when she might be interested in a man? None would likely want a widow with five intractable children.

On the heels of the thought, guilt swept in. William wasn't even gone a year yet. She certainly oughtn't be having thoughts about finding another husband.

"Ma? Everything all right?" Zoe asked.

Susan blinked back to the present. "Yes. Fine."

Wash strode out in the lead, and they all fell in behind him.

Thankfully, Aidan must have been worn out by his dip in the cold creek and the long day, because he trailed along beside her without his usual boisterous chatter and exploratory side-trips. She didn't think her patience had enough foundation to keep chasing him down after the day they'd had.

The city was loud, with taxi-carriages in nearly every shape and size and hills steep enough to make her catch her breath. It was a good thing it rarely snowed this close to the ocean, for if a carriage had to take such a road in snow or ice, they would likely skate straight past the wharves and right into the bay itself. But my, the view! She paused at the top of one hill to take in the scene.

Sunlight glinted in a long swath across the surface of the Prussian blue Pacific, and out a little way, several forested islands dotted the landscape. Despite the bustle and noise, for such a view, she could happily live here.

She hurried to catch up to the children, turning her focus to the architecture.

Many of the buildings in the heart of the city were russet brick or stone structures. Even in Wyldhaven, they'd heard about the fire that took out most of this district a few years back. Residents had decided to reconstruct with safer materials, it seemed.

Wash found their boardinghouse only a few minutes later, and they were directed to their rooms on the second floor. Susan was glad when they decided they would meet in thirty minutes to go down for dinner—she needed a moment to simply sit and rest! They left Wash in his room and entered their own.

Susan was relieved to see that the chamber was comfortably furnished and clean. It had a small window overlooking the street below, and there was even a vanity and mirror in one corner.

Zoe plunked onto one of the room's two narrow beds and rubbed her temples. "I'm exhausted."

Susan unwound her scarf. "We all are." She knew Zoe would be up half the night studying, and she worried about how little sleep Zoe had been getting in recent months, what with all the work she'd been doing to help Mr. Haversham with the Wyldhaven school. Not to mention that soaking in the creek this morning. "Are you warm enough?"

"Yes, Ma."

"Not feeling at all sick, are you?" Even as she asked Zoe the question, she placed a hand to Aidan's forehead.

"No, Ma. I'm fine."

Thankfully, Aidan's temperature felt normal. "We should all try to get a little nap before dinner."

"Can't." Zoe brushed away her comment. "I have to find a watchmaker."

Susan paused in mid-removal of her coat. "A what?"

"A watchmaker. Wash's watch stopped working because of the water." She made a face in Aidan's direction. "So, I want to see if it can be repaired. As a Christmas present. He's done so much for me, especially since Pa's passing, that it's really the least that I can do."

Susan hung her coat on the knob of the brass headboard and paced to the window. She hadn't missed the way Zoe's cheeks pinked a little. She pressed her hands together. "I realize we will have to repay him eventually. But we don't have the money for it on this trip."

"Oh, I already have that figured out. I'll just give up meals. Unless of course, the cost of repairs will be more than that. I need to find a watchmaker and ask about prices. I'll go down to the desk right now while Wash is resting."

"But Zoe—" Susan spun from the window.

The door clicked shut, and Susan sighed. When Zoe was determined to do something there really was no stopping her. But she couldn't simply skip all her meals on this trip!

She glanced down to find Aidan looking up at her. He held up a dime. "Belle gave me this to buy some candy, but Zoe can have it to help fix the watch." Large tears pooled in his big blue eyes.

Susan tugged him close to her side and lifted her eyes to the ceiling as she rubbed his back.

Most days, she felt overwhelmed by parenting five children all alone. But moments like this kept her going.

Chapter 6

Zoe poked her head out of their boardinghouse room door and checked the hallway to make sure Washington wasn't in sight. Seeing that the way was clear, she quickly went down to the front desk and asked the woman there if she knew of a nearby watchmaker.

"Oh yes. There's one not two blocks from here. If you hurry, you can catch him before he closes for the evening."

Zoe glanced at the clock behind the desk. If it was only two blocks, she should have time to get there and back before dinner! She should run up and tell Ma, but she would only say not to go. And tomorrow would be consumed with testing. She wouldn't have time to do much then. Besides, she'd be back before Ma even had time to worry. She walked all over the place in Wyldhaven without an escort. She'd be fine.

She thanked the woman and, with instructions in hand, set out to walk to the store. She gloried in the peach and aqua sunset shot through with gold as she took a street perpendicular to the water. My, but this was a beautiful city! Maybe she would come back here to teach someday.

The shop was easy to find, and the bell above the door jangled as she entered.

A nice-looking older man stood from where he'd been bent over the counter. He had sandy curls that were fading to silver in a few places and the most appealing color of brown eyes she'd ever seen. They fell somewhere between chocolate and caramel. She noticed, because one of his eyes was magnified very large by a pair of spectacles that had three round lenses lowered over the main rectangular one. What an interesting contraption!

The man removed them and offered a smile. "Welcome to Harrow's Timepieces and Repairs. How may I help you?"

"Fascinating!" Zoe made the exclamation before she thought better of it and then figured she ought to explain. "I've never seen a pair of eyeglasses like that before."

The man angled them so she could get a better look. "Each of these lenses gives magnification. If I slide down two, the magnification is increased. And again, with this third one." He looked to the door expectantly. "Is someone accompanying you?"

Zoe waved a hand. "Oh no. I walked down alone."

The man set the spectacles on a soft cloth that had a lot of little gears and tiny brass parts on it. "I see. Are you in the city alone?"

Zoe chuckled, a little uneasy over his probing questions, but also curious. "What tells you I'm not from around here?"

The watchmaker shrugged. "Any woman from Seattle would know how dangerous the streets are in the day, much less with dark coming on."

"Oh." Zoe turned to check the quickly falling dusk outside. "I'm in town to take the teaching exam tomorrow, and our boardinghouse is only two blocks from here. My question shouldn't take long, and I'm sure I'll be fine on the way back."

The man carefully folded the corners of the piece of material on the counter inward to cover the small parts. "My name is Elijah Harrow."

Zoe dipped a small curtsy. "I'm Zoe. Zoe Kastain. Pleased to meet you, Mr. Harrow."

He smiled. "Likewise. Now, what can I do for you?" He folded his hands on the counter and gave her his full attention.

"Well, since I'm in a bit of a hurry to get back to the boardinghouse, I won't tell you the whole story. But I have a friend. And suffice it to say, his great-grandfather's pocket watch took a dip in a creek this morning. And now, it's stopped working."

Mr. Harrow's eyes sparkled. "It's a little cold for a dip in a creek."

"Oh my, yes! It was!" Zoe shivered just thinking about it. "It was my little brother's fault, you see—but I said I wasn't going to tell you the whole story. Anyhow, I'm just wondering if you think you can fix it? The watch means a lot to my friend."

Mr. Harrow tilted his head. "It really depends on the watch. Do you have it with you?"

Zoe's shoulder's slumped. "No. I was hoping you might have an idea of the cost so I could know if we can afford to get it fixed. Then if we can, I'll get the watch and bring it to you. I'm hoping to give it back to him as a Christmas surprise."

"I see..." The man smoothed his hands over the counter. "Are your mother and father at the boardinghouse?"

An ache kicked to life in Zoe's chest. "My ma is. In fact, I need to hurry back so she doesn't worry since I didn't tell her I was leaving. But my Pa...he passed on last spring."

"I'm very sorry to hear that. I lost my own wife not long ago." The man's expression softened with understanding.

Her ache grew. "I'm sure you miss her."

He nodded. "Very much."

"Do you ever try to remember what life was like before? My sister is a painter, you see. And she's amazingly talented, if I do say so. She painted a picture of our family in a wagon on the way to town. She captured Pa's smile to perfection. But try as I might, I can't seem to recall his laugh. Or his voice." Zoe batted a hand through the air. "Sorry, I'm rambling again."

Mr. Harrow smiled, if it was a bit sadly. "I understand your wish. It would be lovely to hear my wife's voice, even once more."

Zoe didn't want to linger in melancholy thoughts the night before her big test. Past experience had proven that she didn't sleep well when she let herself wallow in too much misery. "So, you can't give me a price until you see the watch, is that right?" At his nod, she continued, "I understand. I'll try to bring it by tomorrow, but I have a test, so I'm not certain how long that will take."

"Two bits."

Zoe blinked at the man.

He bobbed his head. "If you bring me the watch, I'll do my best to fix it for two bits."

"Oh! You've no idea how happy that makes me!" Zoe couldn't suppress a little hop. "Yes! I'll get the watch here tomorrow, somehow."

He smiled and reached for his jacket, which hung on a coat tree behind the counter. "Now, how about you let me walk you back to the boardinghouse so your mother knows you're safe."

"Oh, I don't want to put you to any trouble."

"Nonsense." He slid his arms into his sleeves. "It's not anything I wouldn't do for any other paying customer."

"Well if you're certain, I'll say thank you in advance so I don't forget."

He smiled and held the door open for her, then locked it behind them. "I'm certain a lovely young lady like you would not forget."

Zoe was thankful to feel her grief lifting. It came in waves, and sometimes she wasn't expecting the staying power of it. Today, it seemed like she might be able to get past it. "I do try to mind my manners. But sometimes I just get so excited about one thing or another that I forget where I am." She blushed. "Like just now. I can't imagine what made me blather all this to you."

Mr. Harrow clasped his hands behind his back as they trudged up the hill. "It's not a prob—"

"Oh Zoe! There you are!" Ma rushed down to them with Aidan's hand clasped firmly in hers. She was bundled up in her long coat with a wool cap on her head, as was Aidan.

The sight reminded Zoe how chilly it was. She'd left her own coat in their room. She wrapped her arms around herself as she and Mr. Harrow paused on the sidewalk.

"You gave me such a fright!" Ma leaned to enfold Zoe in a relieved embrace. "This is the city! Not Wyldhaven. You can't go running off on your own without—" Ma's gaze settled on Mr. Harrow.

Ma's breath puffed a little cloud before her, and Mr. Harrow remained still, with his hands still clasped behind his back. But there was a little crinkle at the corner of each eye, and his gaze swept from Ma's cap to her boots and back again.

Zoe motioned to the man. "Ma, this is the watchmaker, Mr. Harrow, and you'll never believe the good news!"

"Susan Kastain." Ma extended her hand. "Thank you for escorting her back."

Mr. Harrow bowed over Ma's hand, but he never took his eyes off her face. "Elijah Harrow. And your daughter is enchanting. It was my pleasure. One that has now been doubled."

Zoe glanced back and forth between the two adults.

They were still looking at one another, and Mr. Harrow hadn't released Ma's hand. And of all things—Zoe squinted to see better in the fading light—was Ma blushing?

Zoe shuffled her feet. "Mr. Harrow has offered to fix Wash's watch for two bits, Ma."

"Is that so?" Ma extracted her hand from Mr. Harrow's and nudged Aidan forward. "This is my son, Aidan. Aidan, meet Mr. Harrow."

"Hiya." Aidan stretched out his hand. "Do you have kids that I could play with?"

Settling a restraining hand on Aidan's shoulder, Ma said, "Aidan. That's not an appropriate question upon a first meeting."

But Mr. Harrow didn't seem offended. He merely chuckled as he bent to shake Aidan's hand and meet him at eye level. "I'm afraid I don't. My wife passed away, and we never had any children."

For some reason, the man tossed Ma a glance as he said the words.

Zoe reached to take Ma's arm and turn her back toward the boardinghouse. It brought the ache in her heart roaring back at full speed to see Ma looking at another man the way she used to look at Pa. "Thank you, Mr. Harrow, again, for walking me this far." She meant the words as a dismissal.

But the man continued doggedly in their wake. "I'll just see you all back, if you don't mind?"

"Of course, and thank you." Ma spoke before Zoe could think how to politely dismiss him.

But thankfully, the door of the boardinghouse lay just ahead.

They paused at the entrance. Mr. Harrow gave a little bow and, in that quiet steady voice of his, said, "See you on the morrow then?" But for some reason his attention was yet again fixed on Ma and not on her.

Ma nodded and fiddled with her scarf. "Yes. I'll bring the timepiece myself. Say...midmorning?"

"I'll look forward to it." Mr. Harrow took his leave without much more conversation other than to say, "Until tomorrow."

And for the fact that she'd liked him so much on first meeting him, Zoe was unaccountably relieved to see the man walking away. She tugged on Ma's arm. "Quick, let's get back to our room before Wash sees us."

She snuck up the back stairs and checked the hallway, then darted to their room and held the door for Ma and Aidan.

Safely back inside, she plunked down onto her bed. She pushed thoughts of Mr. Harrow from her mind. What she'd thought she'd seen was probably nothing. She needed to concentrate on what to do next. She had to figure out a way to get Wash's watch without his knowing.

She angled a glance to where Aidan sat slumped on the other bed, legs swinging in boredom. The little shyster had helped damage the watch; the least he could do would be to help fix it.

"Aidan, I need your help." Zoe leaned back on her elbows.

Aidan sat up. "Whatcha need?"

"You are going to help me steal Wash's watch."

Ma gasped. "Zoe Elaine Kastain! Whatever are you speaking of? Think of what you're teaching Aidan!"

Zoe conceded with a chuckle. "Okay, borrow it." She quirked an eyebrow at Aidan to make sure he got the point.

Leaping from the bed, he rubbed his hands in glee. "This is going to be fun!"

Zoe rolled her eyes. If they could pull this off without raising Wash's suspicions, it would be a miracle.

Aiden bounced on his toes. "How are we going to do it?"

"At dinner time, I need you to ask to see his watch, and then you must distract him so that I can tuck it away."

"Zoe!" Ma exhaled. "All of this seems rather clandestine. Wouldn't it simply be better to tell Washington what you'd like to do for him?"

Zoe shook her head. "Ma, it's for a Christmas present." She pegged her little brother with a look. "One he wouldn't need if it weren't for Aidan here."

Ma wrung her hands. "Yes, but suppose someone sees you taking the watch? They might think you a thief!"

Aidan gave a little pump of his fist. "That would be amazing! Imagine! Zoe could go to jail! I bet the jail in this town's a lot bigger than Sheriff Callahan's back home!"

Ma's eyes grew a little bit wider. "Aidan Kastain! There is nothing exciting about such a thing!"

Zoe had to agree. There would be nothing good that would come of anyone thinking her a thief. "We'll just have to make sure that doesn't happen. I'll make sure no one sees me."

Ma opened her mouth, and Zoe figured she was just about to lay down a denial. But Aidan beat her to the punch. "Don't worry, Zoe. You won't have to steal it!"

Zoe narrowed her eyes and hurried to speak before Ma could regain her thought. "Whatever do you mean?"

Aidan was prevented from replying by a knock on their door.

It was Washington, there to fetch them for dinner. And Zoe could only pray that whatever Aidan's plan was, it wouldn't cause too much ruckus!

Chapter 7

Downstairs in the dining room, individual tables were set in three rows. The matron instructed them to pick any one they liked. They chose an empty one toward the near end of the middle row. Washington held a chair first for Ma, and then for Zoe.

Aidan didn't even let Wash sit down before he blurted, "Can I see your watch?"

Zoe bit back her exasperation. Subtle, Aidan was not.

Wash eyed Aidan as he tucked his napkin into his lap. "You have to be careful with it. It belonged to my great-grandfather, and I'm hoping I'll be able to get it fixed."

Aidan stretched out one hand. "I'll be *real* careful with it. I'm right sorry I caused it to get damaged." He blinked puppy dog eyes in Wash's direction.

Zoe turned her chuckle into a fake sneeze.

Ma rolled her eyes and then pinned Zoe with a glower that said if Aidan ended up in Sheriff Callahan's jail one of these days, it would be all her fault.

Zoe held her breath. This would be the critical moment. If Aidan blurted the wrong thing, he could give away the whole plan.

But her little brother, for once in his life, had played his cards perfectly.

Wash reached into his pocket and then handed the gold watch and chain to Aidan, who oohed and aahed over it as a woman set water glasses by each of their plates.

"This sure is fancy! Look Zoe, it has a horse and wagon engraved on the front!" Aidan jostled in his seat as he worked his way to his knees so he could lean to show her, and at the same time, he swung his free arm wide, knocking Wash's water glass right into his lap.

Wash gasped and shot to his feet. Water dripped from his lap, but at least he'd managed to save the glass. He set it on the table with a firm *thunk*.

They all stared for a moment.

Zoe's conscience pricked her. Poor Wash. By his expression, he was doing his very best to batten down a whole wagon load of frustration. His jaw bulged in and out. Then he muttered, "Never leave yourself behind."

Zoe frowned. Had she heard him right? What did he mean by that? She might have asked, but it was clear he'd been speaking the words to himself, and she didn't feel now was the right time to probe.

"Sorry." Aidan did a good job of sounding contrite. "You better go change. Zoe can hold onto your watch until you have someplace dry to put it." He reached for Zoe's hand and carefully tucked the watch into her palm, and then folded her fingers closed over it as if to show Wash how safe the watch now was.

With a sigh, Wash turned for the stairs. "I'll be back."

They watched him go until they were sure he couldn't see them any longer, and then Zoe and Aidan burst out laughing.

Zoe ruffled Aidan's hair. "You are quite the thespian, little brother. Nicely done." She handed the timepiece to Ma and was happy to see that even Ma had a bit of a smile on her face over the whole affair.

Wash woke on the morning of Zoe's test, feeling groggy and ill tempered.

Aidan hadn't been expected on the trip, so the Kastains had only reserved a room with two beds, but since Wash had an extra one in his room, he'd offered that Aidan could stay the night with him. He wasn't sure what had possessed him to do so after the imp had soaked him twice in one day.

No, that wasn't true at all.

He knew exactly what had possessed him. He'd wanted to show kindness to the younger brother of the beautiful soul that was Zoe Kastain.

She was sugared ginger and sunshine and vivid blue skies. Next to her, he felt like vinegar and gray clouds.

Especially today.

Sure, he might not be at a place where he was confident enough in his ability to provide for her that he was ready to start courting. But if he reached out a little, showed more kindness, even when he didn't feel like it, then maybe some of Zoe's vibrancy would make him a better man. He could hope so, anyway.

The problem was that once Aidan had been in his room—even after he'd fallen asleep—Wash had feared that if he slept too heavily, he would wake up to find the mischievous Aidan had disappeared and was lost forever in the city. So, every whisper of sound had woken him.

But thankfully, he'd made it through the night. A good strong cup of black coffee would go a long way toward righting his outlook. He would also keep his distance from Aidan today. Just staying dry would also improve his mood. Thankfully, they'd decided at dinner the evening before that he would accompany

Zoe to her test while Mrs. Kastain ran some errands about town with Aidan. That meant his attitude had improved already, since most of his day would be spent in a disaster-free zone.

Yawning expansively, he reached out and ruffled Aidan's hair. "Wake up, kiddo. We have to get a move on."

Aidan was one of those irritating morning people who popped right out of bed and started chattering from the first breath. And by the time Wash knocked on the other door to escort the women down to breakfast, he could hardly wait to get into a carriage alone with Zoe. She chattered sometimes too, but she did know when to hold her tongue, and even if she was in a talkative mood, her stories never seemed to irritate him.

Breakfast was a short affair. Zoe, as usual, was chomping at the bit to get to her test early. They made plans to meet back at the train station this evening, and as he and Zoe bid Mrs. Kastain farewell and sank into the taxi that would take them to the Territorial University of Washington, he could tell that Zoe was as nervous as a lone fly in a box full of frogs.

They were the only two in the cab. She sat on the bench across from him, rocking a little and studying a few papers in her lap. Her lips moved as she recited things back to herself. With his elbow propped against the sidewall of the carriage, he watched her. Glints of sunlight streamed through the cab's window and caught in her hair. For most of the train trip yesterday, she'd left her hair down while it dried, and he'd never before realized how much he loved the color of those red, wavy locks. Today, she'd pinned it up, but wisps of curls had slipped out to frame her face, and she kept blowing one out of her eyes as she studied.

He took a breath and forced himself to look away. With her creamy skin, a smattering of freckles, and those dark-lashed blue eyes of hers, she was beautiful in a way that drove home his earlier realization of how inadequate he was for taking care of her.

He wanted to be in the cavalry. What kind of life was that to offer a woman? He would constantly be traveling and at the beck and call of his commanding officers. Hardly ever home and in danger when he wasn't.

He rubbed his palms against his knees. No matter how attractive he found her or how he might wish to make her his wife, he'd best remember that she deserved a better life than that. Much better. Zoe needed a man who would be steady and constant and make her rethink when she got one of her fancy ideas. He wouldn't be able to do that if he was gone all the time. Yes, it would be best if he didn't allow these feelings to go anywhere. Best for her, and that was really what mattered.

The horse's hooves clip-clopped a soothing tattoo against the cobbled street. And despite how the busyness of Seattle had set his teeth on edge yesterday, he had to admit there was a certain melody to the sound of a waking city.

Zoe whimpered a little sound, drawing his gaze back to her. The notes in her hand trembled.

He leaned forward, propped his elbows against his knees, and laid his hand over the paper, making sure he had eye contact before he said, "Relax. You're going to do just fine."

She worked her teeth over her lower lip. "I'm just not certain. I've never gotten top marks in mathematics, and—"

"The only one who ever beat you was Kin."

"—there are certain regions of geography that I probably don't know as well as I should, and—"

"You always took top marks in geography."

"—I never even started to school until I was twelve! What if there are things I don't even know that I don't know? We've spent so much to get me here to take this test. If I fail, I know

Ma will still love me, but it will be such a disappointment to her and—"

"Zoe!" With a chuckle, Wash took both her hands in his. "Take a breath."

She did but gave him a little exasperated roll of her eyes.

He squeezed her fingers and rubbed his thumbs over her knuckles. "Last year, you told me something about becoming a teacher. Do you remember?"

She blinked at him blankly.

"You told me you felt like God had called you to this, right?"

She nodded. "Most definitely, which only adds more pressure! What if I—"

"Zo." Wash kept his voice low and steady.

"Yes?"

"First, this doesn't have to be a one-time-and-you're-out-if-you-fail prospect. If you don't pass, you'll just come back and take it again, because you know this is what you are meant to do. You remember Moses? When God called him to take the children of Israel out of Egypt? God gave him everything he needed to accomplish that task. Same with building the temple. There are verses that talk about the skilled workmen. And you are that, Zo. Definitely skilled at what God has called you to do. You are great with kids, and have a knack for explaining things in simple, understandable ways. God won't leave you without the tools you need to do what he's called you to. And you've done your part, right? You've studied and done your very best to prepare for this."

She nodded, and he felt some of the tension leave her hands. She blew at that strand of curls again.

He smiled. "Good. Then that's all you can ask of yourself. I think you're going to pass. But if you don't, you'll study some more, and you'll have a better understanding of your areas of weakness. Then you'll come back and take it again."

She still looked uncertain, even if she had relaxed a little. It was time to bring some levity to this.

He smiled at her. "I'll be right by your side through it all, but if there is a next time, can we please leave Aidan at home?"

Zoe threw back her head on a laugh that tinkled like Christmas bells.

Wash grinned. He liked the sound of that. Liked the sound of it a lot more than he should since he'd just been telling himself he wasn't the right man for her. He released her hands and sat back.

Zoe pulled in a long, measured breath and then blew it out slowly.

And drat if that action didn't draw his gaze to her lips. He squirmed and fiddled with his Stetson where it rested next to him on the seat. How far was it to their stop, anyway?

His answer came just then as the driver of the cab thumped on the roof. "Territorial University of Washington to the right."

Wash felt relieved as they stepped out and stood on the sidewalk. Distance from the beguiling Miss Zoe Kastain would do him some good about now.

Zoe eyed the building as she adjusted her satchel on her shoulder. "I can do this."

He nodded and stuffed his hands into his pockets so he wouldn't be tempted to reach out and brush that curl from her face. "Yes, you can. I'll be waiting and praying for you."

Her eyes softened. "I can't thank you enough for all you've done for me since Pa passed, Wash. Anytime I've needed a listening ear, you've been there. It's meant a lot."

"I'm happy to be of assistance, Zo." More than she knew. More than he ought to be.

She gave him a little wave and trotted across the street to disappear into the building. He gripped the lining of his pockets, trying to decide where he should spend the next few hours, and it was only as the emptiness of his pockets registered that he recollected he'd never gotten his watch back from her the evening before.

He'd have to remember to do that before he got home. He needed to take the watch apart and see if he could fix it as soon as possible.

Chapter 8

Zoe clutched her satchel to her chest as she stepped into the large testing room. Several women and a couple men already sat throughout the area, each at a separate table.

A matron in a black dress stood from a desk at the back of the room and strode toward her. Her raven-colored hair was pulled into such a tight bun that it gave her dark eyebrows the appearance of winging upward on the outer edges. Eyes the color of a winter pond glittered without welcome.

Zoe swallowed and took a step back. Her heart thudded against her breastbone.

The woman pinched her lips together and held out a bony hand. "Come, come. Give me your letter of permission."

"Oh. Yes." Zoe fumbled through her satchel to find the letter she'd received granting her a spot in today's testing. She thanked the heavens that she hadn't been holding her satchel when they'd all gone into the creek. What a disaster that would have been!

She handed the letter to the matron, who narrowed her eyes and took the longest time to study it, as if she might think Zoe was trying to deceive her.

Satchel clutched close once more, Zoe licked her lips. "Is everything in order?"

The woman lowered the letter and handed it back to her. "I suppose it is. Name?"

"Zoe, ma'am."

The matron rolled her eyes. "*Full* name!"

A couple of the other test takers snickered.

Zoe felt her face warm. "Zoe Kastain."

"Very well, Zoe Kastain. Please take a seat at an empty table. Testing will begin in thirty minutes. Until then, you will study quietly without talking, understand?"

"Yes, ma'am."

Without another word, the woman returned to her desk.

Zoe sank down at one of the empty tables next to a pretty brunette.

The girl leaned toward her and whispered, "Don't take her harshness to heart. She spoke to all of us just the same way. I'm Fern."

Zoe had never been more thankful for a friendly face. "I'm Zoe."

"Silence!" The matron snapped from the back of the room.

Fern rolled her eyes and made a little face.

And Zoe felt one of the chains of tension inside her snap free. Followed by another. And another. She took a cleansing breath, and closed her eyes. *Father, You called me here, like Wash said. Help me to be calm. To remember everything I've studied. And to think clearly. And if it happens that I pass this test, then I'll be the best teacher I know how to be.*

She felt much calmer after that, and when, thirty minutes later, the matron set the test before her, she picked up her pen and set to work without even a tremor in her hand.

※

Susan stood outside the jeweler's store with Aidan's hand clasped tightly. He'd been antsy all morning, and the last thing she wanted was for him to run off when she was alone with him.

The boy could move faster than a striking rattler. One moment, he would be by her side, and in the next instant, he could be out of sight. She didn't need that kind of stress today.

But that wasn't the reason for her hesitation outside of the shop. No, not at all. She took a breath and blew it out slowly.

The truth was, last night, Mr. Harrow had unnerved her in a very appealing way. She had never been one who'd given stock to stories of people falling in love at first sight. After all, she and William had been friends from the time they were young people and hadn't fallen in love until years down the road.

So yes, indeed, it had been disturbing to have her heart go all aflutter at her first glimpse of the man—a total stranger—the evening before. He was handsome—maybe more than some— but certainly she'd been around handsome men before and had never felt like a schoolgirl with her first infatuation.

Something about him had settled soul-deep before he'd even said two words last evening. Maybe it was his fathomless eyes that had seemed to carry such profound peace and yet sorrow at the same time. Understanding had hit her the moment he'd revealed that his wife had passed away. Of course, that would be a point of connection. Yet, there had been more.

And it was the more that terrified her.

"You okay, Ma?" Aidan jostled her hand.

She gave herself a little shake. "Yes, dear."

Whatever had attracted her to the man so viscerally could only be fleeting and needed to be pushed aside. She and her children would be going back to Wyldhaven tonight. And she'd likely never see him again.

Between now and then, she only had to have a conversation with him and not stumble all over herself. She could do that, right?

"Ma!" Aidan sighed. "Are we going inside?"

"Yes. We are." She pushed the door open and a bell jangled above her head as she stepped inside.

And there he was. Bent over the counter, working on a small clock.

He glanced up. His eyes widened a little, and he leapt to his feet, snatching his spectacles from his face. He smiled. "Hello."

Though she could tell he meant the greeting for both of them, his gaze never left hers as he said it.

"Hello." The word emerged on a bit of a squeak. Feeling her face heat, she swallowed and tore her gaze from those deep pools of chocolatey caramel.

All around the walls, every space was filled with different styles of clocks. Some were small and round. Others were long and rectangular with little figures at the top and pendulums tick-tick-ticking. The minute hands on each clock clicked over to the quarter hour, and suddenly, the whole room was filled with a beautiful cacophony of chimes and cuckoos.

"Wow!" Aidan exclaimed loudly, covering his ears with his palms. "This is great!"

It wasn't long before the noise receded and Susan swept a little motion with her hand. "You have a lovely store."

Aidan darted over to a large clock that stood taller than her head.

"Don't touch it, Aidan!"

Shoulders drooping, he glanced over his shoulder. "Yes, Ma."

"Where do your hands go?" Susan prompted.

With a sigh, Aidan clasped his hands behind his back and glanced at her for permission to proceed.

She nodded. "Thank you. You may look but not touch while I have a conversation with Mr. Harrow."

"Yes, Ma."

As she turned to face the counter, Mr. Harrow smiled softly. "Good to see you again." His eyes held a softness that revealed the depth of his meaning.

She remained where she stood, feet seemingly rooted to the floor. Could it be that the man was feeling some of the same things she was? And why was she, at her age, so flustered? She didn't know the first thing about this man. He might not even be a believer.

His lips tilted up almost imperceptibly, and his voice lowered when he said, "You can approach the counter, and I promise I won't bite."

Susan felt her face heat. "Ah." She jolted into action, fumbling through her reticule for Washington's watch. "I have the timepiece here." She stepped closer, laid it on the counter, and then snatched her hand back to her side.

His gaze held hers as he reached for the watch, and that imperceptible smile was suddenly very perceptible. "Do you just have two children?" He lowered his gaze to the watch and assessed it, pressing the spring to open the cover.

"No. I have five." She was relieved to say so. Perhaps that reminder would return her feet to solid ground. No man would want to take on a woman with five children in tow.

As he laid a pocket watch on the counter, he lifted his gaze to hers. His brows arched. "Five! I'm sure that keeps you busy."

She focused on the clocks on the wall behind him. "You have no idea."

He opened his mouth as though ready to speak, but then snapped it shut again. He worked for a moment with the watch, and soon the face of it lay beside the casing. "Well, the two of your children that I have met have both been very charming."

Susan tossed a glance toward Aidan. Seeing that he was still fascinated by a cuckoo clock next to the door and not touching it, she returned her attention to Mr. Harrow. "Thank you. Zoe is my second born. She has an older sister named Belle, and then between Zoe and Aidan are twins, Sharon Rose and Shiloh"

Mr. Harrow worked at a tiny screw as he tossed a glance toward Aidan. He raised his voice. "The only man among women, are you, son?"

Aidan gave an exaggerated sigh. "Yes, sir."

The man smiled. He flipped her a glance before returning his focus to the watch. "I grew up in a large family myself. I always wanted to have several children, but that never happened."

He stated the words matter-of-factly, and Susan found herself wondering what the reason was. Had his wife been unable to conceive? Or had she not wanted children? Either way, he must be very lonely. She couldn't imagine what her life would have been like after William's passing if she hadn't had the children to distract her from her grief.

She stepped closer to the counter. "I'm sorry you have been alone."

He lifted one shoulder. "My work has kept me busy. The shop has definitely prospered in the last few months."

Susan tilted her head. She had a feeling that what he was actually saying was that he had thrown all of his grief into nonstop work, which had made the shop prosper.

"I can't imagine what I would've done if I didn't have the children."

"It has definitely been the most difficult time of my life."

"When did your wife pass?" Susan felt her face heat. "I'm sorry. It's none of my business." She fiddled with the strings of her purse.

"No. It's fine. Cassie passed away a week before last Christmas."

"William left us at the end of March. But he had been sick for a long time before that. He was shot by an outlaw and never quite recovered. But in many ways that time helped prepare me for life without him, because he was incapacitated for much of it."

Behind her, the bell above the door jangled. She turned to see who had entered, but no one was there.

"Aidan!" Her eyes darted around the store. He wasn't here! She dashed to the door and burst onto the sidewalk, looking both directions.

She caught a glimpse of him turning a corner into an alley.

"Aidan! Stop!" As she charged after him, she heard Mr. Harrow calling for her to wait, but he didn't know Aidan like she did. The boy would run until he was exhausted, and then he would be lost. She had to keep him in sight!

He must have been upset by her mention of William's death. Careless! Why hadn't she thought?

Skirts raised enough to allow her to run, she turned the corner. "Oh, thank heavens."

Aidan was just ahead, back against the bricks of the store and one foot propped up behind him. He studied his hands, fiddling with his fingers.

Susan stopped by his side and took a couple of breaths.

He glanced up at her, then back down at his hands. "Sorry. I shouldn'ta run."

Susan couldn't reprimand him. She only reached out and hugged him close as she pulled in a few more gulps of oxygen. As much as she had grieved for William, she couldn't imagine what it must be like to have been a seven-year-old, now eight, trying to process a father's passing.

Footsteps approached, and she turned to see Mr. Harrow cautiously drawing near.

Heavens, what was the man going to think?

But there was no censure in his expression. Instead, he looked contrite. He squatted to Aidan's level. "I'm right sorry we upset you."

Aidan only sniffed.

Balanced on the balls of his feet, Mr. Harrow rubbed his fingers along his jaw. "Was your Pa a God-fearing man?"

Aidan nodded. "He made us go to church every Sunday, and licked us good if we misbehaved during service."

Susan chuckled at Aidan's interpretation. The truth was, William had let Aidan get away with a good many shenanigans during services. But the time he'd brought a toad to church and dropped it down David Hines' shirt? He *had* received his just reward for that.

Mr. Harrow interlaced his fingers before him. "You know what the Good Book says, right?"

Susan's pulse quickened. So, the man was a believer.

Aidan pushed back from her, swiping at his cheeks. "What?"

"It says that if a man believes in Jesus, that the moment he leaves this earth, he's in the presence of his Lord."

Aidan pondered for a moment. "And there's no pain in heaven, right?"

Mr. Harrow nodded and stood. "The Bible says that too."

After another moment's pause, Aidan tucked his hand into hers. "We can go back to the store now."

As they turned to do that, Susan smiled her gratitude to Mr. Harrow.

He gave a swipe of one hand as if to say it was nothing.

They had just started back down the alley when from behind them, there came a whine. They all three turned.

At the back end of the alley, there was a door that must be the rear entrance to a business. It had a set of rickety steps leading up to it, and a black and white dog lay partially beneath them. Upon seeing that they'd stopped, it lowered its head and scooted toward them on its belly, inching out far enough that they could see its tail wagging.

Aidan gasped. "Ma! It's the dog from the train station!" He rushed toward it.

Susan hurried after him, warning bells clanging caution in her mind. Something wasn't right.

"Oh, Ma! It's hurt!" Aidan fell to his knees by the dog. He started to reach out to pet it, but the dog growled low in its throat. "It's okay," Aidan crooned. "I won't hurt you." He reached for the dog again.

"Aidan, don't—"

But this time when his hand settled on the animal's head, it made no sound. It rested its muzzle on its paws and its tail thumped a beat against the dirt of the alley.

Aidan looked up, eyes pleading. "We can't just leave it here. Look, something happened to its leg."

Susan bent to see. Sure enough, the dog had been in a fight of some kind. Its back leg and part of its front shoulder were matted with blood. Susan pushed out a breath of despair. There really wasn't anything she could do for the dog. Not when they had to be back to the train in a few hours.

"Aidan we—"

"We'll bring the dog back to my store." Mr. Harrow spoke over her.

She looked at him. He nodded. "I know you are leaving again in a few days. But you can come back to see it tomorrow, and—"

"Tonight." She shouldn't have interrupted, but she didn't want him to misunderstand. "We go back to our home tonight."

There was the barest hint of a twitch near one of his eyes. "I see. Well..." He looked down at the dog. "That doesn't change the fact that I can take care of the dog."

At that moment, another higher pitched whine drew their attention to the space beneath the stairs.

"Oh, Ma! Look!" Aidan exclaimed.

Before Susan could think to caution him, Aidan had scrambled beneath the stairs. He emerged with two skin-and-bones puppies clutched to his chest. The puppies wriggled and wagged their tails. They appeared to be about six weeks old. One was pure white with one black ear and two black paws. The other was spotted like the mother.

Susan pressed a hand to her chest. "Oh, these poor creatures." Even worse, she had a feeling that the bone they'd given the dog the day before might be responsible for its injury. Some other hungry dog must have come and fought her for it.

Mr. Harrow sighed. "They can come too."

"Ma, we can take the puppies, can't we?" Aidan's eyes pleaded. "They can go in a box when we're on the train. I'll watch them! I promise!"

Wide-eyed, Susan turned to look at Mr. Harrow.

He raised one shoulder. "They do look old enough to be parted from their mother. I can keep one, but not all three."

Susan looked back at the puppies. They already had Jinx at home and couldn't take another dog, but they could keep them until they found good homes for them. She gave Aidan a firm look. "We can't keep the puppies, understand? If we take them back to Wyldhaven, we can only care for them until we find someone else who wants them."

Aidan grinned from ear to ear. "Okay. I'll find homes that are close so I can go visit them real often!"

Susan chuckled. "That will be fine."

Mr. Harrow cleared his throat. "And maybe you'll let me write to you?"

Susan's gaze flew to his.

He motioned from the dog to Aidan. "You know, so I can let the boy know how the dog is faring." There was such an innocent, hopeful look in his eyes that Susan couldn't prevent a smile.

"Well, if it's only to tell us about the dog, I suppose that wouldn't be improper."

Mr. Harrow grinned. "I'll keep my letters on topic, you can be sure." His warm gaze remained fixed on her face, and he lowered one eye in a quick wink.

Susan felt her face heat.

Heavens!

Who would have thought that she might need a fan during the heart of a Seattle winter?

Chapter 9

Zoe blew out a noisy sigh and folded the test booklet closed. She'd looked over all her answers multiple times and felt confident that she'd answered every question to the best of her ability. She glanced around the room. She hadn't realized that she was the last one working.

The matron's lips were pinched even tighter than normal as Zoe approached her desk. "Wondered if you were going to complete it before your time was up."

"Oh, I've been done for a while but was just checking over my answers."

The woman sniffed. "If you were confident of the answers the first time you put them down, you wouldn't have needed to do that."

Zoe blinked. What must it be like to be such a sourpuss all the time? Maybe the woman had been through a great tragedy. Or maybe *several* great tragedies. But Zoe didn't figure it was her place to pry. "When can I expect to hear back?"

"We'll mail you."

"Yes, ma'am" Zoe clung to every last ounce of politeness she could muster. "Do you know when that will be?"

The woman sighed and gave a little roll of her dark eyes. "In a few weeks."

Zoe supposed that was all the information she was going to get. "All right. Thank you for taking time to proctor the test."

"Doctor the test? Are you asking me to change your answers?!"

"No, ma'am. *Proctor* the test. You know, sit here and keep an eye on all of us."

"Oh." The woman's brows slumped. "None of the others thanked me. Are you trying to score higher marks than you deserve by buttering me up?"

Zoe sighed. "No, ma'am. Have a nice day." She turned and walked away before her penchant to blurt her feelings had her saying something she really would regret.

Wash and his smile were such a welcome sight when she left the building that she couldn't resist throwing her arms around his neck for a quick hug.

He smiled and set her back from him. "What was that for?"

"For simply being my friend and the kind one that you are."

Wash glanced back toward the building as they walked away. "Test that difficult?"

Zoe wobbled her head. "I'm fairly certain that I knew most of the answers. The essays will be telling. Did I remember to write down everything I knew about mollusks? I simply can't recall what I even wrote right now. My brain feels like a bowl of Ewan's hot chili."

Wash frowned. "That bad, huh?"

Exhaustion hit her in a wave, and she looped her arm through his. "Just get me back to the boardinghouse so we can gather our bags."

Wash lifted one hand to hail a taxi.

"What did you do with yourself all day?"

He shrugged. "It was sunny for this time of year, even if not very warm. But I was bundled up. I walked down to the water and then ate lunch at a little diner. You hungry?"

Zoe suddenly realized she was. "Starving!"

He pulled a paper-wrapped sandwich and an apple from his coat pocket. "I thought you might be. Brought these for you."

"Heavenly!" Zoe munched quietly, and when they got back to the boardinghouse, Wash asked the taxi to wait while he ran up to get their bags.

Ma and Aidan would have already left for the station. Zoe felt a zip of excitement shoot through her exhausted body. Had Ma been able to get the watch fixed? She certainly hoped so. She couldn't wait to see the look on Wash's face when she gave it to him.

Wash returned within a few minutes, and not long after, they settled onto the bench in train car number nine, across from Ma and Aidan.

Zoe and Wash gasped and fawned over the puppies and laughed at Ma's story of how Mr. Harrow had gotten soaking wet while giving the mama and her two pups a bath.

"And the mama dog wasn't hurt near as bad as we first thought!" Aidan exclaimed. "When we left, she was sniffing around Mr. Harrow's clock shop. And Mr. Harrow is going to write to me so I can know how she's doing!"

Ma fidgeted and blushed.

Zoe narrowed her eyes. "Is he, now?" Seeing that Wash was distracted with one of the puppies, Zoe leaned close to Ma. "Was he able to fix it?"

Ma nodded and surreptitiously slipped the fob from her reticule. She pressed it into Zoe's hand. Then she stood. "Aidan, how about we go down to the dining car and see if we can buy the puppies some milk?"

Zoe appreciated the fact that she was giving her some space to give him the watch in a little privacy.

"That's a great idea!" Aidan lurched to his feet and trailed after her. But he dashed back only a moment later. "You two will watch the puppies while I'm gone, won't you?"

Zoe chuckled. "Yes, Aidan. We will."

Wash leaned forward and returned the white pup with the black ear to the box with the other one. He rested his elbows against his knees, and they watched the puppies in silence for a moment. Both curled into a tangled heap and seemed to be settling in for a nap.

Perfect. Zoe cleared her throat. "Wash?"

"Yeah?" He yawned and scrubbed his hands over his face and then looked at her, and the impact of his gray-green eyes suddenly had Zoe at a loss for words. He frowned and straightened. "You all right?"

Swallowing, she held the watch out in an open palm.

"Oh." He reached for it. "I've been meaning to ask you for that back."

"Open it."

His brow furrowed, but he followed her instructions. The moment the cover sprung open, a soft ticking sound could be heard. His eyes widened and lifted to hers.

She smiled. "Mr. Harrow is a watchmaker. He was able to fix it. That was Ma's errand that she had to run today."

Wash cleared his throat and looked back at the timepiece. Then his eyes narrowed a little. "Wait a minute. Are you the reason I got a glass of water in my lap at dinner last night?"

Before she could stop it, a chuckle burst free. "Aidan should be in theatre, right?" She held up a hand. "In my defense, I didn't know his plan was to soak you for the second time that day."

The gold fob looked small in Wash's big hand as he studied it. He swallowed. "Zoe, I know you can't afford—"

She laid a hand on his arm. "It didn't cost so much as you might think. I have a feeling Mr. Harrow gave me a rock bottom price. But I was thrilled he could fix it for you. I know how much it meant when your pa gave it to you. Aidan even pitched in the money Belle gave him to spend on candy for the trip." She smiled. "Happy Christmas, Washington."

His throat worked, and, if she wasn't missing her guess, that was a sheen of moisture in his eyes.

His hand settled warmly over hers. "Happy Christmas, Zoe."

Dear Reader,

This has probably been my favorite of the Wyldhaven Christmas novellas to write, because it is an introduction to two future books in the series. I'm not sure when I'll get to Zoe and Wash's stories, or to Susan and Elijah's, but their stories are already brewing in my mind. (Sounds kind of scary, right? Haha)

Have you ever been in the position Wash was in where you are trying to help someone and seemingly everything keeps going wrong? Or in Zoe's position of a high stress situation with the one delay after another?

It's the fire that brings out the precious metal in us all—if we can let go of the slag. God often uses times of trial and frustration to grow us to be more like Him. In the book of James, chapter 1, it says this: *Consider it pure joy, my brothers and sisters, whenever you face trials of many kinds, because you know that the testing of your faith produces perseverance. Let perseverance finish its work so that you may be mature and complete, not lacking anything. If any of you lacks wisdom, you should ask God, who gives generously to all without finding fault, and it will be given to you.* May that give you strength the next time you need it! I know I often go back to those verses in times of difficulty.

If you enjoyed this story, **please leave the book a review**. It doesn't have to be long, but every review helps spread the word, and the world needs more uplifting stories!

I haven't forgotten about the Carver siblings. They play a small part in the next novella. And I'm very excited to share it with you because it is the prequel to the next full-length book in the series that will come out late next year, *Songs in the Night*.

You can find all the books in the Wyldhaven series here on my website.

Merry Christmas!
Lynnette
BONNER

Parson Clay's Christmas Pup

Novella Six
WYLDHAVEN

Chapter 1

Preston Clay woke a few days before Christmas, feeling like his throat might be on fire.

He groaned.

Perfect.

Not only had an avalanche prevented him from traveling east to visit with his parents this holiday, but for the past few weeks, he had been battling a nagging illness that seemed to now have caught up with him.

He slipped one hand from beneath the covers and fumbled across the night table for the cup of water that he had left there the evening before. Mercy, but it was cold in his room! How could he feel half frozen and half ablaze all at once? His hand settled around the cup, and he lifted his head enough to take a few sips. But each swallow may as well have been filled with razor blades. Giving up, he returned the cup to the bedside table and withdrew beneath his warm feather tick.

He was supposed to ride out to Camp Sixty-One today to perform a Christmas service, but he didn't think he was going to make it. All week, he had been pushing himself even though he didn't feel well, but this morning, the illness had tipped over into outright agony.

He would have to send Kin to the camp on his behalf. Kin could at least let them know he wouldn't be able to make it.

And maybe Kin could even read the passages from the book of Luke about the birth of Christ to the assembly.

Preston smirked. Wouldn't that be a picture! Kin leading a church service! If only he could be there to see it.

Across the room the door squeaked on its hinges, and Tommy poked his head inside. "P-Parson?"

Preston feared what might happen to the poor, simpleminded young man if he were to come down with whatever this ailment was. He didn't want to subject him to this unpleasantness. "Tommy, I need you to go out and close the door, okay?" His voice rasped and he paused to swallow. "Can you get Kin for me?"

Tommy hesitated. "Kin d-done went to f-finish Miss Dixie's s-sleigh."

Preston's eyes slipped closed. Yes. He should have remembered that Kin was finishing up that project. Now how was he going to communicate with Camp Sixty-One?

And, much as he hated to admit it, he needed Doc, but he didn't want to send Tommy down to town on his own. Though he was trustworthy most of the time, sometimes Tommy lost track of the task he had been given and wandered off. Preston didn't want him wandering around in this weather, especially when he was too ill to go looking for him if he strayed from his assigned task.

"Okay, Tommy. I need you to let me sleep for a little bit longer okay? Just close the door and sit by the fire and paint in that book that Aurora gave you."

"F-fire's almost out."

Preston grunted. True. Even if Kin had banked the fire before he left, it would be low by now. And the first week that Tommy had come to live with them, he'd almost started the hearth on fire. Ever since then, they'd had a rule that Tommy was not allowed to do anything with the stove or the fireplace.

Willing himself to be strong, he pushed the covers back and sat up on the edge of the bed. Cold slapped him like an avalanche. Every muscle tightened up, and his right calf went into a spasm. He gritted his teeth and stretched out the leg, then forced himself to stand. The room spun. He grabbed for the footboard and missed. He went down to the floor in a heap. Old words that used to be part of his everyday life spun through his mind. He gave himself a little shake. *Forgive me, Jesus.*

He banished the curses and refocused. Now what?

He simply didn't have the wherewithal to try again. He grabbed the corner of the tick and tugged it on top of himself. But dash, this floor was cold. He rolled over so that part of the tick now lay beneath him. And with that, his strength was gone. Yet Tommy still remained patiently by the door.

Preston didn't have what it took to go put wood on the fire. "Put on your coat, okay, Tom-Tom?"

Tommy chuckled at the nickname. "Okay. I like to p-paint."

"I know. Paint me a real nice one, and I'll put it up in the kitchen when I get better."

Still, Tommy hesitated. "You get b-better?"

"Yes. I'll get better. I just need to sleep. You stay in the house, you hear? Promise me."

"T-Tommy p-promise."

"Good lad." Preston closed his eyes then and willed away the wave of dizziness swirling in his head.

He heard the door squeak and then click shut. Relieved that Tommy had listened to him and not come too close, Preston allowed himself to return to the oblivion of sleep.

Aurora McClure walked through the beautiful chill of this winter morning with her songbooks clasped in her arms. As she crossed the wooden slats of the Wyldhaven Creek bridge near town, she admired the patterns ice had created along the river banks. Only the very center of the creek remained unfrozen, and that likely would be covered over in the next day or so. Her breath puffed in a cloud before her. It was so cold that the snow squeaked beneath her boots. Despite the chill, she felt light of heart. In just a moment, she would be in the warm church and able to spend the next blessed hour in Preston Clay's presence.

Her face heated at the improper thought.

Just because the parson was single didn't mean he was looking for a wife. Not to mention, what did she know about being a parson's wife? Sure, she played the piano and could sing, but she didn't have much to offer beyond that. Preston was likely looking for a woman who knew a sight more about the operation of the church. And, if she were honest, he likely didn't want the daughter of a soiled dove for a wife either.

She'd best compose her thoughts before arriving at the church. It wouldn't do to have Preston pestering her about the cause of her flushed cheeks. The thought of explaining to him only made her blush more.

Ever since she'd come to town posing as a boy to hide from the brothel owner who had wanted to press her into service and lived with the parson and Kin for several weeks in the guise of a lad, both of them treated her like a younger sibling. So, all of her daydreams were likely for naught because Preston would never see her as anything other than the young girl who had deceived him.

Preston.

Listen to her go on! Even if using his first name was only in her thoughts, one of these days, she was going to slip and call him Preston to his face, and then where would she be?

She took the church steps carefully, for they were thick with frost. But when she stepped into the entryway, the building was still cold and dark.

She frowned. On the days when she and Preston went over the music for Sunday's services, he always started a fire ahead of time to warm the place while he went over his sermon notes. So where could he be? Perhaps he had lost track of time and would be here in a few minutes. It wouldn't hurt her to get the fire going this time.

She took kindling from the box by the old wood stove that stood at the back corner of the sanctuary and set about making a fire that was soon spreading heat. Still, Preston had not arrived.

She paced to the side window of the sanctuary that looked up the hill toward the parsonage.

The path between here and there remained empty. And there was something oddly still about the scene that made her take a second look. What was it?

Last night's fresh layer of snow did have footprints in it. Had Preston left the house? Or had someone else walked the path? Maybe she should practice that hymn with the difficult chord changes. She started to turn from the window but stilled.

There was something...her focus honed in on the parsonage chimney then. That was it. No smoke. On a cold day such as today, she couldn't imagine that the cabin Parson Clay shared with Kin and Tommy was warm enough to go without a fire.

Something wasn't right.

She tucked her coat close about her and took the trail up the hill. At the parsonage door, she knocked. "Parson?"

A moment later the door creaked open. Only Tommy's face was visible in the opening.

She smiled. "Morning, Tommy. How are you today?"

"I'm c-cold. But P-PC has r-rules. T-Tommy's not allowed t-to make a fire."

Aurora put her hand on the door. "And you are a good man for following the rules. How about if I come in and make you one?"

He tilted his head, obviously uncertain if that would break Parson Clay's rules.

"Is the parson here?" She searched the yard as she waited for his response. Everything lay under a quiet blanket of snow.

Tommy stepped back and opened the door a little wider.

As she stepped inside and closed it behind her, she noted that Tommy wore his thick winter coat. She rubbed her hands together. It really was almost as cold in here as it was outside. The one room encompassed a kitchen on one end and living quarters on the other. A quick sweeping glance revealed that Preston wasn't here. Her gaze landed on the closed bedroom door, and her heart thudded. "Where's PC, Tommy?"

She felt her face heat at the familiar term. Years ago, Kin had started calling Parson Clay "PC," and the nickname had sort of grown on the community. Many of them called him that now. But never her. She'd always stuck to formal address—except in her thoughts. But a flick of a glance at Tommy showed he thought nothing of it.

He shrugged. "He's s-still s-sleeping."

Aurora frowned. Still sleeping? That didn't sound like Preston at all. When she'd lived here, he had always been the first one up. And right at the crack of dawn. "Maybe you should go check on him?"

Tommy shook his head. "He g-gone down. H-he t-told me to p-paint in m-my b-book. Want to see?"

Gone down? What did he mean by that?

Tommy's feet shuffled.

She forced a smile. "Sure. Show it to me while I get the fire going." She felt pleased that Tommy seemed to like her gift so much. She had originally thought it might keep him occupied while Parson Clay studied, but Tommy had been so taken with the gift that he painted several times a day. She would soon need to get him another book of paper. It didn't matter that most of his pictures couldn't be deciphered. It was the joy he got from the process.

As she made a fuss over Tommy's painting of a horse—nothing but brown blobs on the paper—and got the fire going, Aurora's mind scrambled to decide what to do. She couldn't just go into Preston's room to see if he was all right! That would be unseemly. But neither could she just leave him alone without knowing what might be wrong. "Gone down" kept ringing in her mind.

With the fire crackling cheerily, Aurora stepped back and dusted her hands. "There. The house will soon be much warmer. Did you get some breakfast yet?"

Tommy shook his head. "Nope."

Aurora's worry mounted. "Did PC get up at all this morning?" He shook his head. "H-he's sick."

She studied the closed bedroom door. "How sick?"

Tommy shrugged. "He gone d-down."

That did it.

"Okay. Go sit at the table, and I'll get you some breakfast in just a minute. You can paint some more until I come."

Tommy trotted to the table proclaiming his love of painting.

Aurora squinted at the pine door. When she'd lived here, there'd been only one bedroom, but after Tommy moved in, the parson and Kin had constructed a second one that Kin and Tommy now shared. But she knew the parson had remained in the original one.

The room she now needed to enter!

Aurora approached the door and tapped softly. "Parson? You okay in there?"

When there was no reply, Aurora's pulse gave a little stutter.

Chapter 2

Aurora turned the knob on Preston's bedroom door, and pushed it open just a crack. "Preston?" Drat! There she had done it and let his name slip. She really needed to get a handle on her thoughts and not think of him in such familiar terms.

Had he heard her? He still hadn't responded. Aurora pressed farther into the room. "Parson?"

He made a little groaning sound—from the floor!

Aurora's pulse spiked. Gone down indeed!

She scurried a little closer. At least he had pulled the thick quilt from his bed! All she could see was his tousled sandy brown hair poking from one end of where he'd rolled himself up in it.

Her hand trembled as she reached out to tuck the blanket away from his face. He had a sheen of moisture on his forehead! Without further thought, she sank to her knees beside him. Instinctively, she laid her hand against his skin. He was burning up! And was that—she leaned a little closer. Small red dots covered the column of his throat.

She needed to fetch Doc right away! But what about his fever? She made a quick decision. First, she needed to cool him. She dashed from the room and scrambled into the kitchen.

"Breakfast?" Tommy asked hopefully.

"In a minute, Tommy." She grabbed a basin and pumped the handle on the kitchen pump. "Parson Clay is very sick. I need to help him for a minute. You keep painting, all right?"

"All right."

That was one thing that could be said for Tommy. He was very compliant.

Aurora searched the cupboards for a rag, and, thankfully, the parson and Kin hadn't done much, if any, rearranging since she had lived here, because everything seemed to be in about the same place. She found the rags, hefted the bowl of water, and then dashed back to the cabin's main bedroom.

Heaven help them if any of the Wyldhaven gossips ever learned that she was in his room tending him alone! But she knew Doc wouldn't tell, and she also knew enough about fevers to know that the sooner she got this one to come down, the better it would be for Preston.

"Parson?" She congratulated herself for not using his given name. "You have a fever. I'm here to help." She wasn't even sure if he was lucid enough to understand her. But since he made no response, she took that as permission. She sank onto the floor beside him and dipped the rag in the cool water, then wrung it out. Leaning close, she dabbed the rag across his forehead.

He jerked away.

"I know it's cold. I'm so sorry. But it's important that we get your fever down."

Whether he'd heard her words, or whether he had adapted to the cool cloth, she wasn't sure, but it didn't seem to bother him so much after that. Aurora laid the rag against his neck until it was warm to the touch; then she put it back in the water. She kept dipping and ringing and dabbing.

But she couldn't stay here much longer. The parson needed Doc. Why hadn't he sent Tommy on that errand? Yet even as the question filled her mind, Aurora knew she wouldn't let Tommy go into town on his own either. But what Tommy could do was sit here and cool PC while she ran down. She dashed back into the dining room. "Tommy? I need your help. Can you come here for a minute please?"

In his usual compliant way, Tommy rose and followed her without question.

She showed him how to run the rag along Parson Clay's forehead and over his neck. "Just like that, okay? I'm going to fetch Doc, and I will be right back. You keep doing this, all right?

Tommy nodded. "Tommy h-help PC."

"Yes good. You help PC, and I'll be right back." Willing herself not to panic, Aurora dashed down the hill into town. Twice, she skated on the ice and almost fell, but each time, she managed to right herself. She burst into the boardinghouse and was relieved to see Dixie manning the main desk. "Oh Dixie! I'm so glad to see you." She laid a hand over her chest, and gulped a few breaths. "I need Doc. Is he here?"

Dixie's brow furrowed. "He is. He's just eating breakfast. He had a very late night. Whatever is the matter?"

Aurora pressed her palms together. "There's something awfully wrong with Parson Clay. I was to meet him at the church this morning to go over Sunday's music, but he didn't arrive. When I went up to the parsonage to check on him, I found Tommy in a cold cabin, and Parson Clay has a fever like I've never felt before. And I think maybe a rash."

Dixie's eyes widened and she dropped the pen she'd been holding. It rolled off the desk and clattered to the floor but she paid it no mind. She hurried toward the dining room. "I'll send him right up."

Aurora breathed a sigh of relief that Doc happened to be here. "Thank you. I'm going to hurry back. I'll meet him there." When she arrived at the parsonage once more, she was thankful to see that Tommy had followed her instructions and was still putting the cold compress on the parson's skin, except he hadn't been as adept at ringing out the rag and now the parson and one end of his tick were soaking wet.

She ought to have realized that would be a problem. She reached for the rag in Tommy's hand. "Thank you, Tommy. I can take over from here. Doc is on the way, and as soon as he gets here, I'll make you breakfast. Go back and finish your painting."

Thankfully, it was only a few minutes before Doc panted into the room. He frowned at PC on the floor and the water everywhere. "What happened?"

Aurora felt a little sheepish. "He must have fallen before I got here. And I had Tommy wiping him down with cool water while I came to get you."

Doc grinned. "Well it looks like he did a fine job of it."

Aurora looked at the mess in consternation. "Will it make him sicker?"

Doc shook his head. "We won't want to leave him wet like that for long, but the most important thing was what you did, and that was to cool him down." He motioned to the bed. "Help me get him back onto the bed. Then we can find dry blankets." He set his black bag by the door and came to bend over the parson. "Preston? Can you wake up? We're going to help you back to your bed."

PC moaned a little, and his eyelashes fluttered. His gaze settled on Aurora and a frown immediately puckered his forehead.

"Come on." Doc tugged the blanket free and grabbed Preston's arm.

PC wore only a pair of long underwear! Heavens! She hoped Doc didn't have time to notice the flush in her face as she grabbed PC's other arm and they hauled him to his feet.

He swayed so severely she thought he might fall right back down.

"Whoa!" She surged to wrap one arm around his back.

Doc did the same, and, between the two of them, they managed to get PC seated on his mattress.

"'S cold." He shivered.

"We'll have you covered back up in just a moment," Doc consoled. "Lie back against the pillows."

As PC complied, Aurora hurried to the chest in the corner. When she'd lived here, there'd been extra blankets in there. And thankfully, as with the kitchen, nothing seemed to have changed. She lifted the whole stack out and turned back for the bed.

Doc set his medical bag on the bedside table and opened it to fish around inside. "If you don't mind stepping from the room, I'll do a quick examination, and then we'll know more what we are looking at."

"Of course." Aurora quickly spread the blankets over PC and then took the wet tick with her as she left. She draped it over a couple chairs near the living room fireplace.

Out in the kitchen, Aurora added wood to the stove and fumbled her way through scrambling eggs and making toast for Tommy. When she poured him a glass of milk, she noted that her hands trembled. She *thunk*ed the pitcher down by Tommy's glass and smoothed her hands over the front of her skirt. She looked out the window at the world that looked so pure with the fresh blanket of snow. How was it that, even on a day like today, sickness could sneak in and wreak its havoc?

Tommy looked forlornly at his plate and then glanced up at her. "P-Parson always m-makes me oatmeal."

Aurora laid a hand on Tommy's shoulder. "For today, just eat the eggs and toast, all right? Next time, I'll know that you want oatmeal."

Tommy shook his head. "T-Tommy don't like eggs."

Aurora sighed.

What was it she had just been thinking about Tommy being compliant? But she didn't suppose it would hurt her to make a pot of oatmeal. At the very least, it would keep her occupied. What was taking Doc so long?

When the oatmeal was finished and Doc still had not emerged from the bedroom, Aurora put her energy into scrubbing down the kitchen cabinets. She was only halfway finished with the task when Doc stepped into the room.

He set his doctor bag by his feet and then straightened to face her with a frown.

Her heart stuttered. "Is it bad?"

"It's not good. I'm afraid he has measles."

Aurora staggered to the table and sank into the nearest chair. Measles could be deadly.

Doc gave her a look. "Now don't go giving up before we've even begun the battle. You know that Rose Pottinger had pneumonia a few years back, right? And my treatment saved her. And the mortality rate for pneumonia is much higher than for measles. Parson Clay is strong. He can beat this. But..."

Her gaze flew to his. "But what?"

His lips pressed into a grim line. "You've been exposed. Have you had measles before?"

Aurora felt her eyes widen. "Not that I know of." She gasped! "I didn't expose Dixie, did I?"

He frowned. "Did you cough on her? Or touch her?"

Aurora shook her head. "No. In fact, I remained close to the boardinghouse entrance as I spoke to her because I wanted to return here quickly."

"Then I'm sure she's fine. But I'm afraid I'm going to have to insist that you remain here in quarantine."

Aurora flew to her feet. "What?!"

"Only for a few weeks."

"A few weeks! I can't stay here unchaperoned for one night, much less weeks! Do you know how the tongues will wag?" Her face blazed. Why was she forever blurting the first thing on her mind?

Doc sighed and stared out the window for a moment. "I'll have to find you a chaperone, then. Someone who's already had measles. Besides, your stay might be much shorter than that. There is another sickness called German Measles. It appears to be measles at the onset, but has a much shorter duration and is less contagious. If it is that, the parson will be better by Christmas, and you'll be able to go home. Well, maybe not home." He cast her an apologetic look.

"Why not home?"

"Because I've seen too many cases of pregnant women giving birth to babies with defects if they contract German Measles during pregnancy."

Aurora frowned. Whatever was he talking about? No one was pregnant back at the Rodante place where she lived. Then a thought struck her. She gasped, eyes widening! Despite the craziness of the day she was experiencing, joy flooded in like a crashing wave. "Liora's expecting?!"

Doc blinked. "She hasn't told you yet?"

Aurora shook her head.

"Well, then, you'd best keep that tidbit of information to yourself. I'm obviously too tired, or I wouldn't have let it slip."

Aurora nodded. "Since it looks like I'm going to be stuck here for a while, what can I do to help?"

"I was just about to get to that." Doc hefted his black satchel. "I will go down and get a few things that I need to treat him. But then I have to ride out to Camp Sixty-Three today. It is my normal day for a clinic out there. If I show you what to do, can you stay here and care for the parson?"

"Wait. Why are you allowed to leave, but I'm not?" Aurora frowned.

Doc smiled apologetically. "I've had both rubella—that's the formal name for German measles—and measles. Once you've had them, you can't get them again. In fact, I'll check with Dixie. She may have had them as a child as well, and that would rule out any possibility of you having exposed her."

"There's Kin too. He's out there somewhere. I haven't seen him, but would PC have been contagious before this morning?"

Doc sighed. "Yes. I thought of that. I'll have to track him down."

Aurora nodded and then promptly frowned. "How soon can you find a chaperone? I don't want the parson being bad-mouthed about town on account of me wanting to help him."

Doc seemed to ponder on that for a few moments. "Well, Tommy there will be here, so it's not like you are in the house with him alone. And there's really no one else to do what Preston needs right now. I think folk will be understanding. I'll call a town meeting and try to find someone for you by this evening."

Aurora lifted a hand of resignation. "That will have to do, I suppose."

Doc nodded. "I'll be back in ten minutes. While I'm gone, please boil some water to make him a medicinal tea. And if you could keep the fires going good and strong, that would be best. I've given him a good, strong dose of cough syrup. That might make him a little off his head, so don't be too alarmed if you notice that. The syrup should also help bring his fever down a little."

"All right." Aurora nodded, relieved to have an assignment to tackle while he was gone. "I'll go check on him as soon as I finish washing these cupboards."

Chapter 3

Preston felt a damp cloth against his brow and turned his head into the agreeable chill of it. A woman spoke softly in a pleasant voice, but he couldn't quite make out what she was saying. He tried to open his eyes, but his lids were heavy. Too heavy. And his tongue felt thick. Like it used to when he drank too much on a Saturday night.

The woman crooned a few more words. The voice was so familiar. "Ma?"

The cloth stilled.

He wished he could open his eyes to see her.

He fought to think through the morning. Was it really Ma? He remembered he'd fallen trying to go put wood on the fire. Then Doc had been here. And someone with him. They'd helped him back into bed. Doc had given him some vile tasting medicine, and he'd been able to taste the alcohol in it. Next time he'd have to refuse, but he supposed the good Lord would forgive him for breaking his vow since he hadn't known what was in the syrup Doc had urged down his throat until he was already swallowing. And, whooee, was it doing a number on him! Even with his eyes closed, waves of dizziness rocked him. He may as well be adrift at sea.

The woman murmured again, and the cold cloth found his neck this time. That was not so pleasant because it raised an itch he knew he dared not scratch. If he did, it would only grow worse.

It had to be Ma.

When he'd missed the train for back east because of the avalanche, he had worried that he might never get to see her again. Had she really come? And had she brought puppy? He frowned and tried to think past the sludge of his mind. Puppy? Was that the right word? No, not puppy. Poppy. Poppy with her beautiful black hair and ruby red lips and ready laughter.

The rag resumed its ministration. He licked his lips. "Did you bring puppy?" He frowned. Why was her name so hard to say?

The feminine voice shushed him. "You're going to be fine. Can you lift your head?" He felt a hand slip behind his head, and the cool rag swiped along the back of his neck. He shivered. The boat rocked more violently this time.

If Ma was here, he hoped Poppy had come to her senses and come too. His tongue felt like a stick in his mouth. "Water."

"Of course. Here you go."

The hand slipped behind his head once more, and he felt the touch of the glass against his lips. Never had a few sips of water satisfied so well.

He dropped his head back to the pillow and fumbled for the woman's hand. Her fingers were small and cool in his. Did Ma always have such small hands? He couldn't seem to remember. But Poppy... Her hands had been tiny. So tiny. He'd loved to watch her play the piano with those slender fingers flying over the keyboard. He frowned. Piano? No. Poppy didn't play the piano. "Poppy?"

The small hand gave his a squeeze. "I'm sorry. You don't have one."

Don't have one? "Don't have one what?" The words rasped razor blades in his throat.

"You don't have a puppy."

He felt the muscles of his forehead tighten. That was certainly true. He hadn't had Poppy for a long time. But Ma knew the story. "But I've wanted her since Christmas 1882."

The rag continued its ministrations. "Maybe this year then."

He nodded. At least he thought he did. "Maybe she'll come."

"She'll come."

He relaxed then. The boat quit rocking, and he lapsed into sweet sleep.

Aurora frowned at Preston as he drifted off. His breathing grew more pronounced, and his mouth gaped slightly.

No wonder he was so thirsty. The sickness must be causing him to breathe through his mouth. She'd have to remember to keep giving him liquids. It wouldn't do for him to become dehydrated.

As she returned to the kitchen with the bowl of now tepid water, she pondered over his ramblings about a puppy. Had he been disappointed over not getting one the Christmas of...was it 1882 he had said? He would have been just a boy then.

She knew he'd planned to go back east to visit his family this year but had been prevented from doing so by the avalanches that had blocked the tracks. Perhaps that disappointment had stirred the distant one in his fevered mind.

But it didn't matter what had brought it up. What mattered was that the parson needed a puppy! She couldn't go back and soothe the disappointment of a boy, but she would do everything in her power to make that request a reality this Christmas.

But...where was she going to find a puppy?

She would ask Kin as soon as he returned. He had his ear to the ground all over the place! He would know a family around here somewhere who had a litter they needed to part with!

Her heart felt lighter at just the thought. It was the perfect thoughtful gift. Nothing too intimate, but one that would let Preston know she cared.

Maybe that would jostle him out of his ambivalence toward her.

She set about chopping potatoes for a lunch soup with a song in her heart.

Kin Davis was in his shed out at his pa's old place, working on the final touches of the sleigh that Dixie Griffin had hired him to make for Doc. He had just added the last stroke of red paint when he heard someone hail his name from out in the yard. His pulse spiked. That was Doc! After all the work Dixie had put in to keep this sleigh a secret, it wouldn't do for Doc to see it before Christmas day.

Kin snatched up a rag and hurried from the shed, closing the door behind him. He wiped the red paint from his fingers as he smiled at Doc across the yard. "Morning, Doc. How did you know I was here?"

Doc waved a hand. "Ewan McGinty said this was likely where you were."

Kin clenched his teeth, but made sure to keep his smile in place. He didn't want Doc to wonder why he was frustrated. But Ewan knew very well that he was here working on Doc's present. The old troublemaker had likely hoped to ruin Doc's Christmas. He was likely still sore that Dixie had never given him any consideration and had married Doc.

"Been a while since you came out to this old place, hasn't it?" Doc glanced around. "I see you've done considerable work on the cabin."

That was an understatement. Back when Pa was alive, the cabin had been so gap-sided that Kin hadn't been able to keep it warm in winter even with a blazing fire in the stove. But when Parson Clay had first come to town, he and Kin had lived here for a while, and the parson had showed him some tricks for temporary chinking. After they'd moved to the parsonage near the church, Kin had decided to put in real chinking as he could afford it. And then he'd added a couple windows and replaced the porch and steps. He'd even planted a couple apple trees in the field out back, and maybe one of these days, there would be a proper orchard. But next on his list was converting the old shed into a proper barn.

Doc angled him a look. "You aren't making moonshine in that shed, are you?"

Kin decided that the truth was probably his best defense. He held up a hand to reveal the remnants of red paint. "Just working on a little Christmas surprise that I didn't want a certain someone in town to see." He held his breath. Now he just had to hope that Doc would think he meant the parson and wouldn't pry for more details.

"Speaking of a certain someone...."

Kin released his breath. Thankfully, Doc seemed to be on a mission.

"Listen." Doc said. "I'm here because Parson Clay has come down very sick. I need to know who you may have spoken to before you came out here today?"

Kin shrugged. "I was in the alehouse for a bit last night. But this morning I came straight here without seeing anyone. Well, other than Tommy. He was already up by the time I left the house." Come to think of it, it was odd that PC hadn't already been up when he left today.

Doc rubbed a hand along his jaw and seemed to be pondering.

Kin felt his concern mount. "How sick is PC?"

Doc slapped his horse's reins against one palm. "I think he has the measles. You ever had them?"

Kin nodded." Had them twice when I was a kid. One time was a lot worse than the other."

Doc blew out a sigh of relief. "That likely means you had both types. Which means the chances of you passing it along are much lower. That's a relief. Because I could really use your help."

Kin stuffed the rag into his back pocket. "Happy to help anyway I can. What can I do?"

"Aurora grew concerned when PC didn't show up for their weekly music preparation this morning. She went into the parsonage. She's never had measles, so I have placed her under quarantine. She can't leave the cabin. For that reason, I need to call a town meeting to see if I can find a woman who has had measles to stay with her there."

Kin grinned. PC would be fit to be tied over such a breech in propriety. But then, so would Aurora. After her original foray into folly when she arrived in town posing as a boy, she'd swung completely to the other end of the pendulum and gone out of her way to conform with expectations. She really must have been concerned to go into the parsonage like that—even with Tommy there. He couldn't help a chuckle. Imagine how flustered she was right about now! Oh, he was going to have fun giving her a hard time about this one!

Doc cleared his throat and quirked one brow.

Kin composed his features. "Okay. So, you need me to ride around and spread the word about the town meeting?"

Doc nodded.

"What time do you want folks to arrive?"

Doc was already reining his horse towards the south. "Let's say three o'clock this afternoon. I'll take all the homes towards the south and the east. You handle the north and west."

"Will do." Kin saddled and mounted his horse. He put his heels to his mount's flanks and rode out, but he was still chuckling as he did so.

Aurora was definitely going to hear about this from him!

Chapter 4

Maude Carver sat with her brothers near the fire they had built in the Kastains' yard. Kane had bagged a wild boar, and they were rendering the fat into lard and getting ready to set most of the meat to smoking. Kane had insisted this was a way for them to bless the Kastains for giving them such a good deal on renting the room in their barn, but Maude was just glad she would be around to eat some of it too. Her mouth watered at the thought of smoked pork—fried with a little fatback—and green beans and mashed potatoes on the side... My, she missed Ma's home cooking.

She stirred the pot of lard and watched Kane and Seth add the roof to the smokehouse with the help of Aiden Kastain. Kane had constructed the smokehouse from a hollowed-out log. He and Seth had stood it upright and then driven long pegs through it to form shelves to place the meat on. The pegs could be removed so that each shelf could be layered with meat before the next pegs were added for another layer of meat. Her brother was pretty ingenious, even if she would probably never say so to his face.

When Kin Davis rode into the yard, Maude straightened and smoothed her skirts. When Seth gave her an eye-roll and a grin, she felt her face heat. Despite Seth's teasing, she couldn't resist returning her attention to the rider.

No matter how handsome the man was, he clearly didn't have eyes for her. She'd seen him paying special attention to Zoe Kastain. And once or twice to Aurora McClure, who lived at the Rodante spread a few miles from here. But he'd never even so much as given her a second glance.

And today didn't appear to be any different.

Kin swung down from his horse and strode toward Kane, hand outstretched. "Howdy."

"Davis." Kane took his hand and gave him a nod. "I believe Mrs. Kastain and her daughter Belle headed into town to their shifts at the diner."

Kin rubbed his chin with the back of one hand and assessed the smokehouse. "They'll have heard the news already, then. I can't stay. Just dropping by to let everyone know that Doc has called for a town meeting to be held in the church at three this afternoon."

The two puppies that Aidan had brought home from the trip to Seattle cavorted onto the hard-packed dirt in front of the barn, yapping and tumbling over one another. Jinx dashed around the corner of the building and dove into the fray as well. For a moment, all three dogs yapped at the top of their voices, and then Jinx tumbled onto his back and let the puppies pin him down. All three dogs paused in their play, tongues lolling, to stare at the humans who stared back at them.

"Cute pups," Kin said. "Where'd they come from?"

"I rescued 'em in Seattle. But Ma says I can't keep 'em." Aidan hung his head for a just a split second before he jerked it up, eyes bright. "You don't want one of 'em, do you, Kin? I know you'd take real good care of one."

Kin chuckled and shook his head. "'Fraid I can't take one, A. I'm heading to Seattle myself, sooner than later."

Maude's ears perked up. He was?

Kin's feet shuffled as if he hadn't actually meant to let his revelation slip. He motioned to the Appaloosa in the corral. "I thought Joe Rodante was keeping the horse?"

As if it recognized it was the center of attention, the horse whinnied and pranced a circle around the enclosure. Its breath puffed out in roiling clouds.

Kane layered in the top shelf of meat. "I've been fetching it, mornings, bringing it here, then taking it back again, evenings. Teaching it to walk on a lead. Also helps it get used to voiced directions."

Kin nodded. "Smart. How's it behaving?"

Kane motioned for Seth to help him, and they lifted the roof of the smokehouse into place. "Got spunk. That's for certain. But smart too. Training's coming along right well. Even was able to stay in the saddle for a few seconds yesterday."

Maude snorted softly. The shortest few seconds she'd ever seen. When the horse had sent Kane sailing over the corral fence, she'd rushed to his side certain he'd, at the very least, have the wind knocked out of him, but he'd leapt to his feet almost before she reached him, laughing and pleased as punch that the Appaloosa had let him settle into the saddle. She rolled her eyes, even now. He'd be lucky if he ever got that stubborn critter trained.

Zoe Kastain appeared on the porch drying her hands with a towel. She'd been around a lot the past few days, since school had let out for the Christmas holiday. "Hi, Kin!" she called.

Kin's face lit up like a Christmas lantern as he spun to face her and strode to the porch.

Maude sighed and reminded herself to stir the lard.

Kane ruffled a hand over Aidan's hair. "Looks like we get to take a break this afternoon and ride into town. How'd you like that?"

"Boy howdy, would I!" Aidan spun in a circle, cheering his excitement.

Kane and Seth joined in, mimicking his excitement.

Maude wished they would hush so she could hear Zoe and Kin's conversation, but just as Aidan dashed off on Kane's instructions to go wash in the house, Kin mounted his horse. He reined toward the trail that led to the Rodante place, but he paused for just a moment, looked right at her, and tugged the brim of his hat in her direction. His lips tilted into a secretive smile, as if he might have been aware of her scrutiny this whole time.

She froze, and by the time she recovered enough to lift a hand in farewell, he'd already turned his amused attention to the trail.

She sighed and plunked her hands on her hips.

When she responded like that, what did she expect from the man? He likely thought her a cold hard shrew!

By the time Kin finished his rounds of the homes to the north and west and arrived at the church, Doc had the building warm, and several families were already gathered in the room. Kin removed his hat and shrugged out of his duster. He hung them on the pegs in the entry and then stepped past the partition and into the sanctuary. From across the room, Mrs. Griffin raised her brows at him. He grinned and gave her a nod. Her sleigh was completed. And it was a beauty. He'd built in a special compartment for Doc's medical bag, added a boot with locking shelves for his apothecary, and even added a back seat in case Doc needed to transport a patient somewhere.

A woman cleared her throat by his side. He glanced over to find Mrs. Holloway.

"Is my husband's horse still alive?" she whispered, keeping her focus on the main part of the room.

Kin chuckled. "Yes, ma'am. Saw it just a bit ago. Kane said the training is coming along right well."

She smoothed her hands over her skirt. "If I had known how much stress that present was going to cause me, I might have reconsidered my choice."

Kin tucked his fingers in his pockets. "It will all be worth it when the day comes. Don't you worry."

"I hope so!"

"What do you hope?" Marshall Zane stepped up beside his wife.

Her eyes flew wide and she gave Kin a look that pleaded for rescue.

"Your wife was just telling me how she hopes Christmas is going to be beautiful for everyone in Wyldhaven this year."

Marshall Zane settled a hand on his wife's shoulder. "My Jac. Always thinking of everyone's happiness. One of the reasons I fell in love with her." He smiled down at her.

Something about the look raised a lump in Kin's throat. He tore his gaze to the floor. "I'll just mosey to the back so there will be plenty of seats for everyone." The couple was so consumed with each other, that they didn't even seem to notice his departure. He supposed that was the way it ought to be. But it amused him to see the normally gruff, all-business marshal, devolve into a puddle of sentimentality whenever his wife was around.

Would there be a woman who turned him to mush like that someday? Hang fire, he hoped not!

He strode to the back wall and leaned against it, propping his foot up behind himself as he studied the room.

Of course, the Hines family was here. And right on the front row. Mrs. Hines wouldn't fail to attend a town meeting. She might miss out on some juicy bits of gossip to pass on to the people who came to shop in the mercantile. Next to them sat the Kings. The Kastains were there and the new Carver family. He couldn't withhold a grin as he remembered the surprise on Maude Carver's face when he tipped his hat to her earlier.

Since he was behind her and off to one side now, he allowed himself to study her. She was petite, but her every action showed she was a woman who could hold her own if it ever came down to it. On the other hand, she hadn't handled her brother's illness in the best manner. Stealing from folk didn't sit right with him, but he had plenty of skeletons in his own closet, so maybe he oughtn't be so judgmental about that. In the end, they'd come around to doing the right thing. She was slender but filled out it all the right places, and that hair... Had he ever seen a color quite like it? It reminded him of maple leaves in the fall. And with those soft eyes of hers, she was fetching. Right fetching.

Jackson Nolan settled against the wall next to him. He glanced from Maude, to Kin, and back again with a knowing grin on his face." You ain't the only one to notice the new girl in town."

Kin did his best to look nonchalant. He shrugged one shoulder. "I'll be leaving soon." He had no desire to fight Jackson over a girl he wasn't really interested in. Looking and acting were two different things.

Jackson gave him a squint. "First I heard. Where you off to?"

Kin adjusted his boot to a more comfortable position on the wall. "Think I'm going to search out work in Seattle."

"When you leavin'?"

Kin shrugged again. "Few days, maybe." Truth was, he hadn't quite decided yet.

"What!?" Jackson folded his arms and thankfully returned his scrutiny to the main part of the room. "Well, I wish you all the best. I'd come with you, except Pa would never let me."

Kin pondered on that. He supposed that was one benefit to no longer having a pa. Except... He swallowed. PC had been more of a pa to him than his own pa had been. Guilt piled atop his appreciation as he thought about the reason for this meeting.

He had known PC was sick. Why hadn't he checked on him before he had left the house this morning? If something happened to the man, he'd never be able to forgive himself.

At the front of the room, Doc called the meeting to order. He explained about PC maybe having the measles, and a ripple of horror filtered through the room.

Kin gritted his teeth and tried not to think about how deadly measles could be.

Doc explained that once you've had the measles you couldn't catch them a second time, and how Aurora had been concerned when the parson didn't show up this morning and had gone in to check on him. "She's there at the parsonage with him now," he said.

From the front row, Mrs. Hines gasped. She and Mrs. King exchanged a look.

Doc cleared his throat. "The lad Tommy was in the home the whole time." He gave special emphasis to those last two words, his gaze drilling right into the two women on the front row.

Kin felt the tension in his shoulders. He would like to properly educate those two. If either of them even so much as whispered a hint of scandal about either PC or Aurora, he would give them a piece of his mind. Because neither the parson nor Aurora would stoop to anything immoral, and the whole town knew it.

When Doc got to the part explaining that he needed to go out to Camp Sixty-Three and Aurora was under quarantine and needed someone who had previously had the measles to stay with her and help tend the parson, the room fell completely silent.

If Kin knew the townspeople, either Charlotte Callahan or Mrs. Griffin would have been the first to volunteer. But Mrs. Callahan had been working like crazy making desserts to sell in the boardinghouse diner, and he knew she'd taken several private orders that she had to fulfill before Christmas. And Mrs. Griffin had baby Ellery to care for. Mrs. Holloway would also volunteer, except here right before Christmas, she had quite a bit of sewing to complete for the presents that townsfolk had ordered from her. Mrs. King might volunteer, if not for Mrs. Hines sitting by her side. And Mrs. Hines likely wouldn't step into the parsonage for the next two years for fear of contracting measles.

Zoe Kastain had told him earlier this afternoon, that she had never had the measles before. And her mom and Belle both were needed to work their shifts at the diner. So, who did that leave?

He blinked. Maude Carver was suddenly standing, hand slightly raised.

Doc acknowledged her with a smile. "You've had measles?"

She nodded. "When I was a kid."

"Excellent! I know you are new to our community, and we appreciate your help." Doc glanced back at Kin. "Can you escort Maude up to the parsonage?"

Chapter 5

Preston woke, feeling like a new man other than a pounding ache in his head. But exhaustion lay on him like a lead blanket.

He squeezed the bridge of his nose and tried to think what day it might be. Hadn't he fallen on the floor? How had he gotten back in his bed? How long had he slept? Was Tommy okay? Kin would likely have returned and be taking care of him by now. Still...he'd best check.

"Tommy?" The word croaked from his throat, but at least it no longer felt like he was downing razor blades every time he swallowed.

The door creaked open, and, to his surprise, it was Aurora, not Tommy, who poked her head inside. "You're awake!" She smiled cheerily. "How are you feeling?"

"Better. Thirsty."

"Of course. Here." She strode quickly to the bedside table and lifted a glass. She sank down next to him. "Can you sit up a little?" She leaned across him to grab the other pillow.

As she propped it behind him and held the glass for him to drink, he studied her. He frowned.

First, what was she doing in his house? And in his bedroom, no less? Even if he was fully covered beneath a mound of covers, his parishioners would certainly not understand.

Second, why did she have such distractingly beautiful eyes and lips that tempted a man to wonder what they might feel like? Taste like?

He pulled his head back from the glass and shuttered his eyes. Yes. This was better. Much less temptation with his eyes closed.

"Did you get enough?"

He nodded. And yet, where one thirst had just been quenched, another of a much more personal nature had just been ignited. He clenched his fists beneath the covers.

She laid a hand across his forehead. "Your fever is much improved." She said the words like she might say 'Your forming of letters is much improved' to a child just learning to write.

The tone set his teeth on edge. He wasn't an invalid that he needed her here helping him.

"When I saw you on the floor earlier, it really gave me quite a fright."

His eyes flew open. "You found me? What were you doing in here?" Too late, he realized his frustration had made his tone sound angry. It was this sudden confounded attraction. He was a man of the cloth! Attraction to a woman, especially one he served with each Sunday, wasn't a freedom he was at liberty to enjoy.

Not to mention his past. He'd hate to bring danger into another woman's life. The thought of Poppy made his jaw ache as an old familiar regret tugged for his attention.

Aurora stood and clunked his half-full cup back onto the nightstand. "If you must know, when you didn't show up for our meeting this morning, I worried that something was wrong, so I came to check on you and Tom. And it's a good thing I did too! You were passed out on the floor right there!" She stomped to the door and paused to give him a glower. "I'll be out here preparing dinner. Just call if you need anything else."

She left without so much as a backward glance, and Preston realized she'd left him with more questions than answers. Had she been the one who'd helped Doc get him back into bed? What did she think of a man who couldn't even remain on his own two feet?

He wanted to groan.

This business of being ill was not something he enjoyed. Definitely not.

Kin nodded to Doc that he'd be happy to escort Maude to the parsonage.

Since he'd had what Doc claimed were both kinds of measles as a kid, he had planned to continue sleeping in his room at the parsonage. But now, it looked like maybe he and Tommy would be giving up their beds for a couple of girls.

As the meeting broke up, Kane Carver said a few quiet words to his sister, and then he and Seth headed out. Maude stood to one side of the room, waiting quietly for him. Kin said goodbye to Jackson Nolan, retrieved his hat, and swung on his coat. He swept a gesture to the doors, indicating she should precede him.

She gave a little dip of her knees and then headed outside. The church steps were still very icy, and, without thought, he took her elbow to assist her. When they reached the bottom, she gave him a little glance before she stepped away from him.

He was a little disappointed. He'd thought she might flirt with him, at least a little. Maybe he'd misunderstood her scrutiny this morning. But really, what did it matter? He'd only been hoping for a little entertainment. He wasn't interested in her. He'd be leaving town in just a few days, anyhow.

Right. From here on, he would keep his hands to himself. He thrust them deep into the pockets of his duster and pointed the way to the path up the hill.

"Just there."

"Thank you."

What did one talk about with a woman, anyhow? Sure, he'd had plenty of conversations with Zoe and Aurora, but they were more like sisters.

He was still pondering what topic to broach when from behind them, he heard a shout. "Hey Kin!"

In all honesty, he'd never before been so happy to hear someone yell his name.

He turned to see Jackson Nolan jogging up the hill toward them. Jackson cast Maude a quick glance as he panted, "I forgot that Pa wanted me to ask you if I could borrow your...shovel!"

Kin turned his snort of laughter into a sneeze. And he could tell by Jackson's red neck that he knew just exactly what that sneeze had been.

"Your pa wants to borrow my shovel."

"That's what I said, ain't it?"

Kin thrust his tongue into his cheek and nodded. "All right." With his hands still in the pockets of his duster, he swept a gesture to Maude. "This here is Maude Carver. Maude, meet Jackson Nolan."

Jackson was grinning from ear to ear when he stretched his hand in Maude's direction. "Pleased to meet you, Maude Carver." He swept her with a glance from her head to her toes and back again, hanging onto her hand the whole time.

Maude was nearly as red as Jackson by the time she had extracted her hand from his.

Jackson strode along jauntily beside them. "So where are you from originally, Maude?"

She swept a gesture to the east. "Over Montana way." The words were so soft-spoken that both Kin and Jackson had to lean in to hear them.

"I've always thought Montana must be a beauty of a place," Jackson said. "I plan to go visit someday."

Maude's eyes lit up like the sun had just risen. "Oh! It is beautiful! Just across the valley from our house, the Bitterroots stretched across the sky. My, I do miss that view."

Kin surreptitiously dropped back and let Jackson and Maude continue their conversation.

And lo and behold, once they reached the parsonage and Kin and Maude were standing on the porch, Jackson bid them farewell, and started down the trail.

"Don't you want me to get you that shovel?" Kin hollered loudly.

"Oh!" Jackson turned back, face blazing red.

Beside Kin, Maude gave a little titter.

Jackson gripped the back of his neck, grinning because he knew he'd been caught. "You know...I just remembered where Pa's missing shovel got put. I don't think we'll be needing yours after all."

Kin lifted his chin on a laugh. "Kind of figured as much." He turned for the door but paused because Jackson and Maude were exchanging a long, lingering look. Finally, he rolled his eyes and cleared his throat. "You coming?"

"Yes." She spun to face him, hands clasped before her.

Kin pushed open the door and held it for her. They both stepped inside.

Aurora stood at the kitchen stove cooking up something that smelled tantalizing. And dash it all, if she wasn't pretty as a picture.

"Hey, sis." He greeted her as he closed the door and shrugged out of his coat. Maybe teasing her a little would get his mind back into a sibling frame of mind. "Or should I say brother?" He chuckled and gave her a wink.

She rolled her eyes at him and stuck out her tongue. Then her gaze settled on Maude. "Oh, it's you! I'm so glad. I've been wanting to get to know you a little better ever since you came to town." Aurora approached, hands outstretched, and Maude looked a little wide-eyed when Aurora enfolded her into an embrace.

Kin hung his hat on its peg and roughed his fingers through his hair as he watched the two. Aurora didn't know a stranger, and it appeared that Maude didn't have an outgoing bone in her entire body.

Aurora was already introducing Tommy. "And the parson... he's sleeping in the bedroom there. You'll meet him later, I'm sure." Aurora motioned for Maude to follow her to the kitchen. "Do come in. I've just put a pot roast on, and I need to mix up a batch of biscuits. Then they'll be all ready to just add milk when it's time to mix them for dinner. Do you like to cook?"

Maude's answer, again, was so soft that Kin couldn't make it out. But he was glad to let Aurora take charge of making conversation with her.

He had just decided to head into his bedroom and catch up on some of his reading when Aurora spun back to face him.

"Oh! Kin! I almost forgot. The parson keeps mumbling about a puppy. I think he didn't get one some Christmas when he was a boy." She shrugged. "I was having a hard time making out exactly what he was saying. But I did catch that he wants a puppy. Do you know of anyone in the area that has any?"

Kin couldn't have been more surprised if she had pulled out a gun and shot him.

PC wanting a puppy? There couldn't be anything further from the truth. Whatever had given her that idea?

"Are you certain the parson said he wanted a puppy? He *is* feverish you know."

Aurora fluttered a hand through the air. "That's just it. People let down their inhibitions in situations like that and tell you what they really want from their heart. I'm telling you, I heard him say he wanted a puppy that he didn't get for Christmas."

Kin gripped the back of his neck. How was he going to get the parson out of this one? He was still trying to decide what tack to take when Maude spoke up. "Aiden Kastain has two pups that he needs homes for. He rescued them in Seattle while they were there for Zoe to take her teaching exam. Right cute little things."

Aurora flapped her hands and hopped up and down. "Perfect!" She clasped her fingers under her chin and gave Kin a pleading look. "Do you think you could go and pick one out for me tomorrow since I won't be able to go? He called it a her."

Kin frowned. "Who called what a her?"

"The parson. When he was mumbling. He called the puppy he didn't get a her. So, if one of the pups is female, bring that one. If they're both females, bring the cutest one."

Kin's mouth gaped. The parson would be all sorts of bent out of shape if Kin followed through on her request. But Aurora didn't give him the opportunity to decline. She bounced toward the kitchen, as excited as a calf on a frosty morning.

Kin sighed. If he did bring her a pup to give to the parson, he'd better plan on moving to Seattle sooner rather than later; otherwise PC would have him doing every menial chore around the place in retaliation.

Maybe the day after Christmas.

Yes. That would be a good day to leave. It would give him one last day to enjoy a high point with all the people who had been so good to him in Wyldhaven.

Chapter 6

Aurora couldn't have been happier when Parson Clay emerged from his room two days later as she was cooking breakfast. He was dressed but still looked a little pale.

He did a double-take upon seeing her at the stove, paused, and propped his hands on his hips. His inscrutable gaze settled on her and remained.

"Morning." She pressed her lips together as she turned the sausage patties. Was he surprised to see her here? She'd been taking care of him for the past several days, so she didn't see why he would be.

"Morning." He continued to watch her. And now a set of butterflies were giving wing in her stomach. Was something out of place? She glanced the length of herself. No. Other than the fact that she wore a grease-splattered apron, she hadn't forgotten to do up a button or anything like that. Maybe it was her hair? She blew at a loose strand. Perhaps. But it wasn't like she could pause her cooking to run and redo the braid she'd looped around her head this morning.

Maude, who was churning butter in the corner, paused and studied the man for a moment and then, with a smirk, continued her task.

"Morning, P-parson." Tommy smiled hugely from his seat at the dining table.

Aurora determined to put this new tension she was feeling on the back burner. She hurried to the cupboard to fetch a mug so she could pour Preston a cup of coffee.

Behind her, she heard him pull out a chair at the table.

She took a calming breath as she filled his mug. This was her fault. They'd always shared an easy camaraderie. If she hadn't let her emotions run away with her, this tension wouldn't be crackling in the air. She had never spoken a word of her feelings to him, but he must have sensed something amiss. So, she would work doubly hard to return her frame of mind to one proper for a young woman to feel for her parson. Appreciation for the Word that he brought to her each week and nothing more.

Speaking of appreciation, they all had things to be thankful for this morning.

Doc had come by the day before and proclaimed that the parson was doing so well that he must have had only the German measles after all. And everyone had breathed a sigh of relief. It would have been terrible to have an outbreak of the more serious variety just before Christmas. The parson figured he'd contracted the sickness out in one of the logging camps, but he didn't know which one. That had been one of Doc's main concerns.

As she approached the table with his cup, she determined to converse as if nothing had changed between them. Because nothing *had* changed. "Are you sure you should be up? You still don't look the best." She only realized how insulting that might sound after he gave her a grumpy squint. "Sorry." She set the coffee before him and hurried to rescue the eggs before they burnt. A hint of smoke touched her nostrils. Tommy's oatmeal! She snatched the pot from the heat. Goodness, this fluster was so unlike her. Thankfully, the oatmeal was only singed a little on the bottom of the pan. She'd add an extra teaspoon of sugar to help cover the taste, and Tommy wouldn't likely even notice.

Parson Clay lifted the cup in a little salute. "Thank you." He took a couple of sips and then scrubbed a hand over his face. "What day is it?"

"Monday." She held her breath, knowing what was coming.

He winced. "I missed Sunday services?"

"Yes. But don't worry; Sheriff Callahan read a few verses of Scripture and gave a short message." Not that she or Maude or Tommy had been able to attend. But she left that part out. She determined to keep things positive. "I'm so glad you are feeling better before Christmas. Doc says as soon as you are able to care for yourself, that Maude and I can leave. I'll stay at the Kastain place in the barn with Maude for a few days till he sees if we are going to get sick. Apparently German measles are bad for expectant women and—" Now her nerves had her blathering things that oughtn't be told. "Well, never mind about that."

Preston studied her, brow furrowed slightly. "What?"

Her face flushed, and she quickly scooped food onto a plate. It wasn't even appropriate to discuss such things with other women, so what had made her blurt it in mixed company?

As she approached the table with his plate, his gaze roved over her face, that quizzical frown still on his brow.

Heavens! Was her face as red as it felt?

"Here. Do you like scrambled eggs? The sausage was in your icebox. I hope it's okay that I cooked it. You weren't saving it for anything special, were you?" She set it before him and hoped he didn't notice how the plate rattled a little against the table before she snatched her hands back and wiped them on her apron.

Preston was still scrutinizing her with those amazing dark-lashed eyes of his. But thankfully, he must have decided to let the matter drop. He lifted his fork. "This is perfect. Thank you."

"I w-want oatmeal," Tommy proclaimed.

"Yes!" Aurora blew out a breath of relief as she spun toward to the sideboard. "Coming right up, Tommy."

When she set the bowl before Tommy, she noted that Preston hadn't started eating yet. "Is everything all right?"

He nodded. "Soon as you and Maude have your plates and are seated, we can say grace."

Why did he suddenly make her so nervous? If she wasn't all a-jitter she would have thought of setting the table properly. But he'd caught her off guard, emerging from his room just as she finished cooking. "Yes. Of course."

She spun to fetch plates, but Maude was already there holding a filled one out to her along with utensils. There was a hint of humor about the girl's eyes.

Aurora lifted her brows and mouthed her thanks, and then they both sat.

The parson bowed his head. "Our Father, we thank you for this food, and we ask..."

As he continued the prayer, she wondered that she had never noticed how deep and mellow his voice was before. It washed over her like lavender oil. Calming and relaxing. She felt her jitters easing away.

She wondered if Kin had picked up the puppy yet. He'd left earlier this morning to do so. He still didn't seem to agree with her assessment that the parson had been mumbling about wanting a puppy. But she knew what she'd heard. So, despite the fact that Kin had been trying to talk her out of the gift for the last couple days, she remained determined that the parson ought to have a happy Christmas. After all, he had hoped to spend the holiday with his family back east, so the least she could do was try to bring him a little joy. She'd insisted that Kin fetch her the pup and let the consequences of the gift be on her head. He would see; the parson was going to love it!

She wondered though... Was today the right day to give him the puppy? After all, he was just coming out of an illness and might not feel up to dealing with the rambunctious antics of a scrappy pup.

Besides, it wasn't yet Christmas. She made a quick decision. She would wait to give the dog to him until Christmas day. No. Giving it to him on Christmas might seem too intimate. Christmas Eve, then. That would be perfect. That would give him a couple more days to recuperate.

A sharp pain slashed through her shin. "Ow!" She jolted. And then her face flamed anew.

Apparently, the prayer had been over for who knew how long, and she'd been sitting there with her head still bowed.

From across the table, Maude was laughing at her in that silent way of hers.

Aurora didn't even dare to glance at the parson. She simply lifted her fork and tucked into her food. The sooner the meal was over and the dishes washed, the sooner she and Maude could make their escape.

And maybe once she was away from Preston's constant presence, she would be able to put a damper on these runaway emotions of hers.

Standing in the yard at the Kastain place, Kin did his best to bite back his humor as Aidan fawned over the pup he'd come to pick up. Aurora had said she wanted a female or the cutest one. And as luck would have it, the female fit both criteria.

"The parson is a good, God-fearing man," Aidan crooned to the puppy. He had the poor dog clasped under one arm and was petting her so hard that her ears laid down. "You know, on account of he's a parson and all. So, he's gonna take real good care of you. And Kin lives there too, so if you ever need anything you can just go ask him, and he'll help ya."

Kin swept a hand over his mouth and met Zoe's amused glance above her brother's head. He squatted down before the boy and reached out to adjust the dog to a more secure position in Aidan's arms. "Actually, I'm not going to be there for much longer." Which reminded him, he really needed to have that conversation with PC that he'd been putting off.

"Wait. What?" Zoe plunked her hands on her hips.

Too late, he realized he'd let the cat out of the bag. Maybe if he just ignored her, she'd let it go. He continued to talk to Aidan. "But Tommy will be there, and he's real gentle with animals. I bet he'll even let her sleep at the end of his bed."

Zoe's feet shuffled. "Kin Davis, whatever are you going on about?"

Kin stood and shrugged one shoulder. "Think I'll head to Seattle and see if I can find some work. I've about tapped out my resources here. Same people keep giving me odd jobs, and sometimes I feel like they are giving them just to give me something to do. I don't want to take advantage like that. Besides"—he glanced across the snow-covered field beside the barn—"it's just...time to move on. PC has cared for me long enough."

From the corner of his eye, he saw Zoe tilt her head. "You know he's happy to do that."

"Yeah." He gripped the back of his neck. He said the word, but he wasn't so certain. Truth was, he and PC had butted heads more often than not in the past few months. Mostly because PC didn't like some of his choices. The man would never be happy until he'd taken a knee and confessed his need of a Savior. And he just wasn't certain he'd ever come to that point. Religion was fine for some, but he didn't need it. Moving on would just be easier. He needed a little space to breathe.

"Well." Zoe gave a definitive nod. "We are going to have a going-away shindig for you then."

Kin pulled a face. "Please don't go to the trouble. No one will miss me much. It's not like I contribute a lot to the town."

"Kin Davis, listen to you spouting nonsense! No. You are not making an escape without everyone having the chance to say goodbye. You just leave the details up to me." She flapped a hand at her brother. "Aidan, I know saying goodbye is hard, but you can run see the pup every Sunday after church, if you want to. I'm sure Kin needs to get on his way."

Aidan gave the pup a kiss on the top of her head and finally handed her over. Large tears pooled in his eyes, bringing a lump to Kin's throat. With the puppy tucked into the crook of one arm, he ruffled a hand over the boy's head. "It takes a real man to make the best decisions for his animals. You've done the right thing."

Aidan swiped an arm across his eyes and sniffed.

Behind Aidan's back, Zoe made a little shooing motion that told Kin it was time to cut the strings. He tucked the puppy into his largest saddlebag and then swung onto his mount. His horse swung its head around to eye the puppy for a moment, but then must have decided the creature was harmless.

Kin tipped his hat in Zoe's direction, but as he rode out of the yard, he sighed. When Zoe got a bee in her bonnet there was no stopping her, so he didn't suppose there was much he could do.

But he wished he'd been able to escape town without a bunch of hoopla.

He was only halfway back to town when he met Maude and Aurora hurrying along the road toward him.

Aurora gasped and marveled over the cuteness of the puppy as she lifted it from his saddlebag, while Maude stood back in that quiet way of hers.

Aurora held the puppy up before her. "Aren't you just the most adorable thing ever?" she cooed.

The puppy wriggled and swiped at her face with a pink tongue, which sent Aurora into a fit of giggles.

Kin smiled at the sight. Of course, the pup loved Aurora. Who spent more than five minutes in her presence without falling in love with her?

Except for him. Well, he loved her like a sister. But maybe there was something wrong with him. Why wasn't he ready to settle down and find a good woman yet? Maybe he never would be. Maybe all those beatings he'd taken from Pa had broken something inside him.

He gritted his teeth and pushed the thoughts aside. "Aren't we taking her to the parsonage?"

Aurora shook her head and tucked the puppy close. "I've decided to let the parson recover for a few more days. I'll give her to him on Christmas Eve. Until then, I'll just take her back to the Kastains' with me. I'll be staying there for a few days." With that, she waggled her fingers in farewell, and she and Maude continued down the road.

Kin rolled his eyes. If she'd known that this morning, it would have saved him from making that slip about leaving in front of Zoe.

Maybe he wasn't so broken after all. Maybe he was just smart.

Women were just compact bundles of trouble wrapped up in pretty packaging.

Chapter 7

By Christmas Eve, Preston Clay felt like a new man. It amazed him how a couple days of good food and rest had rejuvenated his body. He would count this as a Christmas blessing—especially since he had so many things to do between today and tomorrow.

The first of which were the gifts he wanted to deliver to a family out at Camp Sixty-Four. They had three of the cutest kids he'd ever come across. And they had wormed their way into his heart. Mostly because both the parents were taking in the Word he shared each month and actually putting it into practice. They'd never heard the truths of the Scriptures before they'd started attending his services, and it gave him great joy to see the Word of God flourishing so effectively in the lives of this little family.

Thus, he was doubly thankful to be feeling better because, for several months, he had been whittling toys for their three children for Christmas gifts. He would take them out tomorrow. He only hoped that he would be able to deliver them without word getting to other families who also had children. He didn't want to hurt anyone's feelings by making them feel left out, and yet he couldn't possibly have presents for every child in every camp. But that was a worry for tomorrow. For today, he needed to get them wrapped.

With Tommy painting quietly in his book, Preston went out to the table in the yard with the carvings, the roll of brown paper, and the spool of pink and white twine that he had purchased at the mercantile. He swiped a section clear of snow.

Often in the summertime, they would eat out here. But today, he simply wanted to be outdoors for a bit of fresh air after being cooped up for so long. Though there was still snow on the ground, the day was unseasonably warm. And it felt good to be in the sunshine. Who knew when they would have another sunny day around these parts?

He had just finished tying the last bow on the last package when he heard footsteps on the path up from the church. He glanced up.

Aurora strode toward him, her brown hair fluttering from beneath a knit cap.

His pulse spiked, and then his teeth slammed together. Tarnation!

He'd hoped that once she moved out of his house, he would be able to get her out of his mind. Yet just the sight of her treading the path toward him had all the confusion resurfacing.

He squinted, then propped his hands on his hips. Was that a dog in her arms? Since when had Aurora gotten a dog?

She looked up then, caught his scrutiny, and flushed prettily.

He wished she wouldn't do that, because it made him envision things like caressing his thumb over those rosy cheeks of hers.

"Good evening." With the dog cuddled up beneath her chin and her green eyes sparkling at him above its head, she presented a heartwarming picture.

One that shouldn't be warming his heart at all. He dipped his chin. "Aurora."

Her feet shuffled, and she suddenly glanced down shyly.

He gritted his teeth. This new tension between them was all his fault. He never should have let himself think of her in any way other than as a friend and fellow servant of God.

She lifted him a quick look before returning her scrutiny to a patch of snow that remained on the table. "When I was tending you...you said something about not getting a puppy for Christmas, in 1882, I think it was." Without another word she stretched out her arms to set the dog on the table before him.

His brows shot up. What in the world?

"I...I know you had wanted to go back east to see your family this holiday. And I'm sure it was a great disappointment when you were prevented from doing so. And I wanted you to have a happy Christmas. To that end..." She swept a little gesture to the dog. "Merry Christmas, Pres—Parson Clay."

For the first time in a very long time, Preston found himself speechless. He glanced down at the puppy, for he suddenly realized that it was indeed a pup and not a full-grown dog.

The puppy looked up at him, mouth slightly open as if it were smiling and happy to meet him.

He curved one hand around the back of his neck. Drat, but it was a cute little thing. Mostly white with black splotches and one ear that didn't seem to want to stand upright. Yet...he had absolutely no recollection of any disappointment over not getting a pup as a boy.

He fought through the haze of memories from the days when he'd been fevered and laid up in bed. What had he said that had given her such an impression?

He remembered first thinking that she was Ma. And he'd been asking Ma about—the realization hit him. Poppy!

A chuckle burst free before he could stop it.

Aurora clasped her fingers beneath her chin in that way she had when something thrilled her. "Oh! I knew you would be happy. I'm elated."

He reined in his humor and roughed a hand through his hair. He really ought to tell her to march this dog back to wherever she'd gotten it from. He didn't have time for a dog! He was constantly on the go. Traveling out to the camps. Not to mention that it was just one more mouth to feed on his meager salary.

But, hang it, one look at the sparkle in her eyes and he found himself saying, "Thank you. It's very cute."

"*She's* very cute. And yes, she is."

Perfect. Not only had she given him a dog, but a female one that might one day saddle him with a litter of puppies. "Does she have a name?"

Aurora scratched the dog behind one ear. "Well, of course you can name her anything you want. But she's a scrappy little thing with a lot of joy and energy. If I were to name her, I'd name her Allegra."

He frowned. He had no idea why that was a good name for a dog with 'joy and energy.'

Aurora withdrew her hand and tugged her coat closer about herself. "It's a musical term, you see. Well, really, the term is allegro, but that's a male ending. So, a female needs the feminine ending..." Her voice trailed away. "I sense you aren't as thrilled with her as I first thought. Kin tried to tell me you didn't want a dog, but you truly did say you wanted one when you were out of your mind with fever. Was I wrong?"

He'd said he wanted Poppy? Confound it, that was no good. When was his heart going to get the message that she was obviously sticking to her guns? And all for many of the reasons that he'd been telling himself earlier were the wherefores of why he should never get married. Poppy didn't want a pauper. She didn't want a teetotaler. And she certainly didn't want a man of the cloth.

Realizing Aurora still waited for his answer, Preston considered his reply. He wouldn't hurt her for the world. And that meant that suddenly he very much wanted this dog. "No. I'm just—you've taken me by surprise is all. Allegra will be a perfect addition to my life."

"So, you're not upset?"

"Upset? How could I be upset about such a cute little critter?" He reached to pet the dog at the same moment she did. His hand fell on top of hers. Neither of them moved. They simply stood across the table from one another with his hand over top of hers.

He'd never realized before that she had a callus on her chin. Likely from the violin she often played at church. A vision of him taking her face in his hands and placing a kiss on that callus popped into his mind. He pushed it away.

Not today. But someday. And if he was surprised by the thought, it was no more than he was surprised by the realization that he cared for her deeply, and that those feelings were not as recent as he'd first thought.

He let his thumb caress over her fingers.

She flushed prettily as she snatched her hand from beneath his and shoved it in her coat pocket. "Merry Christmas, Parson Clay."

She'd slipped earlier and almost said his name, and he suddenly very much wanted to hear her say it. "Preston. You can say it. I call you Aurora all the time."

She kicked at the snow. "That's different."

He tilted his head. "Just this once then, as part of my Christmas present."

With her toe still diligently working at digging that hole in the snow, she lifted him a look from beneath her brows. "Fine then. Merry Christmas, Preston."

He grinned. "Merry Christmas, Aurora."

Dear Reader,

I loved writing this first foray into Preston and Aurora's relationship. Their story is going to be the next full-length book in this series which will release next year called *Songs in the Night*. I can't wait to show you that cover and share their story!

If you enjoyed this novella, **please leave the book a review**. It doesn't have to be long, but every review helps spread the word, and the world needs more uplifting stories!

Wondering what's going to happen with Kin's send-off? And how all the Christmas presents are going to tie-up? The town of Wyldhaven always rallies around to support their own! And I'm sure you'll be pleased by how all these novella's tie together! I invite you to read the next episode of this series titled *Kin Davis's Christmas Send-Off* on the next page.

You can find all the books in the Wyldhaven series here on my website.

Merry Christmas!

Lynnette
BONNER

Kin Davis's Christmas Send-Off

Novella Seven
Wyldhaven

Chapter 1

Kin Davis woke on Christmas morning with a pickax of pain beating at the inside of his skull. He moaned and rolled over—onto something hard and cold. He pushed back and pried one eye open. An empty, brown, embossed-glass whiskey bottle lay on the bed beside him. The cork sat on the nightstand that stood between his and Tommy's beds.

Kin grunted and reached for it, but just that little movement made the room sway like a bough in a storm. He changed course, flopped back to his pillow, and clutched his head instead.

And what was that weight pinning his foot beneath the covers? He pushed at it to give his feet more room, but it didn't budge.

He lifted his head. Allegra, the black and white puppy Aurora had given to PC as a Christmas present yesterday, lay at the foot of his bed watching him. Her tail thumped up and down a few times, but other than that she didn't move.

He dropped his head back to the pillow. "Allegra. Bad girl. Get down." There was no force to the words however, and the puppy knew it. She didn't budge.

PC had consigned her to a crate in the living room, but Kin had a vague recollection of hauling her up onto the bed in the middle of the night because she had wandered into their room and wouldn't quit whimpering.

From across the room, Tommy giggled. "L-Legra likes to sleep on y-your bed."

"Yeah." Kin squeezed thumb and fingers to his temples.

"P-PC not g-gonna l-like that b-bottle."

Remembering the cork, Kin fumbled a hand for it without looking.

A fist pounded on the door, sending a railroad spike through Kin's temples.

"Merry Christmas, boys!" Parson Clay called, loudly. "Breakfast will be ready in five minutes."

Right. It was Christmas Day, and Zoe had organized that blasted going away party for him later this afternoon. He really needed to say something to the parson before then. He hadn't even told him he was leaving yet.

"I l-like breakfast."

Kin could hear Tommy scrambling out of bed and into his clothes.

Even the puppy gave a yap and jumped down from his bed. He heard its claws *scritch*ing across the boards of the wood floor, and then, in the next instant, a sound like tinkling water filled the room.

"Uh-oh!" Tommy exclaimed. "PC's not g-gonna l-like that either."

With a knot of frustration in his stomach, Kin lifted his head. Sure enough, the puppy had relieved herself just to one side of their bedroom door. His lip curled. "If that's her way of saying Merry Christmas, I hope she figures out a different way by this time next year."

Tommy laughed uproariously and slapped his thigh. "You f-funny, Kin."

Kin willed himself to push past the pain and swung his legs over the edge of his bed. He would have to clean that up, but for the moment, he couldn't bring himself to move. All he had the gumption to do was cradle his head in his hands. "I'll clean it, Tommy. Just go out carefully so you don't step in it."

Kin sat very still as the door creaked open and Tommy and the puppy left. From the nausea that roiled every time he moved, he might be cleaning up more than puppy leavings by the time he was through. Why did he do this to himself?

He heard movement by the door and glanced up.

Parson Clay stood in the frame, hands propped on either side. He swept Kin with a disappointed glance and then dropped his focus to the floor. "Tommy, bring me that puppy."

Kin didn't move all through the parson's scolding of the puppy, his putting it outside on the rope he had tied off to the front step yesterday, and the commotion that went on as PC had Tommy help him clean up the puddle.

Though he had planned to do it, in his current state, he was thankful that the parson had stepped in. He was also thankful that the puppy had jumped off his bed before offering her little Christmas surprise. The smell of the lye soap that the parson liked to use to scrub the floors was pungent, yet it had the smell of home about it.

Kin frowned. Had he come to think of this place as home? It certainly had been a better home for him than what Pa had provided after Ma's death. Ever since PC took him in, he'd had a warm bed and a full belly.

PC never said a word the whole time he cleaned and scrubbed the floor. Kin was still sitting on the edge of his bed with his head in his hands when he heard PC's distinctive footsteps approach and stop before him.

Kin winced against the light as he looked up.

PC stood with his hands on his hips, giving Kin that particular look he had whenever Kin had disobeyed one of his rules.

"I've tried to help you, Kin. Given you Truth. Given you the only answer there is to a happy life. But you keep throwing it all away." PC gripped the back of his neck, looking sorry to have to say his next words. "We can't keep doing things the way we've been doing them."

Kin felt his guilt slam home. PC was right. The man had done more for him than anybody had since Ma's death when he was twelve.

"I've got Tommy to think of now, too," PC continued. "He looks up to you, and the example you're setting for him isn't one I can let slide."

Kin lifted the empty whiskey bottle from beside his pillow and set it on the bedside table. "You're right. And that's something I've been meaning to talk to you about."

He worked his jaw back and forth trying to come up with the right words. He'd been planning to move to Seattle for months now, but the truth was, now that it came down to it... He glanced at the whiskey bottle. Living with the parson at least made him exercise some restraint. If he headed out on his own and went to Seattle, would he degenerate into the man Pa had been at the end?

Kin swallowed, suddenly realizing that was exactly what had been holding him back from making the announcement to PC. Sure, he'd mentioned his plans here and there to a few of his friends, but it was different to say those same words to this man who had essentially raised him for the past several years. The man who always made it so clear that Kin could do better. The man who'd never condoned but always forgiven.

"What's that?" The parson's question made him realize he had never finished his thought.

Outside, the puppy yapped to be let back in, and in the main room, Kin heard Tommy open the front door and coo softly to the puppy. Kin fiddled with the top edge of his blanket. "I'm leaving. Moving to Seattle." The brief flick of a glance he raised showed the parson's teeth clamped and a bit of a flinty look in his green eyes.

"I heard about the party. Wondered if you were even going to tell me. When are you planning on leaving?"

Kin felt his shirt pocket. He'd fallen into bed fully clothed the night before. Sure enough, his ticket was still there. "I leave tomorrow. Bought my seat on the train yesterday."

The parson roughed a hand through his hair, leaving several sections poking up at odd angles. "Right. Well, it's Christmas. You better come out and get some of my Christmas sausage pie. Then I have presents for you and Tommy." Without another word, he spun on his heel and stalked away.

Kin scrunched his eyes shut. He'd done it. There would be no getting out of this now—especially considering the parson seemed like he was through putting up with his drinking.

Kin flopped back onto the bed, but he only laid there for a couple seconds before the call of nature pressed for his attention. He sat up and scrubbed a hand over his face. Whooee! He could really stand some time with his toothbrush, too.

Chapter 2

After breakfast, PC declared that the dishes could soak in the sink for a few minutes. He took the chair by the fireplace and urged Kin and Tommy to sit on the settee.

But Kin knew what came next, and he had presents of his own to retrieve. He motioned for PC to give him a moment and then stepped into his room. From the bottom of his clothing chest, he withdrew two packages, one larger and heavier than the other, then returned to the main room and took his seat next to Tommy.

This year, there was no tree. Mostly because PC had been so sick and had only recuperated a couple days ago and because Kin hadn't thought of it. But neither he nor PC needed a tree, and Tommy didn't seem to miss it either. Had the poor simple-minded man ever had a tree on Christmas? They didn't know much about how Tommy was raised. He'd come to live with them when the outlaw gang he lived with had all been arrested.

Kin rubbed his palms down his denims. He should have thought of getting a tree. Tommy ought to have a tree.

PC cleared his throat and lifted his big brown Bible. Like he'd done every Christmas since Kin came to live with him, he read the Christmas story from the book of Luke.

Kin listened, but just like always, he found the story a bit implausible. Sure, the parson believed it was all true, and

Kin had sat through enough sermons to understand the gist of the message conveyed. He believed in God; he really did. And he believed God had plans for good men like the parson, Sheriff Reagan, Marshal Zane, Deputy Joe, or even simple-minded Tommy. But God didn't need a washout failure of a fellow like him.

The parson had preached a sermon not long ago about how the Bible declared that Moses and Abraham were both called friends of God, and how every person could be too. But Kin had no doubt in his mind...he was no friend of God. He doubted that the good Lord even knew who he was, except maybe to mark down another checkmark in the "failed" column next to his name.

PC snapped the Bible shut, and Kin realized his mind had wandered.

Beside him, Tommy rocked in excitement, hands pressed together between his knees. "Baby Jesus w-was b-born on C-Christmas!"

The parson smiled softly at him. "That's right. He was, Tommy. And why was he born?"

Tommy thought for a moment. "To d-die so our bad stuff d-don't c-count."

PC nodded. "That's right, Tommy. Anytime you do something you know you shouldn't, all you have to do is ask God, and He will forgive you."

"Tommy p-pray."

"That's right. And praying is just talking to God like you are talking to me right now." The parson grazed Kin with a glance.

He pressed his lips together and fiddled with the string tied around his top package. He was no fool. He could tell when PC was really speaking to him even though the words were directed at Tommy.

Prayer might be good for some people, but he was tough enough to make it on his own.

"W-we get p-presents now?" Tommy grinned hopefully.

PC chuckled and teased, "Presents? What presents?"

Tommy wasn't fooled. He laughed. "Th-those ones in the b-brown paper!"

Even Kin couldn't withhold a smile.

The parson looked over at him. "What do you think, Kin? Should we open presents now, or later when we get back from the Callahan's?"

"Hmmmm..." Kin rubbed his chin, pretending to be deep in thought.

Beside him, Tommy laughed all the more. He pounded his fists on his knees. "N-now!"

Kin ignored the throbbing in his skull and shrugged one shoulder. "I think Tommy's vote counts for more than yours and mine. I guess we have to do it now."

PC nodded. "Seems so."

"Yay!" Tommy thrust his hands in the air.

PC reached for the smaller of the two packages by his side. He handed it to Tommy. "All right, Tom-Tom. Open this one."

Tommy gleefully tore into the paper without bothering to untie the string. Inside was a wooden box with a couple of drawers. The top lid of the box was hinged along the back edge. At first, Tommy looked perplexed, but then he lifted the lid. "P-paints!" he exclaimed, dropping the lid back into place and clutching the package to his chest like a toddler hugging a kitten.

Kin grinned. He was glad he and PC had agreed together on what they should get Tommy. He lifted his package for Tommy. "And this is for you too."

"Another?!" Tommy tossed his set of paints down on the settee next to him, and snatched the package Kin held out. The paper on this package didn't last any longer than the other. "P-papers!"

Helping him finger one of the pages, Kin said, "It's special heavy paper so you can paint on it."

"I l-love it!" Tommy suddenly had tears in his eyes. "I ain't n-never g-got no p-presents on C-Christmas before."

Kin felt his jaw go slack. He exchanged a look with PC, wishing he had spent more money to get Tommy a few more presents.

PC seemed just as taken aback. Silence hung heavy in the room before he finally said, "Well, Christmas isn't all about the presents that we get, is it, Tommy?"

Tommy shook his head. "It's about Jesus b-being b-born."

"That is right. And now that you have Kin and me, we'll make sure you get a present each Christmas."

"Tommy l-like that." With a huge grin on his face, Tommy stroked his fingers over both his gifts, first one and then the other.

PC had a soft look about his eyes. "I know you do. Now... should we let Kin open his present? Or do you think I should take his back to the store?"

Tommy laughed. "K-Kin likes p-presents too."

Batting Tommy with the back of his hand, Kin pretended to take Tommy's gifts from him. "That's right, I sure do. In fact, I think I like your presents!"

Grinning as he hugged his paint and paper close, Tommy turned his back on Kin. "N-no, Kin! Y-you get y-your own p-presents!"

Lowering his volume, Kin leaned close to Tommy and eyed the parson across the room. "You think PC got me something good?"

Tommy giggled uproariously. "Y-you have to open it to f-find out."

Kin and PC exchanged a smile, and then the parson handed over the parcel. It was a little smaller than the one Tommy had gotten. Flexible, yet firm. Likely a book of some kind.

But there was something resigned about the pinched-lip look PC gave him.

Kin felt caution rise up inside him.

He slowly tugged the bow of the pink and white string off the package, then pressed the paper open. Inside lay a leather-bound book with the words Holy Bible pressed into the front cover.

Kin swallowed and ran his hand over the smooth leather. How much had such a beautiful book cost the parson? More than Kin was worth, and that was certain. Especially since it wasn't likely a gift he would ever use. But because the parson had given it to him and he knew the book meant a lot to the man, he would value it and take it with him. "Thank you. It's beautiful."

The parson planted his elbows against his knees, clasped his hands, and studied the space between his feet. "I know you think you don't need it. But I pray there will come a day when your eyes will be opened and that you'll find life in those pages."

"Yes, sir." And now it was time to get them on a different subject before he had to sit through more of a lecture. "Here." He handed over the other package that still remained by his side.

The parson gave him a look that indicated he knew Kin was avoiding the subject, but he seemed willing to let the matter slide. He turned his focus to the gift.

Kin pressed his lips together as the Parson slowly unwrapped it. Was he going to like it?

He had purchased it months ago after saving up all the money he had earned last summer by selling Dixie Griffin fish for her boardinghouse.

"Well, I'll be..." PC reached into the box and pulled out the first of the books, *An American Commentary on the Book of Matthew*. He blinked a couple of times.

Kin motioned to the box. "There's a whole set."

"I see that. This is very thoughtful of you, Kin. Thank you so much."

Kin nodded. "Heard you mention to Marshall Zane that you would like to have a set. Jerry Hines ordered them special. All the way from New York City."

Beside Kin, Tommy squirmed. "Only b-books? Tommy n-not like b-books."

PC chuckled. "Well it's a good thing this gift wasn't for you then, isn't it? Want to go paint at the table?"

Tommy hopped up from the settee. "Tommy like to p-paint!"

Kin exchanged another smile with PC and set to gathering up the paper wrappings while PC settled Tommy at the table and helped him understand how to use the new watercolor set.

The parson settled one hand on Tommy's shoulder. "Just for a little bit, all right? As soon as Kin and I get the kitchen cleaned up, we've been invited to spend the day with the Callahans."

Kin sighed as he tucked the brown paper into the bin by the fireplace. He had forgotten momentarily that he had promised Mrs. Callahan he would come and eat Christmas lunch with them. And then when PC had been prevented from going back east to be with his family, they had invited him also. He supposed if PC was going to be there, it would be less trying than if he went on his own. He always appreciated how the town of Wyldhaven made him feel like he belonged, but that didn't lessen his feeling of awkwardness whenever he was invited to someone's family event. It was a constant reminder that he was an orphan with no family of his own.

Well—he glanced to the kitchen where PC had set to washing up the dishes—no one other than PC. But he didn't really count as a pa, since he was only a few years older than Kin. A big brother, then.

Kin grinned. A big brother who was glowering at him because he hadn't pitched in to help yet. "Coming," he called.

Chapter 3

Kin couldn't help but grin as PC knocked on the Callahan's door.

Tommy was so excited that he couldn't stand still. He jiggled up and down, clapping his hands. "We g-get to have Christmas d-dinner!"

Kin nodded. "That's right."

"Tommy l-like Christmas d-dinner." He said the words just as Mrs. Callahan opened the door.

She chuckled. "Well that's just what we want to hear around here." She stepped back and swept the door wider. "Please come in."

Sheriff Reagan was adding wood to the fireplace when they stepped into the parlor. He stood and stretched out one hand toward the parson. "Welcome! Merry Christmas."

Marshal Zane and his wife, Jacinda, who was the sheriff's mother, sat on the settee.

The parson shook the sheriff's hand first. "Thank you for having us."

"Of course. Our pleasure." The sheriff reached in his direction. "Kin."

Kin clasped his hand. "Sheriff."

They exchanged greetings with Marshal and Mrs. Holloway next.

The two women rushed off to the kitchen then, and Kin inhaled a big lungful of the scents wafting his way. Mmmm, he was starving, even if he had gone for a second slice of the parson's sausage pie at breakfast. If he didn't watch out, he'd be wiggling worse than Tommy in a moment.

He mostly held his silence while the parson and the other men made small talk. It wasn't long before Mrs. Callahan came in to announce the meal was ready. She led them to the dining room and pointed out chairs for everyone.

And my, could these women cook!

The Sheriff had bagged a wild turkey, and somehow Mrs. Callahan had made that bird just as tender as could be. There were mashed potatoes and the most delicious gravy he'd ever had the pleasure of consuming. There were green beans as well as canned cranberries that the sheriff had apparently ordered in special just for his wife. There were bread rolls that melted in your mouth, and plenty of fresh-churned butter from the fresh milk Mrs. Callahan purchased from the Kastains each week. And then, as if that wasn't enough, she brought out a pumpkin pie, and an apple pie, and a dried cherry pie.

And, of course, Kin didn't want to offend her, so he had a slice of each. By the time she brought coffee, Kin didn't think he could swallow another bite if he were paid. He was very thankful when he could follow the men to the parlor and sink onto the floor next to the fireplace.

Tommy sank into one of the wing-back chairs and put one hand over his stomach. "Tommy hurts."

PC chuckled. "I bet you do, as much food as you put away." The parson pegged Kin with a look. "Kin there is the only one that put away more than you did."

Kin placed his own hand over his belly. "Kin hurts."

Everyone chuckled.

The sheriff leaned back in his chair with his coffee cup balanced carefully on one knee. "I understand you're going to be leaving us, Kin?"

PC squirmed a little in his seat.

"Yes, sir." He studied how the firelight played on the oak floorboards beside him.

Mrs. Callahan bustled in then, stood behind the sheriff's chair, and placed her hand on his shoulder. "Right then. Shall we open gifts?"

Kin felt a little bit of panic zip through him. He hadn't thought about getting gifts for the Callahans. Why hadn't he thought of that?

The sheriff angled himself to look at his wife over his shoulder. He frowned. "Gifts? I was supposed to get you a gift?"

Mrs. Callahan chuckled. "Reagan Callahan, do go on with you."

Kin couldn't help but admire their easy camaraderie.

Even the parson was smiling, though he had lowered his gaze to the space between his feet.

Mrs. Callahan smacked her hand against her husband's shoulder. "Reagan is putting you all on. I think we should give the first gift to Tommy. What does everyone else think?"

The Sheriff gave an exaggerated long-suffering sigh. "What? I want to go first!" He grinned then.

Tommy smiled. "Y-you can go f-first."

Everyone chuckled as the sheriff reassured Tommy he'd only been joking.

And as Kin admired the homey scene, he realized how much he was going to miss all these people when he left tomorrow.

Reminding himself not to go all sentimental, he glanced at PC and was thankful to see him pull a small envelope from his back pocket. At least they could stay without the embarrassment of not having a gift for the Callahans. And he was thankful for that because he was looking forward to watching the Sheriff open his present on account of how he had helped make it happen.

As if she too were remembering, Mrs. Callahan gave him a nervous little smile and clutched her hands beneath her chin. There were more packages beneath the tree than there were people in the room.

Mrs. Callahan handed the first one to Tommy. It was small and flat and square. Tommy had not lost any of his enthusiasm for tearing open presents, and, in no time, he had the paper torn away. The gift was a beginning primer. Tommy exclaimed and fawned over the pictures.

Mrs. Callahan, who had once been the town's schoolteacher, gave the parson a glance. "If you would permit me, I would like to start coming by and seeing if I could teach Tommy to read."

The parson gave a nod of approval. "Of course. I think that's a grand idea."

Sheriff Reagan handed another package to Tommy. This one was a new set of clothes sewed for him by Mrs. Holloway. Just as PC had taught him over the past few months, Tommy politely expressed his thanks, though he was much more taken with the book.

The next two packages were handed to the parson. Mrs. Callahan had sewn him a blue silk scarf.

She flushed a bit when he thanked her. "I do hope it's all right. Jacinda helped me with it quite a bit."

"It's perfect," PC said. "It will come in very handy on these cold mornings."

"Along with..." Mrs. Holloway pointed for him to open the other package that was from her and the marshal.

It was a soft sheepskin coat. Leather on the outside and fluffy wool on the inside. The parson thrust his arms into the sleeves. "It fits perfectly. Thank you."

The sheriff fished under the tree for more presents, and Kin had to chuckle at how antsy he felt with anticipation to see the man open those boots.

But the next two packages were handed to him. He hadn't expected that. He'd thought the remaining packages under the tree would be for the Holloways and Callahans.

"This one first." The sheriff tapped the smaller gift. "But Kin, before you open it, I just want to say a few words."

"Uh-oh." Kin offered a good-natured grin, but a swirl of queasiness swept through his stomach. He never much liked being the center of attention.

"Wyldhaven has been your home for a lot of years."

Kin nodded. "Yes, sir. Ever since Pa moved us here right after Ma passed." He did his best to dispel the nausea at the thought of those years. He tried to push away thoughts of the failure his father had become, but again the question he'd pondered this morning reared its head. Was he destined to become like his pa? Clenching his teeth, he focused on the Sheriff.

"Well, Charlotte and I want you to know that you are welcome to come back to town anytime, so we got you a little something to keep Wyldhaven on your mind while you are away."

Kin dropped his focus to the parcel. These were good people.

"Go on and open it."

With the reality of his future hanging over his head, Kin slowly tore the paper from the package. Inside was a small wooden box. He opened that to reveal a beautiful gold compass. The cover was engraved with an image of Wyldhaven's Main Street. "It's beautiful." Kin ran his thumb over the engraving.

Mrs. Callahan clapped her hands. "Oh good! I'm glad you like it. Belle Kastain did the drawing, and Jerry Hines embossed the lid himself."

Kin felt a lump in the back of his throat. "This means a lot. Thank you."

The sheriff smiled. "Our pleasure. That's so you will always be able to find your way back to us."

Kin swallowed. He had never considered himself sentimental. But hang it, if he didn't have something stinging his eyes. He quickly tore into the next package. It was another sheepskin coat, just like PC's. "This will come in handy on my trip. Thank you." He made sure to make eye contact with both the marshal and his wife.

Mrs. Holloway dipped her chin. "You're welcome. I sewed those myself. The sheep were from the Nolan farm."

"That makes it all the more special." Kin smoothed his hands down the front of the coat, relishing the soft feel of the suede leather.

It was as though every gift given to him today was intended to remind him of this place. The Bible would remind him of PC and his constant, unwavering reiterations of its message. The compass with a picture of Main Street and the coat made by Mrs. Holloway and from Nolan-spread sheep. He wouldn't be able to escape any memories with all of those reminders.

Chapter 4

The sheriff angled to look at his wife. "All right, Charlotte. Your turn." He lifted one of the packages from under the tree and thrust it toward her.

The marshal stood and swept a hand to the spot on the settee he'd occupied near his wife. "Here, sit."

Mrs. Callahan flushed prettily and sank down next to her mother-in-law, but her gaze was fixed on her husband across the room in the armchair near the fire. "What did you get me?"

The sheriff shook his head. "Open it and find out."

"Very well." Mrs. Callahan took her sweet time untying the string from around the package, and then she gasped. "Oh! Reagan!" She lifted a section of cream lace from the packaging. "It's absolutely gorgeous!"

The sheriff was grinning from ear to ear. "Thought you might like that."

"Now you." Mrs. Callahan flapped her hand toward the biggest box under the tree.

Kin couldn't withhold a smile. He was thankful that he had been able to help Mrs. Callahan in some small way to be able to give her husband the gift she had wanted to—even if she didn't know it was him.

The sheriff lifted the box and gave it a gentle shake.

But Bill Giddens must've packed those boots carefully because no sound emanated from the box.

"Hmm..." The sheriff turned the box this way and that. "It's somewhat heavy. But not overly so."

Mrs. Callahan's eyes sparkled, but she wasn't giving away anything.

Mrs. Holloway chuckled. "Oh Reagan! Do just open it." To the room in general she said, "He's been this way since he was a boy. Always has to investigate before opening it."

"All right. All right. I'm getting there. But you can't rush the joy of Christmas." With his eyes closed, the sheriff lifted the lid from the box. He gave the package a sniff. "Smells like leather." He opened his eyes then, and they continued to grow wider as they took in the boots in the box.

Everyone in the room chuckled. His pleasure was obvious.

"Charlie!" he exclaimed. "However, did you afford such a fine pair?" He removed one of the boots from the box and angled it to examine the embossing in the firelight.

Mrs. Callahan gave a shrug of one shoulder. "Well, if the truth be told, I had some help with that. I knew I didn't have the money, and I was so disappointed, but Kin gave me an idea. And it was a good one too! I've been baking pies and selling them in Dixie's boardinghouse for weeks now."

The sheriff looked up and pegged Kin with a look. "Wait a minute!"

Kin found himself thinking one of Tommy's favorite phrases. Uh oh. He had a feeling a cat was about to crawl out of a bag.

Mrs. Callahan blinked. "What is it?"

The parson sat straighter, giving Kin a curious look.

"There's still one more package beneath the tree." Kin tried to divert everyone's attention, but no one took his bait. Kin winced a little and wrinkled his nose at the sheriff. He could tell the man was putting two and two together.

And sure enough, the sheriff threw back his head and slapped his thigh in laughter. "Kin Davis, you are a sly old dog."

Mrs. Callahan still looked confused. "Reagan please do fill the rest of us in!"

The Sheriff gave his wife a sheepish look. "I'm betting that you have been selling apple pies in Dixie's Diner?"

Charlotte nodded.

Kin studied the floor near his feet as the sheriff laughed again.

"Kin caught me checking the street to make sure you weren't in sight. I was just about to carry our bushels of apples across the street to sell to Jerry Hines so that I could buy you that lace. But Kin convinced me to sell those apples to him. He was returning them to our cellar when you saw him coming out. He later told me that it was on account of he wanted a slice of your apple pie today. But now we know the truth. He knew you needed those apples so you could buy me those boots."

"Oh, Kin!" Mrs. Callahan crossed the room and bent to give him a hug. "You are such a dear!"

Kin puffed out a breath of relief. At least the sheriff had only put half the story together.

As she retreated toward the couch, Kin looked down and scuffed at a mark on the floor with his boot. "It wasn't anything. And the fact that I got to be here to see you both exchange those gifts was repayment enough for my troubles." *Just sit back in your seat and don't think on it anymore.*

But in the next moment, his hopes were dashed. "Wait a minute!" Mrs. Callahan exclaimed, spinning to face him and plunking her hands on her hips. "After the Carver siblings stole my money, I wasn't going to have enough to order the boots! But when I arrived at Mr. Giddens place to tell him I couldn't get them after all, he said someone had already paid for them. You avoided my questions that day when I came to the parsonage to ask if it was you, but... if you paid Reagan for those apples, you surely wouldn't have wanted the present of the boots to be ruined when the money was stolen. I'm asking you straight out, Kin Davis, in front of witnesses...it was you, wasn't it?"

He raised a gesture that he hoped conveyed that he didn't know the answer but would prevent him from having to tell an outright lie. "I'm sure Bill Giddens would be happy to tell you who did it now that Christmas is past." He pointed quickly at the one remaining package under the tree. "Don't forget there's still one more present."

"Oh, no you don't, Kin Davis! You aren't going to weasel your way out of this! I got the stolen money back when the Carvers turned themselves in. Kane made sure his siblings repaid me every cent. So, do I owe you money or not?"

Kin shook his head. "You most certainly don't owe me any money, Mrs. Callahan." But knowing he was caught, he couldn't help a grin.

Mrs. Callahan plunked her hands on her hips. "You said it wasn't you!"

He shook his head. "No, ma'am. I do believe if you think back, you'll realize that I never once said it wasn't me."

She shook a finger at him. "Don't you leave today before I give you that money. That was very sweet of you. Thank you so much."

Kin gripped the back of his neck, embarrassed to have everyone in the room staring at him. But it was the quick nod of approval that PC gave him, that kicked him right in the heart. He scrambled to the tree. "Look here. This one says it's for you, Mrs. Holloway." He thrust the package toward her.

And, thankfully, everyone turned their attention to watching her open her gift.

She angled a coy glance at her husband. They'd only been married less than a year. "What did you get me, dear?"

Kin grinned. Why was that the first question most people asked when handed a gift?

The marshal didn't miss a beat. "Garden seeds. I know you'll want to go to work planting them just as soon as the weather warms enough." It was patently obvious that he was joking.

Mrs. Holloway wrinkled her nose at him. Inside her package were yards and yards of various materials. Mrs. Holloway oohed and aahed over each one. Here she exclaimed about how this material was perfect for new curtains. And there she exclaimed over the softness of a long piece of silk. Finally, she stood and moseyed to her husband's side. She curved her hands around his arm and looked up at him. "You know just how to please me, dear. Thank you so much."

The marshal gave her a quick kiss and a smile. "You're welcome."

"Now, you might be wondering why I don't have a package under the tree for you." She swished her skirts a little, and Kin marveled over married people flirting with one another.

"I hadn't noticed," The marshal winked at her.

"Well, I didn't forget you. But I'm awaiting the delivery of your gift. It should be arriving at any moment."

The marshal winged one brow upward. "Delivery?"

She nodded. "Indeed. And I'm just as much in debt to Kin for helping me get your gift as Charlotte seems to be."

Again, all eyes in the room focused on him.

Kin waved a hand. "It wasn't anything."

"Oh, it was too! Kin you are too modest." She returned her attention to her husband. "There was that avalanche, you see. And your gift was on the train. Kin helped me ride out to get it. You remember that day he and I were running errands?"

The marshal grinned. "I knew there was something fishy about that whole scenario."

Mrs. Holloway batted her lashes at him. "There was indeed, but when you see what I got you, you'll forgive me, I promise."

As if her words had summoned it, a knock came to the door at that precise moment.

"Oh! That must be Joe now!" Mrs. Holloway hurried to open the door. "Come on, everyone. You'll all want to see this!"

The marshal frowned as they all followed his wife out on to the porch. "Joe has my gif—" He froze and stared.

Joe stood in the yard with that beautiful Appaloosa colt prancing on the lead rope.

As if by mutual instruction, everyone moved to the Callahans porch rail and leaned against it, leaving the marshal and Mrs. Holloway standing at the top of the steps.

Deputy Joe grinned up at them. "Merry Christmas, everyone!"

They all returned the greeting, and then Mrs. Holloway stretched her hand toward the colt. "The dam and sire are the ones we saw on our wedding tour."

"I don't know what to say!" The marshal descended the steps and rubbed his hands down the horse's neck as he accepted the lead rope from Joe.

Mrs. Holloway clasped her hands before her. "The thing is, he's still green broke. Kane Carver has been working with him for several weeks now, but he still has a way to go. The one I ordered came down sick right before they were to put it on the train, and they sent this one instead."

The horse bobbed its head and blew, then whuffed at the marshal's hat, nibbling at the rim.

He laughed and ducked away. "He's beautiful, Jac! I couldn't be more pleased!" The marshal pulled his wife toward him, and

Kin had a feeling this time, he wouldn't just be offering her a peck of a kiss.

Mrs. Callahan stepped back by the door. "Let's all go back in where it's warm, shall we?"

On that note, it was time for him to mosey on out of here. He offered his thanks once more to the Callahans, retrieved his gifts, and then paused in the doorway of the parlor. "If you all will forgive me, I need to go and speak to the Carvers before I leave town in the morning."

Deputy Joe, who had come in from outside and was seated on the hearth, raised him a look. "Kin, swing by our place a little later, would you?"

Kin nodded. "I can do that right after I speak to Kane at the Kastain place. Couple hours from now be all right?"

The deputy nodded. "That will be perfect. See you then."

With that, Kin retreated. In the yard, he skirted around the marshal and his wife, who were still sweet talking with one another, and fetched his mount from the barn.

He pulled in a full breath of the crisp mountain air and swept a glance up and down the road as he kicked his horse into a trot toward the Kastains'.

He sure was going to miss this place.

Chapter 5

Kin rode his mount into the Kastains' yard and dismounted before the hitching rail.

Kane Carver must have heard him coming, for he was stepping out of the barn just as Kin started toward it.

Kane stretched out one hand. "Davis. Good to see you. The Kastains are all in the house there."

Kin shook his hand. "Actually, you're the man I've come to see."

Kane frowned. "I am?"

Kin suddenly felt a bit awkward about what he had intended to propose. "You are." He didn't want the man to think he was offering him charity, so he'd best proceed with caution. "You see, tomorrow I'm leaving to go to Seattle. Not sure when I'll be back."

Kane nodded. "Heard as much." He grinned. "You might be breaking my sister's heart by riding out so soon after we've arrived."

Kin felt warmth in his face. He studied the side of the barn. "Well—I'm not—I'm just not in a place where—"

"Relax!" Kane pounded a palm against his shoulder. "Just pulling your leg a little."

Relieved, Kin pressed ahead. "Well, the reason I stopped by is that I have this place... Used to be my pa's. And I inherited it when he passed on." Kin kicked at a mound of snow. "It's not much. But it's bigger than the room you three are sharing in the barn there." He tipped a nod toward the building. "My cabin has two bedrooms, and a good cook stove. And it's nice and warm. Wondered if you would be interested in renting it while I'm in the city?"

Kane folded his arms.

If Kin was any judge, that was a bit of a hopeful look on Kane's face, and yet there was caution too.

"How much?"

This was where Kin knew he had to continue cautiously. He didn't want to offend the man's pride. "Well, here's the thing... I'm riding the train to the city. And I can't take my horse with me. I plan to ask the Kastains if I can board him here in their barn, since I know they have room. A dollar fifty a month is the going rate. And that's about what I was thinking to charge for rent on my place. I know it's a little more than you are paying here now. But if you agree, you could just pay the rent to the Kastains on my behalf to cover the boarding of my horse. That is, providing they agree to board him for me."

"Of course, we agree."

Kin spun to see Zoe Kastain standing on the porch.

She nodded. "Yes. We'd be happy to."

Kin felt a wave of relief sweep through him. He had wanted to finagle a way to get the Kastains a little bit more money each month, and also help the Carvers. If Kane Carver agreed, it looked like everything would work out. He looked back at the man.

Kane leaned into his heels and seemed to ponder the offer. Finally, he said, "I'll agree, on one condition."

Kin felt his hopes deflate. "What's that?"

"That you let me pay two dollars a month rent. We both know that's more in line with what's regular around these parts."

Kin grinned and stretched out his hand. "All right. You keep the extra fifty cents and we'll settle up when I come back." If he ever came back. "Zoe can give you directions to the place when you are ready. String on the door latch is out. Just go on in and make yourselves at home."

"Will do!"

It gave Kin pleasure to see the excitement in the man's eyes. Must be a relief to have a real place to house his family.

Zoe stepped to Kin's side and looked up at him. "Are you coming back?" She searched his face.

He swallowed. Zoe had always seemed to be able to read his mind.

She folded her arms against the cold, still scrutinizing.

He whipped off his new sheepskin coat and settled it around her shoulders. He gave her a wink. "I'll come back for certain, if you tell me you'll be waiting for me."

Zoe flushed and clutched the lapels of his coat as she studied his face. "Kin Davis, do go on with you."

Kane Carver chuckled and tipped his head toward the barn. "I think I'll go back inside where it's warm and leave you two alone for a bit. My brother and sister will be happy to hear the good news. All the best to you." Kane disappeared into the barn, sliding the door shut behind him.

But Kin barely heard him go. He folded his arms against the chill breeze and studied Zoe. Was the fact that she was blushing a good sign? Truth was, he knew that she and Wash maybe had feelings for one another. And while he would court Zoe in a heartbeat, he didn't want to tread on Wash's territory.

Zoe dragged her focus to the side of the barn.

"Do I have a chance?"

She tucked her lower lip between her teeth. "Kin, you know I've always valued your friendship."

And there it was. Wash had beat him to it. He gave her a gentle sock on the arm. "Don't go getting all in a dither. I was just joshing with you a little."

Her eyes turned soft as they searched his face. "You do know that I love you like a brother, right?"

He swallowed. Nodded. However, a rock settled into his stomach. No matter that she had meant to soften her rejection, somehow she'd actually heightened it. He forced himself to say, "I'll always love you like a sister, too."

Her shoulders slumped in relief. "You are going to be on time for your party, right?" She took off his jacket and held it out to him.

He swung it on and gave her a nod. "Wouldn't miss it for all the world." He would dread it from now until it was over. But because Zoe had put it together for him, he wouldn't miss it.

She gave him a little wave and trotted up the stairs of the porch and disappeared into the house. And he couldn't help but feel like maybe his last remaining draw for being in Wyldhaven had just been severed.

※

Since Deputy Joe had asked him to stop by and the Rodante place was close, Kin decided to ride that way on his return to town. When he rode into the yard, a woman he didn't recognize was hanging sheets from the clothesline. She was older with a bit of gray in the faded brown hair at her temples.

He swung down and tipped her a nod. She must be a new resident that Mrs. Rodante was trying to help.

She scanned him up and down and then pointed toward the house. "Deputy and his wife are in the kitchen there. Reckon you must be the fellow the deputy said would be stopping by. He said to tell you to come on in."

"Obliged." Kin touched the brim of his hat and then took the steps up to the porch. He felt a bit awkward walking in without knocking, but he figured maybe the deputy had a reason for telling him just to enter. He pushed the door open and poked his head inside. No one was in sight, but the woman had said that Deputy Joe and Liora were in the kitchen.

Closing the door behind him, he strode in the direction of the kitchen.

He was striding past the dining table when from inside the kitchen, Mrs. Rodante gave a little titter. "Now Joe, do be serious. I've been trying to get you alone all morning so I can tell you something, and I can't speak when you won't stop kissing me."

Kin froze. He wasn't about to walk into the kitchen now. He plunked his hands on his hips. Should he retreat and knock on the front door, after all?

"But it's Christmas." The deputy murmured. His voice was low and intimate. "Shouldn't a man be allowed to kiss his wife as often as he wants on Christmas?"

"I suppose he should, but there's really something I need to tell you. So, step back." Though she tried to sound stern, she laughed again.

"You're no fun," the deputy groused.

Kin couldn't suppress a grin.

Definitely not the right moment to announce himself. Retreat it was, otherwise he'd be eavesdropping.

He turned and took a step toward the front door.

"I'm with child, Joe. Merry Christmas."

Mrs. Rodante's words froze Kin in place. A huge grin bloomed.

There were several beats of silence, and then Deputy Joe finally said, "Well, I'll be." There was another moment of pause before Joe continued in a husky voice, "Come here."

This truly wasn't a conversation he should be overhearing. On tiptoe, Kin beat a hasty retreat to the front door. Once he was on the front porch, he grinned and scrubbed one hand over his face. He couldn't be happier for the Rodantes. He waited a few minutes and then knocked loudly.

Deputy Joe opened it, grinning from ear to ear. "Kin! Welcome. Come in."

Kin swiped off his Stetson and stepped over the threshold. "You look happy."

Deputy Joe folded his arms and appeared lost in thought for a moment, but then his grin broadened. "I am. I truly am. I've just learned that I'm to be a father."

"You don't say!" Ken did his best to look surprised. "Congratulations."

"Thank you. Thank you so much. What can I do for you?" the deputy asked.

"Uh..." Kin twisted his hat through his hands. "You asked me to stop by."

Deputy Joe snapped his fingers. "Right!" He called toward the kitchen, "Liora. Kin is here."

Mrs. Rodante bustled in drying her hands on a towel. "Merry Christmas, Kin." She smiled. "We're so glad you were able to stop by. I know we will see you at your farewell gathering this afternoon, but Joe and I wanted to give you a little something to express our thanks for helping us as you did when Ruby was...killed." She cleared her throat and blinked rapidly a couple times.

"That's really not necessary. I didn't do all that much."

"You are too modest by far. We never would have recovered our stolen property or found out what happened to Ruby if you hadn't acted as you did."

"Well, ma'am..." Kin's feet shuffled. "I was only doing what anyone in that situation would have done."

Deputy Joe clapped him on the shoulder. "Nevertheless, we heard you were headed to Seattle and thought that maybe this would come in handy." He thrust a long, lidded oak box in Kin's direction. The top of the box was inset with a round medallion, and brass screws held the edges of the box together. The front of the box had a brass keyhole.

Kin's heart pounded. He looked at Deputy Joe. "Is this what I think it is?"

The deputy grinned. "Open it. Oh!" He dug into his pocket. "Here's the key."

Kin opened the lid, and sure enough, inside, snugged into a bed of red velvet, lay a brand-new Colt revolver. The placard in the lid read "COLT'S PATENT FIRE-ARMS MANUFACTURING CO." Kin was speechless. He had his pa's old pistol, but... "This is one of Colt's latest designs!"

Deputy Joe grinned broadly. "Here tell they're coming out with a new one, but for now, yes, this is one of the most recent models. And..." He reached to the mantel above the hearth and took down two boxes of cartridges. "I got you these too. You never know what you might come up against in the big city. Always good to be prepared, I say. And I know you'll handle it safely."

"Thank you!"

"You're welcome. Merry Christmas." The Rodantes spoke the words in unison, and then they all laughed.

Kin hated to rush off so soon after receiving a gift, but he really needed to get back to town if he was going to be on time for his send-off. "If you'll forgive me, I better get going. I don't want to experience Zoe's ire if I'm late for her gathering."

"We understand." Deputy Joe waved off his apology. "We're just about to head that way ourselves."

"Yes. We are. I was just in the kitchen putting the finishing touches on a batch of sweet rolls that I'm bringing."

Kin's mouth watered. "All the more reason for me not to be late, ma'am. You make the best sweet rolls around."

She smiled. "Thank you. I'll save you the biggest one."

Kin wished she would offer him one for the ride back into town—to sort of get his appetite whet—but of course he couldn't mention it.

Deputy Joe stretched out his hand. "We're sure going to miss you 'round these parts. Don't be a stranger, hear?"

"No, sir. I mean, yes, sir. I won't."

As he strode to his horse and tucked the new revolver into his saddle bags, Kin couldn't help a chuckle. Seemed like several of the townsfolk had wanted to give him parting gifts without making a show of it at this afternoon's gathering. And when he thought about it, he supposed that was one thing that made Wyldhaven special.

Everyone was kind without wanting to get credit for it.

Chapter 6

A weariness washed over Kin as he trotted his horse back toward town. If this day had revealed anything to him, it was how much he appreciated the town of Wyldhaven and all the people who meant so much to him. Was he really going to follow through and get on that train tomorrow?

He gritted his teeth. He had to. Because how would it look for the whole town to come to a going-away shindig and then have him decide to stay?

Besides, though he admired and appreciated most of the people in town, it wasn't like he had anyone to stick around for. There were PC and Tommy, but he would come back to visit them. Someday. Maybe after he had a family.

The thought crashed through him, and he couldn't suppress a bark of laughter. After he had a family? Where had that thought come from? He reined his horse around a pothole in the road.

True, there weren't really any women in Wyldhaven for him. Sure, he admired Zoe. A lot. But he wouldn't barge in there, knowing how Wash felt about her—even if Wash had never admitted as much. Besides Wash was a much better man than him, and Kin couldn't see Zoe ever putting up with his shenanigans.

Belle was gorgeous, and at one time, he'd thought about pursuing her, but she'd grown quiet and distant over the past couple years. Hard around the edges. Besides, he'd heard she was planning on leaving Wyldhaven herself.

There was also Aurora. But she'd never given him any indication that she was even the slightest bit interested in him. She treated him more like a brother. He smirked.

The new gal, Maude... She was cute—no, more than cute—pretty, but a bit too quiet for his liking.

No. When it came right down to it, there was nothing holding him here. And if he stayed, what kind of adventures might he miss out on?

All this angst was simply a few jitters over the unknown future. But he could do this. He *wanted* to do this.

His horse trotted into town on the road just behind Dixie's Boardinghouse, and standing behind the building, Dixie, Doc, and Butch Nolan were admiring the sleigh he'd built for Mrs. Griffin as her gift to her husband.

He grinned and reined to a stop.

"Kin!" Mrs. Griffin flapped a hand for him to get down and join them. Then she wrapped both her hands around her husband's arm and rested her head on his shoulder.

Doc glanced his way. He had baby Ellery—who appeared more like a cocoon of blankets—resting in the crook of one elbow. "You made this?"

Kin lifted one shoulder. "Yes, sir." It hadn't been that hard to figure out. He'd studied a few of the sleighs in the Seattle shop when Mrs. Griffin had asked him to take that trip for her after little Ellery's early arrival.

Doc strode in a circle around the sleigh. "It's amazing, Kin!"

"Thank you. I'm glad you like it. Here, let me show you a few things." He strode to the rear of the sleigh and showed Doc the hidden compartment he'd built into the back to house Doc's medicines. "The cabinet locks so you can keep stuff from being stolen. And here..." He strode to the floorboards where the riders' feet would go and lifted the hinged tops of the compartments he'd built into the flooring. "You can put hot bricks in here to keep your feet warm as you travel. Or," he shrugged, "it could be another place for storing supplies, if you prefer." He lifted a finger and pointed out the areas where axels could be strapped in. "I also made it so that, in the summertime, you can pull off the runners and add wheels instead. The axels and wheels will have to be stored separately as I couldn't quite figure out a good place to store them on the sleigh itself. But I don't think that will be too much of an inconvenience."

"Certainly not! You seem to have thought of everything."

Pleased to see how excited Doc was, Kin scuffed at the snow with his boot. He could go on explaining how he'd put the windbreak up front or tell about the extra padding he'd given to the seats, but Doc would discover those things soon enough on his own.

Butch Nolan gave a loud whistle. "Shore is the pertiest sleigh I ever did lay eyes on, Kin."

Kin smiled. "Thank you."

Baby Ellery gave a little bleat from Doc's arms and poked one arm out of the blanket, waving it in the air.

Dixie straightened. "And that's our cue to head back inside." She pressed one fist into the small of her back and gave a little stretch. "My, but I need to find someone to help me keep the boardinghouse rooms clean. I scrubbed all the floors yesterday, and my body simply isn't as young as it used to be."

Doc wrapped one arm protectively about his wife's shoulders. "I wish I had more time to help you."

She waved a hand. "You're practically run off your feet, yourself. I'll post an ad on the bulletin board at the post office come Monday. I'll even throw in a free room and food to sweeten the deal." She held out her hand to Mr. Nolan. "Thanks again, Butch, for keeping it for me until today."

Mr. Nolan pumped her hand like a man on a firewagon about to lose his home. "My pleasure, Mrs. Griffin. My pleasure!"

Kin gathered up his reins, ready to get his mount to the livery and then head to the party, but Mrs. Griffin stopped him with a hand to his arm as Butch Nolan rode away.

"I'm actually glad you stopped by. Do you have a few minutes to come up to the house? Flynn and I got you a little something to show our appreciation for...well, not just for the sleigh. We..." She paused and blinked a couple times.

Kin frowned. Was she fighting back tears over his departure? He swallowed. He'd always admired Mrs. Griffin, maybe more than any other person in town, because she always believed in him. Whenever he failed and found himself in trouble with PC, if he ended up on her doorstep to sell her a catch, she would give him that knowing smile of hers and give his arm a squeeze. It conveyed that she still cared for him and that he could do better the next time without a word being exchanged. But to think that she cared for him enough to cry at his departure? He'd never thought that would be the case.

Mrs. Griffin offered a watery smile. "Well..." She dabbed at her eyes. "We just got you a little something to let you know we're going to miss you. Do you have time?"

Kin nodded. "A little, yes ma'am." He grinned to ease the moment. "Don't suppose they'll start the shindig without me."

She laughed. "True. I suppose not. Follow us then."

Doc led the way up the boardinghouse stairs to the apartments they shared with Rose Pottinger.

Kin swiped off his Stetson as they stepped inside.

Mrs. Pottinger was knitting by the far window. She offered Kin a smile. "Oh good. You came up. I do hope you'll forgive me for missing your send-off later. These old bones don't take to the snow and ice anymore."

He curled the brim of his hat into one hand. "It's fine, ma'am. Please, stay inside where it's warm."

Mrs. Griffin hurried to Doc's side. "Here. I'll take her. Can you get the gift?"

Doc nodded and disappeared into one of the bedrooms.

Mrs. Griffin bounced the baby, who seemed determined to let her mind be known now.

Kin felt awkward standing with the two women without conversation, but with the baby squalling as she was, there wasn't much point in trying to strike one up.

After just a moment, Ellery calmed to a low fuss.

He swept his hat toward the baby and called, "Good lungs."

Mrs. Griffin smiled as she continued to bounce. She cooed her next words as though she was speaking them to the baby. "Yes. I'm afraid she has only just begun to state her opinion on certain things."

Doc emerged from the bedroom with a brown leather valise in his hands. It sported a red bow tied to the handle. He smiled as he presented it with a little flourish. "From us to you. We hope it will make your travels easier and that you'll use it to come home to visit, once in a while."

"Thank you." Kin turned the bag this way and that, admiring the buffed shine of the leather. "It's beautiful! I only had my old knapsack, so this will be right useful."

Mrs. Griffin gave her signature squeeze to his arm, still jostling Ellery a little. "Merry Christmas, Kin. Do come back to see us. Now, if you'll excuse me, I think I'm going to have to deal with this little miss's needs. I'll be over to the church in a few minutes."

"Thank you, ma'am." He lifted the valise. "This means a lot."

"My pleasure. I'll miss our little chats in the boardinghouse kitchen. And my patrons will miss your fresh-caught fish!"

He smiled. "I'm sure there will be another young man you can talk into fishing for you. The pay is good. Aidan Kastain or Grant Nolan, perhaps. You can make it a competition and get twice the fish."

She chuckled. "I'll have to ask their parents, but that's a grand idea."

Ellery resumed her squalling then, and Mrs. Griffin disappeared with her into the bedroom.

Doc stretched out his hand and grasped Kin's in a firm grip. "Davis, God bless you as you go. Remember the truths you've learned here in Wyldhaven, and don't ever lose your giving spirit, son."

"Thank you, sir. I'll do my best."

Doc saw him to the door then, and Kin realized he'd better hurry up to the parsonage before the gathering commenced so he could leave all these presents in his room.

He took his mount to the livery, hastily unsaddled him, and then skirted around the back of the church and tromped up the hill to the parsonage by the back way so no one who might already be at the church would see him and call out.

Each family had given him these gifts in private, and he didn't want to embarrass anyone by having to explain where everything had come from. People might start comparing, or worse, feel badly if they hadn't gotten him something. Some of the gifts were worth more than others, but each one held a special place in his heart, and that was what mattered.

Chapter 7

Kin stood in his room, drawing deep breaths and willing himself to find the courage to walk down that hill and say goodbye to everyone. All his chats with various families today had been hard enough. And those hadn't really been the final goodbye. He'd known he would see each of them again at Zoe's get-together.

However, now...this seemed so final. It *was* final.

Yet, he was leaving to pursue his dreams, so shouldn't that mean something to him? Shouldn't he be filled with excitement instead of dread?

Hang it, he wanted a drink. And that right there was the main reason for his dread. He was turning into his pa. He didn't want that. And yet, each time he decided he was done with drink, he would have a moment where he caved in to the craving and wake up the following morning suffering the aftereffects and the regret.

How did I seed such a weakling? When're you gonna become a man, son?

He could hear the words as if Pa was standing right here in the room with him.

He inhaled. Held it. Shook out his hands.

A knock sounded on the front door.

He released the breath in a whoosh, took up his hat, and strode out to see who it was. Likely someone here to fetch him for the gathering because he was running late.

When he swung open the door, Wash stood on the porch, thumbs hooked in his beltloops, sporting that familiar, friendly smile.

And blast if Kin didn't feel a bit of a sting in his eyes.

Wash had been a friend since they were still in the schoolhouse that used to meet in Mrs. Griffin's boardinghouse dining room—back when Mrs. Callahan was still single and teaching. Actually, Wash had been more like a brother. He had understood Kin's difficult childhood and silently supported him through it. On mornings when they would go fishing before school, Wash would bring him paper-wrapped sandwiches because, though he'd never said it, he'd known about how Pa used to spend all their money on drink, leaving Kin's belly aching and empty.

"Afternoon," Wash said. "I'm here to fetch you for the shindig. Zoe's beside herself, thinking you decided not to come." He grinned. "That might be a slight exaggeration, but you know how she gets."

Kin chuckled and reached for his coat on the peg just inside the door. "Sure do. But I wouldn't do that to her."

Wash looked down and scuffed one boot against the boards of the porch. "Before we go down..." He dug something from his coat pocket and held it out to Kin. "I made this for you."

Kin hesitated, simply looking at Wash's outstretched hand. He couldn't quite tell what Wash held, but somehow, taking it seemed like the final link in the chain that would take him from this place. He stepped past the threshold and pulled the door shut. Still he didn't reach for the gift. He'd gotten Wash a gift too. He'd planned to tell him about it at the end of the gathering, but maybe it would be better this way.

Wash cleared his throat and blinked. He gave his hand a little shake. "Go on. It's not going to bite."

Kin smirked and accepted the gift.

It was a furl of leather. When Kin unrolled it, he saw that it was a hand-sewn holster with a belt. The belt had several loops to hold bullets, and the buckle was plain but sturdy.

Wash shifted. "Deputy Joe told me about the Colt he got you. I sized it real careful like so's it would fit it just right."

"It's great." Kin couldn't disguise the gravel in his voice. He cleared his throat. "I got you something too. You stop by and see old Bill Giddens tomorrow after I leave, and he'll give it to you." He hoped Wash would like the pair of black boots. He'd had old Bill make them just like the Cavalry units wore so that, when Wash joined up, he'd have a set that fit well and were comfortable, instead of the assigned ones that were often ill-fitting.

"You didn't have to do that."

Kin lifted the holster. "You didn't have to do this."

Wash's lips tipped up. "Guess that's what friends are for." He held up one hand.

Kin hooked his thumb with Wash's, grasped his hand, and then gave him a friendly shoulder bump.

And that was about enough of that, or he was going to start blubbering like a baby. He motioned to his gift. "I'll just put this inside and be right down."

Wash gave him a knowing look. "I'll wait. And Kin?"

"Yeah?"

"Take care of yourself, would you?"

His throat felt thick—like it might close off at any moment. He nodded. "Same to you." With that, he disappeared back into the parsonage.

He stood for a moment, pulling in a couple calming breaths, and then hurried to deposit the holster in the satchel that the Griffins had given him. But just as he was about to do so, he paused. Why not strap it on right now? It would be good for him to get used to the weight of the gun at his side. Yes.

He buckled on the holster, loaded the Colt, and dropped it in. Resting his hand on the gun's handle, he relished the feel of it in his palm. It was good that he'd have protection in Seattle. After all, it was a lot bigger of a place than Wyldhaven, and one never knew what kind of unsavory characters he might run into. Yes. This was a good feeling.

He hurried out then to join Wash, and they strode down the hill toward the church.

The inside of the church was warm and full of people milling about. Someone had cleared all the pews to the sides of the room, leaving the main part of the room open for fellowship.

A collective cheer rose up as Wash nudged Kin into the room.

Kin felt his face heat. Every eye in the room was on him, and he hated that. Everyone in town knew what a failure he was. What had made them turn out to see off a sorry specimen of a man like him?

From the front of the room, Zoe bounced up and down and clapped her hands. "Kin, could you join me up front, please?"

Kin pressed his lips together. He'd have to remind himself to get her back for this later.

As he made his way through the crowd, people clapped him on the back or his shoulders and murmured kind words.

"Sorry to see you go, kid." Jerry Hines gave him a nod.

"Don't forget about us on your big adventure," Ewan McGinty added. "You've got one last night tonight to partake of my finest bottle."

Kin nodded and pressed forward. Ewan obviously only wanted him in town so's he'd keep spending his money in the alehouse.

When he reached Zoe's side, she looped one hand through his arm and smiled up at him. Looking down at her, he sighed.

Too bad she'd made it so clear that she only saw him as a brother earlier.

"Everyone, if I could have your attention?" Zoe stood on her tiptoes.

Kin grinned. Did she think that made her soft voice sound louder?

The room did quiet, however, leaving Kin squirming inside again to have every eye on him.

"First, Merry Christmas!"

"Merry Christmas!" everyone echoed.

"Here's what we're going to do this afternoon. First, we have food."

A collective cheer rose through the room.

Zoe laughed. "Yes. Thank you to all the ladies who worked so hard to cook for us!"

Everyone clapped.

When the sound died down, Zoe continued. "After we eat, we'll have a time of fellowship. Kin will sit at the head table there, and if you'd like to say your farewells, you can do so at that time."

Kin withheld a grunt. If she'd wanted to torture him for leaving, she was doing a mighty fine job of it.

"Then, to conclude, I've asked Parson Clay to say a few words and pray over Kin as he leaves us." Her voice choked up on those last words and a deeper hush fell over the room.

Kin studied the floor at his feet.

Zoe gave his arm a little squeeze. She looked up at him, moisture shimmering in her eyes. "And while he's gone, we'll pray every day that God brings him safely back to us." She flapped a hand before her face, giving a little chuckle. "Now, let's eat before I dissolve into a blubbering puddle right here in front of you all."

A ripple of laughter filled the room, and Zoe nudged him toward the tables along the east wall. "You first, Kin. You're the guest of honor."

He wasn't hungry. Didn't think he could eat a bite. But he'd fill his plate to the brim if it made this sweet woman happy.

Turned out, he didn't need to worry about trying to eat, because everyone ignored Zoe's fellowship time comment. From the moment he set his plate on the table and sank into the seat Zoe had directed him to, townsfolk started coming over to say their farewells. He would stand and chat with them for a few moments, and then he would just get seated and pick up his fork when the next family would stop by, and he'd have to stand again.

After a full hour, his plate was still full, and he felt like a bobber on a fishing line being teased by a fat trout. Up, down, up, down.

But finally, the line died off, and folks settled in to eating their own food, leaving him to reflect.

Across the room, PC chatted with the new banker and his wife.

Where would he be if the parson hadn't taken him in when he did? He would ever be grateful for the man's kindness, even if he hadn't shown it so well over the years.

As if sensing that he was being studied, PC lifted his gaze and met Kin's across the room. He said a parting word to the Olanns and then strode toward Kin. "We probably should wind things down so people can get home before it gets too dark and the temperatures drop. You ready?" His gaze dipped to Kin's still-filled plate.

Kin pushed it back. "Yeah. Wasn't much hungry, I guess."

A glint of humor filled PC's eyes. "Hard to eat when people won't let you take a bite. I'll give you a few minutes.

Mrs. Kastain's fried chicken is delicious. Give it a try." He nudged the plate back in front of Kin.

Kin accepted the gesture for the loving one it was. He nodded. "Yes, sir."

With that, PC strode to the front of the room. "If I could have everyone's attention, I'll get started with my four-hour-long sermon so's you all can get home before morning."

Kin grinned and took a bite of chicken. PC was right. This must be a new recipe because he'd had Mrs. Kastain's chicken plenty of times, and it had never been quite this good.

PC flipped open his Bible while he let the laughter die down, and then he lifted his gaze to the room. "You all sound like you think I'm joking."

Another ripple of laughter, this time a little uneasy.

When PC grinned, Kin could almost hear the collective breath of relief.

PC glanced back down at his Bible. "In all seriousness, what I have to say is very short. I know you all need to get back to your evening chores. As many of you know, Kin has lived with me for several years—ever since his pa passed." PC raised a direct gaze in Kin's direction. "I've grown very fond of you, Kin." He cleared his throat. "I love you like a brother, and so it was with a lot of prayer and searching that I pondered what the Lord would have me to say tonight. I wish it wasn't goodbye, but it is. Hopefully not for too long. The passage I chose for this evening is really a blessing. It's what Aaron and his sons, the priests of Israel, were instructed to say to the children of Israel. The passage is in Numbers, chapter six, verses twenty-two to twenty-seven. And Kin, as you go out, I pray the Lord passes this blessing on to you. The passage reads this way... *And the Lord spoke to Moses, saying: "Speak to Aaron and his sons, saying, 'This is the way you shall bless the children of Israel.*

Say to them: "The Lord bless you and keep you; The Lord make His face shine upon you, And be gracious to you; The Lord lift up His countenance upon you, And give you peace." ' So they shall put My name on the children of Israel, and I will bless them." So Kin, as you go, I would like to say this prayer of blessing over you. If you don't mind, join me here at the front."

Kin felt the familiar dread of being the center of attention. On top of that, he highly doubted that God had any sort of blessing for him, but out of respect, he would play along.

He wiped his fingers on his napkin and then set it back on the table and met PC at the front of the room.

PC wrapped an arm around Kin's shoulders and gave him a squeeze. "Please bow your heads with me."

Kin dutifully dipped his gaze to the floor.

PC's voice rang out loud and clear as he prayed with confidence. "Lord, I know You see Kin and that You love him so much more than he can even fathom. So, as he goes from this place, I ask that You would bless him and keep him. Make Your face shine upon him. Be gracious to him. Lift up Your countenance upon him. And give him the peace that can only come from You. Amen."

A murmured "Amen" filled the room.

"Thanks for coming, everyone. Feel free to be on your way." PC gave him another squeeze and smiled over at him. He lowered his voice so that, in the din that suddenly filled the church, Kin had to strain to hear his words. "I may not have said it much. But I love you. You have one of the kindest hearts I've ever had the pleasure of witnessing. You are giving. Generous. And strong. Much stronger than you give yourself credit for. And I'm not talking about those muscles you've built up chopping wood for me for all these years."

Kin couldn't withhold a chuckle, even as PC's words washed over him like a balm. He tucked his lower lip between his teeth, embarrassed by such praise.

"You can try to outrun God, Kin. But I'll just tell you from experience, God is faster. You'll never be able to leave Him behind. He'll be there, loping along backwards in front of you and dodging every attempt you desperately make to try to push him out of your way. And He won't even be out of breath." With one last jostle to Kin's shoulders, PC released him. "Right, well, that's enough from me. You'll always have a place in my home."

And with that, PC strode over to help several of the women pack up food and cart it out to their wagons.

Kin stood at the front of the church, watching the hustle and bustle. In the back corner, Mrs. Griffin and Mrs. Callahan laughed together over something. Doc and the Sheriff seemed taken with baby Ellery. The Marshal and Mrs. Holloway stood near them, speaking to Bill Giddens. Wash and his brothers were busy carting pots and pans from the tables to wagons outside. Zoe stood in the midst of it all, directing and organizing.

Beside him, someone cleared her throat softly.

He glanced down and smiled. "Hi, Belle."

She gave a little dip of her knees. "Just wanted to say I wish you all the best on your venture."

"Thank you." He studied her for a moment. "Are you ever going to follow your dream of going to the Territorial University to study art?"

She shrugged one shoulder. "Maybe someday. It's just not the right time yet."

Kin bumped her with his shoulder. "Just make sure there is a right time at some point. You've a talent like none I've ever seen."

She blushed prettily. "Thank you." She lifted her gaze to his then. "Goodbye, Kin."

"Goodbye, Belle."

And as she walked away to join her family, a gaping emptiness filled him. Everyone had someone, it seemed, except him.

Blazes, but he had a thirst coming on. But after Ewan's earlier snide remark, he was just stubborn enough to refuse to drink in his alehouse tonight. Besides, he was hankering for a ride. Who knew how long it would be before he got to ride again?

Cle Elum, then. He'd ride to the Cle Elum Inn. It was a long ride, but cutting through the hills shaved off a lot of the time. And if he stayed up all night, then when he got on that train tomorrow, he could sleep all the way to Seattle and not have to think about all that he was leaving behind.

And wasn't that just a contradiction! He'd just been thinking he had no one here, yet now, he was thinking of all he'd be leaving behind.

Chapter 8

Cora Harrison wearily stepped from the stage in Cle Elum and glanced the length of the worn, gray boardwalk. Some Christmas this had turned out to be. She rolled her neck and hunched into her shawl in an attempt to ward off the damp chill of a clinging fog.

"This is as far as we go tonight," the coachman barked gruffly. "We'll continue tomorrow morning. Be here ten o'clock, right sharp. That ought to give me time to get the wheel repaired."

Cora dropped her head to study the damp boards near her feet. The coach was supposed to have made it to the town of Wyldhaven today. She hoped her aunt wouldn't worry too much. Had she even gotten the message that she was now Cora's only living relative and she was on her way to live with her?

Early in the afternoon, the coach's wheel had fallen into what the coachman had called an axel-breaker. The large hole in the road had been filled with water and thus had its depth disguised. In their case, it hadn't broken the axel but the wheel, which was nearly as bad. It had taken the coachman the better part of the day to cobble together a repair that had gotten them this far, but now it was late and...

She glanced into the shadows of the moonlit street again. Her very last penny had gone to buying her coach ticket. Where was she going to spend the night?

Her valise landed with a thud near her feet. The coachman touched the brim of his hat. "Cle Elum Inn is just there, miss. Don't be late come morning."

"I won't be." She dipped a nod of thanks and, even though she wanted to run after him and beg him for his help, watched him tromp down the street, leading the horses and coach to the livery.

Her stomach rumbled loudly. She hadn't eaten since the apple and chunk of cheese that had served as her noon meal the day before. She'd counted on making it to her aunt's this evening. Now... How much longer until she would get to eat? Just the thought of food made her realize how hungry she was. Perhaps the innkeeper would grant her a tumbler of water. Then she needed to find the leeward side of a building, or perhaps a lean-to to bunk in. It would be a long, cold, and sleepless night, but she'd survived them before.

Hefting her valise, she walked to the door of the inn and pushed it open. Loud, bawdy music greeted her, along with a room filled with rowdy patrons and several buxom women making the rounds of the tables. Though they carried trays, it soon became apparent that food and drink were not all they offered. One woman plopped herself down into the lap of a man and draped her arms about his neck, whispering something into his ear.

Cora's face heated, and she focused on the floorboards, even as she heard the bearded man laugh uproariously at whatever the barmaid had just said. This was no inn! It was a saloon!

How *did* she get herself into these situations? Why would the coachman have sent her here? She might be penniless, but she was still a lady! Maybe there was a city pump where she could quench her thirst. She turned in haste to retreat.

A hand shot out and clamped onto her arm. "Well hello there. I ain't seen you 'round these parts afore." The man's bloodshot eyes travelled a leisurely sweep the length of her, one corner of his mouth tipping into a sloppy grin. "I'd surely 'member the likes o' you."

"If you'll pardon me, sir. I was just leaving." Cora tugged for the release of her arm. Her heart pounded against her breastbone. *Lord of Mercy, if ever I needed an angel of rescue, this would be the time.*

"Awe, come on." The man's grip was like an iron band when he tugged her toward an empty table. "Just one drink. You can't say no to that."

Cora leaned back and dug in her heels. Her valise, which she mercifully maintained her grip on, bumped the chairs of several patrons who glowered at the intrusion. She didn't care how hungry or thirsty she was, she wasn't going to encourage this lecher by agreeing to his demands. "I must insist that you release me at once!"

Cora's humiliation surged when she realized that her raised voice had cut through most of the room's other conversations. Almost every eye in the place fixed on her predicament, and silence fell.

Her captor mimicked her. "I must insist that you release me at once!" He laughed heartily, pounding his free fist on the table he'd dragged her to. His grip momentarily slackened, and Cora wrenched her wrist hard in an attempt at escape. She almost succeeded, but at the last moment, the man's hold tightened.

Pain shot up Cora's arm, and she whimpered. Her pulse thrummed in her ears. Bursts of breath beat against her teeth.

The room lay so silent now that Cora heard a floorboard creak from somewhere behind her.

"I suggest you let the lady loose."

The words, spoken by a man, emerged so quietly, so casually, and yet were such a welcome sound that Cora almost could have thought she'd dreamed them. Her eyes fell closed in relief.

Her captor scoffed. He leaned slightly so he could peer behind her. "Mind your own business, Davis. We're just having a little fun."

"You're drunk, Finn. And the lady isn't having fun. Let her go." This time, though the tone had not changed, his words were accompanied not only by the creaking floorboard, but also by the ratcheting of a gun hammer being pulled back.

Eyes widening, Cora craned a glance over her shoulder to see if she might catch a glimpse of her rescuer, but could only see the shadow of a man before a bright lantern that hung just behind his head. The barrel of his gun glinted in the glow.

Her captor grudgingly tossed her wrist back at her. "Since when do you carry a gun?"

"I guess the only thing that matters to you is that I do." Her rescuer's tone was still low and casual.

"Bah." The man called Finn stomped from the premises.

Cora would have made her escape then too, except she had no desire to follow her captor outside. She rubbed her wrist and spun to face the shadow-man at the bar. Conversations in the room slowly resumed, though many still watched her.

Her rescuer holstered his gun and sank onto the barstool he'd apparently vacated when he'd stood up for her. He didn't give her so much as another glance.

Cora lifted her chin and strode toward him. The least she could do was offer her thanks. She clutched her valise before her in a two-handed grip. Her hands twisted around and around the handle for, now that she stood next to him, she wasn't quite sure what to say.

After a long moment, he turned on his stool, pushed his black Stetson back with one finger, and looked up at her. As the glow from the lantern fell over his face, she was surprised to note that he was much younger than she'd first thought. Maybe just a couple years older than her seventeen. The light revealed coal black hair and eyes almost as dark. The face, broad across prominent cheekbones, might have been nice to look at if his eyes weren't so flinty. Stubble darkened a hard, angular jaw, which currently worked back and forth in obvious irritation at her blatant and prolonged scrutiny.

Feeling the heat that filled her cheeks, she forced her focus to the edge of the bar. "I must thank you." Her dry throat caught up to her, and the words emerged with barely any volume.

The man continued to assess her, maintaining his silence.

She cleared her throat and tried again. "I must thank you, sir."

Apparently done examining her, he resettled his hat and turned back to his drink. "Think nothing of it, ma'am." A dismissal if ever she'd heard one.

"It's 'miss.' And it wasn't nothing." Uncertain where to go from here, she glanced around. Her gaze landed on the barmaid wiping up after a departing customer down the bar. The woman watched her curiously, though her rag moved with purpose.

"Might I trouble you for a glass of water?"

The woman pursed her ruby lips. "Water's free with a meal. But when ya *only* want water, it's two-penny."

Cora's hopes deflated. And, as though to pile high her humiliation, just the mention of a meal sent a loud rumble through her stomach. "Thanks all the same." Her feet dragged toward the door. Would her assailant be far enough away that she could exit unnoticed now?

Behind her a coin snapped onto the bar. "Meal's on me, miss."

Cora spun to face the man. "'Tis most kind of you, but I'll be fine. Thank you."

Just then one of the barmaids breezed past her, carrying a tray of bowls filled with a fragrant thick meat stew. Large slices of cornbread accompanied each.

Cora's mouth watered. She licked her lips. Curse her self-reliant pride.

The man kicked out the barstool next to him and snapped his fingers at the woman behind the counter. "Stew and cornbread for the lady, Adelle. And a glass of"—he assessed Cora with a gaze that took her in from head to toe, and then his lips tipped up at the corners as he turned back to his stein—"water."

The barmaid ladled a bowl of the stew and set it on the bar, adding the bread and water.

Still, Cora hesitated.

Her rescuer glanced at her over his shoulder. "Unlike Finn"—he gave a meaningful tip of his head toward the street outside—"I promise not to bite."

Her pulse spiked at just the mention of that vile man, and she instinctively retreated a step from the exit.

Her rescuer—what had Finn called him?—scrubbed a knuckle over his mouth. She might have thought he was hiding a smirk if not for the fact that his eyes remained serious. He again nudged the barstool with the toe of his boot. "Safest seat in the house."

Cora's stomach rumbled pleadingly. Very well. But she would repay the man just as soon as she was able. She crossed the room and climbed onto the stool. Depositing her valise on the warped floorboards, she threaded one ankle through the handle—a trick she had learned from her dear departed mother to prevent the loss of valuables—and then bowed her head and closed her eyes to say grace.

Beside her, she heard the man give a soft snort.

No matter. She took her time with her prayer. Thanking the good Lord for bringing her safely this far, and even for providing a kind stranger to supply food and drink when she was in need. Lastly, she asked the Lord to see her safely through the night and on to her aunt in the morning.

When she lifted her head and reached for her glass, the man was still staring at her. "I'd be most obliged for your name, sir, so that I might repay you for this kindness when I have the means." She drank a few slow sips, relishing the cool spread of the water over her parched tongue.

"Name's Davis. Kin Davis. And there's no need. I've been helped out of a difficult situation a time or two myself."

"Nevertheless... Is this...inn...a good place to find you in the future, Mr. Davis?" Lifting her spoon, she blew on a bite of the stew, willing herself not to gulp it down like a starved dog.

He shrugged and raised his mug, sipping a slow draught before smacking his lips. "Not likely. You've caught me on my last day in this area. Like I said, no need to concern yourself with it."

The thick stew tasted just as good as it smelled, and she savored the flavors dancing in her mouth. "Very well. I understand if you don't want to tell me where you live. I will simply trust the good Lord to orchestrate that we meet again at a time when it will benefit you most."

He snorted. "It will be a cold day in— Well, I'll just say that I doubt the Lord deigns to even glance my way, miss."

She searched his face. "I'm sorry you feel that way, for it couldn't be further from the truth. Perhaps in repayment for this meal, you'll allow me to pray for you over the coming months that God will reveal His love for you."

He huffed and murmured. "I just can't get away from it today."

"You can't get away from the Lord's love *any* day."

"No. I meant—never mind." He looked down and spun his stein on the bar.

Cora frowned. How could a man be so kind and yet so hard at the same time? *Lord? Perhaps you sent me to this saloon just to reach this man? If so, help me to know what to say.*

Love him.

Cora dropped her spoon. It landed awkwardly on the rim of the bowl and then slipped off the bar, flinging a big spoonful of stew against Mr. Davis's shoulder and across his chest.

Cora's cheeks blazed. Heavens! Surely her hunger had her hearing things! "I'm so sorry!" She had no napkin, so she reached out and swiped at the stew on his shoulder with just her hand. "I've gone and ruined your shirt!" She reached for the piece of potato that was slowly slinking its way down his vest.

Mr. Davis grabbed her wrist. He glanced from her hand to her, one brow arching, and she realized that if she'd tried to grab that potato, she would only have ended up smearing more soup on him.

Something in the way his gaze lingered on her face made her freeze. Her heart beat a tattoo. Was she about to experience his wrath?

Only a moment later one corner of his mouth tilted. "Adelle, can we get a damp rag here, please?"

"Anything for you, sugar." Adelle approached and handed the rag to Mr. Davis while she leveled Cora with a possessive glower.

Did the man have a relationship with the barmaid?

If so, he didn't seem to be paying her much mind. He handed the rag to Cora. "For your hand."

She quickly wiped the sticky mess from her fingers and then folded the soiled area to the inside and turned to wipe his shoulder.

Once more he stopped her. "I'll do it." He took the rag.

She brushed her hands together to dispel the moisture. "I'd be happy to wash those for you."

He smirked and leveled her with a look. "For you to do that, I'd have to take them off."

Another wave of heat swept through her face. She looked down, focusing on a circle of carrot floating in her bowl and trying not to focus on his impertinent challenge. Love him? Not a chance. She wanted a good and godly man when she did choose to fall in love. Surely, she must have been hearing things. *Please, God, tell me I was hearing things?*

Silence was her only answer.

"Can we get another spoon for the lady?" At the back edge of the bar, Mr. Davis set a spoon on top of the rag he'd finished using, and Cora realized he'd stooped to pick her dirty one from the floor while she was trying to banish imaginings of what he might look like with his shirt off.

With pinched lips, Adelle snapped a spoon before her, and Cora murmured her thanks. She set to eating quietly after that, praying all the while that the Lord would deliver her from the sins of her flesh.

Cora broke a chunk off her cornbread and popped it into her mouth. Mr. Davis had not asked for her name, and it really was quite improper for her to even be chatting with him—much less falling in love with him—when they hadn't been properly introduced. She glanced around the raucous interior. This whole incident was really rather unfitting. She would just finish her meal and then try to quietly find a place to sleep. Hopefully, her aunt wouldn't learn of this impropriety forced by her circumstances and think less of her because of it.

Adelle took Mr. Davis's empty mug and slid a full one toward him. He held up a hand. "No, thanks. No more tonight." He folded his hands on the bar.

Adelle glowered at Cora like it might be her fault that the man wasn't spending his money, then snatched up the full mug and sashayed down the bar to foist it on some other poor soul. Cora finished her water and glanced sideways at the man. Shoulders slumped and head bowed, he looked like he carried the weight of the world. He was rugged and worldly. And from the look Adelle had just given her, he likely drank more than he ought to. And often. He was nothing like any of the men who'd attracted her before.

Actually, there had only been one. James Bench. His blond hair was always slicked back with pomade. His chin always clean-shaven. His hands soft from days spent in the library studying. He was a church-going man who never missed a service, and she might have married him, if his head hadn't been turned by Millie LaBelle.

She cast another sideways glance at Mr. Davis. Had the man ever darkened the door of a church? It was the fact that he'd rescued her, that's what. She couldn't imagine what else it could be. She'd never been so frivolous as to fall in love with a man only moments after meeting him!

Fall in *love*? Ridiculous! That did it. She plunked her spoon into her empty bowl.

"Thank you for the meal, Mr. Davis. I'll pray the Lord blesses you for your kindness and generosity. Don't discount His love for you."

The look he leveled on her was filled with weariness. "A real missionary, you are, huh?"

She stood and gathered her satchel. "I suppose you mean that as an insult. But I can only take it as a compliment. The Bible teaches us to go into all the world and preach the gospel. I try to do that whenever I can." She gave a little curtsy. "I bid you goodnight, sir."

She started to the door, feeling his gaze drilling into her back. "The only place with rooms to let around here is this one," he called.

She paused and turned to face him, clasping her hands together. He'd spun on his stool and now faced her, elbow's propped behind him on the bar. "Yes. I understood as much from the coachman. Thanks again."

She rushed out then, before he could try to stop her once more.

Chapter 9

Kin swept a hand down his face as the beautiful blonde hurried out. She'd obviously arrived in town on the stagecoach. He'd seen it pulling up the street as he stepped into the inn. Only a few minutes later, she had entered. So, where did she think she was going to sleep?

It hit him then... She'd been about to leave earlier when Adelle told her she had to pay for the water. She didn't have any money.

He had to go after her. He dropped a coin on the bar to pay for his drink.

Adelle eyed it and then leaned across the bar, blinking up at him provocatively. "Only one tonight? You're just getting started, honey. We could take a bottle and go upstairs, if you like."

It wasn't the first time Adelle had given him such a blatant invitation. He tugged at the brim of his hat. "Goodnight, Adelle. Take care of yourself."

With that, he pulled both the sheepskin coat that the Holloways had given him and his long duster from their pegs by the door, and hurried out onto the boardwalk as he swung them on.

The blonde woman was just disappearing into one of the alleys down the street. He hadn't even gotten her name. He should have asked when she requested his. He would fix that blunder as soon as he caught up to her.

When he hurried into the alley, he saw her settling onto a crate about halfway down. She tugged her thin coat tightly about her. At that moment, the clouds parted, and a shaft of moonlight bathed her in its rays. It caught in her upswept gold hair, and stroked her high cheekbones, as though it too wondered how soft her skin might feel.

He shook away the sentimental feeling. Whoever she was, she was simply passing through. And he was headed out on the morning train.

At the sound of his footsteps, her head snapped up and her eyes widened. She leapt to her feet, studying him warily.

He lifted his palms. "I don't mean you any harm. Surely you can't mean to sleep out here all night?"

She glanced down, rolling a pebble beneath the toe of her boot. "I'm afraid I don't have any other choice. The coach was supposed to bring me all the way to Wyldhaven today. But we had a bit of bad luck, and the wheel broke, so we had to stop here for the night."

"Wyldhaven?" The word hit him like a punch. This beauty was coming to Wyldhaven?

"Yes. My aunt lives there. She's married to a banker."

"Mrs. Olann is your aunt?"

She lifted wide eyes. "She is. Do you know her? Is she well? How is the baby? I sent her a letter before I left the city, but of course I haven't gotten a response while traveling."

Kin stretched out a hand. "I never caught your name."

She hesitated a moment, but then must have decided to trust him, because her slender, cool palm settled against his, and hang it if his heart wasn't suddenly beating just as fast as it had when he took her hand back in the inn. "My name is Cora. Cora Harrison."

He gave her hand a pump and then dropped it like a hot potato. "Nice to meet you, Cora. And to answer your questions, yes, I know your aunt. Not well. They've only lived in town for a short time. But the whole family is well."

Her smile was like the first warm day after a long winter. "That's wonderful. I'm so relieved to hear it. I wasn't certain if I was going to come all this way only to find that they had moved."

Kin shoved his hands deep into the pockets of his duster where he could ensure they would behave themselves. And then when she huddled into her shoulders and gave a little shiver, he immediately realized he had on two coats while she only had one thin one.

He yanked off his duster and then the sheepskin coat beneath it. This he held out to her.

She shook her head. "Oh, I couldn't."

He gave the jacket a little shake. "I insist. Let's get your stuff and I'll give you a ride to Wyldhaven. It's only about an hour and a half from here if we cut through the hills." When she still didn't move to take the jacket, he stepped toward her and swung it around her shoulders, and for a moment, he stood there, face to face with her. She was tiny. Only about as tall as his chin and engulfed in the coat. The only thing big about her seemed to be those wide, searching eyes.

Swallowing, he stepped back. "See, isn't that better?" He thrust his arms into his duster.

She worked to don the coat properly and gave a little nod as she threaded the buttons. "Very warm. It appears I'm once again in your debt, Mr. Davis."

The formality grated. "How about we dispense with propriety and you call me Kin, Cora."

She blinked at him. "I'm...not sure we should—"

"Are the rest of your things on the stage?" he interrupted before she could finish her protest. Cle Elum's streets were no place for any woman in the night, much less a lady like this one.

"Ah, no." She gestured to the bag at her feet. "This is all there is."

"All the better." He nudged her to precede him toward the livery. "My horse will already be carrying two, so the less baggage the better."

Cora snagged up her valise and trotted to keep up with him. He consciously shortened is stride.

"Mr. Davis, I'm not certain I should agree to ride through these wilderness hills with a man I barely know, and unchaperoned at that."

He gritted his teeth. She had no idea what danger she'd be putting herself in by trying to sleep on the streets of Cle Elum. "You were planning to stay unchaperoned on the street tonight."

"Well that's...different."

Different indeed.

He slid the barn door open enough for them to pass through and then pushed it shut behind them. His horse whickered to him from down the aisle. "I promise you'll be safer with me. Besides which"—he flashed her his best smile—"I also promise to be on my best behavior."

She eyed him warily.

He raised a hand. "In all seriousness. My only aim is to escort you safely to your aunt's."

She must have believed him that time because she looked away and said, "You're very kind, Mr. Davis. It's just that... My Aunt... She can be a bit—"

"I was raised by a pastor."

She was silent for a moment. "What?"

Kin hefted his saddle and blanket from the rack and strode down to the stall his horse was in. "The man who raised me after my pa passed away—he's a pastor." If anything would get her to trust him, that might.

She remained silent.

He glanced at her as he worked to tighten the cinch. She had her head bowed and seemed to be praying by the way her lips were moving. He rolled his eyes. He wasn't that scary. He waited until she lifted her head before he said, "Just think, in two hours, you'll be in a warm bed instead of trying to doze in that grimy alley."

"I'm just not certain you understand my aunt…"

He frowned. The woman surely couldn't begrudge him for plucking her niece from the dangerous streets of Cle Elum and escorting her safely to her door. With the horse saddled, he held out a hand to help her mount. "Everything will be fine. You ever ridden before?"

She studied his horse cautiously. "I grew up in New York."

He smirked. "So, I'll take that as a no. No matter." He assessed her skirts. "Your dress looks wide enough. I'll swing you up, and you straddle the horse with one leg on each side. You just have to keep your balance until I lead you outside, and then I'll swing up behind you. After that, all you have to do is hang on. Set your bag down for a moment."

She did. But when he settled his hands around her waist, she gave a little squeak and leapt back. "What are you doing?"

"Easy there, missionary. I did tell you I'd need to swing you on board, you'll recall."

"Oh. Yes. Sorry."

He grasped her waist again, and this time, she worked with him as he swung her up into the saddle. But as she swung her leg over the horse, there came a sound of ripping material.

She gasped and looked down at her skirt on the other side of the horse.

He rounded to examine it himself. "It's just the seam. Sorry about that. I guess I need more practice at judging the width of a woman's skirts."

She pressed her lips into a thin line as she accepted her bag from him. "A man like you surely has had plenty of practice." She gasped at her own impertinence. "I'm sorry. I don't know whatever made me say that."

He grinned, liking her more for the spark of gumption. "So, the missionary has a little bite. I'll be sure to remember that. But for your information..." He slid the barn door open, led her outside, and then shut the door behind him. "I'm not a rake." He swung up behind her and reached around her to take the reins.

She pulled in a little breath and stiffened. "Adelle didn't seem to think that was the case."

Kin huffed. "It's Adelle's job to ignore every standoffish signal a man gives her." He grinned then. "You weren't feeling a little jealous, now were you?"

She gasped. "Certainly not!"

Kin couldn't suppress a little chuckle. He definitely hadn't ever looked forward to a long ride through a freezing night more than he was looking forward to this one.

Chapter 10

The ride home was uneventful. But it was late when they arrived and knocked on the Olanns' front door. Weary as he was, Kin was thankful that the Olanns lived in town in a house they'd built right next door to the Holloways' behind the bank. It would only take him five minutes to get to his bed from here. Fun as his teasing of Cora had been at the front end of the trip, he'd grown weary, and his mind was now focused on tomorrow's train ride to Seattle. The encounter with the beautiful Cora had made him realize something. He was ready for this. He didn't have to become the man his pa had been. He could choose kindness and self-sacrifice. And he would. It would be his way of honoring PC for all he'd done for him, even if he still wasn't sure about his religious views.

Mr. Olann answered the door in pajamas and a nightcap.

Clutching her valise before her, Cora gave a little curtsy. "Good evening, Uncle." She explained who she was.

Kin frowned. Had she ever met her aunt and uncle before?

Cora went on to tell of the situation she'd found herself in, ending with a gesture in Kin's direction. "Mr. Davis was kind enough to escort me here from Cle Elum."

Mr. Olann frowned and consulted a pocket watch. "At this time of night?"

"Yes. I didn't have any money for a room, you see, and he was concerned for my safety if I stayed on the streets."

Mr. Olann squinted at Kin for a moment before finally stepping back to pull the door a little wider. "Very well. Come in. My wife is already abed, as you can imagine, but we'll get all this straightened out in the morning."

Cora dipped Kin a parting curtsy. "Good night and Godspeed, Mr. Davis."

Kin tipped his hat.

As he walked away, he couldn't withhold a grin. He shook his head. The little missionary and PC would get along just fine, he suspected.

It was a bit strange to enter the parsonage through the front door at this time of night. Normally, when he was drunk and coming home this late, he went through his window to avoid a confrontation with PC. But tonight, it wouldn't have mattered. The house was dark and quiet. Only Allegra padded across the room to wriggle a welcome-home greeting.

Tommy snored softly from his bed across the room as Kin fell onto his own mattress, settled Allegra into a mound of bedding at the foot of his bed, and tugged the covers over his shoulders.

For the first time in many days, he slept without restlessness. And when a loud knock cracked against the front door the next morning, he sat up feeling like a new man.

He nudged Allegra from his bed and checked the clock on the nightstand. Still two hours before he needed to be at the train station. His bags were already packed, so he could lounge here for a few moments longer. Whoever was at the door likely wanted PC to come to one of the camps to pray over a sick loved one or maybe to officiate a funeral.

Remembering how conversation with Cora the night before had flowed like they were old friends—after she'd finally realized he meant her no harm and had relaxed a little—he pulled in a long, satisfied inhale. If he were honest, a gal like her could almost make a man wish he were staying in town. But her arrival had come too late. Still, maybe he'd be returning to Wyldhaven sooner than he'd first thought.

He grinned and swung his feet over the side of the bed.

Tommy was already sitting up, watching him. "Y-you look h-happy."

"I am happy, Tom-Tom." For the first time in a long time, actually.

In the front room, Kin heard PC answer the door. Whoever was at the door sounded a bit agitated, but Kin couldn't make out what exactly was being said. He tugged on his pants and cocked his head to listen. But things seemed to have gone silent now. He was just slipping on his shirt when a knock sounded on the bedroom door.

"Kin? Could you join me out here a moment?"

Kin sighed as he finished the front buttons. "Coming." Was it someone else here to say goodbye? Had there been someone who couldn't attend yesterday's shindig?

He strode into the main room, feet bare, and still concentrating on doing up the buttons of his cuffs.

A woman gasped.

He paused and glanced up. His brows lifted.

Mrs. Olann? What was she doing here? Finished with the cuff buttons, he offered PC a quizzical look.

PC thinned his lips and swung a hand to indicate he should greet the woman. He hefted Allegra and moved to tie her out on the porch.

"Ah. Good morning, Mrs. Olann. How may I help you?"

She still didn't face him. "Are you presentable now?"

Kin glanced the length of himself and made a quick job of tucking in his shirt. "Yes, ma'am."

She faced him. A scathing look skimmed him from head to toe. When her eyes landed on his bare feet, her lips pinched into a tight little pooch. Her focus rebounded to his face. "You're going to have to marry her."

For the longest moment, Kin remained stock still. Whatever was she talking about? And then like a bucket of ice water, it dawned on him. "Excuse me?"

PC stepped forward. "Mrs. Olann seems to think there was some sort of … impropriety between you and her niece last night."

Kin's jaw ached. "There most certainly was not! I found Cora in distress in Cle Elum—without a penny for food or drink. I bought her a meal. She planned to sleep on the street since she didn't have any money for a room. When I found out she was Mrs. Olann's niece, I told her I would bring her home. Which I did." He transferred his narrowed gaze to the woman before him. "Without touching her—well other than to ride with her on the horse."

Mrs. Olann gasped. "You rode on the same horse?!"

Kin bit his tongue and willed himself to remember that he'd woken up in a good mood. "Yes, ma'am. There was only the one."

Mrs. Olann turned her gaze on PC. "They arrived at nearly twelve in the morning! And my dear Cora had a rip in her skirt!"

"That happened when I helped her up on the horse!" Kin tossed one hand in the air.

Mrs. Olann lifted her chin a little higher. "She said you'd been drinking, which I know you've a reputation for. Perhaps you don't remember what happened."

Kin thrust his hands into his pockets so he couldn't follow through on the temptation to take her arm and show her the door. He pulled in a slow, measured breath before allowing himself to speak. He made his case to PC. "I had one beer.

One. I remember everything, and I didn't touch her. Ask the girl. She'll tell you."

Lips pinched, Mrs. Olann hummed. "Yes. I did ask her. She has told me exactly what you've said. It sounds to me like you both planned how to present the story."

Kin opened his mouth but, when PC stepped forward with one finger raised, snapped it shut again. "Ma'am, Kin didn't touch your niece. I'd stake my life on it."

Kin felt his shoulders relax a little. At least someone believed him. And at least Cora had spoken the truth. She *had* tried to warn him the night before about her aunt. Perhaps he should have listened more carefully. But even then, he wouldn't have been able to leave her stranded in Cle Elum with no safe place to stay.

"I thought you to be a man of the cloth!" Mrs. Olann snapped at PC.

For the first time, Kin saw PC's jaw bulge. "I am a man of the cloth, ma'am."

"Then I insist that you back me up in fending for the reputation of my niece!"

Kin roughed a hand through his hair. "Have you even met your niece? Before this morning?"

The woman's eyes glittered. "Whether or not I've met her before makes not one whit of difference. I've just learned this morning that it's my burdensome responsibility to care for her, and all in the same breath that she spent half the night galivanting and who knows what with you through the back country, unchaperoned!" She angled a glance toward the door. "Cora! Do come in now."

Cora stepped timidly through the portal, hands curled together in a manner that revealed her distress. Her red-rimmed eyes sought him out. "I'm so sorry," she mouthed.

"Come, come." Mrs. Olann snapped, wagging a hand at her niece. "And do speak with your voice if you have something to communicate. It's improper to murmur and mumble." Mrs. Olann wrapped one arm around Cora's shoulders, but the gesture looked more like it was meant to trap the girl there than to comfort her.

Cora's gaze was still fixed to his. Her eyes revealed more than he'd ever considered possible. She was sorry that her aunt was throwing such a fit, she didn't want him to have to marry her, but at the same time, she dreaded the days ahead of living with such a woman.

Kin gripped the back of his neck and studied the floor. He couldn't marry her! She was practically a stranger, no matter that the night before he'd admired her spunk and unapologetic belief in her God. "I'd like to speak to Cora alone."

Mrs. Olann gasped. She looked at PC. "There! You see! Such unseemliness!"

PC's lips thinned. "I'm not sure how things were done where you are from, Mrs. Olann." He stepped forward and took the woman's arm, tugging her rather forcefully toward the kitchen table on the other side of the main room. "But here in the west, a man is allowed to be a gentleman without having his motives questioned."

"Well! I never!" The woman sputtered and kept glancing over her shoulder to look at them.

Kin tipped a nod toward the opposite wall. "We can talk over here."

Tommy chose that moment to poke his head out of their bedroom. "Kin, c-can I c-come out n-now?"

"Sure, pal. This is Cora."

Tommy smiled shyly at the pretty blonde. "H-hi."

"Cora this is Tommy."

Cora stretched out a hand. "It's a pleasure to meet you, Tommy."

Kin touched Tommy on the shoulder. "See that woman in the poofy hat talking to PC?"

Tommy nodded.

"She's Cora's aunt. I bet if you asked her, she'd be happy to make your oatmeal this morning."

Tommy's eyes sparkled, and he jumped up and down a couple times. "M-maybe she makes it n-nice and s-sweet l-like A-Aurora."

Kin nodded. "I bet she would, if you ask her."

Tommy skipped toward PC and Mrs. Olann, and Kin couldn't withhold a grin. When he glanced back at Cora, she gave him a knowing look. "You're terrible."

He smiled. "Maybe. Figured it might give us more time to talk."

Tears immediately burgeoned in her eyes. "I'm so sorry she's doing this. My mother told me about her, but I'd never met her until this morning." Cora's gaze sought the woman out where she was being prodded toward the kitchen by an enthusiastically bouncing Tommy.

From the kitchen table, PC offered Kin a knowing grin. Kin had halfway wondered if the parson would bail the woman out and make Tommy's morning food ritual himself, but it looked like he was on board with Kin's plan.

Cora glanced down at her hands. "She practically had an apoplectic fit when her husband mentioned me to her this morning. I could hear her yelling all the way in my room down the hall. I don't think she's happy about having another mouth to feed."

It was all starting to make sense now. "So, she's trying to foist you off on me." He immediately recognized the mistake in those words when her tears spilled over to stream down her cheeks. "Not that I would see it as foisting."

"Of course, you would." Cora picked at one fingernail. "And I c-can't marry you. You're not the kind of man I want."

He pushed away the discomfort her words raised. "Hey, chin up." Kin crooked one finger gently beneath her chin, bending down until she met his gaze. "We're not going to let her force us to get married for something we didn't do simply because she doesn't want to take care of you."

But what *were* they going to do? That was the question.

He frowned. "Didn't you write her before you came?"

"I did. But my mother passed, and our landlord told me I had 'til the next day to get out. I mailed the letter before I left New York, but..." She shrugged. "I must have beat it here."

Kin's heart went out to her. "So, your mother passed the day before you left New York?"

She nodded. "Three weeks and two days ago."

Kin's eyes fell closed. And right before Christmas too. He thought quickly. If her snooty aunt didn't want her, he certainly wasn't going to leave this sweet girl living with a stranger. Did Liora and Joe have room? He thought of his departure time that was getting closer by the minute. He didn't really have time to take her out there, but he knew PC would be happy to escort her. "Tell me what your skills are?"

She shrugged. "I was a maid in a hotel before I left New York. I can cook a fair bit. Other than that...not much."

A maid... Kin snapped his fingers. "I've just the place for you." He grinned. "And you're going to love it. Just let me get my stuff and put some shoes on."

She swiped her cheeks and nodded.

Kin emerged a few moments later with all his things and stretched an arm for her to precede him.

PC looked at him quizzically.

Kin wagged his head and kept his voice down. "Neither one of us want to get married. And we didn't do anything wrong."

"I believe you."

"Dixie told me just yesterday morning that she wished she had a housekeeper to clean the boardinghouse rooms now that she's so busy being a mother. It comes with a room. Cora seems to think that Mrs. Olann simply doesn't want the bother of supplying for her."

In the doorway from the kitchen, Mrs. Olann gasped. Her narrowed gaze landed on Cora. "How could you say such a thing?"

But Kin wasn't about to let the woman keep bullying Cora. He placed one hand to Cora's back. "Because she heard what you said to your husband this morning. But don't worry, I have the perfect job for Cora. You won't have to give her a cent."

With that, he reached past Cora and tugged open the door.

PC was there then, arms outstretched for a last hug. "You're sure you don't want me to ride with you to the station? Or take Cora to the boardinghouse myself?"

Kin swallowed as the man's arms enveloped him. "Nah. You've got Tommy to think of. And Wash and Zoe are going to see me off. And I have plenty of time to introduce Cora to Mrs. Griffin before we leave." His throat threatened to close off, but he forced the next words past the restriction. "Thanks for everything."

PC clapped him firmly on the back. "Proud of your actions last night, son. Real proud."

Kin only nodded, unable to look the man in the eye. He motioned to Tommy. "Get over here, Tom-Tom, and give me a farewell hug."

Tommy looked bewildered. "F-farewell?"

"Yeah, pal. But maybe not for as long as I first thought." PC's gaze drifted knowingly to Cora. Kin realized that perhaps he'd revealed too much with that comment. He stretched out one arm to pull Tommy in for an embrace.

"T-Tommy come?"

"Nah." Kin ruffled his hair. "You gotta stay here and make sure PC eats right."

Tommy straightened a little "O-okay!"

PC rolled his eyes and mouthed, "Thanks."

Kin grinned, knowing that Tommy would hound PC from this moment forward about whether he was eating right. He lifted a hand of farewell, then closed the door quickly before his emotions got the better of him.

He directed Cora to the boardinghouse and was thankful that Mrs. Griffin's face lit up like a candlelit Christmas tree the moment he presented Cora and her experience.

"Of course, I have a job for you! Do you have a place to stay? The job comes with room and board."

Cora blew out a breath of relief. "Thank you, ma'am. That would be very helpful."

Mrs. Griffin grinned and flapped her hands. "Oh, I'm just thrilled to pieces! Stay right here, and I'll go get the agreement for you to sign. Then I can show you around. How soon can you start?"

"Um... today?"

Mrs. Griffin gave a little cheer. "Kin, you are a lifesaver! And goodbye again, by the way. I know you probably need to get going. I just saw Wash and Zoe walk by, heading to the livery." She pulled him in for a quick hug before she bustled off to find her paperwork.

There was a soft look in Cora's eyes when she settled her gaze on him. "You know last night when that man Finn took hold of me, I prayed for God to send me an angel of rescue. Only just now did I realize that he actually did."

Kin adjusted his bag on his shoulder and couldn't withhold a chuckle. "First time I've ever been called an angel. I'm just glad I was there to help." He swept his hat to where Mrs. Griffin had disappeared. "Mrs. Griffin will take good care of you and be your friend to boot inside twenty-four hours. You'll find that most of the people in town are more like her than they are like your aunt." He motioned up the hill to the church they'd passed on the way here. "There's even a real good church. I'm sure you'll like that."

She nodded. "I will. Goodbye, Mr. Davis."

He backed toward the door. "Goodbye, Missionary Harrison."

She smiled. "I'll pray for you. God truly does love you and see you. That's what Christmas was all about. Imagine, the Holy Creator of all that we see, leaving His place in heaven to be born in a lowly manger! One day, God's love is going to wash over you so powerfully that you won't be able to understand how you resisted it for so long."

Kin gave her a friendly roll of his eyes. But as he rode on the wagon seat next to Wash and Zoe, doing his best to keep up his end of the conversation, he couldn't help but ponder on her parting words. Did God truly love a washout like him? Could he one day be a friend of God like PC had preached about?

"We're here," Wash announced, pulling the team to a stop. "Why are you looking so pensive all the sudden?"

Kin waved a hand and hopped from the wagon, gathering his stuff while Wash helped Zoe down from the other side. "It's nothing. Thanks again for the ride."

Zoe flung her arms around his neck. "Of course! We couldn't let our best pal from school days leave without one final goodbye."

Wash grinned and stretched out one thick palm. "Until we meet again, Kin."

Kin juggled his luggage to free up a hand. He nodded. And this time the restriction in his throat couldn't be overcome.

So, without another word he hurried into the train station.

But as the train chuffed away from Wyldhaven a few minutes later, Kin looked out the window and smiled.

He would go to Seattle for a little while. But he'd be back. He'd definitely be back.

And as the visage of a beautiful blonde with hazel eyes and upswept hair filled his mind, he knew that what he'd said to Tommy earlier was true. He'd likely be back sooner than imagined.

Dear Reader,

I hope you have enjoyed this array of Wyldhaven novellas this season. I can't wait to share Kin's full story with you in a future full-length book. This silly author's heart has grown fond of him—maybe because he's so much like a real young man who is near and dear to my heart. Oh, and the Carvers will get their stories too, eventually. I have so many books left to write in this series! *Smile.*

One of Kin's reasons for resisting committing his life to God is that he has failed too many times. Have you been there? Have you ever felt like you've dropped the ball so often that God doesn't use or need someone like you? Let me encourage you that it's not true!

Remember Moses? He was a murderer, yet God used him to bring the Children of Israel out of Egypt and to do many other miraculous things. Remember King David? He was an adulterer and a murderer, yet his writings compose one of the books of the Bible that have reached many millions over the years. So just because your past may be scarred by sin, don't let that stop you from choosing life! Do you realize that scar tissue is stronger and more resilient than the skin that was unblemished and clear? Some people like to say that when you come to Christ, He wipes all that scar tissue (from our sin and poor choices) away, but I don't think that's quite right. God leaves at least some of the scars to remind us of where we were before Him.

He also uses those scars to reach others. There may be someone that only you can reach because of your past mistakes. This definitely doesn't mean that we should go out and sin it up. But it does mean that I hope you won' t listen to the devil's lies that tell you you're not good enough.

I'll close with this... If you are like Kin, please be aware that there is hope. God has never yet rejected anyone who fell on their knees before him in repentance. In Christ, there is love, joy, peace, patience, kindness, gentleness, and self-control. All that and so much more can be yours, just by asking.

As you go into this Christmas season, I hope you'll ponder on the true reason we celebrate that holiday, and what it cost Jesus to be born on this earth—all for you. If you were the only one, He still would have come.

If you enjoyed this collection, **please leave the book a review**. It doesn't have to be long, but every review helps spread the word, and the world needs more uplifting stories!

We've come to the end of the novellas, and I don't have an excerpt from the next full-length book yet. But if you are enjoying this series, I know you will enjoy my Shepherd's Heart series too. Book one of that series opens in the Idaho Territory in 1885. I invite you to read the first couple chapters of that book on the next page. It is titled *Rocky Mountain Oasis*.

Also, if you missed some of the earlier episodes in this series, you can find all the Wyldhaven books here on my website.

Merry Christmas!

Lynnette
BONNER

Now available...

THE SHEPHERD'S HEART - BOOK 1
ROCKY MOUNTAIN
Oasis

You may read an excerpt on the next page...

Chapter One

*Lewiston, Idaho Territory
August 1885*

Brooke Marie Baker pressed a hand to her thumping heart and forced herself to breathe normally as she walked into town beside the last wagon of the caravan. Whether she wanted to be here or not, they had arrived. Six months of grueling travel across rugged prairies and mountain passes. Aching back. Aching feet. Oppressive heat and little to eat. Yet she'd be willing to travel on forever if it meant she didn't have to be here. Didn't have to give up her freedom.

This morning, Harry had said they would arrive in Lewiston today, but she had hoped something would delay the inevitable.

The weathered facades of the clapboard houses she walked past and the monotonous creak of the wagon wheels turning over the graveled street proved her hope had been futile.

Along both sides of the road, as they turned onto the main street, people stopped to stare. Brooke didn't meet their gazes but kept her perusal focused on the buildings. Real buildings with boardwalks, stairs, and windows. The last time she'd seen boardwalks had been three months ago at Fort Laramie.

Ahead, someone let out a loud whoop of joy.

She looked down the line of bonnet-topped Conestogas.

The first wagons had come to a stop, and apparently the gathered crowd had been anxiously awaiting their arrival.

Toward the front of the throng, a cluster of men stood, studying the caravan expectantly.

Almost all of them had long, tobacco-stained beards. Not one looked like he was under fifty-five, and several had no compunctions about scratching themselves in public. One man, thick black suspenders holding up his baggy pants, ogled Brooke from head to toe. Then, still scrutinizing her, he leaned to one side and spat a stream of tobacco.

She felt a familiar quiver of fear and glanced away, offering the man no challenge.

"Let's get on with the marryin'," a deep voice toward the back shouted. "I got plenty o' work waitin' for me back ta home." A loud grumble of agreement followed.

An older man scratched at his beard and complained, "You all was supposed to be here two days ago."

"Gentlemen! Gentlemen!" Harry's spurs jangled as he jumped to the ground from his position in the lead wagon. He was using his let's-stay-calm tone—the same one he'd used when Emily Donaldson had discovered the much-too-friendly beaver in the bathing hole back on the Platte and every last woman had rushed screaming from the water. "Give me a moment to gather your brides, and then we can proceed."

The grumblings ceased, and apparently satisfied the men had gotten his message, Harry turned and strode Brooke's way, thumbs hooked into his large silver belt-buckle. "Come on, ladies. Everybody circle up. We're here." His familiar *rap-rap* as he knocked on the side of the first wagon resounded down the street.

Her stomach threatened to empty right there in front of God and everyone. She stepped back behind the tailgate, drew in a long breath, held it, and eased it out between pursed lips. Pushing aside memories of days gone by, she forced her shoulders to relax. While she dared not hope that things would be different this time, neither did she want her nervousness to be apparent.

Rap-rap. He'd reached the second wagon. Only four more to go.

She took another breath and released it on a low whisper. "You can do this. Calm down."

A moment later, he peered around the end of the wagon. "Brooke? I need everyone to meet up front, please. The men have a minister here already."

"I know." The words emerged on a squeak, and she pressed moist palms together, rubbing them in circles.

Harry gave her a sympathetic look. "You don't have anything to worry about. I'm real careful to make sure all the men are honest, upstanding citizens."

Emily Donaldson rounded the wagon, her red-painted lips puckered in aggravation and one dark eyebrow arched. "Comforting, I'm sure, Harry, for a young girl like her." She pierced the wagon-master with a glare.

If only Emily knew. But she didn't. None of them knew anything about her or the real reason she was here.

Harry snorted and stalked off, grousing, "Just be up front in five minutes. And best you follow instructions this time, Emily Donaldson!"

Emily huffed. "What do men know?" She put an arm around Brooke and rested one cheek on the top of her head. "Come on, now." She gave Brooke a gentle squeeze. "No use us trying to postpone the inevitable."

"I suppose you're right." Brooke trailed after her past the row of wagons, feeling sweat trickle down her back.

All the women gathered on one side of the street under the overhang in front of the bank. The men clustered across the way, looking them over like meat on a market table.

She swallowed down the burn pressing at the back of her throat. Of course she hadn't expected anything better. She pressed the sleeve of her dress to the beads of moisture dotting her forehead. If it wasn't so hot, this might be easier to face.

The minister in the dusty street between the two groups raised his arms for silence. "All right, listen up now. To make this as efficient as possible, I will call forward each man. He will present me with his documents, and then I will call forward one of you women, and we'll have a ceremony for that couple, then move on to the next one. My wife and Mr. Preston here—" he glanced over his shoulder at a plump woman and a frowning man standing off to one side, "have agreed to be witnesses, and the hotel down the street has prepared a special meal for the occasion."

A chorus of appreciation rose from the men. The women remained silent. Only one or two even shuffled their feet.

"Oh and one more thing." The minister again gestured for everyone's attention. "Is there a Miss, ah—" he patted several pockets, then finally pulled a paper from the one in his shirt and consulted it "—Brooke Baker, here?"

Brooke blinked in surprise. Could this be a reprieve? Maybe the man Uncle Jackson had pledged her to had died or changed his mind. She stepped forward.

But Harry spoke before she could find her voice. "Yeah, she's here. What do you need with her?"

The minister peered at her over the top of his spectacles. "Miss Baker?"

Mouth dry, she nodded.

"Your intended has asked that I escort you by stage to a town about half a day's ride from here called Greer's Ferry. So you won't meet him until tomorrow."

Brooke's knees nearly gave out in relief, but by some miracle she stayed on her feet. "Oh, thank you, sir." Heat rose up from her collar and into her face. She'd sounded a trifle too gleeful.

Easing to the back of the crowd, she relaxed against the building's warm brick and tucked her trembling hands behind her. Her eyes dropped closed, and she tilted her face to the sun.

One more day. One more day of freedom.

★★★

Pierce City, Idaho Territory
August 1885

Evening shadows stretched long as Sky Jordan placed the last of the supplies onto his pack mule. The leather of the packs creaked as he settled them into place, cinched them down, and made sure everything was in proper order. He stood in front of Fraser's Mercantile, scratching the mule behind its long gray ears, surveying Main Street.

A lone pine tree grew in the middle of the dusty street at the south end of town, its shadow falling due east. Summer crickets chirped lustily from the bushes nearby, and he could hear the occasional *tink* of bottle on shot glass emanating from Roo's Saloon across the street.

From an upper-story window in the Joss house, a Chinese woman emptied a pail of water onto the street, splattering mud on Gaffney's Pioneer Hotel next door and leaving a small muddy patch in the alley between the buildings.

"Sky! You comin' in here? Food's gonna be cold 'fore you ever set down to table!"

A rough, gravelly voice interrupted his perusal of the town. He glanced up at the friendly, round face of Jed Swanson, who leaned over the rail in front of his boarding house.

"Food ain't gonna be fit for hogs if'n you don't get in here," Jed complained, rubbing a plump hand down the front of his greasy, apron-clad belly.

A smile stretched Sky's face. Jed's food always fell somewhere between burlap and leather, but Jed invariably claimed that was because it had been left sitting too long.

"Your food? Fit for Hogs?" Sky taunted, unable to pass up the opportunity to tease his old friend.

"Hmmph!" Jed shook his wooden spoon at Sky. "Mind your manners, or you won't be gettin' any o' my fine fixins." He turned away, slamming the door as he went inside.

Sky gave the mule a friendly slap on the neck, left it tied to the rail, then trooped wearily up the steps to Jed's boarding house, the building next door to Fraser's Mercantile.

The rough wooden door opened on squeaking hinges as he entered. He hooked his black Stetson on a peg in the wall and scanned the room.

The only light in the gloomy confines of the rugged log building emanated from a small oil lamp set in the middle of the dining table and a brightly burning fire in the fireplace on the back wall. The stone and mortar hearth, stacked high with logs on one side, held the wrought-iron hook by which the coffee pot could be swung into the heat of the fire. Off to the left, on the back wall, he could see the dark shadow of the doorway that led to the rooms Jed rented out.

Sky turned to his right. Several men were already seated around the coarse plank table, shoveling food into their mouths as though it might disappear before their eyes, their forks clanking loudly against tin plates. His interest piqued as he noticed his cousin, Jason, sitting in the dim light at the end of the table, his back to the wall. A hefty man with unwashed blond curls covering his head, Jason looked as surly as ever. His large belly, the result of his love of beer, protruded over his huge silver belt buckle, bumping the table.

Sky sauntered casually to an empty chair, sat down with his back to the room, and began to serve his plate, listening to the conversation around him.

Fraser was speaking. "This boy is a lunatic, I tell you, and he wants to court my Alice. She's only fifteen, and I sent her down to Lewiston to get an education, not to court boys. So I told him straight out, when I was down to Lewiston last, that he had better stay away from her. Now, with her being over seventy-five miles from here, that in itself wouldn't give me a whole lot of comfort, since I wouldn't trust that boy as far as I could throw him. But I also told Judge Rand that the boy was not to come around anymore, and if anyone will make sure he don't, it'll be the judge."

Sky's mind wandered to his little sister back home as he added a spoonful of greens to his plate. *Wonder if boys are coming to call on Sharyah already?* She was about the same age as Alice Fraser. He smiled to himself. Knowing Sharyah and her blond curls and beautiful sunny smile, the boys were lined up for a mile outside of the little white farmhouse back in Shiloh. *Dad's probably going through the same thing as Fraser.*

Jed slurped his coffee noisily. "Judge Rand be a good man. Speakin' o' which, I hear tell Lee Chang is up to his ol' tricks again. Nigh on got hisself killed by a trader that came through the other day, way I hear it. 'Cept Chang's goons came to his rescue and ran the feller out of town. He tried to pay the man with some o' that bogus gold he's gettin' a reputation fer usin'." Jed shook his head. "Someone ought to take Chang to court. The judge would see to him, sure 'nuff."

Sky's curiosity lifted his brow. "Bogus gold? What's that all about?"

"You ain't heard that story, yet?" Jed motioned at Fraser with the point of his knife. "Tell 'im, Fraser."

Fraser twisted his mug in a circle. "Louise came to see me a couple months back. Right after the last time you came through for supplies."

"Louise? The Nez Perce woman who brings garden produce to town to sell?"

"That's the one." Fraser nodded.

Sky sawed at his meat, waiting for Fraser to continue.

"Well, she brought me the gold that Chang had paid them the last time they sold to him. He'd taken small pebbles and dipped them in gold. They were only worth a fraction of their promised value. She, Jane, and Running Fawn nearly got arrested last time they were down to Lewiston when someone there discovered the deception, but they managed to convince the authorities that they themselves had been duped. Anyhow, Louise came to me. Wanted me to go and confront Chang about it." He stabbed a piece of rawhide-meat and stuffed it into his cheek irritably.

Sky leaned back in his chair, amazed at Chang's gall.

He knew Lee Chang. His character was questionable at best and downright despicable at worst. He dealt in opium and women and offered no mercy when it came time to pay up for either. But this was the first he'd heard of the man being a cheat.

Max, a miner seated next to Jason, grunted. "Don't see why she didn't confront him herself."

Fraser looked up. "You know Chang—he's got his thumb on just about every individual in the county. The women are afraid that if Chang gives the say-so, all the other Chinese in the area will boycott their business. They would certainly be out of business if he did that to them."

"Hmmph," Jed growled, "that there Chinese is one man this here town could do 'thout. He shorly is a cussed buzzard, that'n."

Fraser huffed his agreement. "And do you know," he leaned forward and pierced Sky with a look, "when I confronted him, the man had the nerve to admit to the whole thing!"

"Does he plan to make it right?"

Fraser wiped his mouth with the back of his hand, chewing the food for a moment before he spoke. "Nope. He said he paid them and they accepted payment and that he hoped they would be a bit smarter next time." He glanced around the table, knife and fork held vertically by his plate in suspended animation, then shrugged. "The man showed no remorse whatsoever. I don't know what else I can do." He stared back at his plate and continued to hack at the black slab that passed as a piece of meat.

"Leastwise you tried. Best you watch your back, though," Jed added. "That Chang, he don't cotton to no one gettin' all up in his business."

Jason gave a low snort from the other side of the table, and Sky looked down to the shadows at the end. His cousin shoveled another mouthful of food, then belched. Seeming to notice that everyone's eyes were on him, he spoke. "This town would be better off if we got rid of all the Chinks. I tell you, I've never met a respectable Celestial. Not one. Always sneakin' and spyin'. Lazy cusses, too." He swiped his greasy mouth on his shoulder, the stain there proof that he did so often.

Max made no sound but nodded emphatically as he shoved a huge forkful of potatoes into his mouth.

"This town wouldn't exist if it wasn't for the Chinese, Jason." Sky kept his voice nonchalant. He picked up his glass and took a drink of water, his eyes fixed on his burly cousin over the rim.

Jason snorted again. "You always were too partial to them Celestials, Sky. If you had any sense, you'd realize the type of scum they really are."

Sky changed the subject. "How have you been, Jason? Haven't seen you for awhile." His tone was friendly, but Jason glared at him.

"You been pinin' away for information on your beloved cousin?" he asked, expression caustic.

Sky, accustomed to his cousin's recent foul moods, shrugged and turned back to his food, praying silently that one day his relationship with Jason would be restored.

Jed's gaze bounced between them as he squirmed in his seat. After a minute, he fixed Sky with a pointed look. "That news about Chang...well, that ain't the only news you missed hearin' about. You need to get to town more often."

The venomous glare Jason sent Jed piqued Sky's interest. "Oh yeah?" He cautiously tried a bite of potatoes. Not too bad this time. Maybe he could smother the meat with them.

Jed's twinkling eyes remained fixed on Jason, and a smile twitched the corner of his mouth as silence filled the room.

Sky looked to his cantankerous cousin, one eyebrow raised in question. Several of the men shifted uneasily. Everyone seemed to know what Jed was referring to except him.

Jason waved away his unspoken question with a flip of his hand.

"Aw! Ain't you gonna tell ol' Sky here about yer plans?"

Jason ignored Jed and scooped another bite into his mouth.

Sky turned his questioning eyes on Jed, continuing to eat calmly.

Jed spoke around a mouthful of meat. "Your cousin is soon gonna be married. Or so he's been tellin' it."

Sky's fork stopped halfway up from his plate and he blinked in surprise. *What woman in her right mind would marry Jason?*

Jason growled, throwing his fork onto his plate with a clatter. "Jed, you wouldn't know a secret if it bit you!" He turned belligerent eyes on Sky. "That's right. I've got a mail-order bride coming in on tomorrow's stage to Greer's Ferry. I'm going to have me a pretty little wife to cook for me...and keep me warm at night." He jabbed his elbow into Max's ribs, a dissolute leer spreading on his face.

Sky set his fork down quietly. Pushing away from the table, he stood and walked over to the blackened coffee pot near the fire. Pouring himself a cup, his movements deliberate and casual, he contemplated the situation. His heart went out to the poor girl. He couldn't remember the last time he'd been so surprised.

"You got a picture of this woman?" He hooked a thumb through his belt loop, watching Jason through the steam drifting up from his mug as he took a sip of coffee.

Jason gave his habitual snort. "Like I'd show it to you. Pretty little thing, though. And young, too. I'm really looking forward to tomorrow night." The lewd grin was back before he stuffed a large piece of meat into his cheek.

"Well, let me be the first to offer you my congratulations." Sky lifted his coffee mug in a toast. "To the happy groom." No one in the room responded; he hadn't expected them to. Turning back he gazed into the fire. A log dropped, shooting a cascade of orange sparks upwards. The silence in the room hovered palpably; only the crackling of the fire and the clatter of silverware disturbed the stillness.

Lord, what should I do? I wouldn't give a dog I liked to Jason. You know I care for him, but... Sky tried to think of a solution. Nothing came to mind.

Weariness weighted his eyes and, remembering he still had to travel home tonight, he set his cup down.

Turning to Jed, he placed a hand on his stomach and grinned. "Best hog swill I've had in a long time, Jed."

Jed grunted, waving his fork in dismissal.

To Fraser, he said, "Been a pleasure, Fraser. See you again soon."

Fraser regarded him with a friendly smile as he wiped the corners of his mouth with long, slender fingers. "Sky, always good doing business with you." Sky nodded and Fraser's eyes held Sky's for a moment, questioning what he was going to do about Jason's situation, before he turned back to his food.

"Good night, gentlemen," Sky said to the rest of the men at the table. The leather of his hat felt smooth against his fingers as he removed it from the peg by the door and pushed it back onto his head, exiting onto the now-darkened street.

The muffled sound his boots made in the soft dust of the roadbed didn't carry far into the cricket-serenaded night. At the rail in front of Fraser's Mercantile, he untied his mule. Leading it further down the street toward the livery, he studied the starry sky. *Jason getting married.* Unshakable heaviness settled on his shoulders.

"Get a grip, Jordan," he grumbled and forced himself to focus on the road ahead as he resettled his hat. There was nothing he could do for the poor woman. And maybe she'd be good for Jason.

With renewed determination to let the matter go, he retrieved his stallion, mounted up, and cantered out of town, leading the mule behind.

Chapter Two

Lewiston, Idaho Territory
August 1885

In the shadow cast by the telegraph office, a man stood with his head bent low over a telegram. He leaned one shoulder into the building as a sardonic smile twisted his lips, and he read the message again.

> It's in the back room STOP Come at your convenience STOP Have men in place STOP
> L C
> Pierce City

He rubbed his hand across his chin, still staring at the paper before him. His first two fingers paused on his chin, and he tapped it slowly twice as he thought. The news was good, but so many plans still had to be made. He peered both up and down the street. Although it teemed with traffic, no one looked his way, so he slipped back around the corner and into the telegraph office.

The operator was just heading out the door. Startled, he pulled his round spectacles to his eyes by the rim. "Oh, hello again—" one side of the paunchy little man's mouth tilted up nervously, his eyes darting across the room to a board with several wanted posters pinned to it "—did you forget something?"

"I need to reply to this message." He made sure his tone and face emanated calm.

The operator quickly returned to his side of the counter and took up a pen. With a shaking hand, he dipped it into the inkwell before him and waited expectantly.

The man dictated, "Coming by stage to Pierce City. STOP. Wait for my arrival." He glanced at his watch. *11:59 a.m.* As the operator reached to send the message, the man leaned across the counter and gripped his shoulder. Jumping, the operator turned toward him with a frightened expression, but he only said, "Wait," and paced across the room to peruse the wanted posters.

Slowly the second hand ticked around until the time read *12:05 p.m.* He nodded at the operator, who was now sweating profusely. "I will wait until you have sent the message."

With shaking fingers, the operator tapped out the message to Pierce City. Once the message had been sent, he allowed his face to soften. He even thanked the operator politely for his help and patience.

Mopping his sweat-covered brow with a white handkerchief, the operator smiled his relief and nodded, face calming.

The man turned toward the door and took two long strides. Then, suddenly changing his course of direction and not bothering to use the gate, he placed his hand on the counter and, in one smooth motion, leaped across it to the side where the now gaping, slack-jawed operator sat. Grabbing the trembling telegrapher by his collar, he dragged him into a small room he could see at the back of the office, pressed the trembling man against the wall, forearm to his throat, and pulled a knife from his sheath under his jacket.

He turned the blade, watching as the light glanced off it and made pleasant patterns on the operator's plump face.

"Be a shame if somethin' were to happen to your missus," he murmured.

The little man clutched at the arm pressed to his neck and nodded vigorously.

"Funny thing about those wanted posters. They seem to pop up all over the place. A man can't get any peace."

This time the telegrapher shook his head. "I have never seen you, I swear."

Chuckling, he pressed the tip of his blade to the soft skin under his captive's eye. The man scrunched his eyes tight.

He grinned. *As though that will protect them from my blade.*

"P-Please. I won't say a w-word."

He let the knife point bite the flesh just enough to draw blood. "See that you don't. I've seen your missus, and it would sure be a shame if somethin' were to happen to such a pretty little thing, if you catch my meanin'." With one last surge of pressure, he pushed away from the shuddering man. "And take the poster down. It's an awful likeness. Makes me look as though I'm some unkempt hooligan."

The operator nodded and, as the man turned to leave, he heard him slide down to the floor. He smirked and sheathed his blade.

Moments later he stepped out onto the boardwalk. Smoothing the front of his coat and squinting into the sunshine, he walked up the street toward the stage that waited for boarding passengers. Tipping his hat, he smiled at a woman with a young child in tow.

★★★

Pierce City
12:03 p.m.

Lee Chang lumbered up the street toward the telegraph office. Opening the door, he eased himself into the small, dusty room.

The office had been shut down several years ago, when the population had dwindled to the point that there were no longer enough people in town to warrant its use, though the telegraph was still operational. An occasional message came through, though, and if someone who could read Morse code happened to be passing by on the street to hear it, sometimes it even got to the person for whom it was meant.

On this day, however, Lee knew a message would be coming through and didn't want to chance someone walking by on the street and hearing the clatter of the code. Especially not David Fraser, who understood Morse code.

Leaning out the door, he scanned the street to be sure no one was near. Finally satisfied he was alone, he eased the door shut. He had just turned toward the desk in the darkened corner of the room when the telegraph began to click and tap out its message. He scrambled for a pencil and paper.

★★★

Lewiston
12:15 p.m.

Brooke placed both hands beside her on the seat to help keep her balance as the stage careened around corners and over bumps, heading toward Greer's Ferry. She tried to ignore the chatter coming from the man opposite her. Brushing a stray curl of hair out of her eyes and tucking it behind her ear, she peered out the window at the passing scenery and tried to swallow the lump of nervousness in her throat.

Wondering what the man she was to marry would be like, she wished again that Uncle Jackson had not sent her away. *I could have gone to work and helped support him.* Even living with Uncle Jackson was preferable to being married to a man like the ones she'd seen yesterday.

But his cutting words still rang in her ears. *You good-for-nothing little tramp. I should have sent you off the moment I became your guardian.* His laugh had been cruel as he continued, *At least I'm getting fifty dollars for the trouble you've been! Congratulations on your upcoming marriage, my dear.* She shuddered, giving herself a little shake to dispel his face from her memory, and forced her mind back to the present.

Besides the minister, who traveled with her to perform the marriage ceremony at the trail's end, two other passengers had gotten on the stage. One, a burly mountain man who resembled how she'd always imagined a mountain man would look—with a long, tangled gray beard. It evidenced the fact that often when he spit tobacco juice, he didn't really spit at all but merely let the juice dribble out the corner of his mouth...a most disgusting phenomenon Brooke had witnessed more than once on the trip. When he'd hauled his considerable girth onto the stage, he'd grunted a greeting, let his eyes rove over her form, and then slouched in his seat with his muddied boots stretched out as far in front of him as they would go. Giving Brooke another appreciative look, he'd rested his head against the side of the coach and fallen fast asleep. His snores would have been enough to harry a hen laying eggs, but any hens in the vicinity had probably already been disturbed by the second personality who'd joined them on the stage.

This man had not been quiet for more than five consecutive seconds since his foot first touched the floor of the stage. His blond, frizzy hair poked from his head in unruly abandon, giving him a rather wild look. He wore a pair of round spectacles that invariably slipped down his nose, and he constantly pushed them back up. He would cease to expound on one topic, and

Brooke would sigh in relief, thinking there couldn't possibly be anything more to say on the subject, when he would begin anew. As annoying as she found the talkative man across from her, Brooke did find that she learned a lot about the area that they drove through.

"There are really some fascinatin' rock formations in this area." He gestured out the window with fingers so heavily laden with gaudy gold rings that Brooke wondered how his slender hand supported the weight. "Take that one down there across the river...do you see it?" Even before Brooke nodded, he continued, "The Ant and the Yellow Jacket."

Brooke regarded him quizzically.

He pushed his round spectacles up on his nose with a bony forefinger. "Yep, the Nez Perce say that the ants and the yellow jackets lived peaceably together until one day, their chiefs got into an argument. The yellow jacket—of course the Indians just call them 'Ant' and 'Yellow Jacket,' like that was their names or somethin'." He chuckled. "Anyway, the yellow jacket chief, he had found this piece of dried salmon and was eating it on a rock. The ant chief comes along, and he is hungry, see? So he gets jealous of the yellow jacket and starts hollerin' at him that he should have asked permission to eat on that rock. The yellow jacket responds, 'I don't have to ask your permission for anythin',' and they raise up on their back legs and start fightin'. Well, the old coyote, who the Nez Perce believe is very wise, comes along. He sees the piece of salmon and those two a-whalin' on each other. He's across the river, so he hollers at them, 'Hey, you two, quit your fightin'!' but they pay no attention. So the magic coyote turned them into those rocks you see over there just like that—" He snapped his fingers. "The coyote crossed the river and ate the salmon, and to this day, the ants and the yellow jackets are feudin' among themselves.

"Yep, sure is some interesting country you have come to Miss... Hey, I haven't introduced myself. I am Percival Hunter." He bowed from the waist, as good a bow as one can give from a sitting position, removing his bowler hat. "And you are?"

Brooke smiled; she was beginning to like this talkative man before her. "Brooke Baker. It's a pleasure to meet you." She extended a hand, which he took and raised to his lips.

"The pleasure is all mine, I assure you."

Brooke pulled her hand away and focused on her lap, not wanting to give him the wrong impression. She was, after all, on the way to her wedding.

Percival cleared his throat. "Well, as I was sayin', this sure is interesting country you've chosen to come visit, Miss Baker." He continued without pause, or Brooke would have informed him that she was not here by her own choice. "Take the ferry we'll use to cross the Clearwater. Did you know that the Greer Ferry, as it is called, was constructed in 1861 by two enterprisin' souls who saw a sure-fire way to make some money off of the gold strike up in Pierce?"

Brooke shook her head, resigned to listening to his prattle for the rest of the trip.

"They built the ferry to aid the miners in crossin' the river on their way to Pierce City, where gold had been found. As I see it, their venture was a lot more profitable than goin' on up the mountain to dig for gold. There are even sleepin' quarters where we'll stay tonight."

The minister, resting his forearms on his knees, added, "The first ferry and sleeping quarters were burnt to the ground a few years ago in the Indian War of 1877 when the Nez Perce used it to cross the river and get away from the army chasing them. They crossed the river on the ferry, then torched it and the cabin so the army would have a harder time following them."

Percival nodded. "That's right. After the war, though, a new ferry and cabin were built. Those are the ones we'll see this evenin'."

"I'm amazed at how much you know about this country, Mr. Hunter," Brooke said.

He grinned and shrugged, indicating it was no big deal. Then, after only a short silence, he went on to tell how the Nez Perce Indians made their camp on the Camas Prairie each fall in order to collect the Camas bulbs that grew there in wild abandon. "All the bands of the Nez Perce come together and place their teepees in six camps over a two-mile radius. It's quite a sight."

He told of many men who, in the winter of 1861, while making their way to the gold camps, were blinded by the brilliant, glistening snow and were never found until the spring thaw. Brooke shivered, but if Percival noticed, it only inspired him.

On and on the stories went, and when suddenly, the stage came to a jerking halt, Brooke was amazed to find that the day had ebbed away. They had come to the place where they would cross the river. But as she looked out the window, she was surprised to see that the river still lay below them a good 1500 feet.

"Now comes the fun part," Percival said.

Brooke felt dizzy as she stared down the precipitous pitch to the water. "What are we doing now?"

Her answer came in the form of the stage driver, who poked his head in the door. "Ya'll can get out and stretch a mite if ya want to. We'll be here a few minutes while we hitch up the tree drag."

Brooke wondered at the term *tree drag*, but as she stepped down from the stage, she saw it was just what it sounded like. The stage driver and the man who had been riding shotgun were hitching a large tree trunk to the back of the stage. Her gaze returned to the river, and her stomach pitched. "We are going to drive down *that?*"

"Yep," Percival answered. A little too gleefully, if she were the judge.

"Well, if I die, at least I won't have to get married," she mumbled under her breath as she gazed at the steep track before her.

Soon they all climbed back into the stage except for the mountain man, who had never gotten off. He was awake now, though, and took the opportunity to stuff another wad of chewing tobacco in his cheek. He considered Brooke wolfishly. "Best hold on tight," he told her, winking boldly.

With a shouted "Gidd'up!" the driver cracked his whip in the air, and the horses lurched into the descent. Brooke gripped the edge of her seat and wondered whether she wanted to look out the window or close her eyes as tight as she could. Deciding that if she was going to die, she wanted to see it coming, she peered out and watched the scenery fly by.

Even Percival held his silence. *Thank goodness!*

It was soon apparent that the log hooked to the back of the stage was what saved them at each corner from launching over the edge of the trail into open space. The horses dug their heels in until they almost sat. Still, the stage careened down the steep incline.

Dust boiled up, whirling into the coach in a suffocating cloud. Choking and coughing, Brooke closed her eyes against the grit. Waving a hand in front of her face did nothing but stir the thick, roiling cloud. Feeling something pressed against her face, she realized that the minister was offering her his handkerchief. Gratefully, she grasped it, tears streaming from her eyes as she tried to see what was happening outside.

Then, as quickly as it had begun, the death-defying ride was over. She slumped back in relief. The river meandered placidly beyond the coach's window. They had made it down, and she was still alive.

It couldn't have taken more than a handful of minutes to plunge down the side of the mountain, but to Brooke it had seemed like an eternity. The coachman pulled the snorting horses to a stop and stepped down to unhitch the tree drag.

Brooke glanced down. Her dark blue dress was literally brown with dust. She touched a hand to her face and patted her hair. *I must look a mess!*

The ferry waited for them on the near side of the blue-green river, a smiling, kind-looking man standing on the landing. Brooke eyed the little raft tied to the bank dubiously. *Ferry was really too grand a term for the wooden contraption floating on the water. Will that even float with the stage on it?*

The horses walked onto the wooden platform with the loud clatter of hooves, and they pushed off into the river. She glanced out the window, looking back at the path of their descent in utter disbelief. *Well, the descent from that ridge didn't kill me; maybe I'll drown crossing the river.*

Her stomach felt like it was tied in knots. The man she was to marry would be waiting for her across the river at the landing. *My dress! I can't get married looking like I've been wallowing in a mound of dirt! Oh, what will the man think when he first lays eyes on me? So much for first impressions.*

She did her best to beat some of the dust from her skirt but saw that it was no use. He would have to take her the way she was. It was his own fault, after all, for not wanting to come to Lewiston to meet her. She'd learned he had paid the minister an extra five dollars to escort her to Greer's Ferry and perform the ceremony there.

The swaying of the ferry stopped. Her hands, fisted in her lap, were white-knuckled, but she lifted her chin. *You can deal with this!* Hadn't she survived Uncle Jackson all these years? If she could survive his beatings, then she could survive the abuses of any man. Hadn't she proved that with Hank? Moving out of Uncle Jackson's house to move in with Hank had been like jumping from the frying pan into the fire. She still had nightmares about Hank, but she was alive. She would be fine. But she must be strong.

Yet she could taste fear at the back of her mouth.

These past months, traveling west, she had not been beaten or abused once. Could she truly put herself back into such an environment? There was no doubt that life here would be the same as back in St. Louis. All men were the same: *Father, Uncle Jackson, Hank.* She shut her mind off from that line of thinking. She would not dwell on the past; she needed all of her strength to face the future.

She took the hand that the minister offered and stepped out into the bright sunlight, raising one hand to shade her eyes from the glare.

★★★

Sky watched the ferry cross the river, wishing he wasn't here, yet knowing he couldn't be anywhere else. Holding a single, yellow, dark-centered daisy in one hand, he reached with the other to flick an invisible speck of dust from the sleeve of his black suit coat. Black, perfectly creased pants encased his legs, tapering down to his highly polished black boots. His black Stetson protected his eyes from the glaring sun as he looked out over the river considering his present situation.

Would there really be a woman on board who had come this far to marry Jason? *Of course, she doesn't know what Jason is like, or she'd never have agreed to marry him.* Then again, maybe she would have. What did he know of the woman coming across the river? Perhaps she would be a bawdy, boisterous madam, just Jason's type. But then he remembered Jason's description of her. "Young and pretty" had been his words. No, he didn't think the woman would be risqué, but he found himself wondering what she *would* be like. *It doesn't matter— no woman deserves to be left to Jason.*

She won't be beautiful, though. She wouldn't be coming west to find a husband if she had any hope of finding one back home. With this thought in mind, he cleared his vision of the beautiful Victoria Snyder, his childhood sweetheart who lived back home in Shiloh, and prepared himself for the task at hand. Reaching up, he straightened the string tie at his throat and banished all concern about Jason. The Lord knew about his future, and this gave Sky the peace he needed to face the decision he had made.

The stage pulled off the ferry with squeaking wheels and the minister descended. "It's now or never, old boy," Sky mumbled to himself as he sauntered toward the coach, twirling the daisy between his fingers.

He stopped several yards off as a small, dusty hand grasped the minister's, and a woman stepped down to the ground. She reached one hand up to shade her eyes from the glare of the sun and Sky saw her apprehensive fear. He knew at that moment he'd done the right thing in coming. All his doubts fled. Jason would have thoroughly ravished the enchanting creature before him, destroying her serene spirit.

She was beautiful. *Very beautiful.* Her hair, though covered in dust, was a curly reddish-blond. Large blue eyes peered out from a tanned face accentuated by high cheekbones and a full, soft mouth. A vulnerable expression tightened her features, and his heart constricted in his chest. Her uncertainty gave her magnetic charm. He took a step closer. She bit her lower lip, drawing his attention to her mouth momentarily before it snapped back to her eyes. Blinking in the sunlight, she slowly focused on his face, her lips pinched together. *She's scared to death!*

Sky saw the surprise in her eyes as they adjusted to the glare of the sun and came to rest on him. He stepped forward, smiled lightly, and, lifting his hat, nodded in her direction. "Ma'am, it's a pleasure to make your acquaintance." He held out the daisy like a peace offering, watching her carefully, his eyes never leaving her face.

She looked down at the flower but did not move for several seconds. Then she took it with one slender hand and glanced back up into his face.

Lifting the daisy slightly, her generous mouth serious, she said, "Thank you." The words held the note of a question, and her voice was moderated so low that he almost couldn't hear what she said.

Sky felt his heart go out to her as he again realized how apprehensive she must be. He wanted to smooth the fearful frown off her brow, but he simply nodded, and they stood looking at one another. He wondered what she was thinking.

She was the first to avert her gaze, bringing her hands together in front of her. Her next words captivated Sky: "If you don't mind..." All color in her face disappeared and something flashed in her eyes. Was it fear? She quickly schooled her features and brought her eyes back to his.

When she spoke again, her words sounded strained. "I would like to clean up before the ceremony." A slight lift of her chin and a glint of determination in her eyes dared him to tell her no, yet her chin trembled slightly.

He carefully kept his curiosity from showing on his face and attempted to put her at ease. "It's a dusty ride down the grade." He gestured across the river to the trail she and her fellow passengers had descended and smiled. "I've made that trip on several occasions myself." Holding his hand out toward the log cabin that functioned as the sleeping quarters at Greer's Ferry, he added, "I don't mind waiting." It was the truth. He was still having a hard time believing that he was here, considering marriage. *And to a woman I've only just met.* He wanted a few more minutes to think things through.

A look of gratitude crossed her face. Nodding serenely, she turned, picked up her small carpet bag, and headed toward the building.

★★★

Brooke sighed in relief, clutching the handle on her bag with both hands as she entered the little log cabin. It had two rooms. The front room contained several bunks, a wood stove, and a long table constructed out of logs sawn in half and laid side by side with the flat sides up. Various utensils hung from pegs above the black stove where a pot of coffee perked cheerfully. The smell of venison stew wafted through the cabin.

The heels of her boots echoed on the rough plank floor as Jack Greer led her to the second room in the cabin.

"You can clean up in here," he informed her kindly. He glanced down at her hands, and his face softened.

She realized her double-fisted, white-knuckled grip revealed more than she wanted others to know.

"If you need anything, don't hesitate to ask."

She nodded mutely, wishing she could think of something to say. As he left, closing the door, she collapsed onto the edge of the bed, her quaking legs unable to hold her upright any longer.

She stared at the wall for several minutes before her thoughts began to register coherently.

She glanced around. This room held a double bed and a chest of drawers.

A small wash basin sat next to the door, fresh water filling the blue pitcher on the table near it. Light flooded the room from the window in the back wall, illuminating a table and two chairs that sat against the wall across from her.

Her thoughts wandered to the man who'd met her when she stepped off the stage. He was very attractive. But that didn't stop the shaking of her limbs as she pulled her dress off over her head. She was thankful that...what was his name? Jordan...? Jason...? She bit her lip. *That's just great. I can't even remember his name. Well, at least he doesn't look anything like those dour old men did yesterday.* Still, she had found Hank attractive too. A man's looks had nothing to do with the way he acted.

Thoughts of the evening ahead assailed her and she glanced at the room's one window. What would her chances of survival be if she made a run for it? She walked over to it, but the window had no latch and couldn't be opened. Sighing, she returned to her bag. *Your only option is to go through with this. You have nowhere else to go.*

Pulling her hand mirror out of her bag, she examined her reflection, wrinkling her nose in disgust at the dirt she saw on her face. Pouring some water into the basin, she washed her face and arms as best she could and then, seeing no towel, dried them on her petticoat, which mercifully had missed most of the dust. Pulling the pins from her hair she brushed it out, plaited a braid, and coiled it at the back of her neck. Wispy curls fell out and framed her ashen face, but she did not take time to tuck them back in.

Removing her only other dress from her bag, a dark green full-skirted frock that had once belonged to her mother, she gave it a brisk snap to dispel any dust that might be on it and settled it over her head. It was her nicest dress, and she felt thankful that she had decided against wearing it on the trip. The fitted bodice had a V of cream lace that came down to just above the nipped-in waist. The full skirt and puffed sleeves of the dress accentuated her slender curves, and the dark green material made her eyes look like emeralds instead of sapphires.

After shaking out her dark blue dress, she folded it up and placed it neatly into her bag with the brush on top. She smoothed the front of her skirt with nervous hands. *I've already taken far longer than necessary. I can do this!*

She opened the door and peeked into the outer room. None of the men were inside. As she started to cross the room, she remembered the daisy. No man had ever given her flowers before. It had been a touching gesture. A spark of hope had sprung to life in her heart when he handed her the daisy, but she had quickly smothered it lest the pain of the inevitable abuse be too much to bear.

Turning back, she retrieved the flower and then made her way outside into the golden sunshine.

Conversation ceased as she stepped out and all eyes turned toward her. The admiration on their faces only added to the turmoil in her soul. She had seen firsthand what admiration could do. It was Hank's admiration of her beauty that had first drawn him to her.

But this was her wedding day, and she determined to ignore the looks. A gust of wind blew a strand of hair into her eyes. Reaching up with one hand, she tucked the curl behind her ear, her eyes coming to rest on the face of the man she was to marry. Somehow his look was different from all the rest.

He was not smiling, but she saw something in his face. What? Concern? Was he worried about her, or was he having second thoughts about marrying her? She fleetingly hoped he might reject her. She would be fine with that. But it wasn't rejection she glimpsed. What then? It wasn't an expression she'd seen on any man's face before.

The minister was the first to break the silence. Gesturing to the hard-packed dirt in front of the cabin, he asked quietly, "Shall we commence?"

Her soon-to-be husband stepped forward and offered her his arm. She stepped up beside him, facing the minister, the yellow daisy clutched in her hand like a lifeline.

Skipping the "dearly beloved" speech she'd heard at so many weddings back home, the black-coated minister launched immediately into the vows. "Do you, Brooke Baker, take this man to be your husband? Do you promise to love him, honor him, and obey him until death do you part?"

Brooke hesitated only a moment before she said quietly, "I do."

"And do you, Jason Jordan—" The minister's words were cut off as the man beside her raised a finger.

"Skyler. Skyler Jordan."

Brooke looked up at him, surprised, and the minister, taken aback, glanced down at the names before him, as though to be sure he had read correctly. He paused only a moment, though, then continued, "Do you, *Skyler* Jordan, take this woman to be your wife? To love her, honor, cherish, and keep her until death do you part?"

"I do." Skyler's voice was firm.

Skyler! Why couldn't I remember that?

"Then by the power invested in me, I now pronounce you Husband and Wife." The minister stepped back, his expression saying he was pleased with a job well done. Clasping his hands in front of him, he looked back and forth between them expectantly, his eyes twinkling.

Brooke's heart sank. They were supposed to kiss.

At first Skyler stood still and unmoving. Then he faced her.

Brooke called on every ounce of self-control in her body to prevent herself from running for the safety of the cabin. She looked up as her new husband ran a hand back through his curly blond hair and resettled his hat, a pained expression in his deep brown eyes.

After a moment more, the minister cleared his throat and frowned. "You may kiss the bride."

Skyler stepped closer, his movements deliberate and casual. Her heartbeat thundered in her ears.

He placed his hands gently on her upper arms and gazed down at her. She wondered what he could be thinking. Then, his dark eyes holding hers, he lowered his head, his lips brushing hers for the briefest of seconds.

Her tense shoulders relaxed as thankfulness coursed through her. He had not kissed her possessively as she had seen so many of the men do the day before. Maybe he really was the gentleman he appeared to be.

But her quick cynicism returned, reminding her it couldn't be true. *So! He's the type that likes to appear the gentleman in public.*

A spattering of applause greeted them as he stepped back from her, and Jack Greer called out, "Congratulations!" Then, turning to the small group of men, he gestured toward the cabin and called, "Grubs on! Come and get it."

Brooke rubbed the stem of the daisy nervously between her palms, its head twirling crazily in a yellow blur, as the men began to turn toward the cabin, leaving her alone with Skyler.

Percival was the only one who approached her. Holding out his hand, he said, "My congratulations, ma'am. This gentleman here," he nodded toward Skyler, "is one lucky fellow."

She smiled at him, allowing him to bow over her hand and offering a murmured thank you, then watched his back as headed toward dinner.

When Skyler did not move for some time, she looked toward him, suddenly aware of the rushing river only paces away. Long fingers draped casually over the front of his pockets, he stood, hands resting on slim hips, his black suit jacket pushed open. He watched her intently. *What's he thinking?* His deep brown eyes were disconcerting, and she turned her gaze to the twisting golden daisy, trying to calm the deluge of butterflies in her stomach.

But he never looked away in the long silence that followed. Finally, out of pure curiosity, she peered back up at him.

"Are you hungry?" he asked gently.

She shook her head, not trusting her voice.

"You should try and eat something; you've had a long day."

When she still did not answer, he took her elbow and turned her toward the house. "How was your trip, other than the last stretch?" He grinned down at her, even white teeth contrasting with his deeply tanned face. His smile was meant to ease her tension, she was sure, but it only added to it.

"It was fine," she managed, before her throat closed completely. This was the time she had been dreading since before the wagon train had left St. Louis. She had told herself she was strong enough to handle the abuse any man meted out to her, but memories of past anguish caused her heart to rebel against her mind's logic. She did not want to go through this again. She berated herself for allowing his apparent kindness and good looks to soften her estimation of him even in a small measure. It would only make the inevitable all the harder to bear.

As they entered the dimly lit cabin, all her fears were confirmed. Jack turned toward them with a knowing smile. "You two newlyweds will have my room for the night. There's food on the table in your room." He paused, a twinkle in his eye as he looked at Skyler, and said conspiratorially, "I didn't know if you would want to eat now or later."

Brooke suddenly wondered why she'd thought this man was so kind earlier.

Skyler nodded in his direction, touching the brim of his hat, but there was no amusement in his eyes as he placed his hand in the middle of her back and gently guided her toward the room she had used earlier.

Visions of Uncle Jackson's whip and Hank's fists danced through her mind. She didn't know what to expect from this man, but she knew that if he were anything like the men she had known, it would not be pleasant. Her heart clawed at her throat as she walked woodenly into the room, and Skyler turned and shut the door behind them. She jumped as the latch clicked and knew by the soft clearing of his throat that he had noticed.

He walked slowly to where she stood, twirling the now limp daisy between her palms, and rested his hands lightly on her upper arms. She tensed noticeably, hating herself for her weakness as tears pooled in her eyes and her legs quivered. Past experience had taught her that things only got worse if you tried to resist, so she waited helplessly.

She was surprised when he led her not to the bed but to one of the chairs at the table, easing her down into it. Taking the daisy from her, he laid it next to her plate. Squatting down on the balls of his feet, he pushed his hat back and looked into her face. She glanced at him momentarily but then turned to stare stubbornly at a knot on the pine-wood wall, not wanting to meet his dark, penetrating eyes. As he placed one hand gently on her cheek, she stiffened. With gentle pressure he turned her face toward him. She looked at him for a brief second, glanced away, and then looked back, studying him intently.

"I will not hurt you." His voice was low and tender. "I promise not to touch you until you say it's okay."

She searched his face, hoping to find truth there, yet unable to believe she would.

His face was placid as she studied him. His fingers trailed down her cheek as his hand dropped back into his lap and he reaffirmed, "I promise. You have nothing to fear from me."

Placing her hands over her face, she couldn't stop the sobs wracking her body as relief washed over her. After only a few seconds, ashamed she had shown such weakness, she stopped as suddenly as she had begun. Pulling herself together, she smoothed her tears away with the flats of her fingers, got up slowly, and walked to the bed. Removing one pillow and the top blanket, she held them out toward him. His eyes never leaving her face, he came closer to accept her offering.

He was turning away. *I have to say something!* When she touched his arm, his warmth seared her fingers and she quickly pulled back, afraid he might somehow misinterpret her intentions. She rubbed her palms nervously in a circular motion, staring at the blue water pitcher on the table by the door, trying to force the words from her throat. When she finally glanced his way and saw his questioning gaze. she was able to find her voice. "Thank you, Skyler," she whispered. She wanted to say more, but no words would come.

He nodded. "Sky. Just call me Sky."

She turned and lay down on the bed fully clothed, too emotionally exhausted to do anything else. Closing her eyes, she let sweet, peaceful sleep wash over her, somehow knowing that, if only for this one night, she could trust her new husband.

If you would like to keep reading, you can link through to the story from my website.

Want a FREE Story?

If you enjoyed this book...

...sign up for Lynnette's Gazette below! Subscribers get exclusive deals, sneak peeks, and lots of other fun content.

(The gazette is only sent out about once a month or when there's a new release to announce, so you won't be getting a lot of spam messages, and your email is never shared with anyone else.)

Sign up link: https://www.lynnettebonner.com/newsletter/

Made in the USA
Columbia, SC
02 June 2024